Irish author **Abby Gree** ... career in film and TV— ... a lot of standing in the ra... to pursue her love of rom... ...combarded Mills & Boon with manuscripts they kindly accepted one, and an author was born. She lives in Dublin, Ireland, and loves any excuse for distraction. Visit abby-green.com or email abbygreenauthor@gmail.com.

Jackie Ashenden writes dark, emotional stories, with alpha heroes who've just got the world to their liking only to have it blown wide apart by their kick-ass heroines. She lives in Auckland, New Zealand, with her husband, the inimitable Dr Jax, two kids and two rats. When she's not torturing alpha males and their gutsy heroines she can be found drinking chocolate martinis, reading anything she can lay her hands on, wasting time on social media or being forced to go mountain biking with her husband. To keep up to date with Jackie's new releases and other news sign up to her newsletter at jackieashenden.com.

A RING FOR THE SPANIARD'S REVENGE

ABBY GREEN

THE MAID THE GREEK MARRIED

JACKIE ASHENDEN

MILLS & BOON

First published in Great Britain 2022
by Mills & Boon, an imprint of HarperCollins*Publishers* Ltd,
1 London Bridge Street, London, SE1 9GF

www.harpercollins.co.uk

HarperCollins*Publishers*
1st Floor, Watermarque Building,
Ringsend Road, Dublin 4, Ireland

A Ring for the Spaniard's Revenge © 2022 Abby Green

The Maid the Greek Married © 2022 Jackie Ashenden

ISBN: 978-0-263-30106-9

11/22

A RING FOR THE SPANIARD'S REVENGE

ABBY GREEN

MILLS & BOON

This is for my beautiful niece, Brída Mernagh Spee.

A ray of light and love who arrived into our lives
when we needed it most.

CHAPTER ONE

Castillo de Santos, outside Madrid

EVA FLORES SHIVERED, even though the sun was shining and the early autumn temperature was balmy. She should be feeling relieved. Happy, even. But she wasn't even sure she knew what *happy* felt like, because it had never been a dominant emotion for her. She knew she'd only ever felt it on distinct occasions.

Before she could ruminate on that unpalatable revelation, she figured that she could work with relieved. Beyond relieved. After a year of trying to sell the *castillo* she'd grown up in, the only home she'd ever known, a potential buyer had finally materialised.

He was due to come and visit now, as a precursor to signing the contracts, and when she'd expressed concern the solicitor had assured her, 'He is very interested. He's the kind of man who wouldn't be taking time out of his busy schedule if he hadn't already made up his mind. He just wants to do this as a formality.'

Still, Eva couldn't help trying to temper her relief with a bit of caution. He hadn't signed yet, and until he did this crumbling mausoleum was still hers, with all its bleak memories, loneliness and massive debts.

The *castillo* had felt like a prison for a long time and it effectively still was. Binding her here until she could get rid of it.

She was walking through the rambling gardens, long since neglected and overgrown since the last member of staff had left.

Eva's gut clenched. She definitely didn't want to go down *that* memory lane. Much better to focus on the fact that soon she could begin her life in earnest and try to put her past behind her.

This place had claimed too much of her time. And yet she still felt a compulsion to walk its paths, as if to lay some ghost to rest. *The ghost of her mother.* A familiar swell of something far more complicated than just plain grief rose up inside Eva. It was grief and anger and a sense of futility. Her mother had dictated Eva's life in such a controlling way that it was only through her death that Eva had been able to get some perspective and enough space to start figuring out who she was.

She halted now at the rusted wrought-iron gate that led into a small walled garden with a fountain in the centre. Eva stepped inside and the heady scent of blooms in their last throes filled her nostrils.

Weeds ran rampant through the cracks in the stones on the ground and in every nook and cranny of the brick walls. She should feel guilty that it had gone to such waste but all she felt was empty. Numb.

She turned around slowly to see the elaborately decorated gazebo in a corner, almost hidden by foliage. A beautiful and whimsical piece of architecture that some previous ancestor had had installed. It certainly hadn't been her parents, who had shared no love at all. Her father had eventually walked out and left them when Eva was eight.

That act had thrown her mother into a deep pit of bitterness and despair and had made her toxic. She'd turned to Eva and used her as an object to project all her betrayal and towering rage, seeing in her daughter an opportunity to make sure she was never hurt in the same way. And so far, Eva could attest, she hadn't been. So maybe her mother's legacy had worked.

After all, it wasn't as if she'd had an opportunity to meet anyone in order to *be* hurt.

Except for—

She shut down her mind. Thinking of him caused a maelstrom of emotions that Eva didn't want to investigate. It always had, ever since she'd first laid eyes on him when she was a teenager. Tall and more beautiful than anything she'd ever seen in her life. Even then she'd known that he connected with her in a way that scared her and that she didn't fully understand.

Her mother had seen it, though. She'd found Eva watching him out of the window one day when he'd been working in the garden. Shirtless. Olive skin gleaming. Strong muscles flexing.

Her mother had drawn her close and said, 'A boy like him is driven purely by brute desires, Eva. You are worth so much more than him. But that doesn't mean you can't remind him of that…'

She'd had no idea what her mother was talking about, but it had become apparent over the years. Her mother had wanted her to entice him. To provoke those brute desires so she could rise above them and laugh at him. To remind him of his place and the fact that she was totally unattainable.

The only problem was that he hadn't been a brute. Far from it. He'd been studious, polite and...*sexy*. Eva had become progressively more and more aware of him, so that by that last summer, when she'd turned eighteen, she'd felt like a tinder box about to blow up with surging desires and aching needs and emotions far too confusing for her to know how to handle.

So she hadn't handled them.

The last time she'd seen him had been here in this space...when it had looked as it should.

She could still remember him, so tall and powerful. Short dark hair. Serious expression. Looking at her with a mixture of wariness, pity and anger. It had enflamed her. She'd desperately wanted to provoke a reaction. And she had.

Her skin prickled at the memory. Unconsciously she curled her fingers over her palms. She could still feel the heat of anger and rage and, worse, the shock of what she'd almost done. The way he'd looked at her with disgust. She'd never felt so raw. So...lost.

She cursed herself for letting her imagination run amok into the past. Today was about the future. And she realised she was mooning around the grounds still dressed in worn jeans, an even more worn shirt and scuffed sneakers. With her hair pulled back messily, she didn't look remotely like the owner of a crumbling *castillo*. If she could still be called an owner when the bank really owned it all.

It was a sorry state of affairs for the last person in the line descending from her mother's illustrious family.

She knew she was the last, because she never intended to have children. Not after what she'd experienced. The thought of having a child sent a sense of terror through her at the thought that she might subject them to what she'd been subjected to. Even with the best will in the world.

Enough. She had to get ready.

She turned around to leave the garden but came to an abrupt halt when she saw someone standing in the gateway. Someone very tall and broad. Masculine. The sun was in her eyes, though, and she couldn't make out his features.

This had to be the potential buyer…but how had he found this garden? The grounds were labyrinthine even to her, and she'd lived here her whole life.

For some reason she felt a shiver of recognition. She put a hand up to try and block the sun. 'Hello. Can I help you?'

The man stepped forward and she realised he was even taller than she'd first thought. Well over six foot. And then she saw his face and the blood stopped coursing through her veins.

It couldn't be.

The man took off his sunglasses, revealing all too familiar deep-set eyes an unusual colour of green and blue. Aquamarine. They'd always reminded Eva of the sea.

When he spoke his voice was deep. 'Hello, Eva. We meet again.'

Eva reeled. Had she conjured him up out of her imagination? Literally willed him into existence?

He wore a suit that was moulded to his very powerful body. She'd never seen him in a suit. It had always been jeans or shorts and T-shirts. Now she was the one in jeans and a shirt—the kind of clothes she had been forbidden from ever wearing. She'd rarely been out of

them in the past year, in a sort of very belated and ineffectual rebellion.

'Vidal Suarez…' She breathed the name she hadn't
even wanted to think of a few moments ago. She didn't
realise she'd spoken out loud.

'You do remember me, then.'

Always. The word popped into Eva's head and she
clamped her mouth shut in case it fell out. Except the
person she remembered had been a young man on the
cusp of his power. Lean and muscular. Not this…this
fully formed man.

'I… What are you doing here?'

He stepped closer and looked around. She could
hardly comprehend that it was him. She felt confused,
wondered if the sun was getting to her.

He said musingly, as if it was entirely normal for him
to be there, 'I always liked this space. Shame it's gone to
seed.' He looked at her. 'But then you and your mother
always did have a careless attitude to the *castillo* and
its upkeep.'

She wasn't imagining him. His words sliced into
her. It had been her mother who had relished the ruin-
ation of the *castillo*. As if the disintegrating state of their
home might make her father realise that he had made a
huge mistake and come back to make amends, fearful of
what people would say. But he hadn't. And the *castillo*
had continued to slowly decline. In spite of the skeleton
staff's efforts to keep it somewhat respectable.

His words seemed to break her out of her trance.
'What are you doing here?' she repeated.

'Aren't you expecting me?'

Too many things impacted upon Eva at once for her

to be able to assimilate them all. The implication of what he was saying was too huge to take in.

'I'm waiting for someone from Sol Enterprises.'

'Sol Enterprises is my company.'

Eva shook her head. 'But…how…? Why?'

But even as she asked the question a memory came back. This same man, seven years ago, saying, *'Some are born to this kind of privilege, Eva, and some have to earn it, but I think it's safe to say that the earning of it is so much more satisfying. For all your privilege, you don't strike me as particularly grateful or happy.'*

The clarity of the memory mocked her.

Vidal was looking at her carefully, and the shock of his appearance made her feel as if the walls of the garden were closing in around her. For one awful moment Eva felt light-headed and thought she might faint. But it passed. She had to move away from here.

She skirted around Vidal Suarez and said, 'We should go to the house.'

'Yes, that would be good.'

As Eva walked down the well-worn paths ahead of him she forced herself to take deep breaths. She'd never expected to see Vidal Suarez again. His life now was so far removed from where she was and from where he'd been.

By the time he had come to the *castillo* with his grounds manager father at the age of twenty he had already been known locally as a prodigiously talented boy who had won a prestigious scholarship to one of Spain's most exclusive schools, and had then gone on to win yet more scholarships to the world's best universities.

It was probably the reason Eva's mother had allowed

him to live here with his father—as long as he helped out during his holidays, of course. For free.

And now he was a billionaire—a tech entrepreneur who had blazed a trail across the world before settling in San Francisco, the global hub of tech innovation.

Eva's mother had taken great pleasure in making Vidal do menial work alongside his father, as if to remind him of his true place. But that last summer Eva had seen him had been the summer his life had changed. He'd made his first million.

Years after the Suarezes had left the *castillo,* and as their own fortune had declined, her mother—who had been following Vidal's well-documented stratospheric progress—had said to Eva, 'You should go to him…ask him for help. He owes us.'

Eva had turned on her mother and said, with barely controlled fury, 'He owes us nothing, Mother. Nothing.'

We owe him. I owe him. She hadn't said it, but she'd thought it.

She could almost feel the weight of Vidal Suarez judging the sorry state of the gardens behind her. She felt guilty, even though there was nothing she could have done about it. All her energy had been taken up in keeping herself and the *castillo* afloat. Not that it had done much good in the end.

Her mother had refused to sell. Had refused to show any sign that she'd struggled since her husband had left her all those years before. Preferring to live in a state of total inertia and denial.

It was only after she'd died that Eva had been able to take control, but that sense of control was suddenly very elusive as questions abounded in her head: *Why him? Why now?*

She had no idea why Vidal Suarez had come back here now, potentially to buy the *castillo*. Or maybe she did and she just didn't want to acknowledge the gut-churning evidence that he hadn't forgotten or forgiven his treatment at her hands. At her mother's hands.

They approached the *castillo* from the front, where a large circular area featured another elaborate fountain that lay sadly dry and empty. A sleek, low-slung sports car—presumably Vidal's—looked incongruous against the shabby backdrop.

The *castillo* itself was an imposing building, a mix of classical and Moorish design. The dramatic arching entrance led into an open courtyard, with pillars around the edges.

Another memory blasted back at that moment—as if Eva needed reminding. Her mother had invited Vidal to join them for dinner one evening. Eva had been mortifyingly excited. Sixteen and full of hormones, and giddy with a desire she'd had no idea how to handle.

Vidal had arrived and he'd clearly made an effort. Eva had thought he'd never looked more handsome in chinos and a shirt. Hair smoothed back. Smelling of musk and earthy spices.

And then her mother had proceeded to talk to Eva about Vidal for the entire evening as if he wasn't there. As if he was a specimen to discuss and not a human being to have a conversation with. As if he was sub-human.

It had been excruciating, and Eva had burned with shame and anger. But even then she hadn't been brave enough to stand up to her mother. She'd pulled invisible armour around herself, so nothing could touch her and she could hide. Hide her feelings and desires.

Vidal had suffered that insulting dinner with innate

pride and a politeness they hadn't deserved. He hadn't joined them again.

And now he was here, supposedly interested in buying the *castillo*. It shouldn't be surprising at all that he was taking an opportunity to dish out a little humiliation of his own. The only surprise was that he hadn't put all this behind him. That he wanted anything to do with the *castillo* and Eva, at all.

Eva led him into the main reception room and winced inwardly at the even sorrier state of affairs inside the *castillo*. Peeling wallpaper, damp patches, threadbare oriental rugs... Portraits of ancestors covered in dirt. Dust sheets strewn over a lot of the furniture—not that they were helping much.

Eva steeled herself to face him again before she turned around, but it didn't work very well. Any steel seemed to turn to liquid as she drank him in—this time without the sun in her eyes.

With his powerful build, short dark hair—almost militarily short—and hard-boned face dominated by those wide deep-set eyes, he oozed a raw vitality that effortlessly eclipsed the crumbling *castillo* behind him.

The clipped dark beard that hugged his jaw only drew attention to his mouth. A wide mouth, with lips generous enough to look almost pretty.

But they hadn't felt pretty. They'd felt hard.

Eva's heart thumped.

Please, not those memories. Not now.

'You're looking at me as if you've never seen me before,' he said.

Eva felt heat rise. 'You look...different.'

'I am different.'

There was a stern tone to his voice that made Eva realise just how much had changed for him. Coming from a humble background, he'd well and truly surpassed all expectations. His wealth was inestimable and apparently he owned real estate in every major city. There was even a bolthole in Hawaii.

Eva wondered if he thought *she* had changed. She felt changed. Bruised and weary after a lifetime of being told what to think and how to behave. She felt vulnerable. As if a protective layer of skin was gone.

That made her conscious of her clothes, and she gestured to herself. 'I was going to change before…' she hesitated '…before you came.'

Those green-blue eyes drifted down and up again. A pulse throbbed deep in Eva's body. A pulse of awareness and something being brought back to life. *Her.* In his presence. As if she'd been dormant until now.

'Not your usual attire…? But then how would I know? It's been a long time. Evidently the demise of the *castillo* hasn't been confined to the building.'

'I think it's pretty obvious that things aren't…the same.'

Vidal took his gaze off her and Eva felt as if she could breathe again. He looked around the space, his hands in the pockets of his trousers. Then he looked back at her. 'Things are different. I can't lie and pretend I liked your mother all that much, but I am sorry for your loss.'

Those tangled emotions churned in Eva's gut. She hid them and lifted her chin, saying in a clipped voice, 'Thank you.'

Vidal shook his head. 'You're still a cold one, I see. Not even a mention of your mother gets you to display a chink of emotion. You two were as thick as thieves.'

Eva looked at him and was genuinely lost for words.

How could he think that? *Because it was true,* whispered a voice. Yes, it had been true in one sense. She'd been a captive audience and acolyte for her mother. 'Captive' being the operative word.

She forced a brittle smile. 'It's a funny thing, perspective, isn't it?' In a bid to get him away from the subject of her mother, she asked, 'How is your father?'

Vidal's hands came out of his pockets. His expression hardened. 'You're saying you don't know?'

Eva frowned. 'Know what?' All she knew were these neglected walls and gardens and the route she took to her job every day in Madrid.

'That he's dead.' Vidal's voice was flat.

Eva balked and struggled to speak for a moment, eventually getting out, 'But…how? When?'

'As if you care.'

She felt defensive. 'I always liked your father. He was kind.'

'More kind than you and your mother deserved.'

Shame coiled in Eva's belly. She recalled a moment when she'd delivered an instruction to Vidal's father on behalf of her mother, who had told her never to talk to him as if he were their equal. After delivering the message, she'd walked away—only to be stopped in her tracks by Vidal.

The sheer surprise of seeing him had had a flush of awareness rising through her body before she'd been able to stop it. The kind of thing her mother had warned her about. Being at the mercy of her emotions…hormones. All weaknesses.

Vidal had looked angry. 'Who do you think you are to talk to your senior like that?'

A mix of hot emotions at his reprimand had made

Eva's chest feel tight. Shame and confusion and something much more complicated. Something she hadn't
understood, even at sixteen years of age. And so she'd
retreated behind that cool indifference her mother had
taught her so well and lifted her chin the way she'd
watched her mother do it. 'Who do you think *you* are to
talk to *me* like this? You're not even an employee here.
The fact that you're here at all is because of the generosity of my mother.'

Even as the words had fallen out of her mouth they'd
felt acrid. Wrong. But it had been safer to hide behind
them than allow Vidal to see the awful churning mix of
emotions inside her. The shame.

Vidal had shaken his head. 'You're a piece of work—
do you know that? Here in your castle that's falling to
the ground, clinging onto nothing but a name and empty
privilege. You're pathetic. Don't talk to my father like
that again.'

For a horrifying moment Eva had felt hot tears
threaten, and she'd known immediately that she was
weak. So she'd forced all the emotion down and locked
it in ice and said, 'You do not have the right to tell me
what to do.' And she'd walked away before Vidal could
say another word and bring all those emotions to the
surface again.

Eva swallowed the shameful and painful memory.
'How…? When did he die?'

'Not long after he left the *castillo*.'

'But that was about five years ago. Was he ill?'

Vidal's voice was stark. 'He was proud. Too proud to
leave his job even though I could support him. He felt
some misguided loyalty to you and your mother. Even
though she felt nothing similar and let him go with no

notice and no compensation. I was in the United States. I offered for him to come and join me, but he didn't want to be "a burden". His words. The cancer was already very advanced and in his pancreas by the time the doctors diagnosed it. He died within months. There was nothing I could do.'

'I'm so sorry. I had no idea.' Eva felt nauseous.

'Why would you? He'd only ever been a faceless, nameless employee to you and your mother. He'd had symptoms of his illness while working at the *castillo* but your mother refused to let him have time off to get checked out. And he didn't want to make a fuss.'

Eva remembered the day Vidal's father had left. He had looked suddenly much older. Clearly in shock at the abrupt nature of his departure. She'd offered to help him, but he had insisted that he was fine and her mother had told her to let him go.

Too many memories. This was what Eva was hoping to get away from by selling the *castillo*. Being forced to relive the past.

She folded her arms across her chest. 'Vidal, why are you really here?'

Why are you really here? Why was he here, indeed? An answer floated into his head before he could stop it. *Because you couldn't forget about her.*

Nonsense, he assured himself. He actually did have a plan for this *castillo*, and it had nothing to do with Eva Flores.

Are you sure about that? mocked his conscience.

He couldn't ignore the distinct sizzle in his blood. And it wasn't so much a sizzle as a lick of flame along every vein. Flames that made his skin tighten with awareness and need.

For this woman? After all this time? Galling. Irritating. He hadn't thought about her in years.

Liar.

Vidal grimaced inwardly. If he was being totally honest, she had slid back into his consciousness from time to time. Usually at inopportune moments when he was with a woman and he suddenly found himself thinking of Eva's cool beauty and haughty airs, wondering where she was and if she was still an ice queen, incapable of cracking even a smile to indicate any kind of warmth.

He could imagine men being fascinated enough to want to see if they could be the one to melt all that ice and find the woman underneath. Because, for a time, he'd fantasised about that. Much as he'd like to deny it.

And now that he was standing in front of her she was both exactly what he'd expected and *not*. But he couldn't put his finger on the difference. She was as beautiful as ever. More so, having grown into her coltish limbs and womanly curves.

Maybe it was the fact that she was dressed down. He'd never seen her less than immaculately put together, even though he'd rarely seen her leave the *castillo* with her mother.

She had been home-schooled. He'd used to feel sorry for her, thinking of her as some kind of hothouse flower kept apart from society, but inevitably if he'd said anything remotely resembling pity or compassion she'd come back with a withering put-down and made Vidal feel like a fool for assuming she was like other mortals.

She wasn't. She was a product of her illustrious lineage and she'd been born to make strategic connections and alliances. As she'd liked to remind him.

His father had used to say to him, 'Just ignore her, son. She doesn't even know what she's doing.'

But Vidal had always suspected otherwise. And he'd been right if that last encounter had been anything to go by, on her eighteenth birthday. She might not have been worldly but she'd known of her effect on him, and she'd done everything in her power to ensure he noticed her so that she could then punish him for it.

She'd moved through the grounds of that *castillo* with all the regal aloofness of a queen inspecting her troops and finding them lacking. She'd found Vidal lacking. Especially when he had refused her.

He could still feel her slim body against his, trembling with desperation. Skinny arms winding around his neck, and that pouting spoiled mouth pressed to his.

At the shocking sensation of all that soft sweetness, so at odds with her very *un*-soft personality, Vidal had almost lost it. He'd almost forgotten who she was and how she'd tormented him. That she was nowhere near worldly enough to take what was bubbling up inside him. A heat so intense that it had almost fused his brain cells. *Almost.*

He'd pulled back and taken her arms in his hands. Pushed her away. She'd looked at him with wide, shocked eyes. Molten brown. Golden. Colour slashed along those aristocratic cheekbones. Silky dark hair had been falling loose from her ponytail.

And there was something else he hadn't seen before. A hint of vulnerability. It had tempered the fire inside him.

He'd taken his hands off her arms and stepped back. 'What on earth are you doing?'

Apart from slowly driving me insane? He'd just managed not to utter that out loud.

But as he'd watched, he'd seen any hint of softness leave her face, to be replaced with something he recognised much more. A cool hauteur far more mature than her teenage years.

She'd shrugged a shoulder. 'I know you want me, Vidi, and it's boring watching you try to resist.'

Vidi. She'd used to call him Vidi. As if they'd had that kind of relationship. As if they'd had any kind of relationship beyond the one in which she went out of her way to torture him.

He'd shaken his head, wondering why he'd ever thought he'd seen a chink of vulnerability. She was about as vulnerable as a tank.

'You are just a girl.'

Fire had lit her eyes, turning them even more golden. 'I'm eighteen today.'

In any other instance he would have wished her a happy birthday. But Eva was not someone he'd been able to behave rationally around.

Vidal had thought of how close he'd come to forgetting all of that at the feel of her body pressed to his, that provocative mouth moving so insistently under his. It had made him harsh. 'Go and find someone your own age to torture, Eva. I'm not available to be your plaything.'

Eva had lifted a hand, about to slap him across the face, when Vidal's lightning-fast reflexes snapped into action. He'd caught her wrist and held it tight, resisting the almost overwhelming urge to clamp his mouth to hers and show her exactly how thin his restraint was.

'Like I said, Eva…go and find someone your own age to seduce. You are the last person I would ever touch.'

He'd dropped her wrist and turned and walked away, filled with more volatile emotion than he'd ever felt in his life. *She was dangerous.*

And now she was right in front of him, causing all those memories and sensations to swirl in his gut.

You came here, a voice reminded him, *because you're weak. Because you couldn't resist knowing if she's still the same. Or has she changed, softened?*

She *was* different, on first appearances, with her worn clothes and that haughty beauty that had matured into something far more potent.

But he suspected the differences were purely superficial. Underneath it all she was the same haughty entitled princess.

His eyes traced the dismayingly familiar lines of her face. Those huge wide-set golden-brown eyes. Strong dark brows. A straight nose. The high cheekbones showing her impeccable lineage. And that mouth... As full and provocative as it had been the last day they'd met but even more so now. Her skin was blemish-free and golden. Silky. Inviting him to touch.

His hand curled into a fist at his side. He said, 'Why am I here, Eva? Because I'm fulfilling my dying father's wishes and because I was curious.'

CHAPTER TWO

Eva swallowed past a dry throat. 'Curious about what?' Her voice sounded croaky. She felt totally exposed, unprepared to see Vidal Suarez again.

He cast a look around the room, his hands back in his pockets, oozing insouciance. He might come from a humble background, but right now he looked far more entitled to be in this majestic space than her.

Was this what he wanted? To gloat at the tables being turned?

A sense of vulnerability made Eva voice that question out loud.

Vidal looked back at her. 'You really think I'm so petty or have the time to come here just so I can score a point?'

In Eva's world, with what she'd learnt from her mother, it was entirely feasible that he would want to do such a thing. She felt confused. 'Well…why, then?'

For a long moment it looked as if he had no intention of telling her, but then he said, 'My father always loved this place and these gardens. Don't ask me why. I did not share his love.'

Me neither, thought Eva.

'When he was dying he said that he'd always wished

my mother had been alive to see the gardens here, and that if I could do one thing for him it would be to save this place and rescue it from crumbling altogether. He knew that once he left there would be no one to tend to it.'

Eva shook her head. 'I can't believe it meant that much to him.'

'Because it means nothing to you. And yet you were born here? And your ancestors built it?'

Eva felt defensive. 'Just because I'm from this place, it does not mean that I have to love it. Is it so wrong to want to live my own life now?'

Vidal looked at her with narrowed eyes, making her feel even more defensive.

He said, 'Not at all. I can see how this place must have stifled you while your peers are living far more glamorous lives. No doubt you already have some hapless heir lined up in your sights, to transport you into a far more salubrious environment and lifestyle.'

For a second Eva thought she might actually laugh out loud. A sharp, semi-hysterical burst of laughter. And then she realised that Vidal Suarez had no idea about her life. He just assumed that because she came from this rarefied world it automatically gave her some kind of passport into a glittery existence. And that she wanted it.

It couldn't be further from the truth, and she'd known that for some time now. But, it was the life her mother had envisaged for her. To marry well and strategically. Her mother had wanted to show her errant husband that even though he'd rejected them, she could still make sure their daughter was accepted into society.

But it hadn't worked out like that. After years of being kept apart from society, when Eva had emerged she'd been woefully ill-equipped to fit into the crowd of her peers. On every level imaginable. She'd had none of the social skills or the knowledge she'd needed to navigate stepping into the fast-moving and cut-throat world of Spanish high society.

She recalled with burning mortification one party that her mother had managed—somehow—to get an invitation for. It had been the eighteenth birthday of one of the heirs of Spain's most elite family.

Having only recently turned eighteen herself, Eva had entered the exclusive hotel ballroom as shaky and nervous as a newborn foal, hating herself for it. The first thing she'd noticed with a wave of cold horror was that she was dressed in a fashion about a decade out of date. These people were sleek and sophisticated, even though they were still teenagers. She was overdone and too fussy. And then, as if they were one person, the entire crowd had seemed to turn to look at her. A hush had fallen over them and someone had sniggered.

Eva had fled to the nearest private space where she could hide. A toilet cubicle. Inevitably, she'd heard herself being discussed.

One girl had said to another in an awed tone, '*That's* Eva Flores? I thought she was an urban myth. How can a girl like us be hidden away for years like that?'

'Quite easily, obviously,' had come the dry response from her friend. 'I mean, did you *see* her? It's as if she's got stuck in a time warp. She's like one of those feral people found in the woods after being raised by wild animals. I don't think she's even wearing make-up!'

The girls had left the bathroom. Eva had crept out and found a discreet side entrance to escape through and had vowed never to go near one of those events again. And she hadn't.

Eva pushed down the toxic memories and cursed Vidal for bringing them back to life. 'What I plan to do in the future is no concern of yours. If you're not serious about purchasing the *castillo* then you can leave. I have engagements to keep.'

Like the one she had working as a chambermaid in one of Madrid's most exclusive hotels. If she was late she didn't need to bother going in again—or so her boss had told her on her first day.

But she would die before she revealed that to Vidal. Bad enough that he thought her an impoverished social-ite. He didn't need to know the full grim reality. Even now, when her mother was dead and gone, Eva felt the strongly ingrained instinct to save face and not let Vidal see a moment of weakness.

Vidal folded his arms. 'Oh, I'm serious about pur-chasing the property. I didn't come here for a reunion… as happy as this one is.'

The mocking tone surprised Eva. The Vidal she'd known before hadn't been a mocking person. He'd been serious. Most of the time. There had been one day when she'd been reading in her favourite private spot, seeking respite from her mother, when Vidal had appeared with some garden implements, obviously helping his father.

Even now Eva could recall the way her heart had skipped and then started beating again in a staccato rhythm. The way her skin had felt hot and how she'd been so aware of her skirt and short-sleeved top. Compared to Vidal, who'd been wearing a pair of board shorts and a worn T-shirt, she'd felt overdressed and totally uncool.

He'd stopped and looked at her over his sunglasses, his mouth quirking slightly. 'Don't you ever meet other people?'

She'd felt acutely exposed. 'I don't need other people.' But the sad truth was that she'd had no friends.

'Everyone needs someone.'

'Did you read that on the back of a cereal packet?' she'd sniped back.

Vidal had just shaken his head, as if sad for her. 'You could smile once or twice, you know. It might actually entice someone to want to get to know you.'

He'd walked away and Eva's chest had felt so tight that it had hurt. In fact she'd always felt desperately lonely, for as long as she could remember. She would have loved to have a friend. Pathetically, Vidal had been the closest thing she'd had to a friend, even though she hadn't been able to engage with him in a normal way. Her mother had made sure of that.

Her mother had used to whisper in her ear: *'You're better than everyone... Don't ever let a man think you want him, Eva... You are the prize, not them... You don't need anyone but yourself.'*

Except for this man, who had always made her feel as if he could see all the way under her skin to where she was so uncertain and needy and vulnerable.

It had taken the death of her mother for her to be fully released from the prison of believing she had to behave a certain way, and even now she found it difficult to trust her own instincts.

Eva forced the vulnerability out. There was too much at stake for her to wobble now. Vidal Suarez was just a man. He didn't possess magic powers. No matter what his various ex-lovers had breathlessly told the newspapers, creating quite the playboy mystique.

Moving towards the door leading into the reception area Eva said, 'Like I said, I have engagements. If you're serious about the property you have my solicitor's details. Feel free to look around and reacquaint yourself, but I'm afraid I have to leave.'

'What kind of engagements?'

Eva stopped and turned around. 'I have to meet some girlfriends for drinks.'

The minor lie was so much easier to say than the truth. The last thing she needed was to see pity on Vidal's face. She'd seen it before and she never wanted to see it again.

'I'm happy to hear you've made some friends.'

Eva's chest hurt. She still had no friends to speak of. Not really. One girl she worked with at the hotel was friendly, but Eva was conscious not to say too much for fear of her finding out that she was *Eva Flores*—an heiress who, improbably, had nothing to inherit, and who went home to an empty *castillo* every day. Would she even believe that Eva needed to work for minimum wage after the life she'd lived?

So, as nice as the girl was, and as friendly as they'd become superficially, Eva avoided all overtures to take it any further outside their work environment. She'd watch her colleague meet her boyfriend at the staff entrance and get on the back of his motorbike to go home and envied her life of freedom.

Eva needed to get away from Vidal now. He was too potent a reminder of everything she wanted to leave behind. Emotions were rushing to the surface and emotions were dangerous. Weakening.

'I have to go and get ready. You can let yourself out.'

'You're not worried about burglars?'

Eva cracked a tight smile. They'd sold off anything worth a cent in the last few years. 'No.'

She turned and walked out, aware of Vidal's gaze

boring into her back. She couldn't believe that he had appeared here after all this time and was apparently serious about buying the property in his father's memory. Surely she should be the one feeling some ounce of sentiment and doing all in her power to cling onto her legacy?

You could go to your father, pointed out a voice.

Eva quashed it down straight away. She'd gone to him, begging for help, before her mother had died, and the way he'd treated her had told her in no uncertain terms that he was not an option. Never had been and never would be.

She was on her own, and if Vidal Suarez was going to be the one to help her get her freedom from the past then she had no choice but to accept it. But once the deal was done she would get on with her life and forget about his moment of gloating glory.

Vidal watched Eva walk out with all the grace of a prima ballerina. Even dressed down and against the backdrop of a crumbling *castillo*, she still exuded the nonchalance and the sense of entitlement of royalty.

He felt something drop inside him. Was it a sense of… disappointment? A sense of something slipping through his fingers? A slight lurch of panic that he might not see her again? But it couldn't be. Eva Flores meant nothing to him. He'd merely been curious as to the state of the *castillo* and to see if she was the same.

And now he'd satisfied his curiosity. In truth, the state of the *castillo* shocked him. He hadn't expected it to be so bad. He felt a prick of concern but quickly quashed it. Maybe some of Eva's bravado was gone, since her mother had died and she'd realised that she would have to sell her family's legacy to survive. But survive she would. Of that he had no doubt. She'd obviously been living here in her ivory tower until she could no longer deny the decay.

And now she was off to socialise with her peers and presumably find a suitable husband.

Vidal swept one last glance around the room. He didn't need to see the rest of the *castillo* to know it would be in a similar state. And he didn't need to be reminded of the poky apartment at the back of the *castillo* where he'd lived with his father. Treated like second-class citizens.

Only the fact that his father had expressed his wish for Vidal to do something about the *castillo* and its gardens had brought him here.

He'd always suspected his father had had a soft spot for Eva and her mother, in spite of the way they'd treated him. Vidal didn't understand it, but he didn't need to. He'd made up his mind about what to do with the *castillo* and once he had done the deal he wouldn't have to wonder about Eva Flores again. She would disappear into the society she'd been bred for and she was welcome to it.

Eva pushed her trolley down the hushed and quiet corridor. Luxurious carpet indicated that this was the VIP section of one of Madrid's most exclusive hotels and the décor was similar to what might be found in any royal palace.

This was her last turn-down service. Every bone was aching after hours of backbreaking work making beds and cleaning bathrooms. But it had helped to stop her thinking about what had happened earlier. With *him*. A man she'd never expected to see again and whom she was pretty sure had never wanted to see her again.

But now she couldn't stop thinking about it. And him. Was he really interested in buying the *castillo* or was it just some kind of elaborate wind-up just to inflict a little payback for her having treated him so badly in the past?

Somehow Eva didn't think Vidal Suarez was that petty. As he'd said, he had better things to do. Billions to accrue. Perhaps the story about his father was true and Mr Suarez really had loved the place. God knew, someone had needed to.

She shivered in the hotel corridor when she thought of the lingering sadness that permeated the *castillo*. Memories threatened to rise again, but Eva focused on the task at hand and gathered up the items she needed for the turn-down service.

She knocked lightly on the door of the biggest suite in the hotel. She wasn't expecting the guest to be present. At this time most guests were out or at dinner. So, without waiting for an answer, Eva said in a loud clear voice as she opened the door with her key, 'Good evening—turn-down service.'

But she came to an abrupt standstill in the doorway when she realised there was a man in the suite, approaching the door with a mobile phone held up to his ear. He saw her, and the shock she felt was mirrored on his face.

They said simultaneously, *'You.'*

Vidal Suarez spoke into the phone curtly. 'I'll call you back, Richard, there's someone at the door.'

Eva couldn't believe it. Vidal. Here. In this suite. Looking at her with unmitigated shock. The jacket, waistcoat and tie were gone. The top button of his shirt was open. It felt curiously intimate to see him like this.

Eva found her voice. It was flat. 'Turn-down service.'

'Is this before or after drinks with your girlfriends?'

'I lied.'

The speed with which she'd admitted that seemed to surprise him. He said, 'Why?'

Eva lifted her chin. She was still holding the turn-down service paraphernalia and standing in the doorway. Someone approached in the corridor. There was a woman's laughter. Soft and sexy. As if she was with a lover.

'Come in,' Vidal instructed, reaching past her to push the door closed before she could decide what to do.

Vidal walked into the vast, opulent suite. Eva had no choice but to follow. He turned to face her in the living area, coloured soft and golden by low lights. The city of Madrid twinkled beyond the windows.

'Why aren't you out?' Eva asked bluntly.

'I had remote meetings so I took them here. Why did you lie?'

Eva swallowed. She felt like squirming. 'Because I didn't want you to know how bad it is.' Or that she had no friends. *Still*.

Vidal frowned. 'Well, it's obvious there's not enough money left to keep the *castillo* intact, but is it worse than that?'

Eva nodded. Vidal's gaze dropped and she was suddenly very aware of her plain uniform of black button-down dress and apron. Hair scraped back. Tights. Flat shoes. Minimal make-up.

He reached towards her and said brusquely, 'Put those down.'

He took the things out of her arms and put them down on a nearby table. Now Eva felt even more exposed.

'How long have you been working here?' he asked.

'About a year.'

'Since your mother died.' It wasn't a question.

Eva nodded. 'We—that is, *I* have huge debts. Mother

borrowed against the *castillo* to keep us afloat, to keep staff. Eventually we ran out of that too.'

'What about your father?'

Eva's father was from one of Spain's oldest family lines. She shook her head. 'Not an option.'

'That's not what it looked like in the press. I was in London too when you appeared beside him at that event.'

Oh, God. He'd been in the same city at the same time.

Eva felt a wash of shame rise up from her gullet. 'It wasn't what it looked like.'

She wasn't going to explain how her father had humiliated her that night, and had shown her the depth of his disregard for her.

Vidal made a sound that told Eva he doubted that, and turned away.

Normally when she came into this kind of suite she was on autopilot, wanting to get it cleaned and ready. It was quite different when she had a moment to take it in. Vidal looked as if he'd been born against this backdrop. The tables really had turned. Now she was the impoverished one. At his mercy. If he decided not to buy the *castillo*—

A flash of cold panic gripped her. She couldn't bear to be trapped there any longer. 'Are you going to buy the *castillo*?' The words were out before she could stop them.

Vidal was at the drinks cabinet. He turned around. 'Would you like something?'

Eva's throat was dry. 'Some water, please.'

Vidal smiled, but it was tight. 'Impeccably polite. You always had that quality at least.'

Eva's face burned. She was glad Vidal was facing away. Her gaze moved over his broad shoulders in the white shirt and down to where it was tucked into his trousers. Narrow hips. Long legs. Muscles moving under the thin material.

He turned around again and her gaze became locked on the middle of his chest. She could see the darkness of his skin under the material. The whorls of dark hair where his shirt was open at his throat.

He came towards her and handed her a crystal glass of sparkling water. She took a quick sip, and almost choked when it went down the wrong way. She'd never felt so gauche. And she'd been brought up to feel as if she was prepared, entitled to enter the most rarefied of spaces. But what she'd realised since her mother's death was just how woefully *un*prepared she was.

Her mother had lived in a dreamworld about two decades out of date. Oh, their name and lineage were still revered in some quarters, but the world had moved on, and scandal in the highest echelons of Spanish society had tarnished the respect they'd once held.

Not that Eva really cared about any of that. Her privilege had kept her apart from the world for too long. She longed for normality. To learn who she really was.

'Okay?' Vidal asked, bringing Eva back into the room.

She nodded. 'Fine.' She handed back the glass. 'I should get back to work. My manager will be looking for me.'

'You don't want to know my answer about buying the *castillo*?'

Eva went still. He was playing with her. She should have guessed. She felt the old familiar urge to hide behind the veneer she knew so well. 'I really couldn't care less, Vidal. If you don't, someone else will—eventually.'

Before Eva could stop him, he took her hands in his. The shock of physical contact rendered her mute. He held them and turned them over and back again. Suddenly Eva saw what he saw—the rough patches and dry spots. The short nails. Unvarnished.

He said, 'Oh, you care, I think. You weren't made for this.'

Eva pulled her hands back and put them behind her back. Struggling to focus on words that suddenly seemed elusive, she said, 'And yet here I am.'

He looked at her. 'Even dressed like this, and with raw hands, you can't disguise your nobility. That's quite a feat.'

Eva felt defensive and exposed. 'You've had your moment of karma, Vidal. I have to go.'

She turned to leave, but before she could get to the door Vidal said from behind her, 'Wait.'

Reluctantly, Eva turned around again. Vidal's face was in shadow, so she couldn't make out his expression, but for some reason her skin prickled. Not just with awareness, but with a sense of something about to happen.

Then he said, 'Actually, I have a proposition for you. It could solve all your problems—short-term and long-term.'

Eva frowned. 'What you do mean, short-term and long-term?'

'I'm talking about your debts and the *castillo* itself.'

He stepped into the light. She could see his expression now. Had it always been so unreadable? *No.* He'd lost his layer of approachability. He was altogether a far more intimidating person.

'I told you it was a dying wish of my father's that I offer to do something with the place…?'

'So you said.'

'Well, as much as I loved my father, I'm not sentimental enough to spend a small fortune on a property that needs a mountain of work for little return. But I have devised a plan that could see it earn its own keep and potentially make a profit in years to come.'

Intrigued in spite of herself, Eva asked, 'How's that?'

'By turning it into an exclusive hotel and event space. The gardens alone, once restored, would be a huge draw. It's the ideal distance from Madrid. Guests could take a taxi into the city or enjoy the bucolic peace and quiet of the estate.'

Eva hadn't ever imagined what might happen to the *castillo*.

Vidal was looking at her carefully. 'It doesn't bother you? The plan I have?'

Eva shook her head. 'Should it?'

'Most people have an…attachment to their childhood home.'

Eva stiffened. She wasn't 'most people'. 'I don't care what happens to it. I just want it gone.'

'Well, that's contingent on one thing.'

'What thing?'

'If you do something for me, in return I will buy the *castillo*, settle all its debts and turn it into a profit-making enterprise. I will even offer you a stake, if you'd like.'

Eva couldn't quite compute this information for a long moment. She'd been facing the prospect of sizeable debts remaining even after the sale. But they would be gone. *And* he was offering her a business opportunity.

Then she recalled what he'd said and immediately she was suspicious. 'What do you want me to do for you?'

Vidal folded his arms. 'I want you to agree to a public engagement with me.'

Vidal watched Eva closely. Seeing her like this in a maid's uniform had thrown him. More than thrown him.

He'd underestimated how impoverished she was. And yet not for a moment had she let that hauteur slip. As if he was the one doing her a favour by being available for a turn-down service.

Eva looked a little stunned. And then confused. 'A public engagement…like an event?'

'No. Like a marriage engagement.'

Eva went white. Something about her reaction made Vidal feel simultaneously insulted and vindicated by the impulsive decision he'd made.

'You want to marry me?' she asked, sounding shocked.

'Not in a million years,' Vidal responded. 'You're the last woman I'd ever want to marry.'

A little colour flared back into her cheeks and, perversely, it made him feel comforted. 'Why go through the charade of an engagement, then?'

'It would look good for me to appear more settled in the short term. I've cultivated a somewhat…lurid reputation in recent years, and it's affecting my business.'

'How?'

'I'm looking for investment in a new project. But I'm finding that the higher the stakes are, the more conservative the investors are. They're jittery. Not sure if they can trust me even though I've proved myself over and over again. You see, they can't quite pin me down. My background is not very palatable, and that makes them nervous too. On the social scene I now inhabit stability matters. Status matters.'

Eva spread her hands. 'How on earth can I be of any benefit?'

'You would add a certain…*authenticity* to my reputation. The elusive Eva Flores. Descended from one of Spain's oldest and noblest lines. Distantly related to royalty.'

Vidal wasn't sure what she muttered in response to that, but it sounded suspiciously like, *That's about all I'm worth.* It hadn't been said with self-pity, though. More with a sense of anger.

'Your glittering social life obviously came to a stand-still when your mother died,' he observed.

Eva realised that Vidal must be referring to the pictures he'd seen of her in London, when she'd gone to speak with her father. He obviously assumed that they reflected her life at the time. The reality couldn't be further from that impression. But she wasn't going to expose herself even more.

She still couldn't really wrap her head around what Vidal was proposing. She shook her head. 'Why would you want to do this with me?'

'As I said, by sheer dint of your birth, you have a status that I could never hope to attain. But by association…'

'Are you sure you want to be associated with some-one who has fallen from grace?' Eva couldn't quite hide the brittleness in her voice.

'But that's it. You haven't been on the scene recently, so you bring no adverse baggage.'

'What about my parents? When my father abandoned us it caused quite a scandal.'

'They never divorced, though, so anything anyone might have said is just idle gossip.'

Just idle gossip. It had been the judgement of their peers that had wounded her mother more than anything. The social ostracism. It would have almost been better if her father *had* divorced her mother, but he'd refused.

Not wanting to lose any of his own money. Her mother had been too proud to pursue it. And Eva had always suspected that her mother had wanted her father to return. Even though theirs had been a very acrimonious relationship.

But that didn't seem to bother Vidal. Because for his purposes Eva still had value. In her name at the very least.

Enough value for a fake engagement to the one man on this planet who could look into her soul without even trying and lay her bare.

Eva's breath quickened at the thought of being literally laid bare in front of Vidal. It was the most terrifying thing she could think of. Terrifying and exhilarating. But mostly terrifying. Terrifying enough for her to resist.

'The *castillo* will sell eventually if you don't buy it.'

'It hasn't in a year. Are you prepared to wait another year?'

The thought of another year watching the *castillo* decay around her was enough to make Eva feel even more nauseous. But she hid it.

'If I have to.'

Vidal shook his head. 'Even now, when you have nothing, your pride won't allow you to be seen with someone you consider inferior. I have to hand it to you—you're consistent at least. Your mother would be proud.'

It was safer for him to believe that she considered him inferior. It gave her a sense of armour.

Curious in spite of herself, she asked, 'How long would this be for?'

He shrugged minutely, as if he wasn't suggesting something totally audacious—asking her to pretend to be his fiancée.

'A month? Maybe two? That's all I need to secure a particular investment.'

Something about the way that he was being so cavalier with his pronouncements made Eva ask waspishly, 'Won't it look worse for you if you're only engaged for a brief time?'

Vidal shrugged. 'Once I get the investment I don't really care about people's opinions.'

'You used not to be so cynical.'

Vidal's face hardened. 'Life has made me cynical. And certain people in particular.'

Eva's heart thumped. 'You mean me?'

'Let's just say that you were my introduction.'

Eva knew it shouldn't hurt to hear him say that. But it did. The irony was that even though life had made her cynical too, she didn't want it. She hated it. And yet it was ingrained within her, and she didn't know if she'd ever be brave enough to be vulnerable or let it go.

Clearly what Vidal wanted here was a form of revenge, pure and simple. For the fact that she and her mother had never let him forget that he was beneath them. And her, primarily, for teasing him mercilessly and for punishing him when he'd rejected her. Humiliated her. Because when he'd walked away from her that day she'd known that she was the one who was lesser in every way.

She folded her arms over her chest. 'Isn't it kind of pathetic? Living out your father's dream to own the property where you both worked and then parade me on your arm like some kind of trophy?'

'It's no more pathetic than your teenage dream to seduce me.'

Eva flushed. 'I was bored.'

'You wanted me—and you still want me.'

You still want me.

The shock of his words landed in her gut like a punch.

'Don't be ridiculous…' she breathed. Terrified he would see that it wasn't ridiculous at all, she unfolded her arms. 'I don't have time for this—I'd prefer to take my chances. I need to get back to work.'

Sudden panic filled her, how long had she been here? It felt like hours and it felt like a nanosecond.

'You go back to work and consider my offer. I'll be here until lunchtime tomorrow. You have until then to let me know that you've realised what I'm offering is your only option.'

Eva turned and walked back to the door.

From behind her she heard, 'Aren't you forgetting something?'

She stopped and looked back. Vidal was pointing at the turn-down things. There was the smallest glimmer of a smile playing around his mouth.

Anger at how easily he thought he could manipulate her made Eva say, 'Do your own turn-down service.' And she walked out, heart thumping so hard she felt almost dizzy.

If Vidal chose to make a complaint about her, she could get fired for this. She was an idiot to have let him get to her. But he'd always managed to get to her—from the moment she'd looked at him for the first time. Their eyes had locked and she'd felt as if he could see all the way into her, right down to where she locked away her most tender feelings, for fear that her mother would trample all over them.

And even though she only had herself to blame for behaving as she had around him, she'd always been hurt by his judgement of her—as if on some level she'd hoped that he could see through the armour she wore to the person underneath, who wasn't remotely spoiled or entitled. Who was, in fact, very lonely. And confused. And full of desires she didn't really understand.

Eva gripped the trolley and pushed it back down the corridor. There was no way she could agree to Vidal's shocking proposition. There was no way she could handle being in close proximity with him day after day. Not when he made her feel so exposed and called to the weakest part of her, where her desires threatened to overwhelm her and emotions swirled dangerously with too many memories to ignore.

She needed to escape the past, not return to it.

CHAPTER THREE

EVA COULDN'T SLEEP that night. In spite of everything she'd told herself, she couldn't stop the onslaught of memories. She wondered if she really had been that awful? To merit a level of antipathy where Vidal would have no problem using her to elevate his own standing?

Yes, said a voice.

There had been countless little aggressions. Some benign and annoying and others much more pointed. Like when he'd been studying for university exams during a holiday and he'd been lying outside, bare-chested and wearing board shorts.

Eva had been sent with a message from her mother, and she'd said officiously, while trying not to ogle his perfect body, 'Mother says you are not to lie about like some vagrant. This is not your home to do as you please.'

The words had turned to ash on Eva's tongue as Vidal had twisted to look up at her, making the muscles in his chest bunch and lengthen. She'd had an acute sense of floundering. Swimming far out of her depth.

'And what do *you* say, Eva?'

The sound of her name on his tongue had been deeply thrilling to her at seventeen years old.

'Have you got an original thought in your head?' he'd asked.

Eva had flushed, suddenly very conscious of her gangly limbs in culottes and a button-down shirt. She'd longed to be able to lounge around like him. His sense of ease had always fascinated her. His innate confidence. She'd felt prickly. Defensive. Aware that he was touching on something that was deeply disturbing—her mother's influence over her. But her mother was all she knew. Her only touchstone in this world.

She'd blurted out, 'What about *your* mother? Did she leave you and your father because you had nothing to offer her?'

Vidal had sprung to his feet so fast that she'd taken a startled step back. His face had gone white and he'd been livid. She'd never seen him look so intimidating.

'Do not *ever* mention my mother again.'

Eva had battled to overcome her sense of intimidation. She'd shrugged minutely. 'My father left too...it's not a big deal.'

Except of course it was. His abandonment of Eva and her mother permeated the walls of this castle and every inch of its grounds like a toxic mist.

Vidal had gritted out, 'My mother did not leave us. She died.' And he'd gathered up his things and stalked off.

Eva had never seen him studying outside again.

Eva thumped the pillow under her head. But when she did finally fall asleep her dreams were no less disturbing than her memories. And when she woke in the morning the lingering tendrils of a vivid nightmare made her re-alise that maybe returning to the past was her only op-tion. Maybe that was the only way to find her freedom.

That morning, Vidal looked at the dawn breaking over Madrid, bathing the city in a glorious halo of gold and pink. Grief clutched at his chest as he thought of his beloved father and mother. And how they had died so prematurely and never got to enjoy the fruits of his labour.

He often thought about the kind of house he would have bought them. The life of ease he would have given them after working so hard. His mother had been a seamstress, and one of Vidal's earliest memories was of the distinctive sound of her sewing machine. Day and night. Soothing. But it had stopped when she'd died and everything had changed.

That was why he hadn't bought a property here yet—it felt wrong without them. His father had looked for a better job, having made a promise to his mother to ensure that Vidal had every opportunity to get to a decent school. She'd known Vidal had a prodigious talent.

Vidal's mother and father had had the kind of love and devotion that was rare. They'd never excluded Vidal either—their love had been big enough to encompass all three of them. And big enough to handle the fact that, after Vidal, his mother hadn't been able to have more children.

His experience of their love had given Vidal a lifelong ambition to replicate what his father and mother had had some day. He'd wanted someone as good and kind and selfless as his mother. He'd wanted that deep and pure connection. The kind of mutual support that was unspoken but stronger than steel.

But over the years he'd become cynical. The world he inhabited wasn't that simple. He'd realised how naive he was, how idealistic. The woman he wanted didn't exist. And yet he found himself clinging to the hope in spite of everything. Hoping that he might find that deep connection and love one day.

So why are you pursuing Eva Flores? asked a voice.

Vidal's mouth firmed. Because, as he'd told her, she was the one who had been his introduction to cynicism. So maybe she was the one who could help him exorcise it.

When he'd first met her he'd actually felt an affinity with her. They'd both lost a parent—her father wasn't dead, but he was gone—and they had no siblings. He'd thought they might be friends. But whenever he had reached out the hand of friendship, and whenever there might have even been a moment of communication, Eva would invariably say something or do something to remind Vidal of his place. Telling him he was not to fool himself into thinking he was her equal.

Even after he'd graduated from university and had begun making serious waves on the tech scene Eva had been coolly unimpressed. The most galling thing to remember now was that even though Vidal had no longer been under any obligation to go back and help his father during his holidays, he had *wanted* to go back. To see her. Endlessly fascinated in spite of himself. Fascinated to know if she was the same.

And each time she was. Only more beautiful and more haughty, if that was possible. As if maturity was only hardening her edges even more.

She was impermeable. And over the years any pity he might have had for her was eroded to nothing. She was born of a legacy and a society that he knew nothing about and wanted nothing to do with. It was in her bones and in her blood.

And yet now she's cleaning hotel rooms.

Vidal snorted to himself.

Only because she's too proud to let her peers see her so impoverished in public.

No doubt she had some plan, once the *castillo* was

sold, to reintroduce herself to the society she'd had to hide from.

He was offering her a fast track to that end. So why wasn't she jumping at the opportunity?

Because it was with *him*. A nobody. Even if he did have billions now, he remained unpalatable to her.

The fact that he still wanted her was utterly galling. But he feared it was a hunger that would not go away until he'd had her.

You want to seduce her, insisted a little voice.

No, Vidal countered.

He was stronger than that.

But before he could stop it a fantasy emerged fully formed to mock him. A fantasy of making Eva come apart under his hands. Of all that haughty froideur melting, to reveal the flesh-and-blood woman underneath who couldn't deny that she was just that: flesh and blood.

He wanted to smash aside that ice and make her admit that he'd always driven her as crazy as she had him. He wanted it more than he needed her to help him secure any investment. And that revelation was enough to make him go cold. She still held him in the palm of her hand. She still mocked him for his weakness without saying a word.

As long as she existed in his fantasies like this he would not be able to move on. But he wanted more than this. He wanted a true connection. Love. And Eva Flores was the antithesis of that.

Coming here, indulging his curiosity, had been a weakness, exposing him. He'd become jaded. Time and experience had only sharpened his interest in what was forbidden. He shouldn't be surprised that Eva had managed to burrow under his skin again and lodge there like a sharp thorn. But it was time to let the fascination go.

Her hold over him was illusory. He wasn't used to not having a woman he wanted. That was all. He'd wasted enough time on her.

He was done.

'I'm afraid Mr Suarez has checked out.'

'But it's only ten a.m.!'

Eva wasn't prepared for the sense of panic mixed with desolation that landed in her gut.

She said, 'He told me that he would be here till lunch-time.'

The concierge, who was new and didn't recognise Eva as being on the cleaning staff, said, 'He checked out last night. I'm sorry I can't give you any more information.'

Eva stepped back, conscious of the people behind her. She went and stood to one side, near a pillar, and tried to figure out what to do. She overheard two women talking nearby in not so quiet voices.

'Did you see her? I'm sure that was Eva Flores.'

'No way. No one has seen her in years. The girl is a ghost. She doesn't exist. You know her nickname was "the girl in the bubble", because she was only allowed out of that *castillo* about three times a year...'

Eva could almost hear the shudder in the voice of the other woman when she responded.

'That place is creepy. It looks haunted. She'll never sell it. She'll grow old there, like her mother. All alone and going mad.'

Eva couldn't breathe. It was as if they'd articulated the nightmare she'd had last night. Of growing old alone in the *castillo*. Bitter, like her mother. *Alone.* Trapped.

Even after she'd woken at dawn she hadn't been able to shake the awful clammy horror of that possibility in her future. So much so that she'd found herself deciding there and then that she would accept Vidal's offer and throw caution to the wind.

She wanted to live.

Maybe letting Vidal have his retribution was the only way of doing that.

So she'd come straight to the hotel and now he was gone. He hadn't even waited. Was he already bored toying with Eva?

She avoided the area where the two gossiping women were standing and went out of the hotel and rang her solicitor. He told her what she'd already feared: Vidal's people had called and said he was no longer interested in buying the *castillo*.

Eva felt sick. But she knew that she had only one option. She had to go and find Vidal and ask him to reconsider. Because he was the only thing that could stop her nightmare from coming true.

Vidal stood in the middle of a glittering crowd on the rooftop of one of London's most exclusive buildings. London was laid out before him in a carpet of lights, its tall buildings piercing the dusky sky. He was among some of the most important people in the country. In the world. Tech entrepreneurs like him. Moguls, models, actors, politicians… Even royalty.

He was a lot more comfortable in these surroundings now, but sometimes he still felt like an imposter. Impossible not to when most people in this space had been born into privilege and took it as their due. He was accepted—but only up to a point. Some people still looked at him warily.

People like Eva.

He gritted his jaw. He hadn't been able to get her out of his mind in the week since he'd left Spain. Ridiculously, he was feeling guilty when he thought of leaving her to her fate, when he owed her nothing. Even worse was the frustration and irritation that she'd managed to leave him feeling somehow at a loss. Exposed in his desire for her.

Vidal finally responded to the incessant chattering of a woman who was desperately trying to get his attention and schooled his features into some semblance of interest, when really his interest was back in Madrid.

So, when a movement out of the corner of his eye made him look to his left, he thought he was hallucinating. Eva Flores was just a few feet away. Immediately standing out in the crowd with her tall, willowy silhouette, wearing a dusky pink wrap dress with one arm bared. Hair pulled back. Minimal make-up. But she didn't need make-up. Her bone structure alone was enough to make people turn and stare.

He heard someone say, 'Who is *that*?'

For one cold, clammy moment he thought he really was hallucinating—that sexual frustration was infecting his mind. He blinked. No, she was still there. It was her. Unmistakably. And as that thought sank in and registered a sense of satisfaction settled deep in his gut. Along with something else he didn't want to acknowledge—*relief.*

Everyone else faded away. His eyes were locked with hers. Her chin had that little defiant tilt, as if to remind him that she was better than him. But she had come because she needed him too badly. Because she had a weakness too.

He'd seen her. So much for sneaking into this exclusive party and getting her bearings before Vidal noticed she was there. As soon as she'd walked in his head had come up, as if scenting prey, and he'd looked around and straight at her.

Nowhere to hide. She had to brazen it out now.

She walked towards Vidal and saw his eyes narrow on her. He wasn't wearing formal dress—a dark suit with a light shirt, open top button. No tie. She imagined how breathtaking he would be in a tuxedo.

She stopped a couple of feet away. She was vaguely aware of a woman beside Vidal emitting a huffy sound and flouncing away.

Vidal spoke first. 'Fancy meeting you here.'

Eva felt heat climb into her face. Vidal was looking at her with something distinctly...*satisfied* in his expression. She chafed against it, knowing that she'd had no other choice. That awful nightmare still lingered, even a week later.

She tried not to sound peevish, 'I went to the hotel the morning after we met, but you didn't even wait for my answer.'

'No, because I realised I'd wasted too much time in Madrid.'

Eva felt a sliver of panic. Perhaps even now it was too late?

She swallowed. 'Well, I wanted to talk to you.'

'Well, here I am.'

Eva looked around. She noticed people near them pretending to be studiously engaged elsewhere when they were clearly trying to eavesdrop.

She looked at Vidal. 'Could we talk somewhere a little less...public?'

'If you don't want to be seen with me in public then you shouldn't have come here.'

Eva frowned. 'I… No… That is, I didn't know where else to find you… I just feel it's too personal to discuss here.'

A waiter came by at that moment, with a tray full of glasses of champagne. Vidal took two glasses from the tray and handed one to Eva. 'Why don't you relax for a minute? You look tense.'

She felt tense. She clutched the glass in her hand. She didn't want to be seen in public. She'd hated these kinds of situations ever since that hideously embarrassing event in Madrid when she was eighteen.

She'd sighed with relief when she'd stepped into this party and realised she'd got the tone right with the dress she'd hired from a designer shop here in London.

'You bring the glass to your mouth and you take a sip—like this…'

Eva's scattered attention was brought back to Vidal, who was taking a sip from the glass that looked impossibly delicate in his hand. Her eye followed the movement of his throat as he swallowed. Little flames danced across her skin, making it rise into goosebumps.

This was crazy. How could she hope to have a rational conversation with him when she was so aware of him and so wound up?

She took a sip and the sparkling drink danced down her throat, as if to mock her for being so serious. She tried consciously to relax, but social situations always made her nervous. She wasn't used to interacting with a large group of people. She'd never really been prepared for it—even though her mother had fully expected her to somehow charm and find a suitable husband after growing up in a bubble. Exactly as those women had said.

'When did you come over?' he asked.

'I came this morning.'

'Where are you staying?'

Oh, God, now Vidal was resorting to small talk. 'Um…a hotel near Piccadilly.'

Eva didn't want to admit that she was staying in a hostel near the train station, and that she had a flight booked to go home first thing in the morning. She'd changed in a bathroom at the hostel earlier, and had got some funny looks when she'd emerged, standing out amongst the backpacker tourists.

She scrabbled for something to say to avoid more questions. 'You look good here.' She stopped. Mortified.

Vidal arched a brow, amused. 'A compliment from Eva Flores? That is high praise indeed.'

Eva cursed herself. 'What I mean is that you…fit in. You've done well.'

Any hint of humour left Vidal's expression. 'For a kid from a minor suburb without a cent to his name and working-class parents?'

She looked at him. 'Well, that's the truth, isn't it? That's something to be proud of. What you've achieved is amazing.'

Yes, it was the truth. So why did her observation irritate him so much? Why was he suddenly so tense?

Because all he could see in his mind's eye was the tired faces of his parents and their red hands. Red from working.

And suddenly that sense of being an imposter was back, looming large over his shoulder. As if Eva's presence was all it had needed to re-emerge. Reminding him that he was only here through the sheer dumb luck of having a higher than average intellect and the ability to work hard.

He hated it that she pushed his buttons so easily. That she still had that power without even saying a word. Just by *being*.

It had been a mistake to think that she could bring something positive to his reputation. To his social standing. She'd done him a favour by turning up here to remind him of that.

But when Vidal opened his mouth to tell Eva that she was no longer welcome at this party, he found himself saying instead, 'Fine, let's go somewhere more private.'

Who was he kidding? His head didn't want Eva Flores anywhere near him, but his body was another matter, and right now his body was ruling his head.

'You don't have to leave. I don't mind waiting.'

They were standing at the elevator. Vidal didn't respond. Eva was desperately trying to maintain her composure, but it was hard when Vidal's hand was big and cupping her elbow. Skin to skin.

The elevator doors opened, and when they stepped in an attendant pressed the ground-floor button. The space was too small. All Eva could smell was Vidal. Sharp and spicy and masculine.

She said, a little threadily, 'You can let me go now.'

Vidal looked down, as if surprised that he was holding on to her. He didn't let go straight away, though. He took his time. Fingers trailing over her skin, leaving goosebumps behind.

Finally, Eva felt as if she could breathe again. The elevator doors opened onto the lobby of what was one of London's most exclusive hotels. Luckily, Vidal's social activities were well documented in the press, so she'd found out about this party relatively easily.

She could have tried to meet him at his London office once she'd found out he was here for the week, but the thought of being refused entry had been daunting. So she'd figured a social event might be easier. And it had been. Until now.

They were outside the building and a sleek SUV with tinted windows was waiting. The driver got out and opened the back door. Vidal extended an arm to Eva. 'Please…'

She didn't move. 'Where are we going?'

'To my apartment. It's not far from here.'

The thought of being alone with Vidal made her feel nervous and excited all at once. 'Can't we just go somewhere like a quiet bar?'

Vidal's jaw hardened. 'Do you want to talk or not?'

Of course she did. That was why she'd come here.

Reluctantly she moved forward and sat into the back of the car. The driver closed the door and Vidal got in on the other side, immediately dwarfing the cavernous space.

The vehicle moved smoothly into the London traffic, barely making a sound. An electric car. They didn't speak on the short journey. The car stopped outside a tall, sleek-looking apartment building. A concierge greeted Vidal and then they were in another elevator, and Eva's stomach swooped as they moved smoothly skyward.

The doors opened, and it was only when they opened directly into an apartment that she realised it had been a private lift. The apartment was breathtaking. Contrary to what Vidal probably thought, Eva really hadn't ever been anywhere like it.

Dark, moody tones were lightened by floor-to-ceiling windows showcasing a glittering view of the London skyline. Massive paintings were hung on the walls, and comfortable couches and chairs were dotted artfully around the space, with coffee tables groaning under big hardback books on photography and art.

Low lamps sent out seductive pools of golden light. It was a far cry from the spartan apartment Vidal and his father had once shared at the *castillo*.

Eva was rooted to the spot beside the elevator doors, which slid closed behind her with a muted *swish*.

Vidal had walked into the apartment, not even checking to see if Eva was following him. He was slipping off his jacket and draping it casually over the back of a chair, heading to what looked like a drinks cabinet.

He said over his shoulder, 'Can I offer you a drink?'

Eva felt so tense she thought she might crack. Maybe a drink would help her feel marginally more relaxed. She'd barely touched the champagne at the party.

'Sure, maybe a small white wine?'

He mixed a drink for himself and duly came back to her with a glass of perfectly chilled white wine. She took a sip quickly, and then saw Vidal hold his own tumbler up and say with a mocking tone, 'Cheers…'

Eva felt very unsophisticated. Sheepishly, she echoed, 'Cheers.'

'Please, make yourself comfortable.' Vidal waved a hand to indicate the vast expanse of his lounge area.

The sheer amount of choice made Eva move instead towards one of the windows. London twinkled and glittered under a clear sky. Helicopters traversed the city with blinking lights.

She was very conscious of Vidal behind her. Watching her. Waiting for her to beg for mercy. For a handout. For help. For her life.

She steeled herself and turned around. 'Look, Vidal, it's obvious you've decided to change your mind about the *castillo* and the...' She trailed off.

'The fake engagement?' he supplied helpfully.

'Why?' she asked hoping she didn't sound too needy. Or desperate.

He came and stood at the window, tumbler in his hand. He said, 'It was a moment of weakness to even want to see you again. See what you might have become. See if you had changed at all.' He looked at her. 'I don't indulge in weaknesses. But you always pushed my buttons, Eva.'

Her insides swooped and dived. 'I was young...'

Vidal looked back out of the window and made a dissenting sound. 'Yet you knew how to patronise those around you before most people could even spell the word.'

Eva swallowed her defence. How could she even begin to articulate what she had only come to terms with in the past year—the depth of her mother's malign influence on her life?

Desperately, she cast around for another way to try and get through to Vidal. 'You said it was your father's dying wish that you do something to restore the *castillo*...'

He responded easily. 'I also said I wasn't sentimental. My father was raving at the end...high on morphine. He thought he saw my dead mother standing behind me in the room.'

Eva had never known Vidal could be so obdurate. Feeling a sense of futility, she looked blindly at the view. 'Your father felt sorry for me, you know.'

'I know.'

'He used to say to me that there was a whole world outside the *castillo* and I had to get out and explore it… find my own way.'

'So why didn't you?'

'It wasn't that easy. My mother became unwell. I had to care for her.'

'And now you've lost precious time in establishing yourself on the scene, and perhaps no one is really that interested in an heiress with nothing but a pile of medieval bricks to her name?'

Eva forced a tight smile. 'You have it all worked out.'

'Because, let's face it, it's not as if you're qualified to do anything else.'

Eva realised this wasn't going anywhere, and she was terrified that the longer she stayed the more likely it would be that Vidal would notice her awareness of him. An awareness that she couldn't hide.

She set her glass of wine on a nearby table. She hadn't even put down her clutch bag. It was still clamped in her other hand. 'I think it's best if we stop wasting each other's time. You should go back to your party, Vidal.'

She forced herself to look at him. His face was cast in shadow as he turned to face her from the window. The glow of the city outside made the lines on it look grim. She sensed he was fighting some kind of inner battle, but she needed to move on and try and seek salvation elsewhere.

'It was nice to see you again…and I'm happy that you are doing so well.'

'Are you, Eva? Really happy? Because you don't look it.'

That nearly felled her. *Happy.* The fact that he'd noticed she wasn't. Her chest felt tight. *Dios.*

'I'm perfectly fine, Vidal. Thank you for your concern. Now, I should go.'

She turned and took a step towards the door, which felt very far away, across an expanse of luxurious carpet.

Vidal said, 'Back to work at the hotel tomorrow?'

Eva stopped. Turned around again. A spurt of anger mercifully diluted her emotion. 'Are you intent on torturing me until the last moment, Vidal? It's not enough to dangle the solution to all my problems under my nose and then whip it away at the last minute? I think you've made your point now—your life was a misery while you were at the *castillo* and now you're wreaking your revenge.'

Vidal stepped out of the shadows. He put his glass down on a table. He shook his head. 'It wasn't a misery, actually. My father enjoyed working there and I enjoyed helping him. It just got miserable when we had to deal with your mother—or when you decided that *that* day would be a good day to subject me to a little torture.'

Eva's heart thumped. She'd never known she'd had such an effect on him. 'Torture? That's a strong word.'

'It felt like torture. Being so aware of you and being so aware that everything about you was forbidden. Your age, your experience, your social status… All far beyond my reach. And yet that didn't stop you from parading yourself in front of me at any opportunity, looking for attention.'

Eva longed to defend herself. She hadn't known what she was doing. She'd had no idea of her effect on Vidal. She'd only known of his on her. She said, almost accusingly, 'I could say the same of you.'

He frowned. 'What are you talking about?'

Eva cursed her runaway mouth. 'The midnight swims

you took. *Naked.* You knew where my room was. You knew I'd hear you.'

A vivid memory sprang fully formed into her head before she could stop it. Late one night, under a full moon, Vidal hauling himself out of the pool in one graceful move, muscles flexing and bunching. Water sluicing down over perfectly sculpted muscles. His back broad, waist narrow. Buttocks muscular. And then he'd turned around, as if aware he was being watched. And Eva's avid gaze had dropped to the dark hair between his legs where, even after a cold swim, he'd been impressive.

He'd looked like a Greek statue. The embodiment of physical perfection. And then he'd looked up and their eyes had met. And Eva had stepped backwards so rapidly she'd tripped and fallen over. Pulse hammering. Feeling like an idiot. Completely exposed because she'd known he'd seen her.

'In case I need to remind you, that was the only time I *could* swim, as your mother had forbidden use of the pool for employees and their families. Not that she ever used it herself. You did, though.'

Yes, she had. And all her raging teenage hormones had been channelled into testing and pushing the boundaries of her newly forming sexuality and provoking a reaction from Vidal.

The days he'd been around had been heady. The days when he hadn't had felt cold, as if the sun had dipped behind a dark cloud. She'd come alive when he'd been at the *castillo*, and the memory mocked her now.

She must have been so obvious and gauche. He'd already been a man of the world, and because of the narrative her mother had fed her Eva had somehow believed that she was as sophisticated as the women he was meeting in America. When in fact she hadn't even been kissed! Which was what had led her to make that audacious move on her eighteenth birthday…which had ended in humiliation and disaster.

How Vidal would laugh at her if he even had an inkling that nothing had changed for Eva since that day. She was as innocent as ever. As unworldly. Except he appeared to believe that up until her mother's death she'd generally been living the high life.

She lifted her chin. 'We can keep going around like this in circles, Vidal, but ultimately we're going nowhere.'

'Do you know what that does to me?'

'What?'

'When you lift your chin like that?'

'Like what?'

'Like *that*. You're doing it now and you don't even notice.'

'What does it do to you?'

'It makes me a little crazy.'

'In what way?'

'You're pretending you don't feel it too?'

Eva's heart palpitated. Surely he couldn't mean…? 'I don't know what you're talking about.'

Vidal gave a short, curt laugh. 'Because I'm still the last man you would admit to wanting when we're not within the grounds of the *castillo*?'

'That was a long time ago…' breathed Eva, horrified that he was mentioning what had happened. Horrified that he remembered. 'It was nothing…a silly moment.'

'It didn't feel silly. It felt very serious. I can still remember how you trembled against me.'

'Stop it.'

Eva's jaw was so tight it hurt. Not content with teasing her with an offer to buy the *castillo*, now he was intent on humiliating her. Again.

'Do you know why I remember?'

'I don't care.'

'Because I haven't been able to get that moment out of my head—or the countless other moments when you intended me to notice you. The inconvenient truth is that I want you, Eva Flores.'

CHAPTER FOUR

EVA HEARD VIDAL say the words but they wouldn't go into her brain. They were in her body. That was where they impacted. Right in her solar plexus. She couldn't breathe. Her pulse was tripping. The tiny hairs were lifting all over her skin. And deep inside, where she hid her innermost secrets and insecurities and vulnerabilities, a pulse throbbed and heat flowed. Melting. Exposing. *Weak*.

'That's not true…' she breathed.

Vidal nodded his head. 'It is. And you want me too.'

She was dizzy. Was it that obvious? Feeling desperate, she said, 'You're the last man on earth I'd want.'

He took a step towards her and she almost stumbled backwards, filled with a mixture of adrenalin, panic, and something far more disturbing.

He said, 'You've wanted me from the moment you saw me, in spite of my status.'

She couldn't lie. Not here, under that gaze. 'Maybe I did…a long time ago. A teenage crush.'

'Pretty strong crush. You kissed me. And when I didn't kiss you back you—'

'You didn't want me then.' She cut him off, not wanting to hear him say what she had almost done in a fit of thwarted passion.

Vidal's eyes darkened. 'Oh, I wanted you. But you weren't ready.'

'And now I am?'

'You're a grown woman, aren't you?'

What he meant by that was that he assumed she was experienced. The thought of him finding out that she was as inexperienced as she'd been all those years ago made her feel nauseous.

She feigned bravado. 'Of course.' And then, 'But what does this have to do with…anything?'

'I've decided that my offer is still open. To buy the *castillo*, settle your debts, and even give you a stake in the business.'

'In return for…?'

'Standing by my side and looking suitably devoted when I announce our engagement.'

'A fake engagement.'

'Of course. I have no intention of marrying you.'

This was said with such assurance that Eva found herself asking, 'But you do intend to marry?'

'Absolutely. Some day. To a woman I can love and respect.'

This caught at Eva on many different levels. Too many to pick apart now. Her chief emotion was hurt, when he shouldn't be touching on her emotions at all.

A little waspishly, she said, 'Then why put yourself through being anywhere near me at all?'

'Because I want you. And because I know I won't get you out of my mind until I've had you.'

Until I've had you.

Something about the crudeness of his language thrilled Eva even as it horrified her. And then she realised that he'd admitted that she'd been on his mind. But somehow it didn't make him seem weak, which was what she might have expected if she'd made such an admission.

'You're saying I'd have to sleep with you?' Eva was glad her voice sounded suitably affronted when inwardly she was slowly going on fire.

'No, I didn't say you'd have to sleep with me. I said that I want you. I am not in the habit of forcing women to sleep with me.'

Eva felt confused. 'But then…if I don't sleep with you…would we still have a deal?'

'Oh, you'll sleep with me—and it'll be entirely of your own volition.'

Her pulse thundered. 'You're very sure of yourself.'

Vidal shrugged minutely but didn't say anything else. He didn't have to. It vibrated between them. This awareness. This *heat*.

It's not going to happen, Eva promised herself.

Being so aware of Vidal and being forbidden to do anything about it was like an ink stain on her skin…she'd worn it for so long.

Apart from that one time when she'd tried to kiss him. And he'd humiliated her, exactly as her mother had warned her would happen if she let herself show any weakness.

She was older now. And, while she wasn't more experienced, she wasn't given to moments of exposing herself with unrestrained passion. This Vidal was infinitely more intimidating. It would be easy to resist him.

She didn't fear that he would coerce her. He was too proud. He'd always had the kind of innate pride that she'd never really had, in spite of her mother's insistence that she had every reason to be proud.

Vidal looked at her. 'Well? What's it to be, Eva? Because either you stay here now or you go, and if you go this time I promise you that we will never see each other again.'

Ridiculous to feel such a lurch of emotion at that thought. Either way, even if she agreed, she would never see Vidal again once they were done. It was abundantly clear that he hated himself for wanting her. And perhaps that would make this easier—it wasn't as if he was even pretending to like her. To charm her. What must it be like to be someone he desired and didn't resent desiring? The thought was provocative.

She felt as if she was taking a leap into a void, but at the same time she had no choice. 'I… Okay, yes, I'll stay.'

There was a pregnant pause during which Vidal didn't respond, and for a horrifying moment Eva thought he was going to tell her that it was all a joke and of course he wasn't going to go through with the deal.

But then he became brisk and said, 'I'll get you a pen and paper. Write down the name of your hotel and room number and I'll have my driver pick up your things. I'll show you around and then you can rest. We can discuss further plans in the morning.'

Eva didn't know what to say, so she just took the pen and paper from Vidal and wrote down the details.

He gave her a quick impersonal tour of the impressive apartment, with its state-of-the-art kitchen, two dining rooms—one formal—and the formal lounge they'd just been in. There was also a less formal one, with soft couches, books on shelves and a media centre.

When he showed her into a spacious suite with its own bathroom, dressing room and sitting room, which clearly wasn't his space, she realised that he wasn't expecting her to fall into his bed that night. She felt very gauche, and also, bizarrely, a little dizzy with how fast this was all happening.

Vidal stood in the doorway and Eva felt the chasm between them. A chasm that she had put there from the first day they'd met. A chasm nurtured and supervised by her mother, for fear that Eva might forget for a minute who she was and speak to Vidal as if he was her equal.

She felt a little lost and hated herself for it.

Before she could say anything, he spoke. 'You know where everything is now. Please make yourself at home and help yourself to anything you'd like. The kitchen is well stocked.'

And then he was gone. The door shut behind him.

Eva sat down on the edge of the bed. For the first time in days…months…even though she was in an environment that was more hostile than friendly, she felt a sense of relief wash over her.

If she could just resist Vidal, and if she could weather the public scrutiny of being by his side as his fake fiancée, then she would emerge with her whole life ahead of her. Free from the past once and for all.

What the hell are you doing, man?

The question resounded in Vidal's head as he stood at his office window, looking out over the city. His driver had just returned with Eva's bag. A small case. It had once been very expensive, but now it was battered and falling apart.

Like the castillo.

Also, his driver had informed him that she hadn't been checked into a hotel—the address had been for a hostel, near the train station.

So what? he asked himself. So she was proud and

hadn't wanted him to know the extent of what she couldn't afford? He could have figured that out from the fact that she was working as a chambermaid in a hotel.

Earlier, he'd told himself he wanted nothing to do with her—and seeing her at the party had confirmed that for him. He'd made the right decision in deciding to cut all ties—leave her to her fate. After all, he owed her nothing. And yet he'd invited her back to his apartment. Because the truth was that he couldn't let her walk away. He might have temporarily fooled himself into thinking he didn't want her, or that his desire would fade, but seeing her here, on his turf, in that dress…all bets were off now. There was no turning back.

Interestingly, she hadn't behaved as he would have expected in his apartment. She'd looked uncertain. Awed. She'd gone to stand at the window and looked out as if she'd never seen such a view before. And then he'd cursed himself. Of course she had—she'd been here before. He'd seen those pictures of her in London, wearing a dress that had barely been modest. Surrounded by equally scantily clad women. Champagne flowing. Men leering.

That lifestyle had only stopped when she'd had to take responsibility for the *castillo* on her mother's death, and she must have resented it so much.

She was just toying with him. Pretending to be in awe. Amusing herself, no doubt. Waiting for him to patronise her so that she could remind him of who she was.

If that was the case, why did it still bother him? He was immune to Eva's games now. *He* would be the one in control this time, manipulating events to suit himself.

He would make the most of her presence by his side to be accepted professionally, in a way that had eluded him up to now.

Once he'd made headlines because of how he'd pulled himself out of the margins of society. Now those same newspapers speculated as to who his parents had been, and just *how* he'd really got those scholarships.

As much as people loved a rags-to-riches story, once you were in the *riches*, and mingling amongst the great and good, it became a different story.

After his father had died, he had gone through a crisis of sorts. Grief for his father, old grief for his mother, and lamenting that he couldn't share his wealth with them had driven him on a hedonistic spiral of wanting to forget the pain for a while.

He'd given himself over to a time of finding transient pleasures, earning himself a reputation as a playboy. People had started whispering things like, *'Well, it's no wonder...look at where he came from... He can't take his success seriously...'*

And that was when his business had started to suffer.

But he'd spent too many years working and sweating to be accepted to fall at the final hurdle. The final hurdle being the fact that no matter how much money or success he had, he needed to prove that he was worthy.

Eva, even with her vastly diminished finances and the fact that her parents had separated all those years ago, was still that exclusive and invisible invitation into a privileged world.

So, no. He hadn't made a mistake in changing his mind. He would improve his reputation by association and by appearing more settled. And if she was using him just to get a step back into her own world then what of it? What did he care where she went or what she did when he was done with her? She would be welcome to return to her peers...to find a suitable husband among the pure bloodlines of Spain's great families.

Out of nowhere an image sprang into Vidal's head of Eva with a dark-haired child in her arms. Smiling, playing, laughing. Before he could stop it, it caught at his gut like a vice. He crushed it. That image was a total fantasy, because Eva Flores didn't have a maternal bone in her body. How could she when he'd never seen her display an ounce of compassion or kindness?

There was no fear of his emotions being involved where Eva Flores was concerned. She was the last woman on the planet he could love. She epitomised everything he didn't want in a partner. She was cold, aloof and supercilious. She was rude and mocking.

But right now she was the only woman he wanted, and his desire burned him. Women didn't ever take up his mental energy like this. He wanted them, he had them, he moved on. She was no different.

Eva woke when the light of the rising sun moved across her face the following morning. She hadn't pulled the curtains closed last night. She realised she was on top of the bed covers and still in the robe she'd found on the back of the bathroom door, after having a long hot shower.

When she'd emerged from the shower she'd seen that someone had delivered her bag and left it just inside the door of the bedroom. Vidal? Her heart had thumped as she'd thought of him coming into the room while she'd been naked in the shower...

She'd slept surprisingly well, considering the circumstances.

She wasn't going back to Spain in the immediate future. She would have to call the hotel. Leave her job. Not that they'd miss her. They had a huge staff turnover. Working there had given her huge respect for all the invisible workers who came and went at dawn and dusk to cater for people like her, who would never have noticed them before.

In fact, her whole experience since her mother had become ill and she'd had to care for her had been a huge eye-opener—and not an unwelcome one. She'd realised how insular her life had been with her mother, and how... rarefied.

She'd gone to a private prep school with other children until she was twelve, and there she had had some friends. But it was as if that had been a turning point, and her mother had taken some kind of a paranoid turn. When Eva had been due to go to secondary school her mother had insisted on her staying at home and being privately tutored. Her mother had wanted to keep Eva apart, as if she was keeping her away from bad influences. Or *any* influences.

Eva had seen her friends from time to time, but gradually she'd realised she was losing touch with their lives. She hadn't been able to keep up with the references they made, and she'd soon stopped being asked to meet them or go to parties. She'd become uncool. Unwanted. And her life had slowly closed in on itself.

Until Vidal had arrived with his father, and Eva's world had exploded into sensations and cravings and emotions that she'd struggled to hide. Emotions that he still affected and that she still had to do her best to hide.

Eva got up and washed and dressed in the casual clothes in her bag. Jeans and a plain white shirt. Sneakers. She pulled her hair back into a low bun and took a breath before leaving the bedroom. Vidal had always been up at the crack of dawn, and things didn't appear to have changed when she found him sitting in the informal dining room by the kitchen.

She was startled when a woman came out, dressed in a uniform. Middle-aged, friendly. She was carrying a coffee pot.

'Coffee is fresh, Miss Flores. Help yourself to anything on the table, or I can make you a cooked breakfast if you'd like?'

Eva shook her head. 'No, thank you, that won't be necessary.'

The table was full of an array of fruit, granola, yoghurts, pastries. She was avoiding looking at Vidal, of course. She'd seen enough of him to know he was dressed in dark trousers and a light blue shirt. Open at his throat.

She sat down at Vidal's right, and the housekeeper poured her some coffee. Eva thanked her. When she'd gone back into the kitchen Eva looked at Vidal, who was watching her. She felt her skin heat and took a quick sip of coffee, wincing slightly.

'It's hot,' Vidal said, a little redundantly.

Eva put down the cup. 'It's good.'

'You slept well?'

Eva reached for some fruit and granola. 'Yes, thank you. The bedroom is very comfortable.'

'Yes, it is. The apartment is a good base for London.'

'You own it?'

'I own the building. My London offices are a few floors down.'

Eva nearly choked on a piece of apple, but managed to swallow it before she embarrassed herself by telling him he'd done well again. He wouldn't take it as it was meant. He'd think she was patronising him.

Thankfully they were interrupted by the housekeeper. 'That'll be me, then, Mr Suarez—unless you need anything else?'

He smiled at the woman and Eva was mesmerised. It transformed his face and reminded her of when he'd been much younger. Less stern. More open.

'That's all, thanks, Mrs Carter. We'll be heading to the States later today, so I'll have my assistant let you know when we're due back. Probably not for at least a couple of weeks.'

The woman nodded and smiled at Eva. 'Goodbye, Miss Flores, I hope you enjoy your trip.'

And then she was gone.

Eva's head was buzzing with questions. 'Who is *we*…? And the States? As in America?'

Vidal said, '"We" is you and me—and, yes, America. That's where I'm based now. In San Francisco. That's where I consider home. London is just my European base.'

Eva absorbed this and felt a spurt of anger. 'I know I've more or less signed myself over to you for this… this fake engagement, but when were you going to inform me about this? And why didn't you introduce me to your housekeeper?'

'I was going to inform you. And I didn't introduce you because I didn't think you would care to be introduced. You never seemed inclined to care much about the staff before.'

Eva was speechless with indignation. But then she realised he had a point. Her mother hadn't liked her to address the staff beyond what was strictly necessary. Even the few staff they'd had left towards the end.

Eva felt piqued. 'Well, for future reference, you can introduce me to whoever is working for you.'

'Making beds and cleaning bathrooms has had an effect on you.' Vidal's tone was dry.

Eva felt like sticking her tongue out at him, but resisted the urge.

He stood up. 'I have a couple of calls to make in my study, but come in in about fifteen minutes and I'll fill you in on the plans.'

The plans. The plans to pretend to be engaged? The plans to share his bed?

Eva went hot and then cold when she thought of Vidal realising how innocent she still was. He *couldn't* find out.

When Vidal had gone, she finished her breakfast and coffee, waited the fifteen minutes, and then went to Vidal's study and knocked on the door.

'Come in.'

Had his voice always been so deep? It seemed to resonate right through her body.

She pushed the door open into a surprisingly bright and modern space, painted light grey, with floor-to-ceiling shelves full of books and another massive window showcasing the spectacular view. Vidal was behind a huge desk with three computers, a laptop, and various other bits of tech equipment.

'Come in…sit down.'

Eva felt as if she was there for an interview.

She sat down on the other side of the desk.

Vidal shut his laptop. 'The reason we're going to San Francisco today is because the investors I'm trying to engage with are due to attend a series of events there over the next couple of weeks. It's too good an opportunity to miss, and the perfect place for us to start appearing as a couple,' he said. 'I had hoped to go back to Spain, to let you gather anything you needed from the *castillo* and tie up some loose ends, but we won't have time now.'

'Oh… I hadn't expected that. I can call my job from here, and there's nothing in the *castillo* that I really need.'

'Clothes?'

Eva thought of all the vintage designer dresses belonging to her mother, which she'd had to sell off to make some money. And then of her own very paltry clothes. Ever since her humiliation at that society birthday party she hadn't trusted her own judgement when it came to clothes—and anyway, she hadn't had the money to buy any.

'There's nothing there for me to pick up,' she said, and then she remembered something. 'Actually, that dress I was wearing last night…it needs to be returned to the hire shop.'

'You *hired* the dress?'

'I can't afford a dress like that.'

Vidal made a note on a pad. 'I'll have my assistant pay them for it—you can keep it. And we'll need to get you more clothes. I'll have a stylist meet us when we get to San Francisco. We'll announce the engagement ASAP.'

To avoid thinking about standing beside Vidal in public and pretending to look besotted, Eva said, 'Who are these investors you need so badly?'

Vidal stood up and went to the window, giving Eva a view of his broad back tapering down to slim hips and the muscular globes of his bottom. Long legs… He was more like an athlete in his prime than a tech nerd.

He turned around and Eva lifted her gaze, but not before she caught the look in Vidal's eye. He knew she'd been checking him out. Damn him.

He said, 'They're people who are very instrumental in the industry—the original disruptors. They have access to the kind of funding that just doesn't exist anywhere else, and the project I'm working on needs the funding they can give.'

'Why are they reluctant to invest? Surely you've proved your track record by now?'

'Because they've become more conservative, and they think that while my business is solid, my personal…volatility is detrimental to their reputation.'

Eva frowned. 'But that's silly. Either your work speaks for itself or it doesn't.'

Vidal's mouth twitched. 'Very noble—and spoken by one who comes from a world where you are trusted and granted access purely because of your name.'

Eva's chin lifted and she didn't even care. 'I didn't know you had such a chip on your shoulder.'

Vidal's mouth turned serious. 'I used not to—until I realised that, much as I'd like to believe otherwise, name and legacy still have a powerful sway. Along with reputation. Especially when millions of dollars are involved.'

Eva bit her lip. 'Do you really think it'll help, having me by your side? Most people over there won't have ever heard of me.'

'They'll find out.'

'Then they'll find out that my parents were separated.'

Vidal waved a hand. 'That's not a big deal. What's more important is that you come from old money and a distinct lineage.'

'You mean *no* money,' Eva muttered.

'Your father still has money.'

She looked at him and tried to hide her sense of hurt and abandonment. 'Really? I wouldn't know.'

'Well, it's obvious that he isn't helping you out.'

'My mother and I didn't see a cent of his money from the moment he walked out of the *castillo*. If the *castillo* hadn't been hers by inheritance from her parents, he would have probably tried to take that too.'

Vidal looked at her. 'So what were you doing with him in London?'

Eva stood up, agitated. 'I don't really think that's relevant right now.'

'You said before that it wasn't how it looked. Tell me how it was.'

'What do you care?'

'Humour me.'

Eva started to pace back and forth, folding her arms across her chest. She turned to Vidal. 'Don't you have things to do before leaving?'

'No rush—private plane.'

Of course. She should have known. She glared at him, hating him for pushing her on this. It was too huge, too humiliating. She couldn't bear to expose herself here... now. Not when Vidal was so remote. Stern. He wouldn't understand.

So she schooled her features, hid her emotion and shrugged minutely. 'It was exactly what you saw—a party. My father just happened to be there too. I partied for a few days...went shopping...and then I went home. That was it.'

Vidal looked sceptical. Eva didn't care. He'd already seen too much. He couldn't ever know the full extent of what had happened that night. It was too painful.

To her relief, he appeared to let it go. He said, 'I need

to go down to my offices for an hour or so, to meet with
my team and make arrangements. Give me the details of
the dress-hire shop and write down your measurements.'

Eva did as he asked and handed him the piece of paper.

He said, 'Pack up your stuff and be ready to go when
I get back.'

'I'm already ready.' Because she literally had nothing with her.

Vidal said, 'Good.' And then he left.

Eva congratulated herself on not letting him see into
her too deeply. And then she realised that she would
have to keep up this level of self-defence for the next
month…two months?

Suddenly that felt more daunting than anything else
she'd ever done in her life.

CHAPTER FIVE

'YOU'VE NEVER BEEN on a private plane before? I find that hard to believe.'

Eva sent a scowl towards Vidal. 'What part of asset-rich, cash-poor didn't you understand?'

'Yes, but I assumed your friends would have offered you opportunities—like on that trip to London, for instance. You hardly carried all your own shopping home on a commercial flight.'

Eva shot him a look across the table between them. It was explicit. *Not. Going. There.*

She was even less inclined to tell him the truth now. He'd laugh if he realised she'd had nothing as frivolous as shopping to bring home. And that she'd flown with a budget airline, squeezed into the middle of three seats.

It had been hard for her to focus since they'd left Vidal's London apartment and driven out of the city to the small airfield where this sleek jet had been waiting for them.

The insides were all cream leather. Carpet so thick it was like walking on a cloud. Polished wood finishes. Discreet staff.

Vidal said, 'This calls for a celebration.' He pressed

a button and a man in a uniform materialised as if from thin air.

'Sir? What can I get you?'

'Two glasses of champagne please, Tom.' Just as the man was turning to leave Vidal said, 'Actually, Tom, let me introduce you. This is Eva Flores. Eva—meet Tom.'

Eva's face felt hot, but she forced a smile. It wasn't the man's fault. Vidal was making a point. 'Very nice to meet you.'

'And you, Miss Flores. I'll be right back.'

Eva looked at Vidal and smiled sweetly. 'Thank you for that.'

For a moment he had an arrested expression on his face and her smile faded.

'What is it? What have I done now?'

He shook his head. And then he said, 'You don't smile very much. Do you know that?'

Eva's chest felt tight. She shrugged as if she didn't care. 'I'm sure I smile as much as the next person.' But she knew she didn't. Before she could stop herself she was saying, 'My mother told me that smiling would give me wrinkles.'

She'd also told her that smiling made her look gormless. She kept that to herself.

Tom returned with two glasses of honey-hued champagne on a tray and handed her one. She took it and smiled again. It did feel a little…unnatural. She made a mental vow to herself to try and smile as much as possible from now on. To unnerve Vidal as much as anything else.

'Here's to a successful collaboration,' Vidal said.

Eva looked at him. 'I didn't know you were such a romantic.'

'Oh, I can be romantic when I want to be.'

The thought of Vidal caring about a woman enough to want to be romantic made Eva feel a little volatile. She took a sip of champagne. Then she put her glass down. She said, 'So how will it work for you? You don't even like me but you're happy to sleep with me?'

'Haven't you heard?' he asked with a mocking tone. 'Men don't need their emotions to be involved. Only their—'

Eva put up a hand. 'Yes, I get it.'

'Sex and emotions are two separate issues. But generally I sleep with women I like. I never said I didn't like you, Eva. What I feel about you is…complex. And challenging. But we don't need to worry about emotions in this instance. All we need is the chemistry that's been between us since the day we first met.'

Eva's breathing felt a little shallow. Had Vidal noticed it even then? Before she'd even been aware of what it was she was feeling? She'd only known it was somehow illicit.

'Don't you care what I might feel about you?' she asked.

Vidal shrugged. 'Not really. I don't need you to like me. I just need you to want me—which you do, but you won't admit it yet.'

I don't need you to like me.

Right at that moment Eva wasn't even sure what she *did* feel for Vidal. *Like* was such an ineffectual word for a feeling which was dark and complicated and intense. She couldn't even hope to articulate it.

'I won't sleep with you,' she said.

Because that would be far too exposing.

'I note you didn't say, *I don't want to sleep with you.* At least you're not lying to yourself about this.'

Eva flushed and avoided Vidal's eye.

'Maybe you'll fall in love with me, Eva, in spite of yourself.'

An electric shock went through her system at the thought of that. Of losing herself so completely. She speared him with a look. 'Fall in love with you? Why would you even want that?'

Vidal shrugged. 'It would amuse me, after all these years of you lodging yourself under my skin like a briar.'

Eva skittered away from such a ridiculous possibility. He was teasing her. 'You throw around the word "love" very easily,' she said.

'Love *is* easy.'

'How would you know?'

Eva had to admit that she was fascinated by this turn in the conversation.

'I saw love between my parents. They supported and respected each other and they were kind to each other. A small thing, but profound. How many couples do you see being kind to one another?'

Eva was speechless. All she could think of was the screaming match between her father and her mother before he'd walked out. He'd said so many awful things to her mother that day that Eva had blocked them out of her memory. She couldn't remember now even if she wanted to. They certainly hadn't been kind to each other. Or her.

'Not many,' she had to concede.

'I won't settle for anything less than the kind of love I witnessed between my parents. Even after she died, my father wasn't bitter. He celebrated her life and their love.'

Hearing Vidal admit such a thing so easily impacted on Eva somewhere very vulnerable.

'How old were you when she died?' she asked.

'Twelve.'

'I'm sorry.'

Now Vidal avoided her eye. 'It was a long time ago.'

'I won't fall in love with you, Vidal. What you describe... I saw the opposite. The lack of love. I don't believe it exists.'

Vidal took a sip of champagne. 'Don't underestimate yourself, Eva. You're only human.'

She rolled her eyes at that. 'What would you do even if I did? What if I became over-emotional and needy and didn't want to let you go?'

'I'm good at extricating myself from any relationship I don't want to be in any more.'

She didn't doubt it. She'd seen a whole new side to Vidal. He hadn't even tried to charm her and still she was doing his bidding, debating whether or not she'd sleep with him or, worse, fall in love.

You are getting something in return, reminded a voice.

Eva had almost forgotten what the objective was. She felt exposed and naive. She was already on a plane en route to America and Vidal had given her no assurances yet.

She sat up straight. 'What about the sale of the *castillo*? Have you been in touch with my solicitor?'

'It's all in hand. My solicitor in Spain is meeting with yours today. I'll have some contracts for you to sign when we get to San Francisco.'

Eva felt even more silly now. It was obvious she'd forgotten the objective here. To gain her freedom—economically and mentally. If that was possible.

'You don't trust me, Eva?'

She felt pinned under his mocking gaze. 'I would have without question before. But things are different now. *You're* different.'

'You're different too. At first I thought only superficially…but now I can see it.'

Eva didn't want to ask Vidal to elaborate, not sure she'd like his assessment. Not sure if it would be a positive or negative thing.

'There's a bedroom in the back if you want to get some rest. We'll be announcing our engagement at a very select press conference when we arrive at the airport. I figured it would be best to do it like that and get it out of the way—nip any speculation in the bud.'

Eva sat bolt upright. 'You're announcing it when we arrive? But what about…? I don't have anything with me except for that dress I wore last night…'

Vidal waved a hand. 'I had my assistant drop some clothes off in your size—you'll find them in the bedroom. Choose whatever you think is suitable.'

Eva felt panic rise. 'But that's just it. I don't *know* what's suitable. I can't trust myself when it comes to fashion.'

'What are you talking about?'

'I had a bad experience when I was eighteen,' she divulged reluctantly. 'I turned up to a very exclusive party wearing the worst possible thing. Years out of date. I was ridiculed…'

It sounded so trite now, but at the time it had been traumatic enough to give her a complex.

'I just don't know if I have the best judgement.'

'Maybe you're right,' Vidal said thoughtfully.

Suddenly Eva felt defensive. 'What's that supposed to mean?'

'The dress you wore in London at the party with your father…that was pretty tacky.'

Eva bit her lip again. *That* dress hadn't been her fault. She'd known it was hideous. But she'd had no choice. If it could even have been called a dress. Two pieces of silver lamé held together with silver circlets that had run up and down each side of her body. Two thin straps were all that had held it up. It had been indecently short.

Then Vidal frowned. 'The dress you wore last night was perfectly acceptable.'

'That's because the girl in the hire-shop helped me to pick it out.'

To Eva's surprise, Vidal stood up and held out a hand. She looked at it, scared of touching him when she felt so exposed.

'Come on,' he said, sounding perfectly reasonable.

Eva knew she was being ridiculous. That the more of a deal she made of it the more he'd know he affected her.

She slipped her hand into his and immediately regretted it. Little sparks of electricity raced up her arm and her lower body tensed. She let him pull her up. They were too close. She realised that she was so much smaller than him, even though she was relatively tall.

If she stepped right into his body her head would tuck in perfectly under his chin. She was overcome with a need to do that, and slide her arms around his waist…

But he was tugging her down the aisle, and she sent up silent thanks that he hadn't seen that moment of weakness. He opened the door and Eva gasped when a luxurious bedroom was revealed. Complete with a spacious en suite bathroom.

Vidal let her hand go. She pretended not to notice, even though it still tingled. 'Wow...this is...impressive.'

Vidal was standing by a rail of clothes. Eva approached with trepidation. She seriously thought she had some kind of dyslexia when it came to clothes and colours.

Vidal pulled out a royal blue trouser suit and held it up in front of Eva. He made a face and put it back. Then he pulled out a knee-length leather skirt and a cashmere top.

'That's nice,' Eva said, reaching out to touch the top.

But Vidal was already putting it back on the rail, muttering something about it being too much like a work outfit.

Then he pulled out a dress—it had short sleeves and was dressy without being too over the top. Lots of different colours.

Vidal handed it to her. 'Try this, with this...' he pulled out a short jacket '...and these...' He added a pair of high-heeled shoes in a colour matching the dress.

Eva held the clothes and shoes in her arms and Vidal made a rotating motion with his finger. 'Bathroom—behind you. I'll wait here.'

Eva went into the bathroom, bemused. It was only when she was standing in her underwear that she realised nothing but a thin piece of board and plastic and a few feet separated her from Vidal. And a massive bed.

She hurriedly pulled on the dress, but when she went to pull up the zip she couldn't reach it. Blowing a stray hair out of her eyes in exasperation, Eva put her hands on her hips.

'Do you need help?' Vidal called.

Eva grimaced. 'Yes.'

'Come out.'

The dress was modest from the front, covering her from the neck down, but it was short, coming to mid-thigh. And the skin of her exposed back prickled. But she couldn't hide in here for ever.

She opened the door. 'I can't do up the zip.'

'Turn around.'

Eva did as Vidal bade, and presented him with her back. For a long moment he did nothing, and then she felt his fingers come to the bottom of the zip, resting just above the small of her back.

She tried to repress a shiver of awareness as he slowly drew up the zip. She was very aware of her plain white bra strap. No doubt he was used to more exciting underwear. She wouldn't have a clue where to start buying anything sexy. Not that she wanted to.

Vidal pulled the zip all the way to the top of her back and pushed her hair over one shoulder. His fingers lingered at the nape of her neck for a moment. Eva stopped breathing. But then his hands fell away and she sensed him moving back.

'Turn around.'

She did. The dress was not like anything she'd have chosen for herself. It clung to every dip and hollow. Vidal's gaze was slowly travelling down over her belly and thighs. And back up.

'You look perfect,' he said.

'Is it appropriate?'

He said, 'With the jacket, it'll be fine.'

The air between them felt thick and charged. The space that had at first seemed cavernous suddenly felt tiny. The bed loomed large in Eva's peripheral vision.

Then he said, 'I have something else that you'll need.'

He turned around and took a box from the top of a

cabinet. A small box with the distinctively familiar colours and logo of one of the world's most famous and
iconic jewellers. Devilliers.

Eva looked down when Vidal opened the box. She
couldn't stop her mouth opening. It was a ring with a
glittering yellow stone, square-shaped and set in gold,
with white diamonds on either side.

'What stone is that?'

Eva was trying not to let Vidal see how confusing
this was for her. She'd never dreamt of a moment like
this, but suddenly she was realising that somewhere in
the deepest recesses of her imagination she *had* allowed
herself to imagine such a scenario. She'd dared to dream
that some day someone might want her enough to pro-
pose. Give her a ring. Not because it was an arranged
marriage but because they loved her.

She burned with mortification to acknowledge that
futile dream now. To acknowledge that she'd been that
weak. Even though her mother had told her over and over
again that love didn't exist. Not for people like them.

*Vidal believed in love. Believed he would find it. That
it was his due.*

That only sent Eva's emotions into a deeper spiral.

'It's a yellow diamond.'

Vidal's voice cut through the rising panic inside Eva.
She took a deep breath. 'It's beautiful.'

Vidal took it out of the box and held it up. Suddenly
Eva's dream felt very real, but very fake all at once.

She reached for the ring. 'You don't have to. I can
put it on.'

'I want to.'

Eva glared at Vidal, but finally gave him her hand.
It felt very small and delicate in his. She was conscious

of her short, functional nails. It felt like a travesty putting such a beautiful ring on such a hand, but the ring slid on and fitted perfectly. Like in a fairy tale. But this was no fairy tale. This was a parody. A punishment. A retribution.

She tried to pull her hand back. He wouldn't let go. She looked at him. He was very close. His eyes were on her mouth and it tingled.

His gaze moved up. 'You know, there's something I owe you.'

Eva's head felt fuzzy. She couldn't think straight. 'You don't owe me anything.'

He nodded and moved closer. 'I do, actually.'

Eva's breath stopped.

'I owe you a kiss.'

Eva tried to move her head, to shake it. 'It's okay, you really don't.'

'But you were so angry that day when I wouldn't kiss you back.'

'I misread the situation.'

'You didn't misread anything. You just caught me by surprise. Do you want to know why I didn't kiss you back?'

'I… Okay…' Eva's tongue felt heavy. She couldn't stop her gaze from moving down to Vidal's mouth. Sculpted and firm. Full.

'Because I wanted to…too much. And you weren't ready. You'd pushed me to the edges of my control. And that day… I almost lost it,' he said. 'But now you're ready.'

Am I? Eva wondered through the haze in her head.

Vidal was moving even closer and sliding a hand under her hair, cupping her jaw, moving a thumb back and forth along her skin. His other hand was on her waist. She was in her bare feet, and he tipped her chin up just before his head lowered towards hers, and Eva was drowning in his eyes, blue and green.

She'd pressed her mouth to his all those years ago and it had been so shockingly inflammatory that she could still recall the burst of heat in her lower body. But it had ended almost as soon as it had begun, when Vidal had pulled back.

You weren't ready...but now you're ready.

His mouth hovered a heart-stopping inch above Eva's. Her head was tipped back, her body curving towards his. Every cell clamoured for his touch. She craved to know what it would feel like to kiss him. She'd dreamed of this even as she'd burned with humiliation because of his rejection.

She'd seen it as a slight—a petty way to pay her back for all of the ways she'd reminded him of his place. But in hindsight he'd never been petty. He'd been confident. He'd pulled back because she hadn't been ready for him. For what he'd wanted to do.

That thought was dizzying and Eva almost fell. But at the last second she remembered that the only thing she had to cling on to was her dignity. If she gave in to Vidal now he would have won. She would be lost.

Abruptly, still dizzy with need, Eva pulled back, dislodging Vidal's hands. The air crackled around them, thick with electricity. She almost felt that if she touched something solid she'd get a shock, it was that tangible.

Vidal didn't seem to be concerned. He stood back. Watching. She felt undone. How on earth would she react if he actually touched her? The prospect was as terrifying as it was exhilarating.

'I told you. I won't sleep with you.'

Supremely confident, Vidal said, 'You will. Of that I have no doubt.' His gaze swept her up and down. 'That dress is perfect by the way. You might just want to fix your hair.'

He was gone and the door had closed behind him before Eva could take another breath. In a fit of irritation at Vidal's sanguinity, and frustration at the way her body ached for fulfilment, Eva picked up a sandal and launched it at the door.

It fell to the ground ineffectually and Eva heard a low chuckle from the other side of the door.

She clenched her hands and went into the bathroom. She groaned. They hadn't even kissed and her hair looked as if she'd been tumbled backwards through a bush. Her cheeks were pink and her eyes were overbright.

She could never claim that she didn't want Vidal— they both knew that she did—but by God she would die before giving in to it. Because she knew deep in her bones that once that happened she would be risking the destruction of every emotional wall that had kept her intact her whole life.

And she certainly wasn't ready for that.

Vidal went back and sat in his seat, his body filled with pumping blood and frustration. She was playing him. She had to be. She wasn't an ardent teenager any more. She was a woman. And something about that stuck in Vidal's gut like a splinter.

What? he asked himself. Did he regret not being the one to initiate her when she'd all but thrown herself at him?

No, he assured himself. Because he knew exactly how

it would have gone. She would have stood up afterwards, made some cutting remark and walked away, having absorbed the experience the way she did everything—as if it was her due.

Hell, she'd probably assumed at the time that it was Vidal's duty to initiate her, so that she would be free to get on with seducing an appropriate husband. Except that didn't appear to have happened.

She and her mother had gone into a decline before Eva could establish herself. Did he feel sorry for her? No. What she'd gone through was no more or less than most mortals. And she'd still had a roof over head. She still had her name and her lineage, like a talisman.

A lineage you're only too happy to take advantage of, mocked an inner voice.

Vidal picked up the champagne and took a large gulp. It tasted bitter when paired with sexual frustration.

Yet she hadn't appeared bitter about working in the hotel. She'd seemed…resigned to it. So maybe her experience had smoothed a few edges. Given her a much-needed perspective on the world and the privilege she'd taken for granted.

The door to the bedroom opened and Vidal looked up. Eva emerged in the dress and jacket and shoes, looking immaculate. Legs impossibly long and shapely. Hair slicked back and tucked behind her ears. Expression as smooth as silk. Every inch the regal scion of an illustrious bloodline.

She stood by the table and gestured to herself, 'This will do?'

Vidal consciously didn't let his gaze drop, even though it took physical effort. The colours of the dress made her eyes look even more golden. She was breathtakingly stunning.

'That'll do.'

She said, 'Thank you for arranging the clothes.'

So polite. For a second, disconcertingly, Vidal was reminded of what she'd been like as a young teenager. Immaculately polite but with a tongue as sharp as a razor. He was almost waiting for her to say something else, but she didn't.

'You're welcome. It's the least I can do to ensure you feel comfortable in public.'

She went slightly pale at that, but before he could question it Eva said, 'If that's all for now, I think I'll lie down until it's time to land.'

'Be my guest.'

She turned and went back down the aisle of the plane and disappeared into the bedroom, leaving Vidal curiously deflated. Sometimes she was as easy to read as a book, and then, like a picture jarring out of focus for a second, it was as if she was someone else. Any hint of revealing anything a mere illusion.

But she could keep her illusions. He didn't care what was going on—he only cared that she fulfilled her part of their mutually beneficial arrangement and, when the time came, surrendered to him and sated the fire in his blood.

He chose not to acknowledge his sense of anticipation of that final moment of capitulation, telling himself it was ridiculous to think that it would eclipse everything he'd experienced up to now, personally or professionally.

Eva was still in shock at the sheer number of press waiting for them at the airport in San Francisco. They'd landed a short time before and some of Vidal's staff had come onto the plane to brief them—all very officious and efficient.

The press were waiting in a huddle at the bottom of the steps to the plane. It was meant to be informal. But Eva didn't feel informal. Her palms were clammy with nerves.

She hadn't slept much in spite of her attempts. Too wound up after that almost-kiss with Vidal. His control had mocked hers. Did he really want her at all, or was he just enjoying watching her tie herself in knots?

She put on the jacket over the dress and saw that Vidal was holding out his hand. 'Ready?'

The engagement ring felt heavy on her finger. She knew they were meant to be presenting a united front, so she couldn't very well avoid touching Vidal. She put her hand in his and tensed against the inevitable *zing* of awareness.

He led her to the door of the plane and the world exploded into flashes of light. Eva flinched. The only time she'd been photographed in a similar way had been in London on that ill-fated trip to see her father.

Not the time to think of that.

Vidal led her down the steps of the plane to the bottom. A PR person directed the questions and Vidal answered smoothly. They'd decided to keep things as true as possible, saying that they'd met when he and his father had lived at the *castillo*.

Vidal said now, 'It was a long friendship that has just recently blossomed into something much deeper. I'm honoured that Eva has agreed to be my wife.'

'When are you getting married?'

Eva felt Vidal tense beside her. But he said smoothly,

'There's plenty of time to make plans…we're going to enjoy our engagement.'

Eva was surprised to find that she was almost believing Vidal. He sounded so…authentic. For a second she was imagining… What if they really had been friends? What if she'd been allowed to talk to him as she'd wanted to on many occasions? Was this some kind of parallel fantasy existence?

And then he turned to her. He said something she didn't catch and then he was cupping her chin, tipping it up.

He arched a brow. 'Ready?'

There was a look on his face that was somewhere between tender and hungry. It disarmed Eva completely.

She wanted to resist…she knew it was important to resist…but it was too late. Vidal's firm, warm mouth was settling over hers and Eva's brain ceased functioning. He didn't deepen the kiss, just held it there for a long moment. And then pulled back.

It took a second for Eva to open her eyes, and when she did she was almost blinded by the pops of light. Vidal's PR person was stepping in and saying something about that being all for now…giving the couple their privacy…and Vidal was leading her over to an SUV with tinted windows.

A driver in a suit was holding open the back door and Vidal helped her in, before closing the door and going around to the other side. Then they were moving smoothly out of the airport and towards the tall buildings Eva could see in the distance.

'Are you okay?' he asked.

Eva felt a bit dazed. Vidal took her hand. She looked at him. 'I'm not used to that.'

'No… I guess not. Sorry, I probably should have prepared you better.'

Eva shook her head. 'It's fine.'

She pulled her hand back, liking how it felt in his too much. She'd learnt a long time ago not to seek comfort or reassurance because her mother had never given it. Another weakness.

She could still feel the impression of Vidal's mouth on hers. Like a brand. It had precipitated a longing such as she'd never felt before. It went deeper than desire. And that was scary.

It was early evening in San Francisco and the sky was a blaze of colour. Eva let herself be distracted as they drove into the city, through the iconic Haight-Ashbury hippy area and the famously vertiginous streets.

Soon they were in a surprisingly quiet, residential part of the city and the car came to a stop outside a very discreet fence with high trees. The gate opened and a man in dark trousers and a matching polo shirt came out.

Vidal greeted him warmly and then came around to help Eva out of the car. He introduced her to the man. 'This is Michael, my house manager.'

The man inclined his head and smiled. 'Miss Flores, it's a pleasure to welcome you here, and congratulations on your engagement.'

Eva shook the man's hand, embarrassed. Surely he must know this was a total sham? They'd never even met before!

He went back in through the gate, carrying their luggage, and Vidal led the way into a space that made Eva's jaw drop. Behind the high fence and the trees was a modern work of art set amidst immaculately landscaped gardens. Stone and glass and steel. Huge front doors.

Eva followed Vidal, entranced, as he led her into a massive double-height foyer. It was modern and minimalist without feeling cold or as if one shouldn't touch anything. The furnishings were tactile and comfortable-looking. Art decorated the walls that weren't glass. And as he led her through the ground floor to the other side of the house they came out to the back, where there was a balcony. Looking down, Eva could see a lower level with a long lap pool.

Silent, she could feel Vidal watching her reaction. Then he said, 'You probably hate it.'

Eva shook her head. 'No, I…really like it.'

'Let me show you upstairs.'

Without thinking, Eva slipped off her high-heeled sandals and followed Vidal in bare feet. He looked back at her and clearly noted the feet. She felt self-conscious. 'Do you mind? The shoes were pinching and I don't want to ruin your floors.'

He shook his head, looking a little bemused. 'Not at all. This is your home too…for the next few weeks.'

Few weeks. Maybe Vidal was already regretting his impetuous plan to fake an engagement with her. Maybe he was already deciding that a week or two would be enough.

They went up to the next level, where there was a comfortable lounge area with a massive TV and media system. And then up another level. Vidal walked her through a formal dining area to a decked area outside. The air was still balmy, even though autumn was closing in. There was outdoor seating and a fire pit, but Eva went straight over to the glass railing and took in the view of the Golden Gate Bridge in the near distance, and all the grid-like streets and houses in between.

Eva said, 'I can see why they called this the New World. It *feels* like a new world.'

And it did. She felt as if a weight had been lifted off her shoulders. A crazy sensation for a property to bestow. But it was true. It couldn't be more opposite to the *castillo*—and maybe that was why it appealed to her so much.

'You surprise me.'

Eva looked at Vidal, who was watching her. 'Why?' she asked. 'Because you assumed I'd only feel at home in buildings that date back hundreds of years?' She shuddered lightly. 'No. Give me the new any day.'

There was a sound behind them, and Eva turned around to see Michael approach.

'Sorry to intrude, boss, but your car is waiting.'

Vidal emitted a soft curse and looked at his watch, then back to Eva. 'I'm afraid I have to go to a meeting with my board, but Michael will show you your room and prepare something to eat. I'll see you in the morning.'

And then he was walking away through the vast open-plan space, leaving Eva feeling adrift.

Michael smiled and said, 'Please, let me show you to your room and then we can discuss your dietary requirements.'

She forced a smile and followed Michael, trying not to let echoes of the past reverberate through her head, when she'd invariably been left to her own devices.

Vidal was not her mother, this was not the *castillo*, and she was not a child any more. She could handle this.

CHAPTER SIX

THE FOLLOWING MORNING, Vidal still couldn't shake the niggling of his conscience at the way he'd left Eva so abruptly last night. She'd looked surprised. A little lost. And he'd almost forgotten he had a meeting, because he'd been so transfixed by watching her reaction to his house.

He'd expected her to be blasé. Judgemental. But she'd seemed enchanted. In fact… He had to concede that the Eva Flores he'd met over a week ago was proving to be quite the enigma.

One minute he thought she was the same cold and aloof girl he'd known, ready to reel him in only to lash out with a sting in the tail, and the next she seemed like someone who bore no resemblance to that person. Someone entirely new.

It was disconcerting.

He heard a sound and looked up from where he sat at the breakfast table, near the lap pool on the bottom terrace. Eva was walking towards him wearing faded jeans and a plain white shirt. Hair down, silky. Simple, classic.

Her face was expressionless and old instincts kicked in. The urge to protect himself while at the same time wanting to get underneath that smooth facade. He'd never met anyone who did it so well as her. She could give a masterclass in superiority without even saying a word. Her mother had been the same.

And he'd almost been feeling sorry for her!

She sat in a chair.

'Good morning,' he said, as his chef came to the table with some freshly baked pastries.

'Santo, this is Eva.'

Eva looked up at Santo and smiled. 'Nice to meet you, Santo.'

Vidal saw the man do a double take at Eva's stunning smile. He almost did a double take himself. Santo left and Vidal caught Eva's eye.

Her smile faded. 'What?'

He shook his head. 'Nothing.' And then, 'Did you sleep well?'

Her eyes widened. He noticed she wore no make-up. She was so naturally beautiful that she really was breathtaking.

'My rooms are…amazing. I'm not used to such modern comforts.'

Vidal realised that the *castillo* might be impressive— but no one could describe it as comfortable. 'I guess not. But you don't ever have to go back to that lifestyle. Speaking of which, my legal team have the contracts detailing the terms of our agreement at my office. Your solicitor has sent an envoy from a firm here to represent you and make sure you're happy with everything. We'll go to the office after this.'

'Okay…'

She sounded hesitant. 'You're not changing your mind?' Vidal asked.

She shook her head and took a sip of coffee. 'No, I

just…can't believe that it's all happening so quickly and easily. The debts are…big.' She looked at him. 'Are you sure *you're* not changing your mind? After all, I don't know that my presence by your side is really going to be worth all that much.'

Vidal told himself that her self-deprecation was just a smokescreen. That maybe she was looking for something more.

He shook his head. 'Not at all. It's a viable business venture, I'm fulfilling my father's wishes, and I will have you on my arm to demonstrate how socially acceptable I am in order to secure an important investment. A win for both of us.'

Silently he added, *And I will have you in my bed, to burn this permanent ache from my body and cool the fire in my blood.*

But it was as if his thoughts had silently communicated themselves to Eva. Her cheeks went pink and she said, 'That's it? By your side? Not in your bed?'

Anticipation sizzled along Vidal's veins. 'Like I said, I have never forced a woman into my bed. They've all come quite willingly. And with great enthusiasm.'

It took her a second to absorb his double meaning and her cheeks went even pinker. 'That's disgusting!'

Vidal was intrigued by her prudishness. 'Not disgusting at all. I like to ensure that my lovers are very well—'

The sound of Santo returning with fresh coffee cut Vidal off. He almost laughed out loud at the murderous look in Eva's eyes. It was going to be *so* satisfying when she capitulated and begged him to make love to her.

When Santo was gone again, Vidal leaned forward and said, 'Don't forget that I've seen all that fire and passion inside you, Eva Flores. You might be able to fool others with that scandalised innocent act, but you can't fool me.'

Eva's hand stopped in the process of moving to her mouth with a pastry. She went very still inside. 'You mean… when I tried to kiss you…?'

But Vidal shook his head.

Genuinely confused, Eva started to say, 'But what—?' And then she broke off. Because she had thought of something.

But surely there was no way that Vidal… The thought of him knowing about that made her feel sick. And more exposed than she'd ever felt in her life. It was her deepest secret. Deeper even than the hopes and dreams she'd told herself she didn't harbour.

She looked at him and shook her head, but he nodded. There was a gleam in his eye. He said, 'I used to watch you.'

Eva kept on shaking her head, thinking of how in those moments she'd felt so elemental. Free. Once Vidal's father had stumbled across her secret place, and she'd got such a fright that—to her shame—she'd threatened to have him fired if he ever told anyone.

She tried to bluff. 'I don't know what you're talking about.'

'Do you still do it?'

No. She didn't. But she dreamt of it often. That feeling of losing herself in the beat and music.

She tried again. 'I don't know what you're talking about.'

'Who first taught you to dance like that, Eva? I know you were teaching yourself when I used to watch you, because you were using online tutorials. You were so determined... I've never seen you look so intent about anything. But someone must have taught you first.'

Eva wanted to curl in on herself and protect that very secret part of her—the part that had loved doing something so forbidden.

But, very reluctantly, she divulged, 'It was our first housekeeper. Maria. She was gone by the time you arrived. I saw her one day, dancing in the kitchen. And she used to sing. Such sad songs... I asked her to show me what she was doing.'

'How old were you?'

'About eight.'

It had been shortly after her father had left and her mother had taken to her bedroom, where there had been either long silences or ranting and raving. Maria had been the only one who had cared for Eva through that time. Until one day when Eva had been down in the kitchen with Maria, who was showing her how to cook something, and her mother had appeared and said coldly, 'The kitchen is not a suitable environment for my daughter. And *I* am her mother. Maria, you may go.'

Eva had been inconsolable. Her mother had slapped her across the face to stop her crying and Eva had never cried again. She'd bottled up all her emotions deep inside and made sure she never showed anything that would enrage her mother.

'You were very good, you know,' said Vidal.

'I... Thank you. No one knew. I didn't want anyone to know.'

'Why?'

Eva emitted a short sharp laugh. 'Can you imagine my mother if she'd seen that? Her daughter? Dancing

Flamenco? She would have cast me out of the *castillo* on the spot. Like she did Maria.'

Vidal frowned. 'She fired Maria?'

Eva nodded. 'She didn't like her influence on me.'

'You were a *child.*'

'I was ten when she fired Maria, and those couple of years when she was with us were probably the happiest I can remember in that place.'

Until Vidal had arrived with his father, and Eva had felt as if she was coming out of a fog. The world had suddenly looked sharper again. And that was when she'd started practising Flamenco again on her own. As if to try and understand or channel all the things she was feeling.

But she didn't mention that. The fact that he'd seen her in those moments was shocking. But also… She'd fantasised when she'd been dancing that he was watching her. Maybe on some subliminal level she'd known? And had revelled in it?

Suddenly it was too much. It was as if Vidal had prised her open and taken out her most precious secret to inspect under fluorescent lighting.

Her voice clipped, she said, 'I don't do it any more.'

'That's a pity. Maybe you'll dance for me sometime.'

She looked at him, her insides clenching at the thought. 'Never.'

'So if you'll just sign here, Miss Flores…'

The solicitor handed her a pen and Eva hesitated only for the barest moment before signing away the property that had been in her mother's family for generations. She felt nothing. Not an ounce of guilt or sentimentality. Just a little numb.

The agreement was more than generous, considering the fact that Vidal didn't owe her a thing. The debts were cleared and she was being given an option of taking a stake in the new business once it was up and running, and a position on the board of managers if she wanted.

Right now, she felt as if she never wanted anything to do with the *castillo* again, but she was wise enough not to burn her bridges.

She was finally free. For the first time in her life. But that numb feeling persisted…as if it was too huge to absorb.

There was a knock on the door and she and her solicitor looked up to see Vidal enter.

The solicitor stood up and closed the folder holding all the documents. 'I think that's everything. I'll check with Miss Flores's representative in Madrid and let you know if there are any loose ends.'

'Thank you.' Vidal closed the door behind the middle-aged man.

The numb feeling started to dissipate as Eva took Vidal in. He was wearing a suit and they had come to his offices, located in the buzzing Mission district. Eva wasn't surprised that Vidal had chosen to be in the hub of the city rather than out in the suburbs where most of the tech companies were based.

'Thank you,' Eva said, beginning to feel the magnitude of what had just happened sinking in.

'You don't mind that you've just signed away hundreds of years of legacy?'

Eva stood up and went over to a window that looked out on a green courtyard area in the middle of the complex. Staff were sitting on the grass eating their lunch. Carefree. Now she could be like them. Except she had to navigate the small matter of resisting Vidal Suarez for a few weeks first.

She turned around. 'Truthfully? No. I'm sorry I can't pretend otherwise. It was not a happy place. Your father obviously saw a vision of how it could have been...and if you can bring it back to some kind of life and benefit people then that'll be good.'

Vidal rested his hips against the desk and folded his arms. 'You always looked very content in your role as lady of the manor in waiting. But you're saying you weren't happy?'

What a loaded question. Eva wasn't even sure how to answer. 'I didn't know anything else. The *castillo* was my world. I wasn't aware of being happy or unhappy.'

But that wasn't entirely true. She knew she'd been happy whenever she'd seen Vidal arrive back at the *castillo* during his holidays.

That had been her first real awareness of the two states—happiness and unhappiness. And she'd been happy when she'd danced. Or when she'd been in the kitchen with Maria, learning how to cook. And dance.

With her mother, she'd never felt any happiness. She'd felt tense. On guard. Pressure in her chest. Wary.

Feeling the past sucking her under, Eva said, 'So what happens now?'

Vidal stood up. 'I have a pretty packed social schedule for the next week—so you're going shopping.'

Immediately Eva felt a sense of panic. 'Vidal, I'm really not—'

'I've enlisted a stylist to go with you.'

'Oh.' Eva knew she should feel mildly insulted, or even ashamed that she didn't have the confidence to know what to buy or wear, but she was too relieved.

'How will I know—?'

'She has a list of the events we're attending and she knows the scene. It'll be fine. I'll meet you for lunch.'

Eva couldn't stop a little burst of surprise. And pleasure. 'I'm sure you're busy…you don't have to.'

'It's fine. I've booked a suitably visible place—it'll be good for us to be seen together as much as possible.'

'Oh, of course.' The burst of pleasure fizzled away.

'So why are you so paranoid about what to wear in public?'

Eva was very conscious of the scrutiny that she and Vidal were under at a table in prime position on the terrace of a very exclusive restaurant on the waterfront. The paparazzi across the street weren't even attempting to hide.

'Um…because of scenarios exactly like this!' Eva said, rolling her eyes.

Vidal raised a brow, obviously waiting for her to go on. Up to now, Eva had to admit that they'd passed quite a pleasant time, conversing about general topics. The stylist was meeting her again after lunch, to continue shopping, and for this lunch date she'd changed into flared trousers and a loose-fitting silky top. Surprisingly comfortable.

'I told you—there was an event when I was eighteen. I thought my dress was perfectly nice. My mother approved. It was only when I got there that I realised how out of touch I was with…*everything*. I hadn't really been out in society since before I was a teenager.'

'You were being home-schooled and you had no friends.'

Eva looked at Vidal. He knew too much. 'Thank you for that reminder.'

He shrugged, as if he hadn't just spoken one of her biggest vulnerabilities out loud. He said, 'I used to feel sorry for you, but then you'd invariably say something cutting and make me remember that you didn't need pity from anyone.'

No—because she'd become adept at maintaining that prickly barrier at all costs. In case Vidal got too close. In case her mother decided he should be humiliated again, like at that dinner.

Eva's conscience hurt as it always did when she thought of that night. She couldn't help saying, 'That dinner that my mother invited you to…before you went back to university…'

'Yes?'

Eva forced herself to look at him. 'I've always wanted to apologise for that evening. I had no idea she was going to use it to just…ignore you like that. To talk about you as if you weren't even there. It was…not nice.'

'I remember you sitting there, avoiding my eye. Why didn't you say something?'

'I was sixteen.'

Vidal was quiet, and then he said, 'You know, I always felt you were older in so many ways. And then at the same time younger. A contradiction.'

She'd felt very young that night. Out of her depth. Hating what her mother was doing but not knowing how to stop it. Wearing a dress that she'd been excited to wear in front of Vidal but realising as soon as he'd walked in that it was all wrong. Too fussy. Too formal. Too young. She'd wanted to be sexy.

Maybe that had been the start of her complex about knowing what to wear?

Vidal popped a grape into his mouth. 'So you're saying that you and your mother weren't co-conspirators, then?'

'Truthfully, how I feel about my mother is complicated. She was all I knew. I trusted her. She told me how to be.'

'My father used to tell me that it wasn't your fault. How could you know any different? And I would give you the benefit of the doubt, over and over again, only to be shut down.'

Eva squirmed. 'I don't think I knew what I was doing. I didn't know how to be any other way.'

Vidal leant forward. 'I think you *did* know what you were doing. At some point you made a decision that teasing me and torturing me and looking down your nose at me was more fun than actually attempting to be a nice person.'

Eva felt as if Vidal had slid a knife between her ribs. In many ways she could see it from his perspective, but she'd just told him more about how she felt about her complex past than she'd ever revealed to anyone else. And he clearly didn't want to revise his opinion.

As far as he knew, she had behaved as she had out of pure spite and badness. Not because she'd been coerced by her bitter mother and because she truly had not known she could be brave enough to trust her own instincts.

Eva had revealed far too much. Vidal was chipping away at her with his questions. And he didn't really care at all. She was just a means to an end. And he was a means to an end for her too. She needed to remember that.

She schooled her expression into one as close to boredom as she could get and looked at her phone. 'It's time for me to meet the stylist again. I should go.'

But before she could get up, Vidal reached across the table and entwined his fingers with hers, sending an electric shock straight between her legs.

'Wha—?'

Before she could even utter the word, Vidal had cupped her jaw with his other hand and was settling his mouth over hers, taking advantage of her surprise to make the kiss intimate. This was no peck on the lips. This was open and explicit and she had no defence.

The touch of his tongue to hers was fleeting, but devastating. Then he pulled back. It had lasted mere seconds—if even that long. Eva felt dizzy. Vidal smiled, but it was more like a smirk.

He kept hold of her hand as he stood up, tugging her up too.

A waiter materialised. 'The bill, Mr Suarez?'

Vidal didn't take his eyes off her, for all the world the besotted fiancé. 'Please... My fiancée here has a busy afternoon. I'm sorry we can't stay for dessert.'

'That is no problem at all, sir.'

Vidal led Eva out of the restaurant, and the heads of the other diners swivelled after them as they went.

Eva was too shell-shocked to do anything but follow in his wake. But when they got outside she recovered her wits. She pulled her hand out of his and said, 'That was sneaky.'

'It was an opportunity to make our union look authentic, and I took it.'

'Please do not do that again without asking me first. I don't like to be manhandled.'

A ghost of a smile made Vidal's mouth twitch. 'You didn't mind at the time.'

Heat pulsed between Eva's legs. No, she hadn't minded at all. That was the problem.

'Haven't you heard? There's a little thing called consent now.'

Vidal stepped close and said, 'Fine. May I take your hand?'

Eva put it behind her back. 'Why?'

'Because there are photographers across the road with their lenses trained on us right now.'

She hesitated. 'What are you going to do with my hand?'

'With your consent, I'm going to lift it up and kiss your inner palm.'

Eva knew that they needed to be seen to be behaving like a real affianced couple. Otherwise what was the point?

She offered him her hand. 'Okay. But no kissing on the mouth again.'

Vidal lifted her hand to his mouth and turned her palm towards him, saying in a low voice, 'There are plenty of other places to kiss, besides on the mouth. It won't be a problem.'

And then she felt the warmth of his breath against her skin and he pressed his lips to her palm, lingering for a long moment. She felt the tip of his tongue and gasped. 'That's cheating.'

He let her go. 'See you back at the house later.'

Eva was still cursing Vidal that evening, while she waited for him in the lounge area. All afternoon she'd been tortured with a slew of X-rated images of him kissing various parts of her body.

When the stylist had taken her to a lingerie boutique it had got even worse. The stylist had ignored her protestations that she didn't need sexy underwear, and as she couldn't reveal why, she'd had to give in and let her do her thing.

Eva had found herself sighing over the wispiest bits of lace with ribbon ties, and bras that looked like works of art more than a device to support body parts. She'd never seen anything so decadent and beautiful.

Feeling guilty, because she'd known it would never be seen by anyone other than her, she'd allowed the stylist to box it all up and add it to the growing collection of boxes and bags.

She knew she was focusing on her irritation with Vidal to try and disguise her extreme anxiety at the thought of appearing in public with him at an event tonight. A charity ball, apparently, and one of San Francisco's glitziest annual social fixtures. And she was also trying to hide the lingering hurt of his opinion of her. But in a way she realised that she could use it to her advantage—as a buffer to keep him from getting any closer.

She heard a sound and turned around, and every rational thought in her head disappeared. Vidal was standing a few feet away in a classic black tuxedo. His full metamorphosis from the son of a humble grounds manager to a titan of industry was complete.

His suit had to be bespoke, because there was no point where the material didn't mould lovingly to his body and his muscles. He was…magnificent. Breathtaking.

His gaze was raking her up and down. Immediately Eva felt conscious, even though the stylist had come back with a hair and make-up team to help her get ready for this evening.

His eyes met hers. They stood out even more against the backdrop of black and white. He said, 'You look stunning, Eva. Truly.'

'I… Thank you.'

She'd been afraid the dress was too dramatic. Red and strapless, with a tight bodice, falling to the floor in a swathe of tulle over silk.

Eva had said to the stylist, 'I'd like to stay under the radar if I can.'

The woman had laughed, 'Standing beside Vidal Suarez? You haven't a hope. Not many could pull this dress off, but with your colouring it'll look spectacular.'

They'd left her hair down, artfully tousled. Thankfully, there was a minimum of make-up.

Vidal said, 'We should go—my driver is waiting.'

Emotion was rising in Eva's chest before she could stop it, and she realised it was a feeling of pride in Vidal that he would not thank her for.

Controlling her emotions had become much harder since her mother had died. It was as if suddenly Eva didn't have to hold on so tightly. As if a too-tight button had finally been released.

And seeing Vidal again was having an even more adverse effect on her being able to control…anything.

'*So* sorry for your loss. Your mother was the most beautiful debutante of her year… I remember it well.'

When the older woman had moved away, Eva said to Vidal, 'I have no idea who that person was.'

'But she knows who you are, which is the important thing.'

And it confirmed for Vidal that he was doing the right thing. *This* was why he had Eva by his side.

After lunch today he'd spent the afternoon distracted and doubting his instincts—*again*. He hadn't expected her to mention that humiliating dinner her mother had invited him to, or to express any remorse. It had been so demeaning, to sit there and listen to her talking about him as if he was invisible. So much so that even now, if he was at a dinner party, he always had a moment of insecurity...a feeling that he wasn't meant to be there. That people might just ignore him or talk over him.

Eva had always pushed his buttons, and there had been too many moments when he'd shown a moment's weakness towards her and she'd punished him for it for him to begin to review the past with different eyes. But there had been something vulnerable about her today, and the notion had lodged itself under his skin that perhaps things weren't as black and white as he'd like to think.

Irritated by the questions she'd thrown up, and by the way her face had become a bland mask again at the end of their lunch, his impulse to kiss her had been as much about that as an opportunity to solidify their fake engagement.

Now Eva's arm was through Vidal's as they moved through the crowd. She was holding on tight. Too tight. He looked down and could see the pinched lines of her face. She was tense. *No.* More than tense. She was scared.

I haven't really been out much in society.

Again, not the impression he'd had of her over these past years.

Not liking how his conscience was pricking at him, Vidal said irritably, 'You *can* smile, you know.'

Eva looked up at Vidal, surprised. 'I'm not smiling?'

'You rarely smile.'

'Maybe you should have chosen another woman to be your convenient fiancée, rather than someone who has a resting serious face.'

There she was. The Eva he knew.

You mean, the Eva you want to know...? suggested a snide voice.

Vidal ignored it. He stopped. 'Self-pity really doesn't suit you, Eva. And you're the only woman I want.'

Her cheeks turned pink. Immensely satisfying. Even when she said through gritted teeth, 'Not going to happen, Vidal.'

He shook his head. 'You really shouldn't back yourself into a corner—it'll make it so much more satisfying for me when you admit defeat.'

When they got back to the house later that evening, Vidal took some calls in his office. As he was going to bed he passed Eva's rooms and saw the door was partway open.

He found himself stopping, even though he hadn't intended to. He could see through to Eva's bathroom, where the door was open, and saw that she was reflected in the mirror. He could see her head and shoulders and face. She was wearing a silk night slip.

It took him a moment to realise that she was making faces at herself in the mirror. *No.* Not faces. She was smiling at herself. Or trying to. But the smiles looked forced and fake.

Then she emitted a sound of frustration, stuck her tongue out at herself and turned out the light.

Vidal quickly pulled the bedroom door closed, feeling as if he'd intruded on something very private.

A weight lodged in his gut that night, and as much as he tried to dismiss it, it wouldn't budge.

CHAPTER SEVEN

THE REST OF the week took on a routine as Eva settled into her new existence. An existence that she found to be far less oppressive than anything she'd expected or experienced before.

She loved the wide open skies of California and the irrepressibly friendly nature of almost everyone she met. She'd taken to walking around the neighbourhood during the day, when Vidal was either in his office in the house or at his offices downtown. When the first person had greeted her with an effusive *'Good morning!'* she hadn't known how to respond. She wasn't used to people addressing her so easily or so casually.

There was a green park near Vidal's house, and Eva had got into a routine of getting herself a latte from the local coffee shop and then sitting in the park while she drank it, watching the world go by. Having been sequestered in the *castillo* for most of her life, she found it fascinating.

She watched the mums, or—probably more likely in this area—the nannies with their children at the playground, their joyful shrieks piercing the air. One small, adorable boy had his two fathers with him.

Eva couldn't recall ever going to a playground as

a child. She thought of Vidal's assessment...*self-pity doesn't suit you*...and scowled at herself.

Her childhood hadn't been conventional. She had her privilege to thank for that. But as she watched the children with their carers this morning, she couldn't help but feel an ache at the thought of all that she'd missed out on. Simple things—like going to a park.

A big shaggy collie-type dog ambled over and Eva smiled, reaching down to give it a scratch. He nudged against her, looking for more attention, and a woman rushed over.

'Ollie, leave that lady alone.' She grabbed the dog by the collar and started pulling him away.

Eva said, 'I don't mind, really.'

But the woman and the dog were gone.

'I didn't know you liked dogs.'

Eva nearly dropped her coffee. She looked up to see Vidal standing beside the bench, a cup of coffee in his own hand. She said, almost accusingly, 'I thought you were working.'

'I was. And then I went looking for you and Santo said you'd gone out for a walk.'

Vidal sat down and Eva tried not to be so aware of his thigh next to hers. He was wearing trousers and a shirt, sleeves rolled up. No tie. She could see the effect he was already having on the other women in the park.

Eva almost felt defensive. 'It's nice around here. Everyone is so friendly. The barista at the coffee shop knows me by name and I've only been going in for a few days. I worked at the hotel in Madrid for nearly a year and barely anyone knew my name. My boss used to call me Eve.' Then she said, 'I always wanted a dog.'

'The *castillo* could have accommodated a hundred dogs—easily.'

'It wasn't an option. My father hated them, and after he left my mother was in no state to even think about something so frivolous.' She looked at Vidal. 'Were you looking for me for something? We're not going out until later, I thought?'

'Nothing has changed. I just spotted something online that you should see…'

He handed her his phone and Eva looked at it—and went clammy with shock and horror. It was that old picture of her and her father at the event in London a few years ago. Eva was smiling, but still looking like a deer caught in the headlights.

'It was inevitable that they'd dig out anything relevant about you,' Vidal said. 'It seems this was all they could find.' Then he said, 'Eva, look at me.'

Reluctantly she turned her head.

'In the interests of full disclosure, I need to know if there's anything in your past that could come out now.'

Eva handed him back his phone. She felt cold. 'Isn't it a bit late for that?'

He said nothing.

Eva said, 'There is nothing to come out. That was it. The sum total of my socialising.'

'You'll have to explain that to me.'

She glanced at him, and then away again. 'Afraid that it might not square with the narrative you've put together about me in your head?'

Vidal sighed. 'If I have a narrative in my head based on that photograph I don't think it's entirely unfair. It's a pretty damning picture.'

'You've participated in a few damning scenarios of your own,' Eva shot back.

Vidal inclined his head. 'Touché. I had my time going off the rails, I'll admit. Hence the need to make some reparations now.'

Eva looked at him, curious. 'Why did you? Did the money and fame go to your head?'

Vidal grimaced. 'It wasn't as simple as that. It was after my father died. I felt a little…lost for a while. Wondered what it was all for when I had no one who cared what happened to me.' His mouth twisted. 'My period of self-pity.'

Eva's heart ached for him. She could understand that feeling of being lost and alone. She said, 'I get it.'

They didn't say anything else for a long moment, and then Eva found the words spilling out of her mouth before she could stop them.

'I went to London not long after your father left the *castillo*, to beg my father to help us. My mother didn't know I'd gone. She would have forbidden me. He met me in his office. I wasn't even invited to his house.' Eva swallowed the pain and bitterness. 'When he saw how desperate I was, he told me that if I did him a favour, he would help. The favour was to accompany him to a party. He put me up in one of the best hotels for the night, and had a stylist come to meet me with an outfit. But when the stylist came she had only that one dress.'

'Go on.'

Eva avoided Vidal's eye. 'The dress was so short I refused to leave the hotel room. But my father came and told me I was making a fuss over nothing, and that if I wanted his help this was what I had to wear. I went with him to the party. At first it seemed okay—I thought I'd been overreacting, even though I still wasn't comfortable in the dress. But then, after a few minutes, I noticed that it was mostly men. There were other women, but they didn't seem to be wives or girlfriends.'

'They were hired.' Vidal sounded grim.

Eva gasped and looked at Vidal. 'How did you know?'

'Because I've been to parties like that. Not that I've ever stayed.'

Eva felt sick. 'I didn't realise what was happening until my father introduced me to a man and made me go over to a private booth and sit with him. He started touching me. And then he put his hand between my thighs. I didn't think. I just threw my glass of wine into his face. I found my father. I was upset, crying…but he told me that if I couldn't entertain his friend then he couldn't help me.'

'What did you do?'

Eva balked at Vidal's question. 'I left, of course. Went home and said nothing. I haven't seen my father or spoken to him since then.'

Vidal was stony-faced. 'Your father tried to pimp you out?'

'Yes.'

'I'm sorry I misread the situation. I assumed it was a social event with your peers.'

Surprised that he seemed prepared to believe her, Eva felt a warmth bloom in her chest. 'I've never told anyone else about it. I was mortified when that picture appeared online.'

'Your mother never knew?'

Eva shook her head. 'It wasn't long after that that her mental health really started to deteriorate. I had to care for her full-time. Until she died.'

Vidal said nothing for a long moment, and then, 'I

assumed that you were making up for lost time—for all those years you were more or less incarcerated at the *castillo* being home-schooled.'

Eva looked away. 'It was a little less exciting than that.'

'So you really haven't been out in society…?'

'No.' Eva forced herself to look at him. 'Maybe that changes your view of the benefits of our…arrangement?'

'I'm a self-made man from a working-class background—no matter what your absence from the social scene might convey, you're still an asset.'

'Even with the dubious company my father keeps?'

'He is unfortunately no different to a lot of men who socialise on that level. It's reprehensible, but it's under the radar.'

'It's disgusting.'

Vidal's jaw clenched. 'It must have been hard to see him like that.'

Eva pushed down the humiliation and the shame. 'I shouldn't have expected anything more.'

Vidal nodded his head towards the playground, where the children were still shrieking and playing. 'I wouldn't have had you down as someone who tolerated children.'

Eva wished that didn't hurt as much as it did. It reminded her of a rare occasion when her mother had taken her out of the *castillo* and into Madrid. They'd found themselves momentarily lost, walking into back streets, with buildings close together. Children had been running freely from one open door to another.

Eva had looked into one house where a family were sitting down to lunch. A baby on its grandmother's knee. A father affectionately scolding a young boy who was running around the table laughing. It had been such an arresting vision that she'd stopped in her tracks and hadn't moved.

Her mother had noticed her fascination and pulled her away sharply, saying, 'You are nothing like them, Eva. You are so much better.'

But she hadn't wanted to be better. She'd envied them.

Eva pushed aside the pang of yearning that lay underneath the terror she felt at the thought of having children. 'I have no intention of having children. How could I when my own mother barely cared for me?'

'And yet you gravitate to this place?'

She looked at Vidal, wanting his focus off her. He was seeing too much. 'Do you want children?' she asked.

He nodded. 'I've always wanted a family. I was lonely as an only child. My mother couldn't have more after me.'

'I'm sorry. I didn't know that.'

'I'd like at least two or three.'

With the wife he intends to love. Because he believes in love.

All Eva could picture when she thought of love was her mother's bitterness and the cavernous empty rooms of the *castillo.*

Vidal's phone beeped and he looked at it. He stood up. 'I have to go back and take some calls. Santo is preparing lunch.'

'I'll be back shortly.'

Eva watched Vidal leave with his loose-limbed grace. She needed time to absorb their exchange. And the fact that Vidal was so open about wanting love and a family. Alien concepts to her. But they impacted on her so deeply that she felt almost winded.

Vidal was right. She had gravitated here to enjoy the sights and sounds of happy children playing.

She stood up abruptly and left the park, taking the opposite way to Vidal to walk home the long way.

He was seeing too much, and she was in danger of forgetting her own life lessons. Lessons that told her she had nothing to offer in the way of warm and fuzzy maternal feelings.

To yearn for that was self-indulgent and dangerous, and she put the blame for exposing that weakness squarely on Vidal's shoulders.

'It's an event hosted by the Spanish ambassador to the United States to celebrate Spanish art and culture.'

Eva was in the back of the car with Vidal. She'd just asked about the evening ahead. She was wearing a dramatic strapless black ballgown, complete with a mini train. The hair and make-up team had coiled her hair up into a bun and she wore rubies at her throat and ears. This was evidently the most formal event they'd been to since their debut on the San Francisco social scene almost ten days ago.

Eva had been fooling herself into a false sense of complacency. Telling herself that she was able to resist Vidal's magnetism. But in the past couple of days it had been getting harder and harder.

He hadn't been going into the office, he'd been working at home, and everywhere she turned there he was. As a constant reminder that he wasn't going anywhere.

That this desire wasn't going anywhere.

Eva looked at where her hands rested in her lap, framed by the black silk of the dress. They were soft and clean. Her nails were neatly filed and polished with a gleaming red varnish. Her toenails too.

Vidal had surprised her earlier by getting a manicurist and pedicurist to come to the house before she'd had to get ready. She knew it was only so that she looked the part, but it had felt like a nice gesture.

She held up her hands now and said, 'Thank you for this. I couldn't have done such a good job myself.'

Vidal looked at her hands, devoid of jewellery except for the engagement ring that sparkled in the light.

'You're welcome. As I said, you weren't made to have worker's hands, Eva. I'm just restoring the natural order.'

Putting her back in her place? She chafed at that. 'I think I've proved that I'm not averse to a little manual labour.'

Vidal, resplendent in another classic black tuxedo, inclined his head. 'I'll give you that. I never would have imagined you'd become a chambermaid.'

Before Eva could think of some witty comeback they were pulling to a stop outside a grand building—one of the city's museums, decked out with a red carpet and lights in the colours of the Spanish flag.

Women in jewel-coloured ballgowns and glittering gems eclipsed the men in their suits as they walked up the steps, framed by flaming lanterns.

Once they were inside, Vidal once again deftly led them through the throng, after handing Eva a glass of champagne. There were typical Spanish tapas being handed out by smiling waiters.

Vidal was soon talking to a couple, and the wife smiled at Eva. She smiled back, conscious of Vidal telling her she didn't smile enough. She'd even tried practising in the mirror one night, until she'd realised she looked ridiculous.

The woman hadn't initiated conversation so Eva was unsure what the protocol was. Then Eva noticed she was wearing a hearing-aid. She put down her glass of champagne and touched the woman's arm. She was about Eva's age. She looked at Eva who signed a few words at her and the woman's face blossomed into a huge smile as she signed back.

You can sign! That's amazing!

Eva made a face and signed, *Not really. Only a little.*

But, together with Eva's rudimentary sign language and some lip-reading, they managed to have a conversation. The woman's name was Sophia and she was there with her husband on a business trip. They lived in New York.

When they left to talk to someone else Eva smiled and waved, buoyed up by the friendly exchange. Sophia had even told Eva to come and visit them in New York.

But then she felt her skin prickle and looked up to see Vidal staring at her as if she had two heads.

'What? Why aren't we moving on? Why are you looking at me like that?'

'Since when can you use sign language? Unless I missed something very fundamental, your mother wasn't deaf. Nor are you.'

A little hurt at his incredulity, Eva said, 'It was a friend at work. My only friend, if you must know. She was partially deaf. She taught me a little. It's really not that hard.'

'Do you have any idea who that was?' Vidal asked.

'Of course not. All I know is that her name is Sophia and she and her husband live in New York. Who are they?'

'He's one of the junior associates in the firm I'm hoping to secure the investment from.'

That sank in. 'Oh…wow. Okay… Did I do something wrong?'

Vidal shook his head. He looked a little shell-shocked. 'On the contrary. He said you were the first person who'd attempted to communicate with his wife. Are there any other skills you've acquired that I should know about?'

Eva felt like giggling at Vidal's reaction. She shook her head. 'Not that I can think of.'

Vidal kept looking at her warily for the rest of the evening, as if Eva was going to suddenly take him by surprise again. She didn't care. She was actually starting to enjoy herself. These events were so much less stuffy than the admittedly few she'd experienced back at home.

And then she heard a familiar beat, and every part of her soul and body went still. *Flamenco*. There was a performance in another room. Like a child following the Pied Piper, Eva followed the distinctive music and stood at the back of the room, watching avidly.

Vidal tugged her forward to sit down, so she had no choice but to follow. She didn't know how long they sat there. She was transfixed. It brought back so many memories of her beloved Maria, and how it was the only thing that had ever really transported her away from the *castillo* and her mother.

I used to watch you.

Vidal. He was watching her now.

She suddenly felt self-conscious, as if her blood was pumping too close to the surface. Beating with too many memories and her desire for him. Flamenco was so elemental it was calling to the most primitive part of her.

She tore her eyes off the show and looked at Vidal, who was still watching her. Sitting back in his seat nonchalantly.

'Sorry, you must have people to talk to. We should get back to the main party. Maybe you should talk to Maria's husband again.'

'If you're sure you don't mind?'

Eva could have stayed there all evening, but she shook her head and stood up. She even smiled. 'No, it's fine.'

Vidal stood up too, and took her hand. Eva wished he wouldn't—especially when she felt so raw.

They went back into the fray. Vidal let go of her hand, but only so he could put his hand on her lower back. It burned through the material of her dress, which suddenly felt very flimsy, even though there were many layers of satin and silk.

By the time they were in the car and heading home Eva felt a little light-headed from everything—the champagne, feeling at ease socially in a way she'd never expected, and from the Flamenco.

Its beat lingered in her blood. She wasn't tired. She was filled with a kind of restless energy. A dangerous energy. Reckless. As if something had shifted this evening. As if a wall had crumbled. An invisible wall that had been holding back her ability to resist Vidal.

Vidal was quiet. The air felt charged between them. Crackling with electricity. Eva tried desperately to tell herself she was imagining it. She was so susceptible to Vidal now, it really wouldn't take much if he wanted to push her into admitting she wanted him.

When they got back to the house Eva slipped off her shoes, and when Vidal said, 'I'm going to have a nightcap on the top floor if you want to join me?' Eva responded far too quickly.

'No. I… No, thank you. I'm tired. I'll go to bed.'

Coward, whispered a voice.

She ignored it. This was self-preservation, not cowardice.

'As you wish. Goodnight, Eva.'

The whole way to her bedroom Eva was wondering why she was fighting her desire. Would it be so bad to give in to Vidal? To let him have his moment of triumph? If it meant that she got to relieve this restless, reckless energy inside her? Was she really so proud?

But when she went into her room something laid out on the bed caught her eye. She went over and realised what it was. She stared at it in disbelief. And then mounting anger. She didn't know how it had appeared like this, but she was becoming used to the life of a billionaire, where you merely thought about something and it manifested.

Here she was, torturing herself, and all the while Vidal was just toying with her. Laughing at her. The poor little rich girl who'd never had any money at all but who had lorded it around the *castillo* like a princess…and then had to get her hands dirty and clean toilets…

And now this.

Eva grabbed what had been left on the bed and marched out of the room to the upper floor, where Vidal was standing with his back to her. Jacket and waistcoat gone. Broad back tapering down to narrow hips and muscular buttocks. The material of his trousers doing little to hide them.

He turned around and she tried not to let his presence distract her. She held up the dress. 'What is this?'

'A Flamenco dress.'

'I can see that.'

'Then why did you ask?'

Eva felt like stamping her foot. 'Why is it in my room?'

'I thought you might like it.'

'Why? Were you hoping for a private show?'

Vidal shrugged, totally unconcerned. 'It's just a gift, Eva. Do what you like with it.'

Eva felt dangerously volatile. 'You want a show? I'll give you a show. And then you can have a good laugh—is that it?'

Without waiting for his response, Eva went back to her bedroom, borne aloft on her anger—an anger she wasn't sure was entirely rational. She couldn't rationalise it. All she knew was that Vidal had always known about one of her deepest most secret things and now he was taunting her with it.

Eva managed to get out of the beautiful ball gown and drape it over a chair. She took off the jewellery she'd been wearing. Then she looked at the Flamenco dress. It was white with black spots and layered frills at the bottom. Classic. She'd always dreamed of owning a dress like this when she'd been teaching herself when she was younger. Maybe that was why she'd had such a visceral reaction.

She put the dress on. It fitted snugly around her chest, waist and hips. The bottom of it felt heavy. She caught it up in one hand and stood tall, with a dancer's straight spine. Her anger had drained away to be replaced by something far more nostalgic.

'It looks good on you.'

Startled, Eva looked at the door, where Vidal was leaning against the frame. He said, 'Try the shoes.'

'There are shoes?' Eva turned around and saw them at the bottom of the bed. Black. She put them on. They fitted perfectly. She said, 'The shoes I had came from

Maria—she brought them to the *castillo* for me. I'd out-grown them after a year, but I had to keep using them.'

Vidal said, 'I really didn't mean the dress to be any-thing other than a gift… After what you told me I or-dered it, and it must have arrived while we were out. The timing was a coincidence.'

Eva felt emotional. Vidal was pulling back layer after layer of her past without even realising what he was doing. He was just using her.

And you're just using him…you're still in control… reassured a little voice.

'Will you dance for me?' he asked.

Eva balked, even though moments ago she'd been so angry she'd offered to do just that. 'Now?'

'Why not?'

'But I haven't done it in years.'

'I'm sure it'll come back to you.'

A part of Eva was curious to know if she would re-member anything of the painstaking practice she'd used to put in day after day. She felt hot, thinking about Vidal watching her—then and now. About how she'd fantasised about him watching her.

'I… Okay.'

It wasn't as if she could make any more of a fool of herself in front of him.

She followed him back upstairs. The decking on the terrace was the perfect surface for the shoes. Eva walked around, getting used to them. *Heel, toe…toe, heel…* She couldn't look at Vidal, too nervous to see his expression.

She walked around like that for a long moment, and then from somewhere deep inside her came a familiar beat. She didn't need music. It was in her blood. Her soul.

She pulled the dress up and felt her feet take on a familiar rhythm. Slow at first. Deliberate. And then building to a faster beat. She started moving, back and forth. The frills of the dress dropped to the floor and she let herself get lost, exactly as she had done all those years before.

Vidal was mesmerised. As he'd used to be when he'd watched her when she was a coltish teenager, with long, skinny limbs. She'd always been graceful but, when she'd danced she'd taken on a grace that had left him in awe.

She'd used to practise for hours. Over and over again. Until she was sweating and dizzy. He knew that if he'd made his presence known she would never have forgiven him. He was intruding, but he'd found this other side of her so intriguing. It had been so *counter* to who she was.

And even now, after years of not dancing, Eva was inhabiting the rhythm and the steps in a way that only a true natural talent could. Her body was shaping itself into the traditional Flamenco pose, arched back, arms and hands making elaborate beautiful shapes.

He was almost jealous of the absorption on her face. And that made him shift against the glass railing. He didn't get jealous over women—much less a woman who wasn't even with another man.

The bodice of the dress was cut low enough to display the swells of Eva's breasts. But this wasn't a dance to entice—it was a dance that mocked men for their desire. It was a dance full of the wonder and power of the feminine.

It was the perfect dance for Eva. Mocking him for his desire all over again. Nothing had changed. And he couldn't even blame her this time. He had given her the dress. Asked her to dance.

And now, with each staccato move of her feet and heels, Vidal's control was fraying to pieces.

Eva came to a stop, breathing hard. As if coming out of a trance, she saw Vidal standing a few feet away, arms folded. He looked impossibly stern. Grim. Eva could feel that her hair had come down and was unravelling around her face and shoulders.

She felt undone. The power of the dance still pounded through her blood, as inexpert as she knew she must have been after years of non-practice. She felt powerful, but unsettled, as if she needed something more.

She needed him.

He was the thing that pounded through her body, gathering force. She'd always wanted him. She would always want him.

No, she told herself. That couldn't be. It would be too cruel. *So don't even go there. Protect yourself.*

But Eva feared it was too late already. The time to protect herself had come and gone.

Vidal, as if sensing the need inside her, walked forward, closing the distance between them. Actually, he didn't look grim. She realised he looked *stark*. As if something had been stripped away from him. She felt it too. Exposed. Raw. It resonated deep inside her. A mirroring need.

He said, 'I won't lay a finger on you unless you ask me, Eva.'

Eva couldn't take her eyes off Vidal's mouth. Wide and firm. Beautiful. She wanted to push aside his shirt and run her hands over his chest.

She knew she could turn and walk away. He wouldn't

touch her. But the memory of him rejecting her rushed back. She took a step back.

She said, 'What if this is all just a chance for you to humiliate me again? Expose me and then reject me?'

His jaw clenched. 'You were too young, Eva. Too young for what I wanted.'

Without even realising, Eva took a step forward. 'What did you want?'

Vidal's eyes were burning dark aquamarine, like a stormy sea. It was thrilling.

'What I wanted was to kiss you so hard that you wouldn't be able to say another spiteful, nasty word. Until you couldn't breathe. I wanted to bare you to my gaze, bare that body you'd been taunting me with all summer. Cup your breasts in my hands and squeeze the firm flesh. Taste your nipples…bite them. Bite that impudent mouth. I wanted to explore between your legs and feel how much you wanted me.'

His explicit words robbed her of breath, of rational thought.

'I…' She stopped, suddenly nervous. Was she really going to capitulate so easily? Let him have his moment of triumph? Eva knew she wanted Vidal above any other man. The thought of any other man being the first to bare her, touch her, made her skin go cold.

This was no capitulation, even if he thought it was.

This was her salvation.

'Eva, if you're—'

She shook her head. 'No. I'm not. I want this. I want you, Vidal.'

I've always wanted you. From the moment I saw you.

Now Vidal looked wary. 'You're sure?'

Eva tilted her chin up in the way she knew he hated.

Arched a brow. 'Maybe you're the one who isn't sure, Vidi?'

Colour slashed along Vidal's cheeks. His mouth thinned. 'Do not call me that.'

'Then make love to me and I won't.'

'Witch,' he growled, as he stepped up close and tugged her towards him, crushed her breasts against his hard chest. He tugged the rest of her hair loose and speared his fingers into the silken mass to cup her head. His other hand clamped firmly on her waist.

She could barely breathe. 'Vidal…please…'

'You're begging…good.'

Before Eva could argue that she wasn't begging, his mouth was on hers and he was kissing her so deeply her legs turned to jelly. He caught her against him, holding her up. Suddenly she didn't care if she was begging. She wanted this.

She lifted her arms up around his neck, straining to get closer. She'd never known a kiss could be so all-consuming. His tongue danced around hers, his teeth finding her lower lip and biting gently.

Her breasts felt full and aching. She moaned softly when Vidal's hand passed over one, cupping the flesh and testing its weight through the thin material of the dress.

Then his hand moved down, and down again, to her thigh. She felt the dress being pulled up until a light breeze danced over her bare skin, and then every part of her blood seemed to flow in a heated rush to between her legs, when Vidal's hand cupped her there.

She gasped and pulled back, dizzy with need. His eyes were so fiery she couldn't look away. His fingers pushed aside her flimsy silk underwear and stroked into her, exploring where she ached most.

Eva could hardly contain the visceral pleasure of Vidal's hand between her thighs. She was shaking with it as his fingers explored deeper, harder. He watched her the whole time, a fierce look on his face. She was panting. She didn't care. She only cared about the ratcheting, tightening spiral of pleasure that was consuming her to the point where she had to cry out as it exploded inside her, sending out waves of pleasure so intense and shocking that she would have fallen if Vidal hadn't caught her up into his arms.

He carried her through the house to his bedroom as Eva floated on a wave of endless little pleasures, before placing her down on the edge of his bed. She looked around dreamily. His room was massive, and dressed in earthy tones. A battered leather armchair in one corner had clothes draped over it. There was a discarded towel on the floor of the en suite bathroom. Curiously intimate details she hadn't expected.

Then she looked up and saw Vidal undoing his shirt. She stood, her limbs still a bit wobbly. She said, 'Wait… let me.'

CHAPTER EIGHT

VIDAL WASN'T SURE how he'd managed to get to his room with Eva in one piece. She was so responsive—in a way that blew his mind. In his deepest fantasies about this woman he'd imagined her being responsive enough to lose all that froideur, but he'd barely touched her and she'd melted into his arms, orgasmed into his hand.

A bell went off in his head even as her fingers got to the bottom of his shirt and he saw he was nearly bared. He caught her hands in his and she looked up at him. It nearly undid him all over again.

Her hair was a wild silken tangle around her face and shoulders. Her mouth was swollen, cheeks pink. Eyes bright.

Exactly how he'd envisaged her. *More*. But he needed to know...

'Eva, wait... When you said you hadn't been out in society much...does that mean that you haven't...been with anyone?'

Even as he asked the question Vidal knew. He saw it in the way she tensed. He should have known from her response just now.

She was looking down, avoiding his eye. He was filled

with disbelief, but also a grim sense of confirmation. Everything about this woman was not as he had expected.

Vidal tipped her chin up so she had to look at him. He caught a glimpse of vulnerability before she hid it. He realised how good she was at that. How she had done it before but he'd dismissed it. His guts clenched.

Somewhat defiantly, she said, 'Would it matter if I wasn't experienced? Would you reject me again?'

Vidal shook his head. 'No way. You are not that girl any more.'

She really isn't, a voice prodded him.

He pushed it aside. *Not now.* He couldn't think of that when his whole body was about to go on fire.

'Keep doing what you were doing,' he told her.

She waited a moment, as if not sure what to do, and then she undid the last button on his shirt and spread it open, pushing it off his shoulders and down his arms. He undid the cuffs with economic efficiency and the shirt fell to the floor.

Eva was just looking at him, wide-eyed, and then tentatively she lifted her hands and put them on his chest, fingers spread wide. She was killing him with the most chaste of touches. He would explode if she touched him—

'I used to dream of this,' she said in a low voice. 'I used to watch you...'

'I know.' Vidal knew his voice was dry.

She looked up at him. 'I wanted to talk to you another way...not like I used to...but I didn't know how. I would try...but then I'd see my mother, or she'd call me...and I'd remember I wasn't supposed to be...' She trailed off.

'Treating me like an equal?'

'Something like that.'

He caught her chin and tipped it up. 'We're equals now.'

'Are we?' she asked, and he heard the quaver in her voice. It made his guts clench harder.

He put his mouth to hers—anything to try and keep the focus on the physical. He didn't want to have a conversation with this woman. He just wanted her. But already it felt as if the sand was shifting beneath his feet and he wasn't able to keep his balance.

The kiss deepened. Eva was so sweet... He'd known she'd be sweet under all those tart comments and reprimands. But not as sweet as this. Eager, but reticent. Bold, but shy.

He slowly pulled the zip of her dress down and it loosened around her chest. He moved back and pulled it down her arms. She wore a strapless bra that did little to contain the plump swells of her perfect breasts. The dress fell all the way to the floor, revealing matching underwear. The merest slips of lace.

Vidal was so hard he hurt. Eva stood by the bed. Tall and lissom. Graceful curves. She was a product of her impeccable bloodline, that was for sure. But he couldn't care less about that. He only cared about how they would fit together, and he knew instinctively that they would. In a way that he'd never experienced before.

He walked towards her, undoing his belt as he did so. Her gaze moved lower. He stopped in front of her and pushed his trousers down, stepping out of them. He hooked his fingers into his underwear and pulled that down too, freeing his erection.

Eva's eyes widened, colour slashing her cheeks. Her breasts rose and fell with her breath and he reached for her, turning her around so that he could undo her bra. It floated away. Then he tugged her underwear down and she stepped out of it.

He stood back. He'd been waiting for this moment for a long time. Eva Flores, naked in front of him. Ready to submit to him. Ready to allow him to finally feel a sense of superiority over her.

'Turn around,' he said.

And when she did he felt all of those things, but so much more. She was looking at him, but she had her arms folded over her breasts. His gaze travelled down to the cluster of dark curls hiding her sex.

Dios. How was he going to hold it together enough to even perform? That feeling of superiority was there, because right now in this instance he certainly had more experience, but somehow the sense of superiority was fleeting as he stood in the face of her innocence. An innocence she was trusting *him* with.

The truth was that he felt humbled, and he'd never in a million years expected this. With her.

'Vidal?'

He snapped out of his trance. He saw the slight tremor in Eva's body. She was unsure, and where once he would have revelled in this unexpected twist of events, he found his immediate instinct was to reassure.

He reached for her and pulled her arms down. She bit her lip but didn't look away. Brave. Something else made his gut clench then. Some unnamed emotion.

'You are beautiful.' He felt exposed, so he added, 'But you know that.'

'I don't...not really.'

'Well, you are. Exquisite.'

'So are you.'

He said, 'Lie back on the bed.'

Eva did. Vidal watched her. He came onto the bed beside her and proceeded to indulge all his fantasies, exploring Eva's body, every dip and hollow, and the sharp points of her breasts, until she was moaning, begging and pleading. Incoherent with lust.

Before he lost it completely, he retrieved some protection and rolled it onto his length. He positioned himself between her legs. She looked up at him, full of desire and trust.

He pushed aside the curious ache in his chest and said, 'This might hurt a little, but stay with me. It'll get better, I promise.'

She nodded. Her hands were on his chest. Giving herself to him. He slowly embedded himself in her slick, tight body, sweat breaking out on his brow with the effort it took not to just drive home and explode.

She was more exquisite than anything he'd ever known. It had never been like this before. With any woman. He felt her tense and he stopped. Gritted his jaw. He could feel her body slowly accepting his. Relaxing.

'Okay?' he asked.

She nodded. Eyes wide.

Vidal pushed deeper. And deeper. Until he didn't know where he ended and she began. Then he couldn't move for a long moment, trying to regain control.

Eva shifted under him and he cursed silently.

She said, 'Vidal… I'm okay.'

He felt like huffing a laugh. She might be okay. He wasn't. Amazingly, he felt like a virgin again. With his first woman. Desperately trying not to make a fool of himself.

He moved. Out and back in. Steady long strokes. Letting her get used to him. He reached under her, shifting her up towards him. She gasped when he went even deeper.

Gradually, any restraint was fast unravelling as their movements became faster, more frenetic, and each chased the pinnacle of pleasure. Vidal willed Eva on. She had to come before him.

Her body was sheened with perspiration. She was clutching at him. He could feel the tremors building in her body and as he slammed so deep he saw stars. She went very still, and then it was as if a powerful wave rushed through her entire body, taking him with her as they climaxed together on wave after wave of intense, mind-numbing pleasure.

Vidal slumped over Eva, utterly spent. Her legs were wrapped around his hips. Her body's inner muscles were still pulsating in the aftermath, keeping him deep inside. Keeping him hard. The tips of her breasts scraped against his chest. She was breathing hard.

With extreme effort he lifted his head. 'Okay?'

Dark tendrils of hair were stuck to her forehead. Her cheeks were pink. Her eyes were glazed. Slowly, they focused. She looked at him. She nodded her head jerkily and said, with a rough-sounding voice, 'Is it…always like that?'

Vidal would have loved to have had the wherewithal to say coolly, *All the time*. But, seeing as he was still deeply embedded in her body, and he could barely think straight, he couldn't be anything less than completely honest.

'No…' he said. 'It's rarely like that.'

Eva wasn't sure how long she'd slept. A day? A week? A month? When she woke she was in her own bed, and the curtains were half open. It was bright daylight. Vidal must have brought her back here. She wasn't quite ready to process the meaning of that—beyond the very obvious one that he hadn't wanted to hang out with her after...

Her brain stalled there. *After...* She couldn't totally rationalise what had happened beyond the physical act. She was no longer a virgin. But the taking of her innocence had been such a profound and amazing experience. She'd even asked him if it was always like that. She cringed now. Maybe he'd brought her back to her own bed because he was embarrassed by her. By her naivety.

Eva groaned under her covers. She was still naked. So Vidal had carried her here naked. After extricating himself from her vice-like grip.

She groaned again.

A robe had been left on the end of the bed. A nice gesture. She sat up and reached for it, groaning again when intimate muscles protested. She went into the bathroom and gasped. She looked a sight. Hair in a wild tangle. Make-up smudged and trailing down her cheeks.

She went cold. Had she cried last night? Tears of ecstasy and joy?

She dived into the shower in a bid to try and scrub away the humiliation. Winced as she found tender spots. Her breasts. Thighs. Between her legs. She could still remember the sheer power of Vidal's body moving into hers. And the quickening, the tightening, that had led to the most extreme pleasure.

No wonder people became sex addicts. She'd only had it once and she was already addicted.

Eventually she came out of the shower, knowing she'd need to face Vidal sooner or later. Hoping he might have gone into the office today, she was dismayed to find him sitting in the informal dining room off the kitchen, having his lunch.

Lunch. She'd slept right through the morning. A pleasure-induced coma. More humiliation.

She took a seat and sat down. Santo appeared with a freshly prepared salad. Eva couldn't meet his eye as she said thank you. She avoided Vidal's eye too. She'd noticed, however, that he was wearing a short-sleeved polo top. And that he looked thoroughly rested. Not as if his life and very being had been turned inside out.

But of course it hadn't. For him it must have been almost—

'How are you?'

Eva nearly dropped her fork. She took a breath. Forced herself to look at Vidal.

He reached over and touched her jaw lightly. 'You have a little burn here. I might have to shave.'

Eva's face went hot. She'd noticed the slight beard rash. Vidal's mark. It was on her skin elsewhere too. She liked it.

'It's fine… I'm fine. Thank you.'

'I didn't go into the office today. I wanted to make sure you were okay… That was intense.'

Some small part of her was slightly reassured to hear him say that. She squinted a look at him. 'It was?'

'Yes, Eva. As much as I'd love to pretend otherwise.'

That reassured her more. If Vidal had been out to make her feel insecure he wouldn't have had to do much. And she knew that wasn't his style.

She forced herself to eat some salad, even though—amazingly—she didn't have much of an appetite. She couldn't stop the images of last night running through her head. Their hearts pounding in unison. Sweat-slicked skin.

Eva dropped her knife and it fell with a clatter.

Vidal had bent and picked it up before she could move. He caught her hand, and she gave up any pretence of trying to eat.

'I think you're afflicted the same way as me,' he said.

She glanced at his plate. Hardly anything eaten either. Vidal's eyes were hot.

A zing of excitement went through her. 'Can we?'

Vidal's fingers intertwined with hers. 'We can do whatever we like.'

He tugged her up to stand and led her from the dining room. Ineffectually, she said, 'But what about lunch… the salads…?'

'We can eat later.'

'We don't have to go out?' Eva was sure that there was an event for them to go to almost every night.

'I've cancelled.'

In Vidal's bedroom, the bed had been remade. Eva's dress was hanging up on the back of a door. She blushed when she saw it. There was no sign of her underwear.

Vidal said from behind her, 'Are you sore?'

Eva turned around. She felt shy. She shook her head. 'Just a little tender.'

Vidal came close and caught a lock of her hair, twining it around his finger, tugging her closer. 'Remember when I said there were plenty of places to kiss you other than on your mouth?'

Eva's breath hitched. She nodded.

'Well, take off your clothes and lie back on the bed, because I'm going to show you exactly what I meant.'

Hours later, Vidal stood by the bed. It was dark outside. Eva was on her front, a sheet pulled up over her bottom, her back long and elegant. An arm up by her face.

He had intended on going to work that morning. But when Eva hadn't appeared for breakfast he'd given in to an impulse to stay at home. He'd told himself it was just to make sure she was okay. Because last night had been... unprecedented. And not just because she'd been a virgin.

It had surpassed Vidal's wildest fantasies. When he'd finally come back to consciousness Eva had been deeply asleep, and he'd found himself watching her for a long time. On some level, he'd been marvelling at what had happened. The fulfilment of so much.

She'd been a virgin.

At every step of the way since he'd met her again she'd confounded Vidal's expectations. The truth was that he thought he'd known her...but in fact did he know her at all?

The lure of leaving her in his bed had been so strong that he'd moved her back to her own bed. She'd barely stirred. His conscience had pricked at the thought of her waking alone, but then he'd reminded himself that he didn't do cosy mornings-after with lovers.

She's different.

Precisely, he'd told himself. All the more reason to make sure there was no ambiguity about her role.

So then he'd told himself he'd wait till lunch. Make sure she was okay and then go to work. But then she'd appeared, and Vidal had known he wasn't going anywhere.

Within minutes he'd been leading her back to the bedroom, and for the first time in his working life he'd blown off meetings to indulge his desires. Indulge in an afternoon of unabated sybaritic pleasure. When even through his wildest days Vidal had never pursued pleasure over work.

Eva was an intoxicating mix of novice and practised

seductress. One minute she'd had him doubting that she had even been a virgin, and the next she'd been blushing from her feet up to her neck.

Once again, Vidal didn't want to move her. He wanted to climb into the bed beside her.

So he moved her. Back to her own bedroom.

She barely woke, and he ignored his conscience. Again.

Had another week gone by? Had two? Eva wasn't even sure. She was in some kind of limbo land, where she would wake late, eat, read or swim, or take a walk to the park, and then Vidal would come home, they'd go out and then, within the most respectable amount of time possible, would leave whatever event they were at and come home and—

Eva blushed now, just remembering the previous night.

She pulled her knees up under her chin, sitting on one of the luxurious seats on the top terrace area.

They had barely made it into the house from the car. They hadn't made it to the bedroom. They'd made love on the first floor, clothes strewn along the way like teenagers.

Eva had got up very early to retrieve them, before Michael or Santo could find evidence of their lust. The staff didn't live in the house, but they arrived quite early each day.

She had also got up early because it had been clear since that first night that Vidal had no intention of allowing Eva the indulgence of sleeping in his bed all night. Until morning. Like regular lovers. That was okay, she'd told herself. It actually helped her to keep a certain amount of perspective and distance, even if both perspective and distance faded to dust as soon as she looked at Vidal.

At least one of them was experienced in that regard. And she could appreciate those strong boundaries because in so many other ways she was losing it...

Eva buried her head in her knees. Vidal didn't have to tell her to smile any more because she couldn't stop. She felt so much lighter. As if a burden had been lifted off her shoulders. For the first time in her life she felt her age. She felt young and free and as if her whole life was waiting for her.

It is, reminded a voice. *Without Vidal. Don't forget why you're here.*

Eva's smile faded. She hadn't forgotten the genesis of this agreement. The fact that Vidal had felt a certain need for retribution. To make her pay for her youthful transgressions. But in the last few days it felt as if something had changed. As if they'd moved on from that. As if...

As if what? As if you're in a real relationship with a man who has already told you that he will marry for love and that you are the last woman he would marry?

Eva scowled now. She hadn't forgotten that. But it felt as if they were finally communicating in the way that Eva had always dreamed of when she was younger. Conversing. As equals.

She heard a noise at that moment and looked around. Vidal was striding out onto the terrace, jacket off, tie gone, shirt open at the throat, holding a glass of what looked like whisky.

Eva sat up straight. 'Hi...' She felt shy around him all the time now.

Vidal said, 'Hi, yourself. Good day? Do you want a drink?'

Eva tried not to be put off by Vidal's breezy nonchalance. She wasn't used to this situation. How to act with a lover.

She nodded, 'Fine, thanks—and, no, I'm okay for a drink.'

It had been an amazing day. She'd gone to the park, had a coffee. Come back, read one of Vidal's books from his library. She'd allowed herself to daydream about her future... But she held all that back, still not completely at ease with divulging everything in her head.

She stood up. 'Actually, I spent the afternoon slaving over a hot stove to make us dinner.'

She ignored Vidal's nonplussed expression and went down to the kitchen, aware of him following her, and suddenly aware of the fact that she was wearing soft sweats and a loose shirt. Hair in a messy bun.

She stopped and turned around. Vidal was right behind her. She gestured to her clothes. 'I'm taking advantage of the fact that we're not going out tonight. Is that okay?'

'It's completely fine. This house is your home too, for as long as you're here.'

For as long as you're here.

Eva's heart hitched. She wasn't imagining him putting down boundaries—they were so clear they could be marked with flashing lights and police tape.

In the kitchen, she pressed a button on the state-of-the-art oven. She said brightly, 'It'll just take a minute to heat it up.'

There was bread and salad, covered over, on the counter.

Vidal put down his glass. 'What is "it"?'

'A chicken casserole with a little twist, I added some harissa—'

'I've eaten already.'

She stopped. 'Oh. You didn't mention you would.'

'Should I have?'

'Well, no... I guess I just assumed that you'd want to eat in as we weren't going out.'

Eva was ravenous for a home-cooked meal. They hadn't eaten a proper dinner in days—just bits of food at various events.

'And so you cooked?'

Eva was starting to feel a tingle of irritation at Vidal's reaction. It was as if she'd done something outrageous. 'Yes. I can cook. I like to cook. Hence, dinner.'

'Since when do you cook?'

'Since I had to, or my mother and I would have gone hungry. Maria taught me how to bake when I was small.'

'Where's Santo?'

'I said he could go home. It's his partner's birthday.'

'Well, like I said, I've eaten already. But you go ahead. I have to make some calls.'

He picked up his glass and was just turning to go when Eva reacted impulsively and picked up a piece of bread and threw it at him. It bounced off his shoulder. He stopped and turned around. Eva felt like giggling—but also not.

'What was that for?'

She lifted her chin. 'For being rude. You could have had the courtesy to tell me you'd be eating out. Every evening I'm expected to trot along in your wake, to every envelope-opening in the city. The one evening we have off, I thought it would be nice to eat a home-cooked meal.'

Vidal came back over to the counter. 'I'm not in the business of "home-cooked meals".'

Eva folded her arms. 'Maybe when you get married

you will be.' She cursed herself inwardly for mentioning marriage.

'I most likely will. And I'm sure I'll enjoy them.'

'But not with me?'

'No. Because our relationship is not about that.'

'Oh, I'm sorry—have I strayed over the invisible boundary marking our relationship?'

'I have a chef and a housekeeper. You're not here because I need either of those things.'

'So what you're saying is that you couldn't care less about me as a person—you're just interested in me as a trophy and for sex.'

Eva felt ridiculously hurt, even though Vidal had never been anything but brutally honest about that. The way she'd been mooning over Vidal just a short while before, telling herself that maybe they'd transitioned to a better place, mocked her.

She said, 'You accused me of not being a nice person, Vidal—but you know what? *You're* not being very nice right now. In fact, you're being a complete—'

Vidal moved so fast he took the word out of Eva's mouth and replaced it with his mouth on hers. Like a brand. Fiery and irresistible.

She was responding before she could stop herself. And then she pulled back, disgusted. 'What are you doing?'

Vidal's eyes were bright, his jaw tight. 'Reminding us both of why we're here.'

'A business deal with benefits and a side of revenge. I remember now. Thank you.' Eva's voice was bitter.

'Damn it, Eva. We're not here to play house. I'll do that with my wife.'

Eva smirked to hide her pain—because the pain she was feeling was indescribable, and it shouldn't be. 'What if you fall in love with someone who doesn't want to play house or cook for her husband?'

'If I love her it won't matter,' Vidal gritted out. 'After all, it's not as if I can't afford to have staff to do all that.'

'I *really* don't like you right now.'

'I don't need you to like me.'

The energy between them was volatile. Crackling with electricity. A short time before Eva had been hungry and looking forward to eating. Now she'd lost her appetite. Another appetite had taken over. Lust. And anger. And a desire to punish Vidal for being so cool and for mentioning his future *wife*.

She pressed a button on the oven and turned back to Vidal. She started undoing her shirt. Which was actually his shirt. She'd worn his shirt like some love-sick girlfriend. Angry with herself as much as him, she tore it off and threw it to the ground.

Vidal's eyes flared with heat when he took in the fact that she wasn't wearing a bra. He breathed out. 'Now we're on the same page...'

He came over and lifted Eva up with effortless strength onto the island in the centre of the kitchen. He spread her legs wide and moved between them. She could feel the heat of his arousal against her, and as he bent his head and surrounded the hard tip of one breast in hot, wet heat, she knew she could exult in this at least. Her effect on him. There was no doubt about that.

She just had to remember that he was only interested in seeing her either on her back, or by his side dressed in couture.

When Vidal woke in the morning the sun was up. He felt disorientated. He was usually up much earlier. His body felt heavy and replete. Sated. Yet still hungry. A sensation he'd only experienced with Eva.

Eva.

The bed beside him was empty. It usually was when he woke. It was as if she'd taken the hint after that first night, when he'd taken her back to her own bed, and now she left before he woke.

It should have pleased him. But he found it unsettling. As if the fact that she was doing it irked him somehow. Which was ridiculous and contrary. *He* was the one who'd made sure she didn't get any ideas.

Did a part of him want to wake up and find her nestled beside him, their legs entwined? *Perhaps*, he told himself angrily, throwing the covers back, *but only so he could make love to her again.*

As he stood under the steaming shower a few seconds later he tried not to think of the previous evening, but he couldn't help it. Eva was right—he'd been rude. Rude in a way that he wouldn't accept from anyone. Rude in a way he wouldn't have accepted from her.

For years he'd taken her to task for her rudeness. But last night it had been him. Because when he'd walked through the house, for the first time he'd noticed little things. Additions. Evidence of the presence of a woman.

Her shoes by the door—the sandals that she'd worn that day, presumably to the park. Flowers on the reception table. He never bought flowers. Bright, vivid blooms. They reminded him of his mother. She'd always had flowers in their apartment, no matter how broke they'd been. A shawl on the back of a couch in the TV lounge. A book left open on a coffee table.

The markers of someone else in the house. Not altogether unwelcome. The kind of things he would have expected of a partner. *A wife.* Not a temporary lover.

So when he'd found Eva on the terrace, in soft sweats that clung to her long shapely legs and one of his shirts, hair down and looking sexier than anything he'd ever seen in his life, he'd found it intensely provocative. Even when she hadn't even been trying to be provocative. Or maybe she had and he was the fool.

He'd reacted to her having cooked dinner like a total boor. But it had pushed him over the edge. The edge of not knowing how to handle *this* Eva. The one who surprised him and confounded him at every turn. The Eva who'd worn her vulnerability on her sleeve for the first time. The Eva who had allowed him to take her innocence but had taken the hint and now went back to her own bed.

Vidal emitted a curse and shut off the shower. Even just thinking of her had his body reacting. His libido was out of control and it didn't seem to be on the wane. Very much the opposite.

A prickle of panic caught at his gut. He should be wanting her less by now. That was usually the way with a lover. Actually, usually he lost interest far sooner. But with Eva he'd allowed himself to believe that their shared past and all she had put him through had added a level to their relationship that put it outside of what he considered normal.

Vidal threw on some jeans and a shirt. He walked past Eva's bedroom and glanced inside. The bed was neatly made and the sun was shining in. This sign of order irked him.

He found her in the kitchen. She was wearing a long button-down dress. Simple but sexy. Hair pulled back and in a loose plait to keep it out of her way. He knew she knew he was there, because she'd tensed.

That irked him too.

'I owe you an apology,' he said.

Eva stopped what she was doing with Tupperware bowls and looked at Vidal. 'For what?'

'You made dinner and I was rude.'

Eva looked away and shrugged. 'It's fine. I should have sent you a message. I shouldn't have assumed you'd want to eat here. You have your routine.'

'What are you doing?'

Eva placed a lid on a plastic bowl. 'I'm packing up the food from last night for Santo—he has an arrangement with a charity for the homeless to donate anything left over or unused.'

'Oh.' Vidal felt off-kilter. Why didn't he know that? How did Eva know that? And since when did she care about charity?

It was very clear to Vidal that things had veered way off course, and without pondering his decision he knew exactly what he had to do now, to be able to put this episode behind him so they could both move on.

It was time to get Eva out of his system.

CHAPTER NINE

'YOU WANT TO go where?' Eva looked at Vidal disbe-lievingly.

'My house in Hawaii. Maui, to be precise.'

Eva was still absorbing the fact that he'd apologised for turning down dinner last night. She thought he'd made up for it by ravishing her to within an inch of her life. It had taken extreme effort for her to get out of his bed before he'd woken to find her there.

'Forgive me if I'm wrong,' Eva said carefully, 'but I'm pretty certain that a tropical island isn't in the guidebook for fake engagement relationships.'

Although the thought of being in a tropical paradise with Vidal was…intoxicating.

'I need to go and check on some maintenance issues, and some friends are having a party there. It's just for a few days.'

'I… Do I have a choice?'

'You always have a choice, Eva,' Vidal said.

But she knew she didn't. Not really. It wasn't as if she'd ever be going to a place like that with Vidal again. The weak part of her that she was slowly embracing and learning not to see as a negative thing begged her just to

give in. What harm could it do? She was already in so
deep with this man...

So Eva feigned as much nonchalance as she could
and shrugged lightly. 'Sure, it sounds nice. When do
we leave?'

'Within the hour.'

All nonchalance was gone. Eva squeaked, 'An *hour*?'

They arrived in Maui when it was still daylight, as Hawaii was three hours behind San Francisco. It was a lush
green paradise and Eva had never been anywhere like it.

A car and driver met them and drove them to Vidal's
property high in the hills, with spectacular views down
to the sea. Eva got out of the car and stood taking in the
view. Vidal came to stand beside her.

She shook her head. 'This is...breathtaking.'

Vidal took her hand. 'Come on, I'll show you around.'

Eva let him lead her into the beautiful white wooden
house perched on the top of this idyllic hill. Dark wood
floors gleamed to a high shine. The windows were all
open, allowing a breeze to flow through, muslin curtains
fluttering gently. The furniture was simple, rustic, but it
looked comfortable. The kitchen was massive, and the
dining room was just inside some tall French doors, with
another dining area on the outdoor terrace. There was an
infinity swimming pool in the garden below, surrounded
by flowering bushes.

An iridescent bird flew through the house and Eva
gasped.

Vidal said, 'You'll get used to it. The wildlife here
makes itself at home.'

He led her upstairs to the bedrooms, all decked out

with en suite bathrooms and the same dark wood flooring. Bright rugs. Massive beds dressed in crisp cotton.

To Eva's horror, she felt emotional. This place was
like somewhere she'd dreamed of but hadn't realised it
till now. Tears stung her eyes, and to her horror, Vidal
noticed.

'Hey, are you okay?'

Eva shook her head quickly and took her hand out
of his. 'Fine…just got a speck of dust or something in
my eye.'

Vidal curled his hand into itself. Maybe this had been a
mistake. For a second he'd have sworn Eva was crying.
And he could understand how she felt, because when
he'd first come here he'd felt emotional too.

He'd intended on this being an almost surgical operation. Bring Eva here, sequester her in his house and
gorge himself on her until she was finally out of his system. Pure sex.

But they'd only just arrived and it already felt as if he
was fast losing control of the situation.

He moved back. 'This is your room. I'm down the
hall.'

Eva avoided his eye. She went to the doors that led
out to a balcony. 'It's beautiful…thank you.' Her voice
was husky.

Vidal's gut twisted. He was about to ask her if she
was okay again, but then a voice came from downstairs.

'Yoo-hoo! Anyone home?'

Eva turned around from the balcony doors. What was
wrong with her? Almost blubbing all over Vidal because
of the spectacular views and the peace of the place?

A woman had appeared in the bedroom doorway, with a massive smile on her face. She greeted Vidal warmly, with a kiss and a hug. Eva felt self-conscious. Too stiff for this relaxed place.

Vidal was saying, 'Chelle, meet Eva Flores—Eva this is Chelle, my friend, intrepid housekeeper, chef and general busybody, who doesn't hesitate to dish out life lessons at every opportunity.'

Eva felt ridiculously shy in the face of the other woman's natural easy-going effervescence. It was if she was realising that all the loosening up she had done since coming to America with Vidal was just a drop in the ocean of how far she needed to go.

She stuck out a hand, tried to smile, but it felt forced. She could feel herself pulling back the old armour that had protected her for so long.

'So nice to meet you, Chelle.' She winced. She sounded so stuffy.

The woman's clasp was warm and firm. Her dark eyes so kind that ridiculously Eva almost felt like crying again.

She let Eva's hand go and said briskly, 'I've left some snacks downstairs, and I'll be back later to do dinner. Hal will be over first thing in the morning, to go over the jobs that need doing.' She looked at Eva and explained, 'Hal is my husband.'

'And they've just welcomed baby number three to their brood.'

Vidal was smiling. No doubt already imagining his own brood some day. The thought made Eva feel even more wobbly.

She said, 'Congratulations. A boy or a girl?'

Chelle smiled. 'A girl. We've called her Lucy.'

'You'll meet them all at the party,' said Vidal.

Eva looked at him. 'Party?'

'It's Hal's fortieth this weekend. That's the party I mentioned.'

'Oh, of course...'

Eva had assumed it was going to be another formal society party. Not a friends' party. This was nearly more frightening to her than the other kind. She was only just getting used to navigating that world. And now she was going to be thrown into another one.

Except, as much as she'd dreaded the society world, at least she'd had some sort of template for it. But parties in the real world? With relatively normal people? She didn't have a clue.

'This food is delicious,' Eva said appreciatively.

And it was. Chelle had left out a veritable feast of cold meats and cheeses, bread and salads. Gazpacho soup. Crisp white wine.

She and Vidal were sitting at the island in the kitchen, the warm breeze flowing around them and bringing scents from the garden.

'Why did you buy property here?' Eva asked impulsively.

'Why not? It's beautiful, as you can see.'

Eva rolled her eyes. 'Yes, but why here specifically?'

'My mother always talked about coming to Hawaii. Her dream was to go on a cruise with my father when they retired and see the world. Hawaii, for some reason, was one of the places she always spoke about.'

'Did they ever come here?'

Vidal laughed. 'They never left Spain. That's why my mother pushed me so hard,' he went on. 'She knew

I was intelligent enough to do something. To get out of Spain and see the world.'

'She sounds like she was a formidable woman.'

'She was.'

Eva remembered seeing something on the way in. 'That's why you called the house Casa Inez? After your mother?'

Vidal nodded. 'Yes.'

'That's a lovely tribute to her. I'm sorry she didn't get to see this place.'

'Me too.'

'I can't imagine wanting to name anything after *my* mother.'

Eva saw Vidal's sharp look.

'You're not sorry she's gone?'

Eva looked at him. Shocked. 'Of course I'm sorry she's gone… I loved her.' She bit her lip. 'But truthfully… I can't say I didn't feel a sense of…liberation. Our relationship was complicated. We were all we had. I can see now how unhappy she was…how it affected her mental health. She was pretty much agoraphobic in the end. She wouldn't leave the *castillo* no matter what. Not even to get medical treatment when she had pains in her chest. I called the paramedics, but by the time they came it was too late. She'd had a heart attack and died.'

'I didn't know that. It must have been traumatic.'

Eva tried not to think of the sheer panic she'd felt. 'It was. I did a course in CPR after she died. I never want to feel so helpless again. What if I could have saved her?'

To her surprise, Vidal took her hand. She looked at him.

He said, 'I know what it's like to watch a loved one die and I know there's nothing you can do.'

'Thank you.'

A moment shimmered between them. Light and delicate. Then Vidal took his hand away and said, 'I'm afraid I have to make a couple of quick calls in the study, but you should explore and rest. Lie by the pool.'

Eva smiled. 'That sounds good.' In truth, she'd welcome a little respite—a chance to get her bearings.

Just before he left, though, Vidal turned at the door. 'Were you okay earlier? You seemed a little off with Chelle?'

'Oh, no!' Eva said, genuinely dismayed. 'It's just… sometimes I'm not sure how to behave around people. She seems so lovely and friendly.'

'She is. She has no agenda. She's one of the most genuine people I know. Everyone here is the same.'

Vidal walked out and Eva couldn't help but feel that it had been some kind of warning: *Behave with my friends.*

He still didn't trust her.

And it shouldn't matter. But it did.

When Vidal emerged by the pool as the sun was setting he took in the view. The view of Eva lying face-down on the lounger. She wore a one-piece. Disappointing. He made a mental note to burn all one-piece swimsuits. Her skin was glistening with sun cream. Lightly golden. Her hair was pulled back and caught up in a bun, exposing her neck.

Vidal dropped his towel onto the lounger beside her and sat down. She opened her eyes. Dark and golden. Amazing to think that once he'd thought them cold and now all he thought of when she looked at him was heat.

She came up on one elbow. She looked deliciously sleepy. 'What time is it?'

'About five. Chelle is going to be back in an hour to get dinner ready.'

Eva turned and sat up. 'Okay, I'll get ready.'

Vidal reached for her, tugging her over onto his lounger, making her squeal. 'Not yet. I have plans for the next hour.'

She was breathless. 'You do?'

'Yes.'

She had her back to him and he slipped a hand between one swimsuit strap and her shoulder, to push it down her arm. The next one followed. He tugged the material all the way down, baring her breasts. He cupped them, testing their firm weight, his fingers trapping her nipples.

Eva moaned and arched her back. She reached behind her for Vidal, who was wearing only board shorts. Her hand finding his hardness and cupping him. Teasing him.

He stood up and pulled her with him. Quickly he dispensed with his own shorts and her swimsuit until they were both naked. Eva giggled. It almost stopped Vidal in his tracks. He'd never heard her giggle. She seemed almost surprised by it herself, putting a hand over her mouth.

He said, 'Do you know how many fantasies I used to have of you in that pool at the *castillo*?'

Eva shook her head. He took her hand and led her to the steps leading down into the pool.

Eva still felt a little hazy from her nap as Vidal led her down into the deliciously cool water. The sky was turning to violet around them. The night chorus of birds was starting up. She wondered if in fact she was Eve and he was Adam. It felt primeval at this moment, as the silky water caressed their bodies and Vidal took her deeper and deeper until she couldn't stand and she had to put her legs around his waist.

She allowed herself to fall all the way into the dream. The dream that this was real and that Vidal loved her as much as she loved him.

It was only later, when Eva was back in the bedroom, her whole body still tingling after what had happened in the pool, that she acknowledged what had gone through her mind in that dreamlike moment.

She loved Vidal.

But that was crazy. She didn't even know what love was. How could she? What she'd experienced from her mother had been some sort of toxic love. And no one else had ever loved her. Apart from maybe the house-keeper Maria.

So it couldn't be love. It was infatuation. Lust-induced emotion. That was it.

Vidal certainly didn't love her. He would fall about laughing if he knew that, of all things, she'd actually fallen for him.

The ultimate revenge.

She pushed the notion of love out of her head and gave herself a quick once-over. She was wearing a strappy red maxi-dress. Sandals. Hair down. Face scrubbed clean. She loved not having to dress up.

Vidal was nowhere to be seen in the kitchen, but Chelle was there. She saw her, and Eva apologised.

Chelle smiled and said, 'Don't be silly—come in... help me. There are some mushrooms waiting to be chopped on the board.'

Delighted to be given something to do so she didn't have to navigate a conversation, Eva smiled. 'Yes, please.'

But Chelle was so friendly and open and easy that it was impossible not to just follow her lead and engage in conversation. Without even realising it, Eva found she was telling her about the *castillo* and her mother.

Chelle looked at her at one point. 'That place sounds crazy—like something out of a gothic novel.'

Eva shrugged, self-conscious. 'I mean, it was amazing... I was very privileged.' How many times had Vidal levelled *that* accusation at her?

Chelle surprised her by squeezing her arm gently. 'It sounds like it was amazing, but not very...homely.'

Eva laughed out loud at the notion, and then put her hand to her mouth as if she was surprised at the sound. She shook her head. 'No, not homely at all. The opposite, in fact.'

The conversation flowed and Chelle poured some wine for Eva. She didn't even notice Vidal standing in the doorway until he said, 'That's quite enough fraternising with the staff.'

Chelle looked up and threw a piece of raw green pepper at Vidal, who caught it deftly and promptly ate it.

She said, 'Don't worry. Thanks to my commis chef here, dinner is ready and I will take my leave.'

Chelle waved goodbye to Eva, who was genuinely touched by the woman's warmth and humour.

Eva had already laid the table outside on the terrace and lit candles. She brought out the plates of food and the wine. Vidal was in a crisp white shirt and faded jeans. Mouthwateringly sexy.

'You didn't have to help prepare dinner,' he said as they sat down.

'I didn't mind. I told you—I enjoy cooking. Although I'm nowhere near Chelle's level of proficiency.'

'She's a trained chef.'

'So she was telling me.' Eva swallowed a delicious mouthful of seafood risotto and a sip of wine and then said, 'You don't cook?'

'I never had to, really. I was either in boarding school then at university or at the *Castillo* with my father. And at university I ate like everyone else—terribly.'

'And then you made your millions, so you could always afford to hire a chef.'

Vidal drank some wine. 'Something like that…'

They were silent for a moment, and then Eva put down her fork. The night around them was soft and dark, like a cocoon. 'You know… I envy you.'

Vidal put a hand to his chest, '*You*, the princess of the *castillo*, envy *me*?'

Eva felt a dart of hurt. 'Don't call me that, please.'

He picked up his glass and said, 'Noted.'

She clinked her glass with his. 'Thank you.'

'So tell me: why do you envy me?'

'Your opportunity to go to university… I always wished for that.'

'You could have gone.'

Eva shook her head. 'Apart from no money, I wasn't bright, like you. I wouldn't have got a scholarship. I left traditional school at the age of twelve. My home-school tutor was a joke. I'd probably barely have scraped through the most basic exams.'

'Lots of people have only a rudimentary education and go on to university.'

'Perhaps… I wanted to do a degree in business and economics.'

'There's nothing stopping you now. It's just a matter

of putting in the work to get the basic qualifications. I would give you the money to do that, Eva.'

She looked at Vidal, horrified. 'I didn't tell you for that reason...you don't have to give me anything. You've done enough. Not everything has to be a transaction.'

Vidal sat back. 'I'm sorry. I didn't mean it like that. But it's a very achievable dream, Eva.'

Slightly mollified, she said, 'Sorry, I overreacted. I just don't want you to think I'm grasping for whatever I can get.'

Vidal sat forward again and shook his head. 'Believe me, you're the least mercenary woman I've ever met.'

Eva smiled and held up a finger. 'Ah, one positive quality in my favour!'

Vidal's eyes gleamed like two aquamarine jewels. 'Oh, you have a few more, don't worry.'

Eva blushed. Ridiculously. She hated it that she craved his approval so desperately.

Vidal looked at Eva in the flickering candlelight. He knew he'd never seen a woman as beautiful. And might not ever again. But there was something even more to her beauty now—a kind of luminescence that had never been there before. She didn't look so serious. So pensive. So...haughty.

In fact, just now, when he'd found her in the kitchen with Chelle, helping, he'd felt like saying, *Would the real Eva Flores please stand up?*

Half idly, he said now, 'Who are you, Eva? Are you this person who really likes to cook and dress down and who isn't remotely mercenary?'

She looked at him, startled. 'What do you mean?'

He waved a hand between them. 'You bear little resemblance to the girl I knew. The one who wanted to slap me in a fit of pique.'

Eva's eyes were dark tonight. He couldn't read them.

Eventually she said, 'Is it so hard to believe that I've changed?'

'Changed dramatically. To the point where I'm wondering if this is all some kind of an elaborate ruse.'

He saw her fingers tighten on her glass.

'To what end, Vidal?' she asked.

'To lull me into a false sense of security?'

'What? So that I can have my wicked way with you? I think that horse has already bolted. And you were the one intent on seducing me, remember?'

'It didn't take much seduction in the end.'

Eva stood up, clearly agitated. She walked over to the terrace railing, her back to Vidal. He couldn't fully understand it but he felt the need to push her…to try and get her to reveal something.

She turned around and her face looked…stark. 'Why are you doing this?' she demanded.

'Because I learnt a long time ago with you never to trust these kinds of moments. Because you'll always come back with some zinger or put-down.'

'Maybe I'm all out of zingers and put-downs.'

Vidal could see that her eyes were shining. With emotion?

This was too much. Who did she think she was kidding?

He stood up and went over to her. She stood with her back against the railing, hands by her hips.

'What's your problem, Vidal?'

There she was. The Eva he knew. Even if she wasn't quite as sharp as he remembered.

He came close, until he could see the golden lights in her eyes.

'My problem is why you think you need to put on this act. It's to no end, Eva. Nothing else is going to happen here. We'll be going our separate ways very soon. There won't be any permanent arrangement.'

Her mouth twisted. 'Permanent arrangement? Since when did you get so arrogant? You told me that I'm the last woman you'd want to marry. Well, don't worry, Vidal, because you are literally the last man I would marry.'

She put a hand to his chest and pushed, but he placed a hand over hers. 'That's all I wanted to say, Eva. Just that you don't need to put in this effort, pretending to be something you're not.'

She looked up at him. 'What if this is who I am, Vidal? What if the girl you knew was the one who was putting on a front and pretending to be someone she wasn't just to survive? Have you ever considered that?'

She took her hand from under his and walked around him and into the house. For the first time in his life Vidal was not sure he knew which way was up any more. And if what she'd just said was true, then the very basis of everything he believed was suddenly in doubt.

'I'm sorry.'

Eva didn't look up from the book she was not reading. She was so hurt and so angry with Vidal that she was trembling with it. His legs and feet came into her line of vision. She hadn't realised he was barefoot. He had very beautiful but very masculine feet.

Her pulse tripped. Damn him anyway.

He tugged the book out of her hand and looked at it,

reading out the title. '*The Tech Revolution*. I don't rec-
ommend it—it's very dry.' He threw it aside.

He came down on his haunches in front of her. Eva
refused to look at him. She felt like a petulant child.

'Eva. Please look at me. I'm sorry.'

She looked at him and hoped her hurt wasn't visible
on her face. She said, 'I can't keep apologising for the
past, Vidal. I know you can't understand it, and I'm not
even sure that I can fully, yet, but I was always aware of
how I was behaving. I just didn't know how to be any
other way. My mother's presence…her influence…was
so pervasive. It isn't an excuse for my behaviour, which I
know was atrocious. I'm just simply trying to explain…'

Vidal said, 'The truth is that it doesn't matter, and I
shouldn't have brought it up. Because we're not here to
talk about the past or even who we are now. We're together for a finite amount of time, and the sooner this
chemistry between us burns out, the sooner we can get
on with our lives.'

Even now, when he'd hurt her and was basically telling her that he didn't care to find out the truth about who
she really was, Eva felt the pull to just cleave to him.
To tell him with her body who she was, even though he
wouldn't notice.

She made a split-second decision. If he could be so
cold, then so could she. She would surround herself in
ice—it wasn't as if she didn't have practice.

Eva stood up, and Vidal rose fluidly too. She walked
to the door and he said from behind her, 'Where are you
going?'

She looked at him over her shoulder. 'You mean you
don't already know? You seem to know everything else.'

She pushed one strap of her dress down one shoulder. 'This chemistry isn't going to burn itself out, now, is it?'

She sauntered out of the room, pushing the other strap down her shoulder. By the time she was at the stairs, the dress was down to her waist. Granted, it didn't take Vidal long to gather his wits, but it had been a very satisfying few seconds catching him off guard.

He recovered soon enough, taking Eva into his arms before she could protest. The grim look on his face secretly thrilled her—because she knew she was getting under his skin.

Good.

Because he was so deep under her skin that she dreaded to think of the day when he would look at her with no interest and she would have to confront her true feelings about him.

Not now. Not yet. Not ever.

'But I've never held a baby!'

'It's like riding a bike…or something,' Chelle said as she handed her baby girl into Eva's tense arms.

Eva had no choice but to hold the baby because Chelle was gone, tending to something for the party.

It was on the beach. A very relaxed and casual affair. Music playing from huge speakers. Flaming lanterns. Tables stuffed with delicious food. Drinks.

Everyone was so friendly and happy. Eva's fears had been quashed straight away, and there was no time to be nervous or worry about how to act or what to say.

She and Vidal had arrived late. Since the other day there had been a kind of fierceness between them. They didn't have conversations. They looked at each other and within minutes they were in bed. Her bed or his—it didn't matter.

That morning, when she'd woken in his bed, she'd made a move to get up, but he'd caught her back and whispered sleepily into her neck, 'Don't go. Stay.'

She'd lain there under his arm for what had felt like aeons. She'd known he hadn't really wanted her to stay, so eventually she'd managed to sneak out and back to her room.

Hal, Chelle's husband, had been at the house the past couple of days, giving Eva a chance to get some space and also to watch Vidal work on the house with him—in shorts, shirtless... The memories of watching him covertly at the *castillo* had been vivid and bittersweet.

But now she was sitting here, terrified, with a live, wriggling bundle of vulnerable flesh in her arms. She was almost afraid to breathe.

The little girl let out a squawk and Eva looked up, but no one was around. She tried jiggling the baby the way she'd seen Chelle do it, so effortlessly, while holding a plate in the other hand and with a toddler clinging to her leg. Miraculously, the baby stopped squirming and opened her eyes. Eva gasped. They were dark brown. Long lashes. In spite of her terror and fear she was mesmerised. She lifted her free hand and stroked the baby's cheek with a finger. It was so soft.

'Oh, you are a beauty, aren't you? Yes, you are...'

Eva didn't even know what she was saying. Nonsense. She felt herself relaxing. Allowing the baby to settle more into the crook of her arm. She felt the same yearning sensation she always did when she saw children or babies, but this time she had no defences to push it back down.

This place…the last few days…the intensity between her and Vidal…had left her exposed.

And now, with this beautiful baby in her arms, she couldn't fight the truth any more. She was undone. She wanted a baby. She wanted a family. She wanted to be healed by the love of a family. She wanted Vidal. She loved Vidal—even though he would never choose her or love her.

'You're a natural.'

Eva looked to her side. Vidal had come to sit beside her. It was as if he'd intuited that she was at her most raw and appeared to make her feel even more exposed.

He frowned. 'You're crying.'

'Am I?' Eva half laughed, half cried. She didn't care. The baby's tiny fist closed around her little finger and she said, almost to herself, 'I always thought I didn't want this…that maybe I couldn't have it. But I do want it.'

The baby mewled again and this time she didn't stop, working herself up into a full-blown cry.

Eva panicked. 'I don't know what to do—'

Vidal deftly took the baby out of her arms and lifted her so that she was draped over his shoulder. He patted her back and after a moment the baby burped.

He looked at Eva. 'She just had some wind.'

Seriously impressed, Eva said, 'Since when do you know about babies?'

Vidal's voice was dry. 'Since Hal has been coming to work on the house and hands me whichever child or baby he's been left to mind that day.'

Chelle appeared again and took the baby back, holding her with that expert ease that Eva could only envy. The baby smiled gummily.

Chelle said, 'It's time for the cake—come on.'

For the rest of the evening Eva couldn't ignore her revelations. She loved Vidal. She wanted a family. She knew instinctively that that was the only way she would be fully healed after the childhood she'd had.

But she'd already told Vidal too much. He was quiet. Distracted. No doubt horrified by Eva's show of emotion and her confession.

When they got back to the house he said, 'I have to make some calls. We'll be leaving in the morning.'

'Oh…okay. Back to San Francisco?'

'Madrid, actually. There's an event to attend. If that's okay with you?'

Eva balked at that. Going back to Madrid? What was even there for her any more?

What is there anywhere?

She ignored the self-pitying voice. 'Of course. That's fine.'

Eva was asleep on a reclined seat on the opposite side of the aisle in the plane. She'd refused Vidal's offer to use the bedroom. The steward had pulled a blanket over her and Vidal had had to restrain himself from snarling at him to let *him* do it. He was jealous, and he'd never been jealous over a woman in his life.

When he'd seen Eva holding Chelle's baby at the party it had stopped him in his tracks. The look on her face…

At first it had been abject terror and horror, and he'd told himself he shouldn't be surprised, because that was exactly the reaction he would have expected from Eva.

But then her expression had softened and changed. Had become one of wonder.

She'd cried.

And she'd admitted that she wanted a baby. And it

hadn't been said with any kind of coquettishness. Or for his benefit. He'd have had to be blind not to see that she was literally admitting that fact to herself for the first time.

And that was the moment when he'd known that this had gone too far. Eva *was* different now. He'd been punishing her for crimes she'd committed while under the influence of a very malevolent presence.

Even Chelle had seen it. She'd pulled him aside while Eva had been talking to one of Chelle's friends and had said, 'That is a very special girl, Vidal. But she's been wounded by life. Don't hurt her any more than she already has been.'

Vidal had been stunned by the fact that one of his best friends was not only defending Eva but warning him off her! But he'd realised that he couldn't in all conscience keep up this charade of a relationship. His and Eva's past had been well and truly exorcised. He'd indulged in every fantasy he'd ever had about her. She'd changed. She wasn't the girl he'd known. Or thought he'd known.

But you still want her.

Vidal looked away from Eva's sleeping form. It was just lust. It would fade. He needed to move on and find the woman he would marry.

CHAPTER TEN

MADRID IN THE autumn was magical. The city was bathed in bright sunshine and russet and gold. Eva marvelled that she really didn't know the city well at all. Maybe, when all this was done, she'd come here and pretend she was a tourist.

She smiled at that thought.

'What's funny?'

Eva looked at Vidal on the other side of the car. 'Nothing…just thinking nonsense.'

Vidal looked serious. Eva was tempted to ask if everything was okay, but she wasn't sure if she wanted to know the answer. He had been distant since the party on Maui. He hadn't touched her, and her body literally ached from being so close to his but not touching.

They'd arrived at dawn that morning. She'd been surprised to find that Vidal had booked them into the penthouse suite of a different hotel from the one he'd stayed in the last time. When she'd asked him about it he'd said, 'I thought you might appreciate not revisiting where you used to work.'

His thoughtfulness had touched her.

They'd had breakfast and changed, and now were on

their way to Eva's solicitor's office to sign final contracts and make sure all loose ends were tied up.

Eva couldn't help feeling that they'd come full circle, somehow...

After their meeting with the solicitor, Vidal waited for Eva to get back into the car, but she stopped. 'Actually, I think I'll walk back. I might go to a museum. Or an art gallery...'

Vidal frowned. 'Why?'

Eva shrugged. 'Why not?'

She held her breath for a second, wondering if he might join her, but he just said, 'As you wish. You need to be back at the hotel by four to meet the stylist and her team and get ready.'

Eva hid her disappointment. 'What is the event later?'

'It's for a charity that funds cancer research.'

Her heart constricted. No doubt he was interested in that because of his father.

She said, 'Okay, I won't be late.'

Vidal got back into the car and watched as Eva crossed the road and started walking. She was wearing dark trousers and a cashmere jumper under a light coat. Flat shoes. Hair pulled back into a low bun. Dark sunglasses.

She looked like any other stylish Madrileña, walking in the sunshine, but Vidal didn't see any others—he saw only her.

The car turned at some lights and Eva disappeared around a corner, and for a second a sense of panic almost overwhelmed Vidal. He'd wanted to go with her—to a gallery or a museum. But at the last second he'd realised that he couldn't. Because this relationship was not about that…and it was coming to an end.

They'd both benefited. It was time for him to let Eva go.

Eva got back to the hotel in good time. She'd enjoyed her walk and had visited a gallery and stopped for coffee. She hadn't been able to shake the feeling of loneliness, though, and she cursed herself. It wasn't as if she wasn't used to it. And it wasn't as if her relationship with Vidal had ever been about going on dates like normal people.

She arrived at the same time as the stylist and her team, and braced herself for the ordeal of being dressed up and done up. But the dress had the power to make her stop in her tracks.

If she'd ever dreamed of being a princess, then this was the dress. It was a gown of sheer tulle, covered with gems, with a diamanté and gold belt around her waist. The stylist kept her hair down and smoothed it into sleek waves. Her make-up was a little more dramatic than usual, with kohl around her eyes and deep red lipstick.

Eva saw herself in the mirror and thought how proud her mother would be if she could see her now. Looking every inch the glittering heiress. Except she'd never really been an heiress to much at all. That was the sad truth. Heiress of a tainted legacy.

She noticed the stylist and the other women around her collectively doing a double take, and one of them blushed profusely. Eva turned around. Vidal was in the doorway, fixing his cufflinks. He was wearing a tuxedo, this time with a white jacket and black bow tie. It made him look even darker and more gorgeous.

Eva could sympathise with the love-struck women.

He looked up and saw her, and for the first time since

they'd left Maui she felt a spurt of hope when she saw how his eyes darkened and his jaw clenched. He might not be touching her, but he wanted to.

'You look stunning, Eva. Truly.'

Now she was blushing. 'Thank you.'

The stylist and her team gathered up their things and said goodbye. Eva thanked them profusely, appreciating so much that she didn't have to figure out all this stuff on her own.

When they were alone, Vidal said, 'Actually, there's something I want to talk to you about before we go. Let's have an aperitif?'

Eva followed him into the suite's reception room. He poured her a glass of white wine and himself a small whisky. She took the glass. 'Thank you.'

The sun was setting on Madrid, and with its autumnal colours the city looked as if it was on fire.

She lifted her chin. An old reflex. 'What is it you want to talk about?'

But she already knew. It was in every line of Vidal's body. Tense. Rejecting.

This was it.

He said, 'It's good news, actually. I've got the investment I was looking for—for my project. I'm going to go back to the States tomorrow, to New York, to meet with the investors and sign contracts. You were instrumental in that, Eva, so thank you.'

'But I didn't do anything.'

Vidal shook his head. 'You did far more than you realise. People were charmed by you. Especially Sophia Brentwood and her husband—which led more or less directly to this result.'

Eva's face felt hot. 'But I didn't even know who they were.'

'Yet you charmed them.'

'I didn't know I could do such a thing. I feel like for my whole life I was being instructed *not* to charm anyone for fear of looking weak.'

'It would appear you have an innate ability to connect with people,' Vidal said, his tone dry. 'Trust it, Eva. Your mother didn't kill your spirit.'

That made her feel ridiculously emotional. 'Thank you…that's a nice thing to say.' Then she thought of what he'd said at the start. She looked at him. 'You said you're going back to New York? You don't need me to come?'

Vidal shook his head. 'No, I don't. After tonight, this arrangement is over.'

Eva felt as if he'd slapped her. Her ears were ringing. Somehow she managed to say, 'Why do you need me tonight, then?'

'Because it's a high-profile event. I can release a statement in the next few days, saying that we've parted amicably after our short engagement.'

'After you sign the contracts for the investment, presumably?'

'That would be prudent…yes.'

The sheer depth of his cold ruthlessness made her breathless. 'So you're just planning on leaving me here like some kind of…left luggage?'

'You deserve to have your life back. Free of debts or ties.'

She'd be tied to Vidal for the rest of her life and he didn't even know it. She knew there could be no other man for her.

'What if I refuse to go tonight?'

Vidal shrugged. 'That's entirely your choice. I'd prefer if you did, as it's a high-profile event, but it won't make much difference to the statement.'

'Why tell me now and not afterwards? That way you would have been assured of my co-operation.'

'Because I didn't want you to think I'd manipulated you.'

'That's noble of you.' Eva was only half mocking.

He looked at her. 'It's not as if we didn't know how this was going to go.'

Eva did her best to look unconcerned. 'Of course.' Then, 'As for the other…the fact that we became lovers…'

Vidal's face became a smooth mask. 'I see no justification in prolonging a temporary affair.'

Certainly no justification as base as prolonging it because they both wanted it. Vidal had had his fun, made his deal, taken his revenge, and he was now ready to move on. Eva could almost admire his clinical efficiency.

She wondered if this was what he was like with all his lovers. Handing them a glass of wine before going out for the evening and telling them coolly and dispassionately that it was over.

Well, Eva refused to be the kind of woman who stormed off in a huff or threw her glass of wine over him—much as she was tempted to right now. Instead, she called on every ounce of the armour she hadn't had to use in some time. She took a sip of wine and put the glass down, then said coolly, 'I'm ready. Shall we go?'

Vidal looked at her for a long moment. Eva met his look. She prayed with every fibre of her being that he was buying her act. Because inside she was breaking into a million pieces.

He drained his glass and put it down. 'Very well… let's go.'

Somehow Eva managed to get through the evening. Her first public event back among her peers in Madrid. The same people who had laughed at her all those years ago, giving her a complex.

Now, they couldn't get enough of her. Air-kissing and declaring that they must meet soon for lunch/coffee/drinks…

She couldn't think of anything worse. She felt as if the walls were closing in on her. She thought of Vidal's open glass house in San Francisco, or his beautiful mountaintop house in Maui and wished she was there, feeling free.

But she wasn't. Because they weren't her homes. She didn't belong there.

Thankfully, just when her feet were starting to scream and her face was aching from forcing smiles, they left.

The journey in the car back to the hotel was silent. Vidal had touched her during the evening, but only the most solicitous of touches. Like a stranger. He might still want her, but not enough. And did she want him to string it out just for the sake of it?

Pathetically, Eva knew that if Vidal suggested continuing the affair, she would probably say yes.

He was doing her a favour by letting her retain her dignity.

Vidal had taken off his jacket and waistcoat and tie, feeling constricted. He paced up and down in the suite. Everything he'd said to Eva earlier had been with the view of doing her a favour. Releasing her from this charade so she could get on with her life and not be beholden any more.

So why didn't it feel like a good thing? Why had it left him feeling edgy and restless and volatile?

Because of the look on her face when he'd told her he didn't need her any more. Shock. And something else that he hadn't been able to decipher.

Of course it would look better if they stayed together for a while longer—a month at least. To let news of the deal sink in. And of course he still wanted her. So much that it had taken all his control to only touch her fleetingly all night. It had been excruciating not to be able to search for and find her hand. Slip his arm around her waist. Smell her scent. Imagine peeling that exquisite dress from her body and making her melt under his hands. Again and again.

But now that he knew everything he couldn't in all conscience keep up the charade. Eva deserved more.

She appeared in the doorway behind him and he saw her reflected in the window. She'd taken off the dress and she was wearing jeans and a top. Carrying a small suitcase.

He turned around. 'Where are you going?'

'I don't see the point in staying. I'm going back to the *castillo*. I believe it's still mine for two weeks? I need to clear out some things anyway.'

Vidal felt a sense that he was falling. 'I booked this suite for you for a month, or however long you need it—until you get your bearings.'

Eva shook her head. 'That wasn't necessary, but thank you.'

Vidal, rarely at a loss, felt at a loss now.

Eva smiled, but it was small. 'Thank you, Vidal, for freeing me from the burden of my inheritance. And for showing me the world. And for...' She stopped there.

Vidal's gut clenched. He felt ashamed. 'You don't have to thank me. I all but blackmailed you into this charade.'

She shook her head. 'I had a choice. It wasn't your fault the *castillo* wasn't selling, and I'm sure it would have eventually. It was no hardship being treated to a life of luxury and glamour. And you didn't have to blackmail me into your bed. I wanted to be there.'

Like in that moment when Vidal had felt humbled before Eva's innocence, he felt humbled again.

She said, 'I wish you well, Vidal. Truly. You deserve to find the woman you'll love and marry her and have your family.'

The thought of that now felt like grit in his mouth. 'You deserve all that too.'

Eva smiled again, but it looked sad. 'I'm sure some day I'll find my people. The ones I really want to be with. They aren't here, in this society, and you've helped me to see that.'

It was a statement Vidal would never have expected to hear this woman make. He'd misjudged her and underestimated her. She deserved her freedom now.

'Let my driver take you to the *castillo*, at least.'

'Okay, thank you.'

And then, she was gone.

Vidal heard the door closing.

He went through the suite to the bedroom, where the evening gown was neatly hanging in its protective bag. Something caught his eye and he saw the engagement ring sitting on the top of a chest of drawers. He went over and picked it up, pressed it into the palm of his hand. He curled his fingers around it so tightly that the gemstones dug into his skin painfully.

He had no right to demand anything else of Eva Flores. He had to let her go. Their past was well and truly exorcised.

About a week later, Eva was in old cut-off shorts and a sleeveless shirt tied at her waist in a knot. Hair tucked up under a baseball cap. Sneakers on her feet so old they had holes in them.

It was unseasonably warm and she wanted to swim in the pool, but the surface was covered in leaves and debris, so she was using a brush to clear it.

She leant forward as much as she could, holding the brush, and then a voice came from nearby.

'Careful.'

Eva might have fallen in if her whole body hadn't frozen on the spot. She'd been hearing Vidal's voice all week, in whispers and echoes around the *castillo*. But this sounded uncomfortably real. Maybe she really was losing it?

She straightened up and looked around. The sun was in her eyes, so all she could see was a tall, broad shape. Much like the first day he'd appeared again.

He stepped forward and she could see him now. Dressed in a three-piece suit. She was afraid to do anything or say anything in case he vapourised. Then she thought about how she looked right now, and of him in his pristine suit.

She gestured between them. 'I think if anything demonstrates how karma works, this is it.'

'No amount of casual clothes or menial tasks can hide true breeding.'

Now she knew he wasn't an apparition. She put the brush down and took off the gloves she'd been wearing to gather up dead leaves and dirt.

'Why are you here, Vidal?'

'Because it took me a week to realise that I'd made a huge mistake.'

Eva's heart palpitated. 'A huge mistake about what?'

'I should never have let you go. Or at the very least that I should have asked you what you want.'

'What I want…?' Eva said faintly.

Vidal came closer. He had an intense expression on his face. 'What *do* you want, Eva?'

What do I want?

Where did she start? A spark of anger ignited. He was toying with her again. She put her hands on her hips. 'It wasn't enough for you to get your revenge? You've come back for more?'

'What do you want, Eva?' he repeated.

Anger mixed with other volatile emotions. What he was asking her was huge. No one had ever asked her what she wanted. Never. She'd been used as a pawn by her mother and then by this man.

Except was that really fair? He hadn't forced her into anything. He'd just presented her with an opportunity. If she hadn't fallen into his bed—jumped!—it would have been a business deal, albeit unorthodox. She would have walked away intact. In every sense.

The fact that she hadn't was down to her as much as him.

And the fact that Vidal was here, in front of her, back at the place where she'd first seen him, made something crumble inside Eva.

She had no defences left. She'd teased this man and

she'd tested his patience. She'd treated him like a lesser being.

'What do I want, Vidal?' She put her hands out, 'What I want is to be forgiven by you. What I want is to be far away from this place. I can't breathe here. The only place I can breathe is with you.'

Vidal came even closer. The intense expression on his face didn't change. His eyes were burning. 'There is nothing to forgive unless you're prepared to forgive me too. The truth is that I love you, Eva. And I think I've loved you from the start, when you drove me so crazy I couldn't see straight.'

Eva felt light-headed. 'I didn't mean to…'

'But you did. And I wouldn't change it for anything.'

Vidal came closer.

'How can you say that? I was a brat.'

He shook his head. 'A beautiful, maddening brat. And underneath that brat was this even more beautiful woman, waiting to find herself and emerge.'

Eva's eyes stung. 'You don't mean it. You…you can't just appear here and say that.'

He lifted a hand and touched her face with his fingers…the barest touch, but it burned.

'Why not? You're the one, Eva. You've always been the one. You never left me. You haunted me for years. I was always going to come back because I couldn't *not*. I think my father knew that there was something between us. I think he engineered it so that I'd have to come back and find you.'

Eva's chin lifted. Old habits died hard. 'You said I was the last woman in the world you'd marry.'

'I was wrong—and cruel. The truth is that you're the *only* woman in the world I'd marry.'

She shook her head. She'd been on her own for so long. She'd never been loved. What Vidal was saying... offering...as much as she wanted it, it terrified her.

'You can't, Vidal. There's something wrong with me. That's why my parents couldn't love me. You'll see...'

Vidal reached for her baseball cap and pulled it off. Her hair fell down around her shoulders and back. He cupped her face in his hands. His familiar scent washed through her.

'No, my love. There was something wrong with *them*. They were twisted. They were bad parents.'

Fear rose up inside Eva. 'What if I am too? You deserve someone who can give you a happy family, Vidal. I don't know if—'

He kissed her, stopping her words. Then pulled back. '*I* know. You deserve to be happy too, Eva. And if we have a family we will be happy...and if we don't we will be happy. Because all I need is you.'

'I'm not imagining this?'

'No—and I'm not leaving without you. As long as you want this too.'

Eva was slowly allowing herself to believe that Vidal was real...that this was real. That the joy spreading through her was real.

'I want this to be real so badly it scares me,' she said.

'It is. Believe me. And I have something for you.'

He let her go briefly, to take something out of his pocket. Eva looked down. It was the engagement ring. He took her hand and slipped the ring back onto her finger.

'What happens now?' she asked.

Vidal smiled at her. 'We leave this place and the past behind us. How does that sound?'

Joy bubbled up inside Eva and she let out a little laugh

and a hiccup. 'That sounds good. Almost too good to be true. I'm scared, Vidal... Scared that this isn't really happening. That I'm just dreaming this up. This moment... I fantasised about you taking me away from here so many times when I was younger...'

A mischievous glint came into his eye. 'I know how to reassure you that it's very real.'

Eva frowned, and then opened her mouth to ask *How?* But she never got to say it because Vidal had taken her hand and jumped fully clothed into the pool, pulling Eva with him.

She rose to the surface, spluttering and laughing and in shock at what he had just done. Vidal broke the surface too and reached for her, two big hands on her waist, tugging her into him.

She wrapped her legs around his waist and her arms around his neck. 'You're crazy!'

He grinned. 'Now do you believe it's real?'

Eva grinned too. She couldn't help it. It fizzed up and out of her. She nodded. 'Yes, I believe.'

Vidal moved them so that her back was against the side of the pool. He took his hands from Eva's waist and started undoing the buttons on her shirt. He pulled the lace cups of her bra down and exposed her breasts to his gaze. The water was cold, but Eva was boiling.

Vidal asked, 'Did I ever tell you about the fantasy I used to have about making love to you in this pool?'

She nodded. 'You might have mentioned it in passing...'

Before he could distract her with his far too wicked mouth, she cupped his face and said emotionally, 'It was always you, Vidal. No one else could have saved me.'

He kissed her. A kiss of benediction. 'You don't need

saving—you need to be loved. And I am going to spend my life showing you how worthy you are of love. But I need you to love me too, because that's all I've ever wanted.'

Eva smiled. 'Is that all? That's easy...'

EPILOGUE

San Francisco

VIDAL WALKED THROUGH the house. The sun was setting and the Golden Gate Bridge in the distance stood out against the blazing sky. He would have stopped to admire the view, but it came a distant second to everything else he had to admire in his life now.

He stopped at the door of his office and admired his favourite view. Eva's head was in her hand and she was poring over a document, wearing new reading glasses that made her look even sexier, if that was possible. Especially when she had her hair up in a messy top-knot and was wearing an off-the-shoulder slouchy top and cut-off jeans. Bare legs and feet.

Who would have known that underneath her *froideur* the princess of the *castillo* was at heart a California girl? She'd even started learning to surf on Maui, and they went back there as much as possible.

This last year had been a revelation. Vidal had realised how hubristic he'd been in assuming he could attain the kind of love that his parents had shared. What they'd shared had been unique. To them. He'd limited himself in wanting what they'd had.

What he shared with Eva was so far beyond what he might have imagined or hoped for. She humbled him every day with the journey she'd taken from what had been an abusive childhood. Something he'd only fully appreciated over time. As had she. With the help of therapy she was finally coming to terms with her complicated relationship with her mother and father.

He couldn't wait any longer. He cleared his throat, wondering if he should be insulted that her studies for a degree in economics and business were more absorbing than him.

She looked up and smiled. Every time she smiled now it made Vidal emotional. So he was emotional a lot. But he took such joy in her healing.

'There you are,' she said.

Vidal smiled too. 'Here I am. Wife.'

'Husband.'

'Love of my life.'

Eva rolled her eyes but kept smiling. 'Ugh…so soppy.'

He came into the room. 'You'll pay for that, Mrs Suarez.'

She stood up and reached for him, wrapping her arms around his neck, her mouth seeking and finding the tender spot just under his ear. She breathed against him. 'Mrs Suarez… I like that a lot. So much more than Flores.'

She pulled back and Vidal took her glasses off, putting them aside. At the feel of her curves against his body he almost forgot his objective. But then he remembered. 'I have something for you upstairs.'

She stopped him for a moment. 'Actually…there's something I need to tell you.'

She looked a little apprehensive, but also excited.

Vidal asked, 'Can it wait?'

After a moment she nodded. 'Yes, it can wait.'

He took her by the hand and led her out and up to the next level. To the terrace, where there was a large box with a bow on top.

'You know you don't have to get me things,' Eva grumbled behind him. 'I have so much stuff I don't even know what to do with it all.'

'Hush, you ungrateful wench.'

There was also an ice bucket with a bottle of champagne in it and two frosted glasses on the low table.

Eva stopped. 'What have I forgotten? Our anniversary? But that's not till next month. Your birthday? That was last month. My birthday isn't until April…'

Vidal put a hand over her mouth. 'It doesn't have to be any occasion. Be patient, my love.'

He led her over and sat her down on one of the seats near the box. Then he crouched down beside it. 'This is a gift I've been meaning to get you for some time…but I was waiting for the perfect… Well, you'll see…'

They'd started trying for a baby not long after their wedding, with Vidal reassuring Eva that she would be an amazing mother. But so far each month had passed with no pregnancy. Vidal knew that Eva was a little worried, even though she wasn't saying anything. So he wanted to give her something to distract her.

'What is it, Vidal?'

He took the top off the box and lifted out a small, furry, wriggling bundle of…

'A puppy!' Eva squealed, reaching for it immediately.

The fluffy golden retriever puppy, delighted to be liberated from the box, promptly weed on Eva and licked her face with enthusiastic kisses. Eva laughed, and then started crying, clinging on to the creature.

Vidal sat beside her, concerned. 'I didn't want to make you cry.'

She shook her head and buried her face in the puppy. Then looked up again, her face wreathed in smiles. 'Happy tears. I've always wanted a dog.'

Vidal wiped away her tears with his thumbs. 'I know, and I've wanted to get you one for so long. I know we've been trying for a baby, and I know you're worried even though you haven't said anything, but I don't want you to be because I'm sure—'

Eva put a hand over Vidal's mouth. The puppy was squirming to be free and Vidal took him from Eva. She took her hand down.

He said, 'What?'

She glanced at the champagne on ice and back to Vidal, and then smiled tremulously, more tears forming. 'I don't think I'll be able to have any of that for a while.'

It took a few seconds for Eva's meaning to sink in. And then he remembered her saying she needed to tell him something. In a daze, he said, 'This is what you wanted to tell me?'

She nodded and took his hand. The puppy slithered off Vidal's lap and started sniffing around the terrace. They were oblivious.

Vidal couldn't say anything—and then he couldn't stop. 'Are you sure? When? How long? How?'

Eva laughed and placed his hand on her still-flat belly. 'I'm about six weeks. I missed a period and didn't want to say anything just in case. But I went to the doctor today. It's early days… She's sure everything is fine, but obviously we have to be careful.'

Vidal took his hand from Eva's belly and cupped her face. He was so full of joy he wasn't sure how he wasn't exploding with it. He said, 'You are going to be an amazing mother, Eva, and you are going to give our child all the love that you didn't have.'

She smiled, and it was watery. He saw in it a mix of joy and trepidation. 'I don't know about that…but I do know that with you as its father we can't go wrong.'

Vidal shook his head. 'Have faith, my love…you'll see.'

And approximately thirty-four weeks later Eva *did* see. She held their dark-haired daughter, Inez, in her arms and she'd never felt such an infusion of pure love and devotion. She knew she would die for this child. She would never harm her.

Maybe her mother had felt like this when Eva had been born, but somewhere along the way she'd become twisted. Eva knew deep in her bones that she was different. She was stronger. And that was perhaps the biggest gift of all.

One day, not long after Inez had been born, they were walking along the beach at sunset. The baby was nestled against Vidal's chest in a sling. Eva was bone-tired but had never been more content. Their beloved mischievous dog, Toto, sped after a ball in the surf—his favourite pastime apart from guarding baby Inez.

They were just one in a number of similar families on the beach at this hour. It was a simple moment, but so profound. And it impacted on Eva so deeply that she had to stop and let it wash through her.

Vidal looked at her and smiled. He picked up her hand and pressed a kiss to her palm.

'Thank you,' she said, and there was a wealth of meaning and love in those two innocuous words.

He shook his head. 'Thank *you*. I thought I knew what love was, but I had no idea.'

'And I didn't know what it was at all!' Eva half laughed and half cried.

But now she did. And so did Vidal. And that was all they needed to know.

Eva wrapped her arms around Vidal's waist and they continued their walk, melting into the sunset and into a lifetime of true love.

* * * * *

THE MAID THE
GREEK MARRIED

JACKIE ASHENDEN

MILLS & BOON

For Eric and Joan

CHAPTER ONE

Spring

THE LITTLE MAID was cleaning his room again.

Ares had come in to prepare for drinks with his father-in-law and there she was, on her knees in front of the big stone fireplace, sweeping ash out of the grate, and humming.

And she kept on humming as he shut the door behind him and strolled across to the chair that stood near the fireplace and sat down.

She kept on humming as if he wasn't even in the room.

He'd thought that humming would irritate him the first time she'd appeared to clear the fireplace, but it didn't. He even liked it. The soft sound of her voice was light, with a pleasing husk to it. Feminine. Soothing.

Mainly, though, he liked that she hummed as if he wasn't Ares Aristiades, CEO of Hercules Security, one of the largest private security companies on the planet and in demand from governments the world over.

Ares Aristiades, ex–French Foreign Legion, scarred and broken and harder than the Greek mountains he'd been born in.

Ares Aristiades, whose heart and soul had died years ago, and now was burdened with neither.

Duty, though, remained, because here he was, visiting his in-laws at their remote mountain compound near the Black Sea. The way he'd done most years since Naya had died. Or at least, the years he hadn't been either in hospital or in the Legion.

This particular maid had cleaned his room every year for the past five years, though it had only been in the last two years that he'd noticed her humming. And the last year he'd become aware that she was a woman and that the plain black dress she wore did nothing to hide the lush curves of a nineteen-fifties pinup.

She had long, honey-gold hair that she kept pinned in a severe bun at the nape of her neck and a sweet, heart-shaped face. Her mouth was full, her nose slightly tilted, her lashes long and looked like they'd been dipped in gold.

The staff here weren't permitted to meet the eyes of the guests, or so his father-in-law had said—a strange rule for staff that Ares didn't see the point of but hadn't been interested enough to argue about—and the little maid never had.

Apart from once, the previous year, as she'd scurried out of his room with her bucket full of ash. Those gold-dipped lashes had risen, and she'd flashed him a wide-eyed glance.

Her eyes had been golden too.

She'd only given him the briefest of looks before hurrying away, but there had been no fear in them, only a kind of awed curiosity.

Which was surprising. That wasn't people's usual response to him. People were usually…disturbed if not downright terrified. Facial scars had that effect, he'd discovered.

He'd thought she wouldn't be back cleaning his room after that, yet here she was, a year later, kneeling in front of the fireplace, once more shovelling ash.

He didn't know what to make of it.

He didn't know what to make of the desire that had ignited the moment her golden eyes had met his. He'd thought that as dead and gone as his wife, but one look from the little maid and it had roared into life, as raw and as powerful as it had been when he'd been young.

He didn't know why he still felt it even though a year had passed since that one brief glance, yet he did.

What was different about this woman, he wasn't sure, nor did he care to think about it in any depth. But it had made him aware that the years were passing, and he wasn't getting any younger. And that he'd made certain promises.

Promises to his father that he wouldn't let the blood of Aristiades die with him.

Promises to his late wife that they would fill their house with children.

Both his father and his wife were gone, but those promises were iron chains, and he couldn't—wouldn't— break them.

His conscience had died with his wife and now all that kept him on the right path was her memory and the promises they'd made to each other.

His father, Niko, had been very insistent that the line of Aristiades must be preserved, especially since they were descended from the mighty hero Hercules. And although Ares had no use for bloodlines himself and it

didn't matter to him if he was the last Aristiades, he'd
sworn to his father he'd preserve it.

But it was for Naya's memory that he'd actually do
it. She'd always loved children and they'd planned on a
big family, and even though she was gone, those plans
hadn't changed. His entire life since she'd died had been
about honouring her, and having children would be another thread to add to that complex tapestry.

However, if he wanted them, he was also going to need
a wife, and really, the sooner the better.

The room set aside for him was stone, its hard lines
made softer with expensive silk rugs on the floor and
velvet curtains. Not that he cared for rugs or curtains or
anything that could be termed 'soft.'

Yet this little maid looked soft, and he liked that more
than he'd anticipated.

'What is your name?' he asked in Russian, assuming she was Russian since she worked here. His voice
sounded rusty and harsh, cutting through the silence like
a rockfall in a quiet valley, but he took no notice. His
vocal cords had been damaged in the fire and he was
long used to that by now.

She gave a start. 'Rose,' she said in her light, husky
voice. Then she turned her head and looked at him over
her shoulder. 'What's yours?'

Her eyes were exactly as he remembered from a year
earlier, like big golden coins, and once again there was
no horror in them. No pity, either, or even compassion
for the massive burn scars that pulled at his skin. She
looked at him as if she didn't see his scars at all.

Such pretty eyes.

The raw flicker of desire burned brighter, higher, yet
he made no move. He wasn't a boy at the mercy of his

passions any longer, no matter how unfamiliar those passions might be these days. He was a man in complete control of himself. A man who could be patient when the situation demanded it.

A man who didn't hide the scars that ravaged his face, a continual reminder of the dangers of pride.

He didn't care what she thought of them. He didn't care what anyone thought of them. They were no one's business but his.

He stared back, letting her look. 'You do not know?'

Her gaze never wavered. 'No. I'm not told the names of our guests.'

Ares was due downstairs in five minutes, and it wasn't appropriate to engage a servant in idle conversation, but Ivan, his father-in-law, could wait.

Ivan was a Russian oligarch with too many fingers in too many pies, and had never forgiven Ares for how his daughter had fallen in love with a lowly Greek shepherd boy while holidaying in Athens. Ivan had objected to the marriage, but Naya had always been a strong woman and she'd wanted Ares. She'd never cared that he lived in a hut in the mountains without a drachma to his name.

Over the years, Ares had increased in Ivan's estimation after he'd left the hut behind and become who he was, the God of War, as he was known in some circles.

Ares didn't like Ivan, though. Not that he was here for Ivan. He was here because Naya would have wanted him to be and so here he was.

'Why do you want to know?' he asked, deciding he wouldn't give it to her yet. She was only a maid, though he had to admit, she didn't much act like one.

She didn't answer immediately, a small crease appearing between her golden brows. Then she dumped the shovel full of ash, and the brush, and turned around to face him. She stood up, ash dusting her uniform, but she didn't brush it away. In fact, she didn't seem to notice it at all.

Her expression had taken on a set look, as if she was steeling herself for something. 'I...need your help,' she said.

Ares stared at her, conscious of an unfamiliar feeling spreading through him. And it took him a couple of moments to realise that what he was feeling was surprise.

It had been a very long time since someone had surprised him, when these days he felt nothing at all. Not even a flicker of an emotion. So it was odd that one little maid should be able to coax it from him.

His legs were outstretched and crossed at the ankle, the black leather of his shoes—handmade by a shoemaker in Milan—glossy in the evening sun coming through the window. She was standing just shy of his feet. Close, even.

Close for a little maid with seemingly no fear of the man who was sitting bare inches away. A man worth billions who had governments in his pocket.

A man who was scarred, yet still physically powerful and who could crush her without effort.

A man she apparently thought could help her.

Ares was not accustomed to being asked for help and he was even less accustomed to giving it.

'Help,' he echoed, tasting the word. 'You think *I* could help you.'

'Yes.' She didn't seem to notice that he hadn't made it a question. 'I have no one else.'

If she was coming to him, then she must indeed have no one else.

He tilted his head back slightly, studying her.

She wasn't tall. In fact, even standing while he was sitting, she was barely at eye level. But there was a determination to her, a stubbornness, he could see it in the cast of her chin. Her gaze met his unflinchingly, though he could see the hint of desperation to it.

Her black dress did her no favours, but it didn't hide the lush promise of those curves either. She had a sweet, womanly figure, which was really all he required in a wife, though why he was thinking that this little maid shovelling ash could fit the bill he had no idea.

Then again, why not? It didn't matter which woman he chose, she'd never be Naya, and that meant one pretty woman was as good as any other. She clearly wasn't bothered by his scars, though, which was a considerable point in her favour. He didn't care what people thought of them, yet he also didn't want to be confronted by distaste or fear over the breakfast table every morning. Or in his bed every night.

'Well?' she asked. Her hands had curled into fists at her sides, though her small, delicate features were unreadable.

A woman used to hiding what she felt, he suspected.

'Help with what?' He really shouldn't be continuing with this conversation, considering Ivan, but now he was curious and more than happy for his father-in-law to have to wait.

Rose stared with a direct, unblinking gaze. It might have been disconcerting for a lesser man, but Ares had never been, nor would he ever be, a lesser man.

Her lovely mouth compressed, and she shifted on her feet at last. Nervous, obviously. Then she darted a gaze at the door, as if she was worried about eavesdroppers.

'They're going to sell me,' she said, the words falling over themselves in their efforts to escape. 'Tomorrow, I think, or maybe the day after, I'm not sure. I don't know where I'll be going or to who, but I don't want to stay to find out. I need to escape somehow, but I've got no money and I've never been out of this compound, and I can't get out of here anyway, not without help, and I know because I've tried. Someone has to get me out and I have no one else to ask.' She took a shuddering breath. 'Please, sir. Please, help me.'

Rose knew she'd said too much the moment the words were out of her mouth. They'd escaped as if he'd somehow tripped a switch inside her, causing all her desperate fears to come cascading out.

She didn't want to sound like a scared little girl. Scared little girls were victims and she was tired of being a victim. She'd been one for her entire life and that had to stop. Here. Now. Today.

The man said nothing, sprawled out in the seat in front of her as if he didn't have one single care in the entire world. Because of course he didn't. Men like him never did. The rich, the powerful, the infamous. All kinds stayed at the compound, and she'd seen them all. She was a house servant, and it was her job to make their beds and clean their fireplaces, scrub their baths and pick up their clothing.

Some were terrible, lashing out with a cuff for no reason at all, and others groped her because she was there, and they thought they had the right. Some shouted at her for some imagined slight, and some made disgusting insinuations, then laughed. Some ignored her like she wasn't even there.

But this man… This man was different, and he always had been.

Rose stared fixedly at him.

He was immensely tall, immensely powerful. Built broad and muscular like the guards that kept watch over the doors of the compound. Except for all their physical strength, the guards seemed small and insubstantial next to this man. They thought they were wolves and maybe they were, but this man was a dragon.

He projected the strength of a giant, the arrogance of a king and the confidence of God himself, and she had no idea who he was that granted him such massive self-assurance, but one thing she was sure of: he could help her.

She'd been cleaning this room for five years and it was only the previous year that she'd risked punishment by looking at him. She already knew he was tall and that his voice was cracked and broken sounding. That he walked silently and with a grace that was almost shocking in a man built so broad.

His scars had been shocking too, but only because she hadn't expected them.

She didn't care about his scars. The only thing she cared about was that he was the only one who didn't paw at her, who didn't try to touch her, or say disgusting things and make crude jokes whenever she was in the room. He didn't shout at her or even make conversation.

He wasn't one of those men who ignored her either, though.

She'd sensed him watching her, and why he did so, she wasn't sure, but it didn't frighten her. His attention felt curious rather than threatening, though again, she wasn't sure why that was. Perhaps it was her humming. Perhaps he liked it.

That was beside the point, though. What mattered was that he'd never made a single move towards her, not one. It didn't mean he was any better than all the rest, but it was a sign that he was at least no worse, and that was as good as she could get in a place like this.

Not that she had a choice now. They were going to sell her tomorrow and he was her only chance of escape.

She stared at him without blinking, willing him to say something, her heart thudding uncomfortably loudly in her ears.

He stared back, in no hurry. As if he hadn't even heard her little speech.

She swallowed, a feeling she didn't understand flickering like a fire inside her.

He wore an exceptionally well-cut suit of dark grey wool; she knew a good tailor when she saw one, she was nothing if not observant. His shirt was snowy white and open at the neck—he hadn't bothered with a tie.

She found herself uncomfortably mesmerised by the glimpse of his throat, though she couldn't imagine why. His skin was dark bronze, the white of his shirt showing it off to good effect, and his hair was darkest black and cut close to his skull. His eyes were startling, a strange silvery green, like a tarnished sea.

He was a man wrought of iron, everything about him hard. Yet there were great gouges in his face, scar tissue twisting one side of it, while leaving the other side almost unmarked. That side was beautiful, high cheekbones, beautiful mouth, straight nose, while the other side was…scar tissue and melted flesh.

Horrifying. Compelling. Frightening. Magnetic.

She couldn't settle on which, but that didn't matter either. She needed his help and she needed it now.

'Who is going to sell you?' His voice was deep and harsh. It sounded like stones scraping over one another.

'The boss,' she said. 'Ivan Vasiliev.'

The man's expression was merely one of polite interest, though it was difficult to tell with those horrific scars clawing his face. He certainly didn't seem worried or upset or even angry as she'd mentioned Vasiliev's name.

Perhaps he knew that Ivan Vasiliev had bought two children through human trafficking networks, and that one had been chosen to be his daughter, while the other had ended up as a servant. Perhaps it didn't bother him. Perhaps he'd even been involved with it himself.

Rose went cold at that thought, but she let none of her fear show. Hiding her emotions was one of the first things she'd learned how to do when she'd arrived here and now it was so ingrained it was automatic.

It didn't matter if he was involved. The only thing that mattered was that he could get her out. Athena had told her she was going to be sold and Rose believed her implicitly. But Athena hadn't known details such as why or to who, but neither of them ever knew those things.

Rose had been brought here as a child, given the bare minimum of schooling, then put to work. She'd never been allowed to leave, not even once, and all forms of communication with the outside world were banned. All she knew was what she'd managed to glean from eavesdropping on conversations and discussions with Athena.

There had been moments over the years where she'd thought about trying to escape, but the practicalities had always defeated her, and so she'd stayed. Yet she'd never forgotten that she was a prisoner.

And now Vasiliev was going to get rid of her, she wasn't even that. She was property.

'I see,' the man said in his rough, scraping voice, the expression on his scarred face impassive. 'And what makes you think I'll help you, Rose?'

'I don't think you'll help me,' she answered bluntly. 'I only hope that you will.'

He was silent a moment, the intensity of his silvery-green gaze unnerving. 'Why me?'

Rose clenched her hands unconsciously. 'I have no one else to ask. There are no other guests and… You are the only one who hasn't tried to touch me. Not once.'

He gave a grating, mirthless laugh. 'That's all? Your bar for trustworthiness is very low.'

Rose ignored the tension coiling deep in her gut. She had to convince him to help her, she had to. He was her last chance. 'I don't need to trust you. I just need you to get me out of here.' She took a steadying breath. 'I'll do anything you want. Anything at all.' She hadn't meant to offer herself, but she would. If it meant getting out of here, she'd let him do whatever he wanted with her. Athena had protected her from most unwanted attention—unlike some of the other women who did the cleaning—and so she hadn't been touched. But that didn't mean she didn't know what men wanted from a woman.

'Anything at all,' the man echoed softly and there was something in his voice that made her shiver, though she wasn't sure what it was. It wasn't an unpleasant shiver either. Strange. His gaze was very steady, not dropping to assess her figure the way some men's did. He stared right into her eyes.

Rose wasn't used to anyone seeing her, really *seeing* her. And not merely as a method by which a fireplace got clean or a bed got made, or as an object to either manhandle or beat. A thing. But seeing her as a person.

She wasn't sure she liked it. It made her insides shift uncomfortably, as if it was a challenge he was issuing and a part of her wanted to answer it. But that was difficult when the impact of his attention felt like a weight slowly pushing her into the floor.

His eyes are beautiful.

She gritted her teeth. She had no idea why she was thinking about his eyes, but she knew she couldn't look away. That would betray fear and betraying fear was just about the worst thing she could do. Fear invited beatings or worse. Strength was all in this place and so strength she would give him.

'So, you would give me your body if I asked for it?' His tone was very casual, as if he asked such things of women every day and with the same unblinking stare. 'Take off your uniform and lay yourself out naked on my bed?'

This is a test.

She didn't know how she knew; she just did. Just as she was clear she would pass it. She'd had such tests before and she'd never failed them.

'Yes,' she said. And then, because she wasn't the only one who could be tested, she added, 'Though you'll have to help me with the zip.' And she turned around, presenting her back to him.

Silence fell.

Her heartbeat thudded in her ears. Her awareness narrowed on him behind her, waiting for the sounds of him rising and coming over to her, taking the tab of her zip and pulling it down.

Her skin prickled.

She hoped he would be gentle, though he didn't look like a man who knew what gentleness was. Perhaps he would be quick then. Quick was good, or so she'd heard from the other maids.

Thank God Athena's protection had saved her from that. Athena had been brought here at the same time as she had, two little girls terrified out of their minds and clinging to each other during the long journey to Vasiliev's house. Athena too had been taken off the streets. Except Athena hadn't been chosen for servitude, she'd been chosen by Vasiliev's wife as a replacement for a daughter who'd died.

She now lived a life of pampered luxury, yet she was as much a prisoner as Rose. It was Athena who insisted Rose spend time with her, even though Vasiliev's wife disapproved. And it was Athena who'd let it be known that no one was allowed to touch Rose or else she'd be distraught, and no one wanted Athena distraught because that made Vasiliev's wife distraught, and Vasiliev would do anything for his wife.

Yes, Rose had been lucky. Rose had been protected. But no one would know if one of Vasiliev's guests decided to avail himself of her. And it would be her word against his, the word of a woman absolutely no one cared about except Athena.

Rose stared at the dusty stone fireplace she'd just cleaned, everything inside her drawn tight. Her jaw ached. Yet still there was silence from behind her.

'The zip,' she said at last, impatient and wanting this to be over. 'I can't do it on my—'

'Your body doesn't interest me, little maid.' The words were heavy as falling boulders and she was shocked to feel a small sting. As if she was disappointed, which surely couldn't be true. She couldn't *want* him to touch her.

She turned around sharply. He was still sitting there

in the chair, having not moved a muscle, his stare as un-yielding as stone.

'I will pay you,' she said, desperation tightening in her gut. 'I don't have any money, but once I'm free, I'll get a job and I can—'

'I don't require your money either.' He tilted his head like a bird of prey, his gaze speculative in a way that made her shiver yet again. 'But I also do not do any-thing for free.'

'So, what do you want?' Her tone was too sharp, the words too blunt, and she knew she was behaving in a way that would normally earn her a punishment. Ser-vants were expected to be invisible, and she'd learned that lesson early on. But she didn't take it back.

'I will need to think on it.' He glanced down at the chunky platinum watch that circled one strong wrist. 'But we can discuss that later. I have an appointment that I am now late for.'

Rose took a silent, shaking breath, her hands clenched into unconscious fists. Hope was dangerous and yet hope was all she had, and she had to know now. 'Does this mean you'll help me?'

He looked up from his watch, his silvery-green gaze enigmatic in the fading evening light. 'Yes,' he said. 'Why not?'

CHAPTER TWO

ARES STARED DOWN at the vodka he was holding, the cut crystal tumbler beaded with condensation. It was good vodka, clean and sharp—Ivan always had good vodka—but Ares found he'd lost his taste for it.

Ivan had poured him a drink and had immediately started into a business discussion that Ares had tuned out. Lately, his father-in-law had started trying to impress him with details of various dealings that Ares had no interest in. Ivan was angling to be a Hercules client, Ares knew. He wanted the highly trained black ops soldiers for his own security staff and the technology that was a Hercules specialty. He'd also mentioned that he had 'capital' and was looking for somewhere to invest it, and maybe he could invest in Hercules.

Ares didn't need any more investment and even if he did the last person he'd get it from was his father-in-law. He didn't want his father-in-law as a client either.

They were in Ivan's private study, and Ivan was standing at the huge fireplace, one elbow on the mantelpiece, his other hand holding a tumbler full of vodka.

He was a tall man and broad, and even in his early seventies, he still radiated the kind of cold power that was common in this part of the world. Power that came from money and the relentless selfishness that all men carried in their hearts.

Ivan was still talking about business opportunities, but Ares wasn't listening. His thoughts kept drifting back to the little maid and what she'd told him back up in his room. About being bought and then sold and how she needed help.

Ares knew that something had broken in him the night he'd tried to save his wife and failed. The beam that had fallen on him, pinning him in place and scouring away a good many of the nerves in his face, had also burned away the ability to feel any kind of emotion. His facial expressions were frozen as was some core part of him, and while some feeling had returned to his face over the years, the part of him that was frozen had remained so.

So, it was strange to find himself…almost on the verge of anger by what the little maid had told him. That Ivan had not only bought her but sold her too. Not that he was particularly surprised about that—Ivan had always been extremely morally grey.

Naya would have been appalled that her own father had been involved in such a thing, and she'd probably demand that something must be done.

That was why Ares had set up Hercules, a security company that went into places governments couldn't risk open involvement in, to fight for people who had no one to fight for them. To protect those who couldn't protect themselves and to even the odds against tyrants. He also provided services to countries who needed help during times of natural disasters or other such catastrophes.

Hercules was Naya's memorial and meant every contract he took on had to be something she would have approved of.

The little maid reminded him somewhat of Naya.

She'd stood in front of him, small and determined, every part of her lush figure set in stubborn lines, as if she'd fight the entire world for what she wanted.

She hadn't been afraid of him—or if she had been, she'd hidden it well—meeting his gaze without hesitation. And when she'd offered herself as payment and he'd called her bluff, she'd turned around, clearly ready to pay up.

He'd been surprised by the kick of lust that had provoked too, though perhaps that had merely been the long years of celibacy speaking. Then again, it wasn't as if he had a shortage of beautiful women all vying for his bed, and none of them had sparked anything inside him, not the way she had done.

Those women aren't warriors. The little maid is.

It was true. Perhaps that was why he'd agreed to help her in the end. Because he'd seen the ember of a warrior in every fierce line of her and he respected that. There was something…admirable in people who were willing to risk everything to get what they wanted, even when they were afraid. Even when they were desperate, and she was; he'd heard it in her voice.

But also, he'd agreed to help her because it was something Naya would have wanted him to do. Most especially when it was Naya's father who'd bought her in the first place.

Naya wouldn't have wanted you to require payment, though.

Ares stared down at his vodka, Ivan's voice a low drone in the background.

No, she would have wanted him to help Rose without requiring anything in return. Especially when Rose probably had nothing whatsoever to give him.

Ares swirled the vodka around in his tumbler, frowning at it, conscious that the unfamiliar feeling of anger collecting in his gut was getting stronger.

Anger at Ivan and the audacity of the man for sullying the memory of his daughter by buying and selling a young woman. He only had Rose's word for it that Ivan had bought her, but there was no question in Ares's mind that she'd been telling the truth. There had been nothing fake about the desperation in her eyes.

So, while his unexpected emotional response was disconcerting to say the least, there was no other option but to help her, regardless of whether she could pay him or not. Naya's memory commanded it.

It wasn't personal. He wouldn't do it because she'd touched him emotionally in any way, or because of that inconvenient spark of desire she'd ignited. He was dead inside, and nothing could reach him, least of all one little maid.

But Naya had been his conscience for years now and she was as ever his guide.

He would help the little maid for her, because she would tell him it was the right thing to do.

The little maid would make a good wife, though.

Ares's thoughts drifted.

Oh, she would, that was true. She was clearly a woman with backbone and the first to spark his interest sexually in years, and he suspected she was also fierce. She didn't seem to be afraid of his scars, or him either.

If he married her, he also wouldn't have to go through the tiresome process of finding a suitable woman elsewhere. He could, of course, but he didn't want to devote any time or energy to what was a relatively minor issue.

And although they hadn't exchanged a word with each other before today, he felt as if he almost…knew her. He'd watched her for two years now, going about the task of cleaning with such focused intensity it was as if she was heading into battle.

Would her approach to pleasure be like that too?

Ares dismissed the thought almost as soon as it had entered his head. It was an extremely inappropriate one to have about an imprisoned woman. Naya would not only be disappointed, she'd be appalled.

'Are you listening, Ares?' Ivan asked sharply.

'No,' Ares said without looking up from his vodka. 'How much do you want for the little maid?'

There was a shocked silence.

Ares lifted his gaze from his tumbler.

Ivan was giving him a narrow look. 'What little maid?'

'The one who cleans out the fireplace in my room every year when I visit. Blonde. She said her name was Rose.'

A strange ripple of expression crossed Ivan's craggy face. 'What do you mean how much—'

'I know you bought her, Ivan, don't bother pretending you didn't. So how much for her?'

He didn't want to get into a discussion about where Ivan had got her, or why. What was important now was getting Rose away as quickly as possible.

Ivan's mouth worked but nothing came out. Then he looked down at his tumbler abruptly and took a healthy swallow. 'I already have a buyer for her.'

No, indeed. The little maid had not been lying.

Ares swirled his vodka in a leisurely movement, betraying nothing of his thoughts. He might have told himself that rescuing Rose wasn't personal, but his anger certainly was, which surprised him and not in a good way. He'd thought his emotions dead and gone and quite frankly he preferred them that way. It did make things simple and he liked simple.

However, he sensed that nothing about this situation was simple and now it was about to get even more complicated.

'Have you? Then I will double whatever has been offered for her.' Buying her wasn't ideal and he suspected Naya wouldn't like it, but it was the quickest way to get her out and with the minimum of fuss.

Ivan's gaze narrowed. 'What do you want with her?'

'Irrelevant. Do you want the money or not?'

'She is…very valuable,' Ivan said slowly. 'Athena likes her and whatever Athena wants, Athena gets, you know this.'

Athena was the Vasilievs' second daughter, spoiled and pampered as any princess. Ares didn't know her since she'd been adopted after Naya had died, but it was clear Ivan was only mentioning her because he'd sensed the resolution in Ares's tone and had decided that now was a good time to drive a hard bargain.

Ares's anger twisted inside him.

Ivan would be wrong.

'If she's so precious to Athena, then why are you selling her?' Ares asked idly.

Ivan took another swallow of his vodka, his gaze flickering. 'Athena is too attached, and the girl is a servant. Athena needs friends from her own social station.'

Ares wasn't interested in what Athena needed. He was

interested in Rose and whatever information he could get out of Ivan about her. 'And the girl? What can you tell me about her?'

Ivan shrugged. 'There's nothing to tell. She has no memory of anything before coming here. I don't know why. She was uninjured when she came to me, so it's not physical.'

A tightening sensation shifted behind Ares's breastbone. He ignored it. 'Nothing? What about family? Anyone who may potentially come looking for her?'

The older man shook his head. 'I have no idea. I don't go investigating the backgrounds of my servants. No one knows who she is and neither does she.'

She has no memories. She has no one. You know how that feels.

Well, he used to. Now, he felt nothing, though he suspected that wasn't the same for Rose. 'So Rose is not her name?'

'She couldn't remember her real name, so Athena gave her one.' Ivan frowned. 'I didn't intend to purchase her, that was a mistake. And I could have got rid of her, but I didn't. I kept her and gave her a safe home.'

This was clearly supposed to be admirable somehow, but Ares didn't find it a compelling argument. 'I don't care what you intended,' he said. 'It is of no interest to me. I will take the girl and I will take her tonight.'

Ivan's expression darkened. 'Tonight? But I haven't—'

'As I said,' Ares interrupted flatly. 'I will pay double for her. And if that is not to your liking, then I will pay you nothing and take her anyway.'

It wasn't something he would have chosen since he didn't relish getting one of his team in to storm his father-in-law's house, especially without going through

the proper channels. He was meticulous about obeying
the laws of whichever country his team happened to be
in at the time. Then again, maybe he should storm the
compound. Perhaps Ivan had bought other people that
Ares didn't know about.

His father-in-law's expression had darkened still further. Ivan was not used to giving ground. Still, Ivan had
never tested himself against Ares; mainly, Ares suspected, because he knew his son-in-law was more in-
fluential and far more powerful than he himself had ever
been.

Ivan wouldn't let it come to that unfortunately. He
knew he wouldn't win that battle, that diplomacy was
the only way he could get what he wanted from Ares.

Pity. Ares hadn't had a decent battle for years. Still,
Ivan would keep.

And sure enough, his father-in-law finally lifted a
negligent shoulder. 'Very well, you may take her. But if
you're leaving tonight, then there are some more important things I need to discuss with you.'

Ares was in no mood to discuss anything with Ivan.
'Not tonight,' he said curtly, before downing his vodka
and rising to his feet. 'I've stayed too long as it is. As
soon as the money is in your account, you will release
her to me.'

He didn't wait for Ivan to respond, striding from the
room and ignoring the older man's grumbling protest,
filled with the sudden need not to spend any more time
in the man's presence than he had to.

Ares organised the transferal of funds, gave a few orders regarding Ivan to one of his teams who specialised
in financial investigation, then packed his bag.

It didn't take long, but it was full dark by the time he made his way to the compound's helipad.

The Hercules Security chopper was waiting for him, its rotors already spinning up as it prepared for take-off.

He ducked into the machine to find the little maid already tucked into the seat next to him with a headset on. She was still in her uniform and appeared to have no luggage about her person whatsoever, not even a hand-bag or purse. Her expression was steely, yet she was also pale, and he thought he could see fear glittering in her wide, golden eyes.

Once, he'd been the kind of man who'd taken his wife in his arms to comfort her after a nightmare. Who'd stroked her hair and told her he'd protect her from all harm. Once, he'd been a man who'd cared about such things.

But that man was dead and gone, along with his abil-ity to provide comfort. He wasn't that man now and he never would be again.

So, all he said was, 'You have no belongings?'

She shook her head wordlessly.

She has nothing and no one.

Something tightened in his chest. He ignored it. 'No documentation?'

Another shake of her head.

'Do you have anywhere to go?'

Again, she shook her head.

Nothing. No one.

It wasn't a surprise. If Ivan had bought her as a child and she'd never left the compound, then of course she'd have nowhere to go.

He regarded her huddled in her seat, clutching at the leather, her jaw set in hard lines as if she was determined not to show her fear. But he could see it. She looked very small sitting there and very alone.

He rubbed at his chest absently, trying ease the unfamiliar ache that had settled there. 'So, what were your plans when you finally escaped?' he asked, because surely she must have had some idea about where she was going to go and what she would do.

She was silent a moment. 'I…thought I might go to Paris,' she said at last. 'I always wanted to go there.'

Paris. She wanted to visit Paris.

'And how were you going to get there?' A tugging sensation had joined the ache, along with the anger he'd felt just before in Ivan's study. 'With what money?'

She shook her head and glanced down at her lap.

No, she had nothing. No money, no documents. No belongings.

'What about family?' It came out sharp, but the anger hadn't gone away, and he didn't like it. He didn't even know why he was angry since she meant nothing to him. 'Do you have anyone you can contact?'

She kept her attention on her hands, every line of her tense. 'No. Or if I do, I don't remember them.'

No family either.

She truly was alone in the world.

Ares rubbed at his chest again, the ache persisting.

'I'm sorry.' She spoke so quietly he barely heard her. 'How did you… I mean, did you…' She paused yet again. 'Are you… Are you my owner now?'

The words made him feel as if there was a sullen fire burning behind his breastbone, outrage joining the heat of his anger.

'No,' he growled. 'I do not own people. I did have to

pay Vasiliev money for you, but it was the quickest and easiest way to get you out. You are free, Rose.'

Her head lifted slowly, big golden eyes almost lost in the darkness. 'But you did have to buy me.'

The sullen fire burned higher. He ignored it. 'It was not my first choice. But freeing you by force would have taken some time.'

Her jaw hardened. 'I have no money, nothing to pay you back with—' She broke off suddenly, her expression tightening, fingers clutching at the seat as the helicopter shifted, lifting off the pad.

She was afraid, he could see that, but she was trying to hide it.

'There is nothing to fear,' he said, letting her know he saw it anyway. 'My pilot is the best in the business.'

Her gaze narrowed. 'I'm not afraid. It's only... I haven't been in a helicopter before.'

She might not have been in a helicopter before, but she was lying about not being afraid. Still, it was better that she be annoyed with him for pointing it out than giving in to her fear and cowering.

At the thought of her fear, the fire sitting in his chest burned brighter, hotter, the sensation so unfamiliar and alien that he couldn't process it. And he wasn't sure why he was feeling it now, when for years he'd felt nothing. He'd always sought Naya's memory for guidance about moral matters, yet now something inside him, an instinct he'd thought long dead, believed that what had happened to Rose was terrible and wrong, and she must be helped.

It was ridiculous. He couldn't understand what it was about her that should ignite any sensation in him at all. Perhaps it was merely physical, some by-product of desire.

'You will have to get used to it, since you are out now,' he said. 'If you want to go to Paris, I will take you—'

'As I was saying,' she interrupted suddenly. 'I have no money to pay you back now, but the moment I do, I swear I will.'

He stared at her. 'You don't have to pay me, Rose.' Her name tasted oddly sweet on his tongue. 'You owe me nothing.'

'Yes,' she insisted. 'Yes, I do. You paid money for me.'

'And I have plenty of money. It was nothing.'

'It's not nothing.' There was an oddly determined look on her face. 'I know how things work. You don't get something for nothing. You paid for me and now I owe you a debt.'

The anger inside him kept on burning, scorching a hole in him. He didn't want it. He'd left his emotions in ashes on the floor of his burned-out house, and he was all the better for it. They weren't supposed to rise like a phoenix to haunt him again.

'You have no money,' he said curtly. 'Even if I did demand a price from you, exactly what are you supposed to pay me back with?'

She didn't look away. 'Well, what do you want?'

He didn't know why in the end he said it. But say it he did. 'What do I want? What I want, Rose, is a wife.'

Rose had prepared herself for the scarred man to want any number of awful things, but wanting a wife was not one of them.

She found herself staring at him in shock.

The unfamiliar movement of the helicopter and the dull, rhythmic sound of the rotors were almost overwhelming even with the headset on, and she was over-whelmed enough as it was.

First, one of the house thugs had come to find her and had dragged her roughly outside. Naturally, she'd been anticipating a beating. Perhaps the scarred man had complained about her behaviour to Vasiliev and now she would be punished for her temerity.

Except she hadn't been punished.

She'd been dragged to the helicopter sitting on the helipad instead, and pushed inside it, a headset jammed on her head.

Nothing had been explained to her, but she was used to being in the dark about everything. She'd sat there, fighting fear, thinking that she was being taken to her new owner already and wondering whether there was any point to leaping out and running. At the same time, she also knew that no, there was no point, not when she had nowhere to run to.

Then, just as despair had set in, an immensely tall, broad figure had appeared from out of the house, illuminated by the outside lights and striding towards the helicopter.

There was no mistaking him. The scarred man. And she knew in that moment that he hadn't lied. He'd promised to get her out and he had.

A thousand questions had tumbled through her head, but then he'd pulled open the door and got in beside her, and every single one of those questions had vanished as quickly as they'd come.

The interior of the helicopter had felt very small, as if it had shrunk somehow, and he was taking up all the room. Every part of him seemed big and hard, wide shoulders, broad chest and powerful thighs. And what room he didn't take up physically he filled with the sheer weight of his presence.

She felt flattened by the force of him and his stare as he'd turned to look at her, the lights from the outside turning his scars into deep crevasses and gouges. Frightening and yet there was a strange beauty to him too. She didn't know how to process it.

She didn't know how to process her feelings either since there seemed to be many of them. Sharp relief that she was leaving. Terror at having to face a world she had only read about, never visited. Regret that she hadn't been given time to bring anything with her—not that she had anything anyway—or even say goodbye to anyone. Not that anyone would care except Athena. Excitement that she would finally see all those places she'd read about. Intense anxiety about what to do next.

Then he'd told her that he'd paid money for her, and while it might have indeed been the quickest way to get her out, it now meant that she owed him. And while he might say that no, she owed him nothing, there was a debt there all the same. A string tying her to him, ensuring she'd never be completely free.

Or at least, not unless she paid him back.

He'd made it clear he wasn't after her body, and so she'd been prepared to offer him money—or at least future earnings from whatever job she'd managed to land. However, it seemed he didn't want money either.

Yet…a wife?

'Why?' she asked bluntly, since she might as well be blunt.

He lifted one massive shoulder. 'I require children. Time is passing and I have no heirs.'

You could use him.

The thought came out of nowhere, creeping through her brain and making her eye him warily. She had nothing and nowhere to go, not to mention only the vaguest idea of how the outside world even worked. There were identity documents such as birth certificates and passports and other things she would need, that she would have tremendous difficulty getting.

But he was clearly powerful, with 'plenty of money' or so he said, and while she trusted powerful, very rich men just about as far as she could throw them, which was not at all, he might be trustworthy enough to be of some use. He *had* been as good as his word and rescued her, after all, and perhaps he might even help further, with money and documents for example.

She already owed him for the money he'd paid for her, and if she asked for more help, she'd only owe him more. But if she gave him something he wanted, that could offset her debt. Something such as being his wife, for example. Which might even suit her purposes anyway since wives had power—certainly Vasiliev's did.

She lifted her chin and held his gaze. 'I could be your wife.'

If she'd shocked him, he didn't show it. 'You?'

The way he said the word, as if he couldn't conceive of a more ridiculous idea, stung unexpectedly and she found herself bridling. 'Yes, me. I know I'm not experienced in anything much except cleaning, but I'm a fast learner.'

'You did hear me when I said I wanted children?'

Rose wasn't deterred. She didn't have the first clue about what being a mother entailed but she wasn't inherently against the idea. In fact, she quite liked the thought of having a family, since she'd never known what it was to have one herself.

You know what that means, though, don't you?

Obviously. She'd have to have sex with him. Well, she'd been prepared to offer that before, hadn't she? It would be fine. She might be a virgin, but she knew all about sex. It had always sounded distasteful to her, but if what some of the others in the compound had told her was true, then it would be over in a few minutes.

It would be worth it if it meant she had freedom.

'I heard,' she said determinedly. 'I can give you children.'

His expression was impassive, yet something glittered in his silvery-green eyes. 'Are you bargaining with me, little maid?'

'I owe you,' she repeated, just so he was absolutely clear. 'But I also need money, a place to go and I'll definitely need documentation.'

'I can help you with those things. I do not require payment for them.'

'You might not, but *I* would still feel as if I owed you,' she pointed out. 'You need a wife who can give you children and I'm prepared to do that in return for all the help you can give me right now.'

He was silent a long moment, staring at her. 'Why?'

'Why marry you, you mean?'

'Yes. I've told you that you have no debt to me so why insist?'

'Because I don't want to feel as if I owe someone. The debt is still there even if you insist it isn't and I won't be truly free until I pay it.'

He said nothing, his expression giving nothing away.

'Well?' she asked.

'You really promise to give me children?'

'Yes. Millions of women do it. It can't be that hard.'

'Little maid,' he said, his voice just a touch too patient now. 'I don't think you fully understand what it is you're offering. Do you really think that having my child to repay a debt is a good idea?'

She flushed a little at that, because that was exactly what she'd been thinking, and opened her mouth to tell him that yes, it was a fine idea, when he went on, clearly not having finished, 'However, if this is something you feel you have to offer, then I have a counteroffer.' His eyes gleamed in the darkness. 'If I marry you so you can feel you have repaid part of your debt, I will insist that we not live together, nor will I claim my rights as a husband.'

Rose frowned. 'But that's not—'

'What I will require is that for the next year, you will spend two weeks of each season at my home so we can get to know one another.'

Rose's heart gave one loud beat that she heard even through the dull sounds of the rotors. 'Why? What's the point of that?'

'I don't think you understand what you are offering, little maid. I don't think you know what being a wife means, let alone being a mother. So, I will offer you the chance to find out.' His gaze was very direct and very compelling. 'If at the end of the year, having spent some time with me, you still wish to give me children, then we will remain married. If you do not, then I will have the marriage annulled and you may go on your way, your debt fulfilled.'

She bit her lip. It wasn't completely what she wanted, and it would mean feeling in debt to him for a whole year instead of getting the kid thing over and done with now. And it was strange that he should be the one with scruples about it. After all, she had no problems with being married to a stranger, so why should he?

Then again, she wouldn't have to live with him. She would have a year of complete freedom…

She almost couldn't imagine it. 'So,' she said slowly, wanting to be sure. 'I'll have a year on my own. To do… whatever I want? Go wherever I want?'

'Yes. I will arrange all the documentation you will need, including finances. I can also arrange for someone to help you set up a bank account, find a job, a place to live, all the things you'll need to start building a life for yourself.'

A little thrill of excitement went through her, the sensation so alien she almost didn't recognise it. A job. A place to live. A bank account. All the things that most people had, that she didn't, that meant she was actually going to have a proper life.

But it also meant more than that.

She hadn't told him the whole truth about her plans for when she escaped—she'd told no one, not even Athena. Never reveal anything, that was the key, that's what she'd learned over the long years in the compound. Be quiet and don't draw attention. Never give anyone anything that they might use against you, including your secrets. Never betray your emotions.

Yes, she had dreams of wanting to see Paris, but that wasn't the whole of it.

What she wanted was to find out who she was and where she came from, and maybe, one day, the family she'd been stolen from.

She'd told him she had no family, but the truth was, she really didn't know if she did or not. She had no memories at all of her life before being taken to the compound.

There was only one thing she could remember and that was looking at some kittens in a shop window and someone saying, 'Wait here. I won't be long.'

Presumably that meant someone had been watching over her—a family member or a friend maybe—but she really had no idea who.

You might not have anyone.

That was a possibility. She might have been some street kid with no one, whom no one even knew she existed, but that thought was too depressing for words and so she tried not to think about it.

The main thing, though, if she wanted to find out who she was then she would need his help. She would need the money and documentation he offered, as well as someone to help her navigate her new life.

It seemed almost too good to be true.

Rose took a silent, steadying breath. 'You'd really do all of that for me?' she asked cautiously, not wanting to get her hopes up. 'And all you require is marriage?'

A strange half-smile twisted his mouth. 'I wouldn't say "all," Rose. Being my wife might not be easy for you.'

She wasn't sure what being a wife involved—if Vasiliev's wife was anything to go by, it seemed to involve a lot of shopping and lying around not doing terribly much—but it didn't sound like the worst thing in the world. How hard could it be? Maybe she'd even like it. Maybe at the end of a year, she'd want to stay married to him.

'Can't be any worse than my life in the compound,' she said.

Oddly, something that looked like amusement gleamed briefly in his eyes. 'I suppose that's true. But, Rose, you must be certain that this is what you want.'

'Of course I'm certain,' she said, and she was.

Perhaps she'd be able to navigate all of that on her own, perhaps she wouldn't; either way, things would be a lot easier with his help. And she was tired of having nothing. Tired of being a victim, of being prey. She never wanted to be prey again. And allying herself with this man would certainly ensure that wouldn't happen.

Being his wife was hardly a high price to pay. It was only for a year and she wouldn't even have to live with him.

His scarred and ruined face remained impassive. 'In that case, I accept your offer.'

Another strange little thrill coursed through her.

Are you sure this is a good idea? You don't know anything about him.

No, she didn't, but she was also short of options. And he hadn't forced her into anything. She'd offered herself to him and he'd declined. He'd even tried to decline her offer of payment. She wouldn't go so far as to say she trusted him, but she was certain that he wouldn't hurt her, and she didn't think he'd betray her.

'Okay,' she said. 'So, how will I know when it's time to visit you? And how will I get there?'

He gave her considering look. 'I will give you some notice and have someone come for you. I have many homes in different locations, so you might even find it enjoyable.'

The excitement inside her grew and she sat there, feeling the electricity of the sensation, half marvelling that she even knew what it was since she couldn't recall ever feeling excitement before.

Ares was now taking out his phone. He didn't look at

her as he made a call, his rough voice filling the helicopter, speaking a language she didn't recognise.

Rose sat in the darkness, finally allowing the hope that she'd tried not to feel, that somehow hadn't died in all the years she'd been at the compound, to join the excitement that was already inside her. It felt like dawn breaking after a long, cold, dark night.

You owe it all to him.

She stole a glance at him, questions filling her head. Why did he want to marry? And why her? He was rich and powerful—all Vasiliev's guests were—and he must have many women to choose from, because he was certainly compelling despite his scars.

Did he really need someone like her? A woman who'd been a bought and sold servant all her life? A nobody who'd been cleaning his fireplace not a couple of hours ago?

It didn't make any sense.

Then again, maybe it didn't have to make sense. Because the main thing was that she was free. And she would have a whole year to herself, doing whatever she liked. Finding out where she came from…

She almost couldn't believe it was actually happening.

Some time passed, though she wasn't sure how long, and then the helicopter was descending. They landed in darkness and a few minutes later Rose found herself being ushered across a landing field and into a long, black car. The scarred man got into the car beside her, and she wanted to ask him where they were and what was happening, but the habit of keeping silent and staying guarded, and watching, was too deeply ingrained, so she said nothing as they drove into the night.

She'd find out soon enough, no doubt.

She must have dozed off because the next thing she knew, they were driving into a brightly lit city, though which one she had no idea. The car stopped outside a big, fancy-looking building, and she was ushered out of the car and up the steps and through the doors. The entrance-way was full of light, ornate chandeliers hanging from a lofty ceiling, and she stared at them, because they were beautiful and there hadn't been any in the compound.

There also seemed to be many people milling around all doing the scarred man's bidding.

He led the way to a bank of lifts and gestured her inside when the doors opened. She wasn't used to any kind of courtesy so the fact that he didn't push her inside or even touch her was almost disconcerting.

She got in, startling slightly as it began to ascend. But she didn't want him, or indeed anyone, to know just how disconcerting all of this was for her, so she kept her expression guarded.

When the lift arrived at the designated floor, she was taken down a long, silent hallway to a door, and when the door was opened and she was ushered inside, she realised it must be a hotel room.

She'd never been in a hotel room.

She had never been in a hotel at all.

Everything was beautifully appointed and there were big floor-to-ceiling windows that gave a nice view out over a city she didn't recognise. Not that she recognised any city, never having been in a city either.

There were several people already in the room, including a man in formal-looking robes who smiled at her.

The scarred man gave her a glance. 'Time to hold up your end of the bargain, Rose.'

She looked warily back. 'What do you mean?'

He nodded towards the man in formal robes. 'The priest will marry us.'

A small, electric shock arrowed through her. 'You mean…now?'

The scarred man shrugged. 'All the documentation you need will be easier to get if you are legally married to me.' His silver-green gaze was enigmatic. 'You do not have to be afraid. I will keep my word.'

He was trying to reassure her, she understood that. But she wasn't reassured, only annoyed. She wasn't some poor, helpless victim. And besides, she knew he kept his word, because he'd told her he'd rescue her and he had.

'I'm not afraid,' she said flatly. 'And I said I would marry you, so I will.'

He gave her another one of those long, speculative looks, then nodded in the direction of the priest.

Ignoring the strange clutch of trepidation, Rose moved over to where he stood, sensing the scarred man's huge, powerful presence at her side.

Her heartbeat was uncomfortably loud in her head as the priest began to say the words of the ceremony, but she didn't hesitate when it came to speaking her vows. And then she listened to his rough, scraping voice saying those same words.

'I, Ares Aristiades…'

Ares Aristiades. So, that was his name.

He didn't look at her as he said the words. She might as well not have been in the room. Not that she cared. This wasn't a marriage in any sense of the word, not yet. That would come later, and really, that was the least of her worries now.

She had greater concerns, such as what was going to happen next.

At the end of the ceremony, there were documents to sign, which she did.

'You don't have a second name?' the scarred man—Ares—asked, the first words he'd said personally to her since the ceremony.

'No,' she said. 'Perhaps I had one once, but I can't remember what it was. I'm just Rose.'

What he thought of that, she had no idea since he betrayed no reaction to the news whatsoever.

A few minutes later, a copy of the document was given to her.

'Here,' said Ares. 'Your marriage certificate.'

Rose looked down and saw her own name. *Rose Aristiades.*

It gave her a little jolt. For years and years, she'd had no last name. For years and years, she'd only been Rose. But now she wasn't. She had a last name now and a connection to someone.

She had a husband.

She looked up at him, but he'd already turned away, heading towards the door. He paused in the doorway and glanced back at her, enigmatic as a sphinx. 'I will see you in three months, Rose.'

Then he was gone.

CHAPTER THREE

Summer

ARES STOOD IN the middle of the villa's living area, looking through the big windows that faced the pool area, the deep, vivid green of the sea beyond it.

The pool was white stone and organically shaped with lots of flowing curves, and an infinity edge facing the ocean. Sun loungers in dark teak with white linen cushions stood around the pool, shaded by large white sun umbrellas. The garden surrounding the pool was lush and tropical, the scent of hibiscus and salt hanging heavy in the humid air flowing through the open windows of the villa.

A woman lay on one of the loungers. She was on her front, her head pillowed on her folded arms, the fading blue dye in her hair no match for the deep honey gold shining through it. The red bikini she wore fitted her as beautifully as he thought it would, lush curves spilling out of it, the sun highlighting a wealth of smooth, golden skin.

A sarong had been draped across the end of the lounger and on the low wooden table next to it stood a tall glass of orange juice and a book.

She'd been here in his villa, on a private island just near Koh Samui in Thailand, for a week already, which left him with only one more week of her presence. A pity, but he hadn't been able to get away sooner.

He'd wondered if she'd keep her promise to him when the time had arrived for their first two weeks. He'd thought the lure of travel might be enough, especially given the gleam he'd seen in her big golden eyes that night in the helicopter when he'd mentioned his different homes. And indeed, that seemed to be the case since here she was.

His wife. The little maid. Rose.

You should not have agreed to marry her.

No, perhaps he shouldn't have. Perhaps the urge that had taken him that night hadn't been one he should have listened to. He'd rescued her, as he'd promised, and he'd have given her all the help she'd needed to build a life for herself. He didn't require payment and he'd made certain that she knew that.

Except she'd insisted. She owed him, she'd said, a fierce light gleaming in her pretty eyes. He'd bought her and so she owed him.

And no amount of telling her otherwise had made any difference, so when she'd asked him what he wanted, he'd told her. And when she'd said she'd be his wife in order to pay him back, he'd said he'd wanted children, thinking that then she'd surely give up insisting on this payment nonsense.

But she hadn't.

She clearly had *not* understood what she'd offered.

So perhaps that was why, in the end, he'd agreed. So he could show her.

Nothing at all to do with not being able to think about anything else but her in your bed.

He watched through the windows as Rose shifted on the sun lounger, burying her head deeper in her folded arms.

Yes, he'd admit to thinking that. Not that he'd touch her, or at least not until she decided to stay married to him—*if* she decided to stay married to him.

But in the meantime, he could deliver her a little lesson in what it meant to wildly promise things you didn't understand to people you shouldn't promise them to. And maybe he'd enjoy her company too. Naya wouldn't begrudge him that, surely?

Not that he'd had time to think too deeply about it in the past three months since their marriage.

He'd been very busy, involved in some new tech development and then a contract negotiation with one of the smaller Baltic states.

But Rose was always at the back of his mind. A puzzle he kept turning over and over, unable to put it down.

He was never interested in people. He was a tactician involved in the business of protecting them, but only as an abstract concept. Yet he couldn't deny that since he'd left her standing in that hotel room in Istanbul, having newly married her, he hadn't been able to stop thinking of her.

He wasn't sure why.

Perhaps it was how she had been the only woman to excite his lust in over a decade. Or perhaps it was how mysterious she was, how no one knew where she'd come from or even her real name. Or maybe it was more to do with how she hadn't been afraid of him, even from the first moment they'd met. Even in that helicopter, full of wariness and suspicion, trepidation and apprehension, she'd met his gaze determinedly as she'd put her offer of marriage to him.

It was clear then that she had no idea what it meant to be your wife, and yet still you accepted.

Out beside the pool, Rose shifted yet again, the sunlight gleaming on her skin.

No, she didn't know. That's why he'd decided to give her a year of freedom for herself, while at the same time, she would spend two weeks every season to get to know him. And if at the end of a year, she did not want to remain married, he would annul the marriage.

Naya wouldn't object to that.

He pulled his phone out of his pocket and glanced at the screen, once more scrolling through the emails one of his assistants had sent him, providing him with all the info he needed about what his wife had been doing for the past three months.

She'd been living in Paris, in an apartment she'd found herself rather than the one he'd organised for her. She'd also found herself a job waiting tables at a local cafe, which she hadn't needed to do since he'd provided enough money for her, and yet she'd insisted on anyway.

Strange when she was the one who'd asked for his help. She was apparently very set on doing things her own way according to the staff member he'd assigned to help her, and did not like to be told what to do. That, he could understand. She'd been a prisoner for so long, and some people would have been beaten down by it.

Not Rose.

She'd adapted very quickly to life outside the compound, learning French and English in rapid succession, as well as opening her own bank account. Apart from some initial set-up money, she hadn't touched any of the funds he'd provided, preferring to live frugally off her own wages at the cafe.

Again, odd when she'd been the one to request the money.

It made him curious. It made him want to know more.

He'd made some initial enquiries to track down where she came from, but so far hadn't had any luck. He'd assumed she was Russian, but maybe she wasn't. Maybe she'd come from somewhere else.

He put his phone away and gazed at her through the windows, the breeze ruffling her hair that tumbled over her shoulders. He had no idea why she'd dyed it blue, but the afternoon sunlight caught gleams of brightness in among the dark blue strands, like a seam of gold at the bottom of the ocean.

Pretty.

Yes. And so was she.

His plan for this next week was simply to get her used to his presence, nothing more, no matter what his body wanted. Sex would happen when and if she decided she wanted to stay married to him, and not before.

He had once been an exemplary legionnaire, a master of himself physically, and impatience had never been one of his weaknesses. Still, it had been a long time since he'd been with a woman, and he couldn't deny a certain…hunger.

A strange thrill wound through him, and he realised with a start that it was anticipation. He'd been looking forward to this. When had that last happened? He couldn't remember.

Yes, you do. Going home after a day on the mountains and seeing Naya.

But that had been years ago, and Naya was long dead. He'd had a terrible lesson in the dangers of allowing his emotions to blind him, and he'd learned it. Love was the weakness. Love had exacerbated the flaws in his pride and his arrogance, making him think that as a descendent of Hercules, nothing could touch him. But he'd been wrong.

He was just a man and not a particularly good one at that.

Moving over to the big glass doors that had been pushed back to allow the breeze to flow into the house, Ares stepped out into the pool area. He walked silently over to the sun lounger where she lay and stopped beside it, glancing down at her.

She didn't stir.

The last time he'd seen her, she'd been in that black dress with her hair in a bun. Now, though, she wore only the bikini, and the curves that had only been hinted at by her dress were on full display. And yes, they were as spectacular as he'd thought they would be. Full, rounded breasts and generous hips and thighs, elegant back, small waist, shapely rear...

Her golden skin gleamed and lust kicked hard inside him. He caught his breath, conscious that he hadn't felt so intensely about anything for years, let alone a woman. He even had the oddest need to run a finger lightly down her spine, see how warm her skin felt, how silky and smooth. Touch her purely for the sensuality of it.

You felt this way about Naya, remember?

Oh, he remembered. He'd seen her that night in a crowded bar in Athens, getting hassled by some lowlife. Dark eyes, dark hair, a glowingly beautiful face. She'd been gracious and polite, but the man bothering her was not and Ares had had to teach him a few lessons in courtesy. Afterwards, Ares had bought her a drink and been captivated instantly and so had she with him. Their physical attraction had been so powerful they'd ended up in her hotel room only an hour later…

He wasn't that young man, completely at the mercy of his body's needs, not any more. The years in the Legion, concentrating on nothing but honing his physical skills and obeying orders, had been well spent. No passing fancy or rogue emotion escaped his control nowadays.

So, he ignored the heat that burned inside him. Ignored the urge to touch her. Physical desire was no match for his will. He'd already decided how this first week would go and it did not include any physical closeness.

For now, he'd let her know he was here, inform her they'd be having dinner together and then he'd retire to his office for the afternoon. That was all.

'Good afternoon, Rose,' he said, his voice a heavy rasp in the peaceful silence.

She jerked, her head lifting sharply, her eyes meeting his.

He remembered those eyes, large and golden. He remembered her heart-shaped face and her small, precise features. The feline tilt of her golden brows, the soft little rosebud of her mouth.

She was beautiful and he hadn't fully comprehended that until now.

Perhaps that was why the lust inside him kicked harder, deeper. Why his fingers curled unconsciously in the pockets of his trousers, clenching tight, as if to stop from reaching for her.

Nothing else would explain this ridiculous reaction to a woman he barely knew. One look at her beauty and a decade of celibacy that hadn't weighed on him at all now felt heavier than an entire planet.

Her eyes had widened, taking him in, shock rippling over her face. Then the shock disappeared as quickly as it had come, her expression becoming as guarded and wary as he remembered.

Slowly, she sat up, treating him to a view of full, pretty breasts almost spilling over the cups of her red bikini, and much to his intense annoyance, the more disobedient parts of himself began to harden.

Theos, what was happening? He wasn't fifteen any more. The mere sight of a woman's breasts in a small bikini top should not make him hard. He'd decided nothing would be happening between them and so nothing would, regardless of what his baser parts were urging.

Clearly noticing the direction of his gaze, she coloured and reached for the sarong, quickly wrapping the material around herself.

He made no comment. There was no point drawing attention to his own interest or her modesty. If she wanted to remain his wife after this year had passed, then they could have that discussion, but that time wasn't now.

'Good afternoon…uh…' she said, her soft, husky voice trailing off uncertainly. 'Mr Aristiades?' Her damp hair had fallen around her shoulders in thick waves, vivid gold glinting in among the strands of blue.

'My name is Ares,' he said, more tersely than he'd intended. 'I am your husband, remember?'

The pink in her cheeks deepened into red, a flash of temper glinting in her eyes. 'I hadn't forgotten. That's why I'm here. Which I have been, for an entire week.'

Intriguing. It seemed she was annoyed with him. He hadn't thought she'd care that he hadn't been here when she'd arrived. He'd even thought she'd enjoy having a week to herself. Yet was that not the case?

'I had business to attend to,' he said. 'As I'm sure my staff informed you.'

'They did, I just thought…' She stopped.

He lifted a brow. 'You thought what?'

'It doesn't matter.' She fussed with the material of her sarong, making a knot between her breasts. 'I'm here anyway. As you ordered.'

He was tempted to push her on whatever it was that didn't matter and why exactly she was so annoyed, but decided it could wait until dinner. Right now, he was here to inform her of his arrival, nothing more.

'Indeed, you are,' he murmured, his gaze dropping to where her hands fussed with the knot of her sarong, drawing attention to the shadowed valley between her breasts. He could imagine undoing that knot and tugging aside the cup of her bikini, letting one full breast spill into his palm…

No. *Theos*, this had to stop.

Ares had to consciously drag his gaze back to her face. Yet again, she must have noticed him looking, because another blush turned her cheeks a deep rose and her hands had dropped away from the knot.

Irritation with himself and his recalcitrant body coiled like a snake in his gut, though a distant part of him found it interesting that she was blushing instead of showing any fear. He'd thought it likely that she'd been manhandled back in the compound because she was beautiful and no doubt there had been men who'd viewed her as something they could take. The chances of her being untouched were remote and so he was expecting fear not embarrassment.

Yet he didn't think it was fear that made her blush.

'You will have to get used to me looking at you, little maid,' he said, since there was no point denying he hadn't been, and since if he was going to teach her exactly what she'd got herself into, he might as well start right now. 'That is what a husband does with a wife. He also does more than look. Especially if he wants children.' He watched her face for fear as he said it, or even trepidation. But there was none.

Instead, that small spark of temper glittered brighter in her eyes.

Three months earlier he'd noticed that spark, the flicker of a warrior spirit, and it seemed that the past three months of freedom had only fanned the flames.

Good. He liked that. It was better than the guardedness she'd displayed earlier and definitely better than fear.

You never wanted a doormat for a wife.

No. No, he did not.

'Fine, then let's get on with trying for them now,' she said tartly. 'Might as well get the first attempt over and done with.'

For a second, he almost laughed and then realised she wasn't joking. She truly did not understand, did she?

'Little maid,' he said with some patience. 'That is not what we agreed on. I told you that claiming my rights as a husband would only happen if and when you decide to stay married to me. And only after a year has passed.' He gave her a direct look. 'And if you decide to stay, there will be no "getting it over and done with" about any attempt at children. Do you understand me?'

She scowled. 'It's just sex. What do you care?'

Ares opened his mouth. Closed it again. Then pondered an appropriate response. She didn't seem to be scared at the thought of sleeping with him. She could be pretending, of course, but he didn't think she was. Had she managed to escape assault while in the compound? Or maybe she hadn't. Maybe she'd become inured to it.

At that thought, the sullen anger he'd experienced in Ivan's study that night flickered to life inside once again. At what might have happened to Rose and how helpless she would have been to stop it. Again, he did not appreciate the feeling.

Over the past three months he'd been steadily gathering information on Ivan and his business. He was still pondering the best course of action, but was erring on the side of armed men storming Ivan's house and legalities be damned.

It was no less than what the man deserved.

'That is something we can discuss later tonight,' he said at last, deciding this was not the time to talk about it. 'Over dinner.'

'Dinner?' She didn't sound any less irritated by this. 'That's what you came here for? Dinner?'

'I am here so we can get to know one another,' he said mildly. 'So, you have some idea about what being a wife means. And dinner is part of that. In fact, I have dinner planned every night—'

'No,' Rose interrupted flatly.

Ares blinked, completely nonplussed. 'No? What do you mean no?'

'You didn't marry me to get to know me.' She was looking distinctly angry now. 'You married me because you wanted children. That's what you said. So, let's have

sex and then I can leave, because I have other, more important things to do than hang around waiting for you.'

Rose stared angrily at her husband, totally forgetting that
she'd decided to take a wary and watchful approach to
him, and not to let her temper get the better of her.

But she'd been waiting a week for him, winding herself up with imagining what would happen when he arrived, and getting herself into quite a state. She was
angry she hadn't been told exactly what these first two
weeks would entail—he'd said it would be so they could
get to know one another, but what did that mean?—and
then even more angry to find that when she'd arrived,
he wasn't here. That he'd been delayed a whole week,
leaving her to stew about what would happen when he
finally arrived.

She knew she should stay in control of her emotions,
that there was a reason she should keep them locked
away, but three months of freedom had allowed her more
emotional expression than she'd ever had in her life, and
she liked it.

Oh, she'd tried to enjoy herself too—she'd never been
to Thailand and his villa on a secluded island was more
luxury than she'd ever seen—but anger felt good, it felt
powerful, and so she indulged it.

That night in the helicopter, he'd told her she owed
him nothing, yet she knew she'd never truly be free unless she got rid of all ties, all obligations, and so she'd
insisted he marry her. He'd agreed. It had seemed like
an excellent plan at the time, but now she'd had time to
process what had happened and, quite frankly, she was
having second thoughts.

It had seemed so clear that night. He'd given her what

she wanted and so she'd give him what he wanted. That was how the world had worked in the compound, and now that she was out, it seemed that was how it worked everywhere else too. Things were bought and sold, sometimes for money, sometimes for favours, sometimes for services, but nothing came for free.

The first month she'd decided that out of necessity she'd use some of the funds her powerful husband had set aside for her, but in the future, it was better not to rely on him. So, she'd found a job and an apartment, and even though she didn't earn much, she made sure she lived within her means and had some left over for savings.

She was enjoying being self-sufficient and wasn't in any hurry to live with him, be a wife to him like she'd seen in the movies or TV. Where wives seemed to worry over the wellbeing of their husbands, have difficulties with children, argue about money and get annoyed about sex.

That didn't look like freedom to her.

However, she *had* promised she'd come to him for two weeks of every season and she would. Except he hadn't been clear what 'getting to know each other' actually meant. She'd assumed it was just another way of saying he expected sex. That was usually what men wanted, no matter what they said.

She was fine with sex. She'd prepared herself for it.

Yet now, here he was, telling her that no, he didn't expect that and in fact what he wanted was dinner. *Dinner.*

It didn't help that he'd startled her awake, his rasping voice somehow insinuating itself in a dream she was having about lying naked on the sun lounger with someone stroking her bare back very lightly, making her shiver and not with fear.

She'd been enjoying it, until he'd said her name and she'd woken up with a start to find him standing next to her, staring down at her.

That silver-green gaze of his was just as haunting as it had been three months earlier, those deep scars just as horrifying. The proud, stark planes and angles of his face just as mesmerising.

He wore a crisp white business shirt, and dark blue suit trousers, and standing there with his hands in his pockets, his broad, powerful figure looming over her, the force of his presence had been like a hammer blow.

He'd looked at her in the way a man looks at a woman he wants, and she knew that because men had looked at her that way before. She'd always hated it. It made her frightened and then angry, because if they'd wanted to do anything about it, she couldn't stop them.

But now, even though she could stop him, it was worse. Because when he looked at her, she didn't feel frightened. She felt…prickly. Shivery. As if she liked him looking at her, which couldn't be right.

She didn't like it. She didn't. And she *did* have more important things to do. Such as continuing the search for who she was. For anything that could give her a clue about her real identity. She hadn't found anything yet, but that didn't mean there wasn't anything to find. She hadn't given up wanting to escape the compound and she had, and she wouldn't give this up either.

Ares raised one black brow again, infuriatingly calm. 'What important things do you have to do, little maid?'

'Don't call me that,' she snapped. 'I'm not a maid any more.'

His other brow rose. 'True. But Rose isn't your name either, is it?'

She wasn't surprised he knew about her origins—or rather, her lack of them. She'd done her research on him as soon as she could. Ares Aristiades, owner of Hercules Security, a worldwide security company that provided military services to governments the world over. There wasn't much about him on the internet, not that she was surprised about that either. He was a man who stayed out of the spotlight, which she could understand given his business and the secrecy that it no doubt entailed.

What other information she'd managed to find was sparse. He'd been born to a hardscrabble life in the mountains of Greece as a shepherd before going into the French Foreign Legion and carving a military career for himself that many would be proud of. Then he'd built himself a billion-dollar company by being one of the best military tacticians on the planet.

A mysterious man with a questionable company and who knew Vasiliev.

She didn't like what that said about him, despite the fact that he'd rescued her. She didn't want to be a wife to a man who condoned the buying and selling of people like herself, or associated with those who did the buying and selling.

No, she didn't like that, and she didn't like him.

Now, she glared angrily at him. 'My name could be Rose. You don't know.'

'It's unlikely.'

'It doesn't matter how unlikely it is, it still could be.' She sniffed. 'Anyway, that doesn't matter. I have decided my name is Rose so that's what it is.'

He regarded her for a long moment, his expression inscrutable. 'You are not the same woman you were three months ago, are you?'

'What? A biddable servant you can do anything with? An object that you can ignore? No, I am not.' She glanced up at him from beneath her lashes, a daring thought occurring to her. If she played with the knot of her sarong, what would he do? Would it irritate him? Would it knock that annoyingly expressionless expression from his face? He'd left her stewing for a whole week and part of her wanted to make him stew too.

Some of the other cleaning women in the compound had whispered about using their sexuality to make men do what they wanted, but Rose had never seen the point of it. If it wasn't going to get her out of captivity, then why bother?

But perhaps she could understand it now. Like anger, there was a certain…power to it. Men were easy to manipulate, or so some of the others had said.

Maybe she could test her own power, see what it did to him. Experiment a little.

She lifted her hand and fussed with the knot, watching him slyly as she did so.

One corner of his twisted mouth turned up, though the rest of his face remained impassive. Was his lack of expression due to all that scar tissue perhaps?

'I am not going to do what you want, Rose,' he said. 'No matter how many times you play with that knot.'

Damn. Either he wasn't open to manipulation, or he didn't want her as much as she'd thought.

She let her hand drop and pulled a face. 'What's the point of getting to know one another? When all you want from a wife is children?'

He gave her a steady look. 'Are you a virgin, Rose?'

After years of staying quiet and still and keeping her secrets, her instinct was not to tell him. But she wasn't in the compound now, and anyway, there wasn't much point in hiding it. 'Yes,' she said, lifting her chin in challenge.

His eyes widened a fraction. 'No one touched you? No one…hurt you?'

The question stung. That she'd managed to avoid what many of the others hadn't made her uncomfortable, not to mention angry. 'Vasiliev's daughter, Athena, was my friend. She…protected me.' She gave him a severe look. 'Not that it didn't stop men from trying to take what wasn't theirs.'

He remained inscrutable. 'I see.'

'It doesn't bother you?' she asked suddenly, wanting to know. 'That you bought me? That I was sold to you? Were you okay with it? Or perhaps you take part in it yourself?'

Again, his expression gave nothing away. 'No,' he said flatly. 'I do not. And no, I was not okay with it.'

'Really? Because you look okay with it.'

'If you hadn't noticed, I do not have a lot of movement in my face.' His voice was terse. 'It does not mean I was okay with it, not in any way.'

That wasn't fair. You thought it might be scar tissue, so why push?

A small thread of guilt wound through her, but she ignored it. Why shouldn't she push? He hadn't told her anything about himself and she needed to know.

'So why were you there? In Vasiliev's compound?'

Finally, an emotion flickered across his ruined face, but she couldn't tell what it was. 'Vasiliev was my father-in-law, once upon a time. I visit him every year.'

Rose blinked, taken off-guard. His father-in-law? She'd made up all kinds of reasons for why Ares would be at the compound. Good reasons, she realised with a start, because she hadn't wanted him to be there for bad reasons. She hadn't wanted him to be like all the others who visited Vasiliev.

That means he was married.

Rose blinked again. 'You're married? I mean, to someone else?'

Ares gave her an enigmatic glance. 'Once. A long time ago.'

'But what happened—'

'We'll talk tonight,' he interrupted, his tone casual yet firm. 'I'll have one of the staff come and get you when dinner is served.'

Then before she could say another word, he turned and stalked back into the villa, leaving her staring after him.

She didn't know what to make of that. She didn't know what to make of him, full stop.

She'd never thought that a man so hard and impassive, so seemingly wrought of iron, would do something so mundane as visit his ex-father-in-law.

It was…interesting, she couldn't deny it. She was married to this man, after all, and while technically she didn't have to stay married to him, she had given her word she'd spend two weeks of every season with him. And she was here now.

Perhaps it wouldn't be such a bad idea to get to know him, as he'd said.

Anyway, that was the least of her worries. She'd been thinking more and more about Athena, still trapped in that place. Kept in luxury and pampered, it was true, but still a prisoner.

Vasiliev needed taking down.

You can help her.

Rose bit her lip, staring sightlessly at the villa. Well,

she wanted to, but how? She had no money and no power. And she didn't know anyone who… Wait a second…

Ares.

Yes, he could help. He had the money and the power. He had the means, and she was his wife. She could ask him, couldn't she? He might not agree—it was difficult to tell what he thought about anything—but… Maybe she wasn't without something to bargain with.

She touched the knot of her sarong, remembering how his gaze had dropped there when she'd fussed around tying it. There had been heat in his gaze and perhaps she could use that. He'd said he wasn't going to do anything no matter how she played with that knot, but was he really as controlled as he made out? He'd declined the first time she'd offered herself, up in that room in the compound, and he'd just refused her now, which meant a straight-up offer of sex didn't move him.

She would have to do something more.

Still thinking, Rose slipped off the sun lounger and walked towards the big glass doors of the villa, stepping inside.

The past week she'd spent here on her own had been very pleasant. She'd done nothing but swim and lie around the pool reading books she'd found in the small library near her own room. In fact, she hadn't been able to get enough of books. She'd been given a bare minimum of an education in Vasiliev's compound, enough to read and write and some basic sums, so in the past three months she'd gorged herself on information.

She loved reading. There was something about escaping into another world and joining the characters of whatever book she was in the middle of, experiencing their journey with them that was very exciting. And it wasn't just fiction she devoured, but nonfiction too, all kinds from science to technology, history to philosophy, and everything in between.

Most of the books in the library were in English, but there were a few in a strange-looking language that she'd discovered was Greek. The script looked familiar to her, which was even stranger, though she couldn't imagine why.

She moved down the wide, breezy hallway, the dark wood of the floor gleaming as she made her way to her bedroom. It was situated in one wing of the villa that overlooked sharp cliffs, a green, translucent sea swirling around the base. The big windows were open to let in the humid air, while slatted screens drawn across them prevented any rogue insects.

A big four-poster bed piled high with white pillows was pushed up against one wall, the frothy mosquito net canopy pulled back. The bed had been made by the villa's staff and she'd run a professional eye over it before she could stop herself. Initially she'd been suspicious of the staff here and had asked the housekeeper many questions about whether they were actually staff who'd been hired and who were paid regularly, since her experience of staff in rich people's houses was that 'staff' was a very loose term. But the housekeeper had patiently explained that yes, the people who worked here were indeed staff and that Mr Aristiades paid them well.

She'd been encouraged by that, but not enough to trust him, of course.

Wandering over to the big dresser carved in a gleaming, dark wood, Rose pulled open a couple of drawers, thinking. When she'd arrived, she'd found the wardrobe and the dresser full of clothes and all in her size. Ares had obviously prepared for her even though she'd brought her own meagre supply of clothing.

Everything was beautifully made, in gorgeous fabrics, and obviously very expensive, and secretly she loved that he'd provided a few extra items. She'd had to check with the housekeeper—the poor woman had the patience of a saint—about why there were clothes in the drawers and the housekeeper had been very clear that they were for her. So, she'd spent at least a couple of hours going through all the beautiful things and admiring them. She'd never had anything so beautiful, and she found herself being slightly less suspicious of him than she'd been before. But only slightly. She still needed to be cautious.

Now, she rifled through a drawer and pulled out a gorgeous silk sarong in vivid golds and blues. There were gowns hanging in the wardrobe, but she didn't want to wear a gown for dinner tonight. She didn't want to look as if she was trying too hard. Yet she also wanted to look beautiful, because if she was going to bargain with him, she needed something to offer. Herself.

Again.

Yes, again. She just had to find out what would move him. What would…seduce him.

She held the sarong up and examined it critically. It was a little see-through, but not too much. At least, she hoped it wasn't too much because perhaps it was temptation he needed. A glimpse of what he could have, rather than everything immediately.

Carrying the sarong over to the bed, she laid it down on the white quilt.

Was she really going to do this? She'd spent years avoiding men's gazes, afraid of their touch, yet now she was considering actively courting one man's attention.

A man she didn't know and didn't trust. A man who'd bought her and married her, yet freed her.

She didn't understand that. When a man wanted something, he took it; that had been her experience and so while she understood him buying her and agreeing to marry her, she still didn't understand why he'd then let her go. Or why he wanted to 'get to know her.' Or 'dinner.' In the helicopter that night, he'd mentioned teaching her what it meant to be a wife, which had been kind of patronising of him, but was all of this part of the lesson?

Whatever, she wasn't here to understand him. She was here because she'd agreed to come, and her word was important to her. And because she'd decided that, since she was here she might as well use him the way he was using her.

She touched the silk on the bed, the material light and insubstantial against her fingertips.

He'd said she was a different woman than she'd been three months ago, and yes, she was. She didn't know what kind of woman she truly was, not when she'd grown up in that place and not when that had moulded her in a certain way, but she wanted to find out. Part of her freedom was the freedom to choose who she wanted to be and she could be anyone, couldn't she?

But how can you ever truly know who you are, when you don't even know who you were?

That would come. She'd find out. She would.

In the meantime, she would choose simply not being a victim. Or a servant or a poor trafficked girl.

She would choose to be powerful. Strong and in control. A seductress.

Let him deal with that.

CHAPTER FOUR

ARES SAT AT the table reading an email on his laptop.
Night had fallen abruptly, as it did in the tropics, the
air heavy with humidity and the scent of flowers. The
darkness was broken by the discreet lighting of the outside terrace, the thick trees and shrubs highlighted with
various spotlights.

Candles in glass hurricane lamps had been placed on
the table, along with a full silver service in preparation
for dinner. Crystal wine glasses and white porcelain,
snowy napkins and a gleaming silver ice bucket for the
champagne.

His staff had outdone themselves and he was pleased.

Except that Rose was late.

It annoyed him, though he tried not to let it. His days
in the Legion had taught him to be adaptable and not everyone was as punctual as he was. Though these days,
everyone ran to his command, and he was not used to
people disobeying his orders.

He did not look at his watch. She was making him
wait, he was sure of it.

Anticipation gathered inside him, though he tried to
ignore that too. The anticipation of an unexpected challenge, because she was unexpected.

He hadn't expected that little scene by the pool, for example, her being cross with him and offering to get the sex 'over and done with' as if it didn't matter. She'd been all prickly, not bothering to hide her annoyance with him at being made to wait a whole week for him to arrive, and he was male enough to find it satisfying that she was impatient. That she'd been thinking of him.

You fool. Why should you care who she's thinking of?

He didn't. But he could enjoy a woman thinking of him, couldn't he? It had been years, after all. He'd also rather enjoyed her trying to tempt him by toying with the knot of her sarong. A long time since he'd played that game with a woman too, and he couldn't deny a certain pleasure in playing it with Rose.

Except he hadn't enjoyed her mentioning Ivan. Or how he'd let slip Ivan's relationship to him. He couldn't think why he had. Maybe it had been her thinking he was a human trafficker, or perhaps condoned it, and he'd felt…angry. Yet again.

He hadn't wanted her thinking that of him, though why her opinion mattered he couldn't fathom.

She was his wife, it was true, but only in a legal sense. Their marriage wasn't based on any kind of emotion.

No, your marriage is based on a debt she feels she owes you.

He frowned down at his laptop, turning that thought over in his head.

That was an issue. She'd never be free, she'd told him that night in the helicopter, not until she'd paid him back, and while he understood her reasoning, he didn't like it. What must it have been like, growing up in Ivan's compound? Imprisoned, knowing that she was property…

The anger that had ignited three months earlier burned

hotter now, smouldering like an ember in his chest, and he rubbed at it, trying to ignore it.

It was terrible what had happened to Rose, but he could not afford to personalise it. He'd learned many things in the years since his wife had been gone, and not allowing his emotions to get the better of his intellect was one of those things.

For example, if he'd known back then that Stavros and his gang of petty thugs would retaliate so violently, he wouldn't have allowed his pride to get in the way and would have paid the protection money they'd demanded. But he hadn't. He hadn't wanted Naya to think him a coward. Aristiades was a proud name, and strong, and he'd refused to bow to weaker men.

Yet those weaker men had torched his house, and Naya had been killed. Her life the price of his pride.

He should never have allowed himself such arrogance. He should have thought things through. He should have thought, full stop.

A soft footfall came from the direction of the double doors that led from the dining room and out onto the terrace.

Ares dragged his attention from his laptop screen.

Rose stood in the doorway. Her hair was loose over her shoulders, the candlelight picking up strands of brilliant honey gold in amongst the blue, and she wore a silk sarong in blue and gold wrapped around her lush figure as a dress, the ends twisted and tied at her nape to create a halter neck. On her feet she wore flat golden sandals, golden ties crisscrossing up her calves.

The silk billowed gently around her in the breeze, and he realised, with a start, that the silk was just a little transparent, giving him tantalising, shadowy glimpses of her curves. Making it very clear that she wore nothing underneath it.

Desire leapt inside him, and he had to concentrate very hard on staying exactly where he was and not moving an inch simply to stay in control.

She came slowly down the steps that led from the doorway to the terrace, the silk swirling around her legs, the fabric parting to reveal a hint of pale golden thigh.

She was beautiful, utterly beautiful. And it was clear that she knew it and that she was using it as some kind of power play, because as she came over to the table, the look she gave him from beneath those thick golden lashes was speculative. Assessing.

His little maid had come to the fight armed and was now sizing up her opponent.

Interesting. Very interesting.

He didn't know which particular battle she wanted to engage him in, or what she thought she was fighting for, but he'd oblige her. He might even allow her a victory if the mood took him, because she couldn't win, not if he didn't let her.

Ignoring the desire that gripped him, Ares rose to his feet. He came around the table, pulled out her chair and held out a hand, inviting her to sit.

She gave a little frown, as if she hadn't been expecting that, but made no comment, sitting down gracefully. She smelled sweet, like lilies, clearly having availed herself of one of the many different bath oils stocked in her bathroom.

Ares pushed her chair in, anticipation gathering in his gut at the coming fight, especially with such a worthy opponent.

It was only supposed to be dinner, remember?

Of course. And it would only be dinner no matter how many games she wanted to play.

Stepping back from her chair, he went over to where the champagne was cooling in the ice bucket and lifted it. 'A drink to celebrate?' he asked casually.

A flicker of irritation crossed her face, as if that wasn't what she hoped he'd say, and then was gone. Carefully and with some ceremony, she adjusted the folds of her sarong. 'Celebrate what?'

Ares couldn't help himself. He was amused at her annoyance and further amused by her attempts to hide it. 'Our marriage,' he said, opening the champagne and popping the cork. 'Though you aren't here for a celebration, are you? You're here for a fight.'

More emotions chased themselves over her face, though they were gone too fast for him to get a good glimpse of what they were. She was much more expressive than she had been three months earlier, as he'd already noted. Had that guardedness been a legacy of growing up in Ivan's compound? Had she had to monitor herself all the time, to make sure she gave nothing away?

What must it have been like for her? Constantly under threat, constantly waiting for an attack. She was a prisoner of war, living with the enemy, nothing but property...

The smouldering anger tugged at the leash he'd put on it, but he dismissed it. Curiosity and desire he'd allow, but nothing more than that.

'A fight?' she echoed as he poured some champagne into her glass. 'What makes you say that?'

'The fact that you are wearing a transparent sarong with nothing on underneath it.' He poured champagne for himself, dumped the bottle back in the ice bucket and sat down. Then he lifted his glass. 'To my beautiful wife.'

Rose did not lift her glass. She stared at him, her chin jutting stubbornly. 'I don't want to fight you.'

Ares shrugged and took a sip of his champagne. 'You want something, though.'

Her pretty mouth compressed with annoyance. Clearly, he was not supposed to have spotted that. 'Well,' she said. 'Since you didn't seem to want what I offered at the pool, I thought I'd give you a preview of…what you said no to.'

He sat back in his chair as another unfamiliar, disquieting emotion flexed inside him. It felt like guilt, though he couldn't think about what. Not that he'd refused her, that had been the right thing to do, and he didn't need to think of Naya to know that. More because of what she'd thought she had to do in order to engage his attention, bargaining for something with her body…

Was that the way it had worked at Vasiliev's? And did she really think he was the kind of man who indulged in such bargains? He'd refused her twice already and still she tried to give herself to him, so it was clear she did.

He didn't like it.

'You want something, Rose.' Might as well be direct about it. 'So why don't you tell me what it is?'

She bit her lip a moment, frowning at him, as if she was weighing something up. Then she said flatly, 'I want your help freeing my friend Athena in Vasiliev's compound.'

He frowned. 'What do you mean Athena? She's Ivan's daughter.'

Rose shook her head. 'She's not. She was bought at the same time I was. I came to the compound with her.'

Ares had to admit to a certain shock.

He hadn't known that about Athena. His mother-in-law had been devastated after Naya's death, and after Ares had been discharged from the hospital and before he'd gone into the Legion, he'd visited both her and Ivan. But she'd taken one look at him and had fled the room. The burns, the reminder of what happened to her daughter, had been too much for her.

She never came when he visited Ivan, and when he'd heard that they'd adopted a child, he hadn't enquired further. He had his own grief to deal with.

Except it appeared she'd hadn't been adopted, after all. Athena was a trafficked child and Ivan must have bought her for his wife, that was the only explanation.

You should have known this. You should have known exactly what Ivan was doing, but you wanted to give him the benefit of the doubt. For Naya's sake.

Ares looked down at the champagne glass he held in his hand, the ember in his chest that despite his best efforts to ignore it hadn't gone out, a constant burning pain.

It was clear he had to do something about this. Ivan had always been…shady in his business dealings, but those first few years, he'd been consumed with grief as well as recovering from his injuries, and he hadn't noticed anything untoward at the compound. Then he'd gone into the Legion and when he'd come out again he'd been shaped into something much harder, all his weaknesses—his pride and all the other, useless emotions that went along with it—shorn away.

Naya's memory was his conscience, his guide as to what was right, and she had loved her father, despite his numerous flaws. So, Ares had ignored his doubts about Ivan, continuing with his visits, doing his duty to Naya.

Perhaps you didn't do anything because you didn't want to. Because you prefer not caring. Because it keeps you safe.

Ares shoved that particular thought away.

'Ivan will not let Athena go,' he said after a moment, still staring into his champagne. 'Not if his wife has any say about it.'

'That doesn't mean I can't try,' Rose insisted. 'She helped me. She protected me. I can't leave her there.'

Ares looked up to find Rose's direct golden gaze staring straight into his. And she didn't look away. There was a steely determination in it, as if nothing and no one would dissuade her from her path, let alone him.

She cares about her friend.

He found that unsettling, even as the fierce look on her face appealed to the warrior in him, sending a flicker of intense heat straight to his groin. It made him want to match her, test her, conquer her. She was even more attractive to him now, all fire and spirit, and iron at her heart.

He didn't look away either. 'So, what are you asking me, Rose?'

'Isn't it obvious? I want you to get Athena out.'

'And I assume you will want to pay me for my assistance?'

'Of course.' She held out her arms. 'If you help me, you can have me. Whenever and however you want.'

Ares's silver-green gaze betrayed nothing. He lounged opposite her at the table, long, powerful legs stretched out, his champagne glass held casually in one hand. Unlike her, he hadn't changed for dinner, still wearing that pristine white shirt and the suit trousers that emphasised his muscular thighs.

The candlelight cast flickering shadows across his ruined face, turning his scars into a horrifying kind of architecture. Part beauty, part nightmare, and unsettling.

This is a stupid idea. He's already said no to you twice. What makes you think he'll agree now?

Well, she didn't know if he'd agree. But she hoped. And this was different. She wasn't a prisoner now and after three months in the outside world she knew more than she had. She wasn't a powerless victim with nothing but her body to bargain with.

And apart from anything else, he wanted her.

Nervous tension coiled inside her. She hadn't expected to put forward her offer so early on in the evening, but not only was he not stupid, he was also very direct. He'd guessed straight away that she'd wanted something from him. Which was fine. She liked his directness, but it didn't leave her with much negotiation room.

'But I've already refused your generous offer,' he pointed out. Irritatingly. 'Twice. What makes you think I'll accept it now?'

Rose grabbed her champagne glass and took a sip. It was very dry and very cold, and she liked it. 'Because you want me.' She glared at him over the rim of her glass. 'I can see it in your eyes.'

His expression was enigmatic, his gaze opaque. 'But you do not want me, Rose. That is the issue.'

Unexpectedly a little thrill pulsed through her. He hadn't denied it. He *did* want her. But as for her not wanting him, well, that was a lie. Sex sounded uncomfortable, yet she wouldn't mind if she had to do it with him. He wouldn't hurt her, she didn't think.

'I do want you,' she insisted. 'I said I'd give you children, didn't I?'

'Sex is not a transaction, little maid. Or at least, it shouldn't be. That is why I said you could have a year to make up your mind about whether you wanted to stay married to me. You should choose it because you want it.'

She frowned, not liking the overly patient tone in his voice. She was very inexperienced, it was true, but she wasn't a child. 'But I did want it. I was the one who suggested the whole marriage thing in the first place, remember?'

His head tilted slightly, his eyes glittering in the candlelight. 'Yes. To pay off a debt I told you that you did not have to pay.'

'I might not *have* to pay it but it's a debt all the same,' she insisted. 'And anyway, you agreed. It wasn't as if I held a gun to your head and demanded that you marry me or else.'

'True,' he said. 'You did not.' And oddly another one of those smiles turned his mouth, as if he was enjoying her responses, making something in her stomach flutter like a bird. It was genuine amusement, she thought, and it lightened his face. He would never be an easy man to be around, his presence was too intense, too overwhelming for that, but it lessened the claustrophobic weight of it. Made her almost want to smile with him.

'What's so funny?' she asked, irritated with how hot her cheeks suddenly felt.

'You are a surprising woman, Rose.' He surveyed her from underneath ridiculously thick, silky black lashes. 'I was not expecting that.'

Warmth shifted inside her, as if part of her was very

pleased to be thought of as surprising by him. Again, unsettling. In fact, he was unsettling all round.

She shifted in her chair. 'What were you expecting then? A doormat?'

'No. I like a woman who speaks her own mind and isn't afraid to match wills with me.'

Again, there was that flutter deep inside her, an excited little thrill. Part of her liked that very much indeed. Liked that a man as iron hard as he was thought she was strong enough to match wills with. And that he wanted her to speak her mind.

He might call you little maid, but he's never treated you like one.

That was very true. Every time she'd been on cleaning duty in his room while he was Vasiliev's guest, he'd never told her what to do the way some did. He'd never treated her like a piece of furniture. He'd been…aware of her.

And it had never made her feel afraid.

You liked it. He interested you.

Rose shifted in her seat again, discomforted. Men were dangerous, especially if you got their attention, and being interested in this one felt threatening somehow.

Yet she *was* interested, she couldn't deny it. What with those horrific scars and being Vasiliev's son-in-law, and the fact that he'd had a wife before her. And being a shadowy businessman that the press seemed to find frightening. Yet also the man who had freed her, who'd only reluctantly agreed to her marriage demand and who'd treated her with nothing but courtesy.

A puzzling man. A man of opposites and contrasts.

His expression was unreadable, those fascinating eyes of his glinting as he watched her.

Something about the way he was looking at her made

her feel hot and restless. 'So, what?' With an effort she tried to keep her voice cool and not sound so impatient. 'Will you help me?'

'Get your friend away from Vasiliev, you mean? Yes, I will help.' He toyed with his champagne glass, his thumb rubbing against the stem. 'As it happens, I've already been gathering information on him. I will have to go through the proper legal channels in order to get Athena away from him permanently, so it might take some time. But she isn't in any immediate physical danger.'

The flutter in Rose's stomach fluttered even harder. So, he'd already been gathering information about Vasiliev. She hadn't expected that. He seemed not to care about anything much, yet... That wasn't quite true, was it?

'I understand,' she said. 'And thank you.' She tried not to give away the depth of her relief or how much that meant to her. 'I can give you—'

'No,' he interrupted calmly. 'You do not need to give me anything. I will help Athena and take down Vasiliev because it is the right thing to do. Nothing more and nothing less.'

She stared at him in surprise. Men, in her experience, were generally not concerned with doing the 'right thing.'

He stared back, enigmatic as a brick wall. Then he said, apparently reading her mind, 'What? Did you think I was like Vasiliev? I've already told you that I'm not.'

Her curiosity tightened. 'So, if you're not like him, then exactly what are you?'

He didn't reply immediately, his gaze falling to his glass for a moment. 'I was a soldier once, a long time ago,' he said at last. 'Then I became a businessman. Now I am building a legacy for someone who was concerned with injustice. Someone who was important to me.'

She had read that he'd been a soldier. A soldier in the French Foreign Legion.

What had happened to him? Was that where his scars had come from? Had he been burned in a military operation? And who was that someone he was talking about? The someone who'd been important to him?

She suspected she already knew—his first wife probably—but asking him about it would be taking her interest in him too far, which, again, might be dangerous.

Instead, she changed the subject. 'Why did you agree? To marry me, I mean?'

He took another leisurely sip of his champagne. 'I told you. I want children eventually. Heirs for my company and a family for myself. You were also rather…insistent.'

She ignored that. 'But why me? There must be lots of other women you could choose.'

He was silent, watching her the way he'd used to do back in that room in the compound, and she felt that awareness build between them once again. An awareness of each other that felt both exciting and dangerous at the same time. And she realised with a sudden lurch that he wasn't looking at her as if she was a servant, and he wasn't looking at her as if she was just another woman either.

He was looking at *her*. The person she was.

Then she realised something else. The enigmatic look on his face wasn't all that enigmatic, after all. Desire glittered in his eyes, along with curiosity, as if he found her just as fascinating as she found him.

Her mouth had gone dry, her heartbeat suddenly fast. Her skin prickled, a shivery, shimmery sensation, like a fine electrical field moving over her body.

'I think you know why I chose you,' Ares said softly. 'Tell me, little maid. Do you know what desire is?'

It was a simple question, the simplest, really, and she didn't know why it felt so charged. 'Desire?' She tried to keep her voice light, ignoring the 'little maid' thing. 'Of course. I was a prisoner. You think I didn't desire freedom?'

'I mean physical desire.'

Oh. She swallowed, trying to get some moisture into her suddenly dry mouth, and when that failed, she took another healthy sip of champagne. She didn't know why the question made her so uneasy.

'Yes,' she lied determinedly.

Ares gave her a look, then put his wine down and pushed his chair back. 'Come here.'

Rose narrowed her gaze. 'What?'

'I won't hurt you. I just want to show you something.' In the flickering light from the candles, his eyes gleamed silver. 'But if you're afraid, I won't force you.'

This was a manipulation, of course, challenging her to make her do exactly what he wanted. Yet she found herself powerless to resist. She was curious and she wanted to know what he was going to show her. Knowledge was power, after all.

Ignoring the sudden clutch of trepidation, Rose pushed back her chair. Got to her feet and moved around the side of the table, coming over to where he sat. And while the scared part of her wanted to keep some distance between them, the braver part, the warrior in her, insisted on coming closer. Standing right at the arm of his chair.

He remained still, his long, powerful body stretched out. And this close, even in the humidity of the night, she could feel his heat, as if that iron-hard body contained a furnace. She could smell him too, a delicious, woody, masculine spice.

She hadn't realised that she could like the heat of a

man and his scent, and that it made her want to get closer, even though she knew she shouldn't.

'You are very beautiful,' he said quietly, staring up at her. 'Did you know that?'

She wasn't, though. Beauty had been valued in Vasiliev's house, but she certainly hadn't been. 'No.'

'Well, you are.' He lifted one hand and held it up to her in silent invitation.

His hand was large, long-fingered and strong-looking. There were scars on his fingers, old and white, standing out against his dark olive skin.

Rose's mouth was very dry. This shouldn't feel so scary. It was just a hand. He wasn't going to hurt her, he'd said, and she believed him. But she was conscious of a certain reluctance, as if touching him would change things, would start her off down a path she didn't want to go down. But still, this was a challenge, and she wasn't going to refuse it.

Slowly, she reached out and placed her hand in his.

His skin was hot, far hotter than she'd expected, and his palm was rough, his fingers callused. He might have been a businessman, yet his hands were those of someone who did hard, physical work.

It was shocking, this touch. She could feel that electrical current ripple all over her skin, prickling down her spine, stealing her breath. And he watched her, his silver-green gaze unwavering as he slowly curled his fingers around hers.

His hand was so warm and so large, engulfing hers completely, containing it in a way that she thought might be threatening, yet it wasn't. It was reassuring, comforting even. But the way her own skin was prickling wasn't comfortable in the slightest.

Her heartbeat was very loud and very fast, and she

wasn't sure why she was so short of breath. She stared at him, unable to look away, watching heat glitter in the depths of his eyes, and something shifted inside her, a fascination gripping tight.

The scars on his face extended down his jaw and the side of his strong neck, disappearing beneath the material of his white shirt, and suddenly she wanted to see how far down they went, maybe explore the differing textures of his skin. The rough and the smooth. He'd be hot, though, she knew that, and he'd feel hard, even where he was burned. Did they hurt him, those scars? If she touched them, would he feel it?

He stroked the back of her hand gently with one callused thumb, the roughness of it pulling over her skin and scraping just enough to send the most delicious shiver down her spine. What would that thumb feel like stroking other parts of her? More sensitive parts?

You know how it would feel. Amazing.

She took a ragged breath, caught in his silver-green gaze, a distant part of her urging her to pull her hand away, while the rest wanted her to leave it exactly where it was, enclosed in his.

After what felt like an endless stretch of time, the air around her feeling too hot and too close, he moved again, turning her hand over so it lay cupped in his, palm up, a pale starfish against his darker skin. Then everything in her tightened as he bent and pressed his mouth gently to the centre of her palm.

She gasped, unable to stop the sound as all the air rushed out of her, her whole body drawing tight. Her palm throbbed, and even as he lifted his head, she could still feel the impression of his mouth. It was as if he'd burned her.

His gaze was relentless, his expression unchanging. But it was his eyes that gave him away. There were flames in them and he let her see them.

An ache pulsed inside her, a deep, heaviness between her thighs, and she could feel the press of her sarong against her bare skin, the brush of it over her sensitive nipples. They felt hard, tight, and her breathing was far too fast.

She wasn't expecting it when Ares let her hand go, and she wasn't expecting not to want him to. She almost protested, but bit down on the words at the last second.

He only sat there watching her. 'That, little maid,' he said softly, 'is physical desire.'

She said nothing, her whole body alive and alight in a way it had never been before. Like Sleeping Beauty waking up, the world was different now and she didn't know what to say or what response to give.

Because if this feeling was desire, then she'd underestimated every single decision she'd made since she'd got here.

Sleeping with him will change you. Irrevocably.

Rose didn't know how or why, but she knew it was true all the same. It would change her. And it made everything she'd done so far, everything she'd planned for this evening, seem like the naive imaginings of a silly, sheltered girl.

She'd thought using his desire for her as a bargaining chip would give her power, but only because she hadn't understood what wanting him meant. She did now, though, and that left her vulnerable.

You can't sit here with him.

No, she couldn't. Suddenly it seemed like the most dangerous thing in the world.

Without a word, she turned around sharply and left him sitting on the terrace alone.

CHAPTER FIVE

Autumn

'I DON'T CARE,' Ares growled. 'Find her and find her now.'
He hit the disconnect button, thrust his phone back in the
pocket of his suit trousers, then turned from the window
he'd been staring through and strode out of the study.

He'd arrived at his Cotswolds manor the night before,
hoping to have some good news for Rose when she arrived today, but everything had gone to hell in a hand-
cart, and he was in a foul temper.

The time had come for Rose to visit for her two weeks,
and after what had happened in Thailand three months
earlier, he'd decided to do things differently this time.

That summer he'd allowed himself to get too busy and
had arrived a week late, not thinking about her in any
particular way, only to find himself brought up short by
a beautiful woman with a stubborn spirit and a blunt,
fierce nature who'd somehow reached inside him and
flicked a switch. A switch he'd had very firmly turned
to 'off' for at least the last decade.

It shouldn't have mattered to him that she'd insisted
on marrying him to pay back a debt. And he shouldn't

have cared that she'd thought paying him with sex in return for freeing her friend was a perfectly valid choice.

He shouldn't have taken her small hand in his, intent on showing her that she'd lied and hadn't the first clue what desire had meant. And he definitely shouldn't have kissed her soft palm, making her turn on her heel and leave him sitting alone on the terrace.

Especially not when he'd known the night he'd taken her from Vasliev's clutches, the night she'd told him she'd marry him, that she had no idea at all what *any* of it meant. Not being a wife, not having children and definitely not a single thing about sex.

What had caused her to walk away, he wasn't sure. He hadn't hurt her, and he'd been very sure that the glitter in her wide golden eyes as he'd kissed her palm had been as much desire as it had been shock. She'd had a physical response to him, that was clear.

He'd wanted to follow her to ask her, but he also didn't want to force his company on her, so instead he'd kept his distance. If she wanted to talk, it would be her choice to come to him, but it was clear that she didn't want to talk since at the end of the week she'd left without even a goodbye.

He'd told himself it hadn't bothered him, but when he'd left himself, he couldn't deny a certain…disappointment.

He didn't often make missteps, but in this case, it seemed he had and that disturbed him. Naya would not have wanted him to upset Rose, but that night he'd kissed her hand, it hadn't been Naya he'd been thinking of.

All he'd wanted was to show her that it was a bad idea to go around offering herself to people without any clear idea of the implications or consequences. She was so inexperienced. Someone had to teach her.

However, the little lesson in desire he'd given her had frightened her in some way and he meant to find out why. And he'd also very much hoped to bring some good news with him this time too, to put at least some of her concerns about Athena to rest, yet that had just fallen through.

Athena had escaped Ivan's compound some months ago and no one knew where she was.

Since Thailand, he'd forwarded the information he'd collected on Ivan to the authorities, and they were now in the process of dealing with him. But Ares had wanted to secure Athena's freedom, then bring her to Rose personally. But that wasn't going to happen now, and he was in a foul mood about it.

You shouldn't be in any kind of mood, let alone an angry one.

That was true, he shouldn't. Which only added to his annoyance. Still, at least he had *some* news to give her, and that was better than nothing. She would be pleased to know Ivan was being handled at least.

He strode down the hallway of the little manor he'd bought on a whim five years ago. He had houses in many different countries since he liked to move around—staying in one place for too long made him restless—but this was the perfect location for an autumn meeting. The large oaks in the grounds had on all their autumn foliage and the rolling lawns were still green. There was a crisp bite to the air, and he thought Rose might enjoy rambling through the woods behind the manor.

She'd just arrived, and he'd instructed his butler who managed the house to show her into the library to wait for him. He wasn't going to let her sit and stew like he had in Thailand. He was going to show her around himself and maybe have a conversation about what had happened three months earlier.

He stopped outside the closed library door, suddenly aware of something else beneath the burn of his irritation. A sparking electricity, a kind of anticipation.

You've been looking forward to seeing her, don't deny it.

It was dangerous thing to admit, though. Certainly, he was looking forward to matching wills with her and having the same kind of blunt, honest conversations they'd had in Thailand. Plus, he liked the thick sexual tension that filled the air whenever they came into contact, a sexual tension she hadn't even been aware of until he'd made it obvious.

She is more sheltered than you thought.

No, it wasn't that she was sheltered, he suspected. It was that she *hadn't* been. Athena had protected her physically at the compound, but no one had protected her emotionally. She'd probably seen the worst men could do to women, and even if she hadn't experienced it herself, that would colour all her opinions of sex and desire.

He couldn't let his own desire goad him into making another slip like he had in Thailand. Nothing physical would happen between them, not until the year was up and she chose it. That was his bottom line.

He would need to go carefully.

Ares put his hand on the door handle and went in.

It was a warm, cosy little room, and his butler had made sure there was a fire burning in the fireplace. Tall wooden bookshelves lined the walls, a couple of worn but comfortable armchairs and a sofa set before the fire.

Paintings of hunting scenes and forests were hung between the shelves, making the room feel very much like the house of an English aristocrat. Which he supposed was appropriate given that it had once belonged to an English aristocrat.

Rose herself stood before the fireplace with her back to him, her small hands outstretched to the blaze. The blue had faded completely from her hair, leaving its rich gold to gleam in the firelight. It was longer than it had been in Thailand, below her shoulder blades, and she had tied it back in a simple ponytail. She was dressed casually in jeans, a soft-looking jumper in stark black, with sneakers on her feet. A cheap black overcoat lay thrown over the back of the sofa.

He remained in the doorway a moment. He'd prepared himself, yet still the gut punch of desire made his breath catch.

How ridiculous. She wasn't in a bikini this time, and every inch of skin was hidden by her clothing, yet all he wanted to do was to lay her down on the hand-knotted silk rug in front of the fire and peel those clothes off her, see what her naked body looked like in the firelight. And whether the rest of her was as golden and felt as silky as her hand had that night on the terrace.

Her small fingers cupped in his palm. Her skin so soft and fragile beneath his mouth as he'd kissed her. The flicker of a flame in her golden eyes…

She turned sharply and he heard her indrawn breath as their eyes met. For some reason it felt like no time at all had passed since he'd seen her, and that they were on that terrace in Thailand still, her hand in his, the desire she hadn't been able to hide alive in her eyes.

The desire he could see burning there now.

He'd shut the door hard and taken a couple of steps towards her before he even knew what he was doing.

Theos, weren't you supposed to go carefully?

Ares stopped himself just in time and from the widening of her eyes it was clear that she'd known exactly what he'd meant to do. She didn't look afraid, but there was wariness on her face all the same, as if he was a dangerous animal and she wasn't sure which way he was going to leap.

She should be wary. You were just about to pounce on her.

Yes, and he should know, better than anyone, the dangers of letting your own desires blind you. Of letting your heart dictate your actions.

He *had* to control himself.

Ares thrust his hands into the pockets of his trousers to keep them contained.

The pulse at the base of her throat, just above the neckline of her soft jumper, was racing. He could barely look away from it.

'Hello, Ares,' she said.

He hadn't been aware that he'd missed the sound of her voice until he heard it again, light, husky, feminine. She used to hum while she'd cleaned the fireplace in his room at Ivan's. He'd never recognised any of the songs, but he'd liked hearing them. He'd found it soothing.

He gritted his teeth, forcing a leash on his hunger. 'Hello, little maid. Welcome to the Cotswolds. I don't think you've been to England, have you?'

The soft curves of her breasts rose beneath her jumper as she took in a breath, and he couldn't look away from those either. 'No. But then you know that already, don't you?'

He did. He knew everything that she'd been doing

since he'd made it his business to know. So, he knew that instead of traveling and seeing a bit more of the world, she'd stayed in Paris instead and worked at her job in the café. Chatted with her co-workers and went home every night to her little apartment.

There was no point denying it, so he didn't. 'Yes.'

'I thought so.' Her chin had that stubborn tilt to it again. 'There's a guy who sits in a car across the street from my cafe. Sometimes he comes in for a coffee, but most of the time he just sits in his car. Except of course when the time comes for me to go home.'

You really think she wouldn't notice? She's far too smart for that.

Perhaps he should have been annoyed that she'd spotted the member of one of his specialist teams that he'd sent to keep an eye on her, but he wasn't. The man was an expert at tailing people and yet still she'd seen him. He liked that. She was, indeed, far too smart.

'It is for your protection,' he said.

'Worried about the risk to your investment?' There was acid in her tone. So much for hoping she wasn't going to be angry with him. But was it only because she hadn't liked being watched or was there something more going on?

'You're my wife.' He met her challenging gaze head-on. 'I want you to be safe.'

'You also want to know exactly what I'm doing, don't you?'

He ignored that. 'Is it me having you watched that's really making you angry or was it what happened in Thailand?'

She stared at him for a second, then abruptly turned back to the fire, holding her hands out once more to the blaze. 'Nothing happened in Thailand,' she said after a moment.

Ares took a couple of steps closer. She was standing very rigidly, though he wasn't sure whether it was anger or fear that was making her so tense.

He couldn't leave it the way he had in Thailand. He needed to find out what was wrong.

'You walked away so abruptly,' he murmured. 'Then I didn't see you again for the entire week. I wanted to give you some space and I thought you might…come to me to discuss things, but you didn't.'

She said nothing.

He had no idea what she was thinking and suddenly that felt unacceptable. This was important. He needed to know if he'd made things difficult for her.

So, he took another couple of steps, closing the distance between them until she was mere inches away. He could see the rounded curve of one cheek, the flames from the fire sending golden flickers over her skin, and since her hair was pulled back and the neckline of her jumper low, he also noted the delicate arch of her neck, the fragile contours of her collarbones and the curve of one small ear. She had her ears pierced and wore small golden hoops.

Pretty. So pretty.

She must have sensed him standing behind her, because he could see how her shoulders tensed. Was that him making her uncomfortable? Was he standing too close?

He should move and yet… He didn't.

'Rose,' he said quietly into the silence. 'We will talk about this, understand me? I am not going to let you walk away a second time.'

Still, she said nothing, her gaze fixed on the flames in front of her, tension radiating from her.

'Rose.' This time he put an edge of command in his voice. 'Look at me.'

She didn't want to look at him. She didn't want him standing so close. She didn't want to be here with him. And she very much didn't want to feel the aching heaviness that sat deep inside her, or the crackling, spitting electricity that prickled over her skin the instant she'd seen him in the doorway.

For three months she'd told herself that her response to him that night in Thailand had been an aberration, a trick of being somewhere new and exciting, and that once she left, once he wasn't in her vicinity, it would disappear.

Yet she hadn't been able to get him out of her head.

Ares sitting arrogantly in that chair, with his big, hard muscled body so close.

Ares cradling her hand in his, slowly turning it palm up and pressing his scarred mouth to it.

The memory of that mouth on her skin had haunted her, and even now, months later, she could still feel the burn of his kiss on her palm.

'This is desire.'

She hadn't known. She hadn't ever known what it was until he'd shown her. Until she'd realised what a fool she'd been, thinking to use sex against him, thinking it didn't matter. And that was the problem. She could feel the power of it inside her now and she knew it made everything different.

Because desire did matter. It did. It wasn't abstract any more, and while being in the outside world had certainly shown her that it was possible to want a man and that sex could be pleasurable, there was a part of her that had never quite believed it.

But she did now. She knew what it felt like to want someone, and she hadn't liked how vulnerable it made her feel, not to mention stupid.

Stupid to have offered herself to him so many times without even the faintest clue about what it meant.

Facing him again after that night in Thailand had felt impossible, the power she'd thought she had an illusion. Wanting him had frightened her, because wanting anything had been a dangerous thing for a prisoner. She'd avoided him the whole rest of the week, which she supposed made her a coward, but she hadn't been able to process this new knowledge about herself with him around.

Rose swallowed. This was silly. He hadn't hurt her—he'd only kissed her palm, for God's sake—so why she was acting like the scared little girl she'd once been, she had no idea. She didn't want to be afraid. Not the way she had been back in the compound. Afraid and powerless, a victim.

No. Not again. Never *again.*

Gathering her courage, Rose turned around and met his gaze.

Instantly all the breath left her body.

She'd known he was standing behind her, she'd felt his heat, but she hadn't realised how close. Only inches away. And he towered over her. So tall, like a building or a tree, like one of the oaks she'd seen through the car window as they'd driven up to the manor. Huge, encompassing, his wide shoulders and muscled chest seemingly taking up the entire world. Before, in Thailand, he'd been sitting down and, apart from that one time as he'd stood beside the sun lounger, she hadn't understood just how tall he was or how that would affect her. One kiss in the palm of her hand had set her alight, but him standing so close, his body hotter than the fire at her back, the spicy, masculine scent of his aftershave all around her, was making her burn.

He wore another expertly tailored business shirt tonight, though this time in black and his suit trousers were also black. He seemed dark, powerful, the very epitome of who he'd been named for, the god of war, and that should have made her afraid, but it didn't.

His mesmerising silver-green eyes reminded her of olive leaves, so startling in his dark and scarred face, and she found herself staring up into them, her breath coming faster, shorter.

'I need to tell you something,' he said. 'I was hoping that since Ivan is being dealt with, I could also bring your friend Athena to you, but I just had news today that it appears she has already escaped.'

He'd emailed her a month earlier to tell her that steps against Ivan were being taken and that he was making enquiries about Athena, and she'd been so shocked that he was actually doing what he'd promised that it had taken her a good ten minutes to reply.

She'd felt helpless to do anything for her friend, and yet Ares, in one fell swoop, had not only brought Vasiliev to justice, but had maybe rescued Athena as well. Except, obviously, he'd been too late.

She swallowed, even now afraid to hope. 'Escaped? But…she's alive?'

'Yes.' There was a strange expression in his silvery-green gaze, one she couldn't immediately identify. 'It seemed she escaped a week before the authorities raided the compound.'

'She wasn't sold? She wasn't taken—'

'No. My sources told me that Ivan was furious, so it really was an escape attempt.' His expression remained as inscrutable as it always was, yet that there was a certain…softness in his eyes. 'I'm sorry I couldn't bring you better news. I had hoped to tell you she was safe and well and that you could see her. But I thought you'd want to know that she got out.'

That look in his eyes was concern, she suddenly realised. Concern for her. As if he cared what this news might mean for her and whether she would be upset.

And an odd feeling spread out inside her, warmth shot through with sparks. No one had ever been concerned about her feelings. No one had ever been concerned for her at all.

No one except this hard, frightening man who apparently cared more than he let on.

That warm, sparking feeling pulsed lightly in her chest, and completely without conscious thought, Rose lifted a hand and touched his scarred and melted cheek.

His eyes widened and she knew a moment of intense satisfaction that she'd shocked him, then the look of concern vanished and something hungry and hot leapt in his gaze.

He lifted his own hand, his fingers closing around her wrist, gripping her firmly. She hadn't forgotten how hot his skin was, not one single iota, and if she'd had any breath left in her lungs, it would have burned away in that instant.

He left her hand where it was, resting on his cheek, but his hold was firm. She didn't know if that meant he wanted her to touch him or not. She still couldn't believe she actually was, but there was no backing away and she knew it.

She'd touched him. She'd crossed a line. And while she still felt vulnerable about wanting him, and afraid about what it would mean for her to go on touching him, she also didn't want to let that fear stop her. She didn't want to keep on being afraid.

He'd done something for her. He'd handed his own father-in-law to the authorities, had tried to find Athena for her. He'd been concerned for her feelings and she wanted to acknowledge that. Let him know that it meant something to her.

Yet at the feel of his burned skin beneath her fingertips, she was consumed by a sudden curiosity, intrigued by how some parts were shiny and smooth, while others were rough. All parts were hot, though, burning her fingertips, making the ache inside her get more intense. Making her breasts feel heavy and her sex throb.

This is desire.

She was breathing very fast, and she knew that maybe she'd made a mistake, that this was a bad idea, yet she couldn't stop, her fingers trailing down his twisted cheek to his hard, scarred mouth. It felt soft beneath her fingertips, so soft. The only thing about him that had any give.

'What are you doing, little maid?' His harsh, rasping voice had become even harsher, guttural almost.

She could barely speak. Her heartbeat was so loud she could barely hear him either, but she kept her fingertips on the softness of his mouth, tracing his lower lip. 'I just… Thank you for trying to help. That means a lot to me.'

His grip on her tightened, just shy of painful, yet he

didn't pull her hand away. 'You do not owe me anything. I've told you that before.'

Rose swallowed. 'I know. I didn't mean it like that. It's just... I can't stop thinking about this. About you...' She dragged her gaze from her fingers and looked up his face. 'Will you show me?'

His fingers closed around her wrist in a convulsive movement, his grip now painful. But she didn't want to show any weakness, so she bit down on the pain. She'd told him she wasn't a doormat, and so she wouldn't be one.

His gaze was now all silver, tarnished and glittering in the firelight, and she could feel that thing crackling between them, that tension, glorious and electric.

Desire.

It didn't feel like a weakness now, not when she could see it burning so clearly in his eyes. He felt it too, didn't he?

'You need to be more specific,' he said, raw and guttural. 'I have not been with a woman in years, and I would...hate for there to be any misunderstandings.'

Shock echoed through her. She hadn't wondered about his love life, not once.

But he'd been married before and even with those burns he was phenomenally attractive. Mesmerising, his presence a force of nature. She couldn't imagine him alone.

'Years?' she asked.

'Not since my wife died.' The words were bitten out, his big body full of tension, as if he was struggling with something. 'But you, little maid... *You*—' He broke off, but she didn't need him to elaborate. She already knew.

For years he hadn't been with anyone else, yet now he wanted her.

Her, the abducted girl no one had looked for and the servant no one thought about; she was wanted by this man. The god of war.

She wanted to ask him about his wife and how long he'd waited and why, and why her? Why now? But the heady rush of power that filled her couldn't be denied, and it felt different to the power she'd thought she'd had on that terrace in Thailand. Then it had only been an abstract concept, about her femininity, her body. Now, though, it was about *her*.

She was the one he wanted. Not just any woman, but her.

It mattered, she didn't know why, but it did, and that made her brave. Even braver than she'd thought she'd be.

Rose cupped his scarred cheek, ran her thumb along his lower lip. Then she went up on her toes and pressed her mouth to his.

He didn't wait, not one second. He pulled on her wrist, tugging her right up against him, and with his other hand resting firmly at the small of her back he held her there. And then he devoured her like a lion with his kill. Open, hot, hungry. His tongue was in her mouth, and she knew a moment's fear that she'd be swept away, caught in a riptide that was far too strong for her. But she only had two options now: either she pushed him away, or she surrendered.

She'd never thought she'd give up all control again, but there was no fighting this. And more, she didn't want to. She wasn't afraid any more. She wanted to go with the tide wherever it took her.

So, she curled her fingers into the fabric of his shirt and kissed him back.

She had no idea what she was doing; she'd never kissed anyone before. But for the past six months everything she'd done had been new and this was just one more new thing. One more glorious, amazing new thing.

His mouth was hot, soft and hard at the same time, demanding something of her that she didn't understand. But she answered that demand all the same, pressing herself against the hard wall of his chest, her tongue touching his as she tried to explore him the way he was exploring her. He made a hungry sound deep in his chest, and the hand at her back was like an iron bar, forcing her even closer to him.

Her entire front was plastered up against his and there was nothing but hardness everywhere. And he was hard. Like the oak tree she'd imagined, or no, harder. An iron figure of a man, unyielding in every way except his mouth.

She shuddered as he kissed her deeper, with a feverish intensity. He tasted of wine or chocolate or coffee, a dark, rich taste that made her realise how hungry she was. So hungry and she didn't even know it.

Then he pulled his mouth away, kissing down the side of her neck, making her tremble as he set his teeth against the sensitive cords there, nipping her so that she gasped aloud. Next, he found the pulse that beat at the base of her throat and kissed her, his tongue on her skin, and she felt like she would go mad if he didn't kiss her lower, run that incredible mouth of his all over her body.

'Ares,' she whispered hoarsely, even though she really didn't know what she wanted, only that she wanted more. 'Ares…'

The hand at the small of her back had somehow slid beneath the hem of her jumper, his rough, calloused fingertips stroking her bare back since she wasn't wearing anything underneath it. And then his fingers moved higher, tracing each vertebra, sending the most delicious chills through her.

But she didn't want him to only touch her back, she wanted him touching her in other places, more sensitive places. Her breasts and between her thighs, yes, especially there.

'Rose,' he growled against her mouth. 'You must know that I was not planning on this. I was not planning on anything physical happening between us until you made the decision to stay married to me. So, if this is what you want, you had better be sure, because I do not think I can stop.'

For the first time she heard the lilt of an accent in his voice. An accent that felt familiar, as if she'd heard it somewhere before. He was Greek, that she remembered, and yet there had been no Greeks in the compound, so how could she have heard it before?

But then that thought was swept away as the grip on her wrist shifted and he was bringing her hand down to rest on his chest along with the other. He released her wrist only to grip her hips, fitting her more firmly against him so the soft, intense ache between her thighs was pressed to the long, hard ridge behind his fly.

'Rose,' he murmured again, more demanding this time. 'I need your agreement before this goes any further. It has been a long time and I do not think I can be gentle with you.'

She understood and again she wanted to know exactly how long it had been, but she didn't want to break this moment with questions. Not now she knew what she wanted and quite desperately.

In the compound she'd been alone. Nothing good had ever happened to her, nothing wonderful. There had been moments of lightness, when she'd spent time with Athena, but they'd been all too brief.

Until he'd walked into her world, and everything had changed. Thanks to him, she had Paris. Thanks to him, she had a job and an apartment. Thanks to him, she had freedom. She had justice thanks to him, and he'd tried to rescue her friend, and now he was giving her something else, something wonderful, and she wanted it so badly she thought she would die if she didn't have it.

'Yes,' she whispered, trembling against him. 'Ares, yes. Please.'

He didn't wait. One moment she was standing upright, held up against him, the next she was lying on her back on the silken rug in front of the fire with him kneeling astride her thighs, looking down at her.

The light from the flames flickered over his scarred face, highlighting the deep twists and gouges of the scars, but she barely saw them. All she could see was the burning silver of his eyes as they looked down at her, avid and hungry, full of desire.

As promised, he wasn't gentle. He shoved the jumper she wore up under her arms, along with her plain black bra, exposing her breasts. Then he bent over her, his hot mouth closing around one sensitive nipple and sucking hard.

She gasped, the sensation so indescribably intense she could barely stand it. The heat of his mouth and the pressure were doing the most incredible things to her. She'd really had no idea at all that it would feel quite *so* good.

He sucked harder and her back arched as she thrust herself up into his mouth, wanting more of this pleasure, this intense sensation, the dragging ache between her thighs becoming more and more insistent.

She lifted her hands, but he gripped her wrists and pressed them flat to the floor on either side of her head, holding them there as he transferred his attention to her other breast, his teeth against her nipple, biting gently and sending yet more sparks cascading everywhere. The feeling of being restrained made the pleasure somehow sharper, except she wanted to touch him.

She wriggled, trying to free her wrists. 'Please, Ares…'

He made a growling sound against her breast, releasing her nipple and raising his head. His gaze was all fire, all sharp intensity. 'What is it?' His voice was stone on stone, grating together. 'Am I hurting you?'

'No,' she panted, trying to get her voice working. 'I just…want to touch you. I want to see you.'

He stared at her for a second, then abruptly released her wrists and sat back on his knees again. Keeping his gaze fixed to hers, he lifted his hands and undid the buttons of his shirt, pulling it open.

The breath left her body and she stared, unable to help herself. The whole left side of his body was scarred, as if he'd been licked by fire, chest and shoulders and abdomen all twisted, melted flesh. Like his face, some parts were shiny, and some were rough, white and stark against the bronze of his skin. But even beneath the scars, she could see the carved outlines of muscles that look like they'd been chiselled from stone. The contrasts of him were beautiful to her in a way she'd never expected.

She sat up, reaching for him, touching the smooth

olive skin of the unburned part of his chest, then running her fingers over some of the tightened scar tissue. All parts of him were so hot she felt burned herself.

He looked like he'd been created in a forge where the heat was so intense that even his skin hadn't been able to withstand the fire. But his bones and his muscles had, the fundamental part of him was granite hard.

He said nothing as she touched him, his hands dropping to his belt and undoing it. He flicked open the buttons of his trousers, before pulling down the zip of his fly. She could hear his breathing, it was as ragged as hers, and beneath her hand she could feel the beat of his heart. Fast, powerful.

Again, he didn't speak as he pushed her back down again, his hands at the buttons of her jeans, pulling at them, undoing them. Then he was jerking down the denim to the tops of her thighs, taking her underwear with them, and somehow the fact that he didn't undress her entirely or himself, was intensely erotic. As if he couldn't wait.

A curse escaped him as he looked down at her, all exposed for him, in a language that was at once foreign to her and familiar at the same time. And a dim part of her tried to puzzle it out, but then he was jerking at the denim, shifting as he spread her thighs so he could kneel between them. Positioning himself, and then stretching over her. And she could feel the hot, hard length of him pressing against her entrance, then sliding in slowly. Deep and then getting deeper.

She groaned. He felt big and it hurt, but it was a good pain. She didn't want him to stop. Strange tears started in her eyes, and then suddenly it didn't hurt any more and there was only him, filling her so completely that she hadn't known she'd been empty until this moment. She hadn't known that she'd ever wanted someone there, but she had. She'd wanted him. He was still for a moment, the blazing intensity of his gaze looking down into hers, and she felt her body adjust. He fit her like he'd been made for her.

Then he began to move, and everything became desperate, the ache inside her building until she didn't think she could bear it. Yet she wanted more, because even though the friction was driving her mad, it somehow wasn't enough.

She twisted beneath him, her hands against his bare chest, her nails digging in, heedless of his scars. 'Ares,' she gasped. 'Ares… More. Please…'

His mouth took hers, her desperate pleas lost, and then his hand was down between her thighs, his fingers applying the most exquisite pressure right where she needed it most. Then he gave one hard thrust and she felt as if the whole world was coming apart and her right along with it.

Dimly, in the corner of her mind that wasn't quite lost, she was conscious of his own movements, faster, harder. Then he gave a low, guttural roar, before he joined her, lying in pieces before the fire.

CHAPTER SIX

ARES LAY THERE for a full minute, completely and utterly stunned. He hadn't expected this to happen, not any of it. He'd thought she'd be upset when he'd told her about Athena, not that she'd touch his face and kiss him. And he certainly hadn't expected her to then turn so soft and hot in his hands that he hadn't been able to resist her.

He hadn't expected to pull her down onto the rug in front of the fire, to be so lost that he hadn't even bothered to undress her properly, his only thought to get inside her as quickly as possible.

What he'd expected was another six months of her getting to know him and mastering his own desire until—*if!*—she decided she wanted to remain married to him.

What happened to your control? You didn't even bother to use protection.

He gritted his teeth, trying not to be furious with himself as well as ignoring the odd possessiveness at the thought of her being pregnant with his child.

He'd promised Naya children and he'd meant to provide them, and he'd honestly thought he'd be more detached about the idea of having children with someone else and yet... He wasn't quite as detached as he'd thought he'd be.

You weren't supposed to touch her. You were supposed to wait.

The fury at himself twisted tighter, but he shoved it away. It was too late to get wound up about it now. She'd touched him and it was he who'd gone up in flames. He'd let himself go too long without a woman, let himself be overcome by desire and by the look in her eyes when he'd told her about Athena, as if he'd handed her the moon and the stars on a plate, and every single one of his controls had vanished.

He had no one but himself to blame for it. He had to do better.

He lifted his head and looked down at her.

Rose's face was flushed, small tendrils of hair that had escaped her ponytail clustered around her damp forehead in tiny threads of gold. Her eyes were very wide, staring at him, the firelight gilding the tips of her lashes.

She looked just as shocked as he felt.

'Are you all right?' His voice sounded even rougher than it normally was. 'I hurt you.' It wasn't a question. He'd felt her tense as he'd pushed inside her. And he'd tried to stop then, but…

It had been years. *Years.* The feel of her, the heat of her, the scent of her body and the sounds she'd made, everything so soft and silky and smooth…

He'd forgotten how incredible it felt to sink into a woman's body, to feel her clench around him, to hear her sighs in his ears as he gave her pleasure. To feel her welcome him and enclose him…ah, *Theos*, how could he have forgotten all of that?

Perhaps he'd denied himself too long and that was why it had been so good. He just missed sex. Nothing to do with Rose in particular.

'It hurt a little bit. But not really.' She was staring at him as if she'd never seen anything like him in all her life. 'Ares...is it always like that?'

He liked that expression on her face. It made everything male in him, the parts of himself he'd almost forgotten, growl with satisfaction. 'Not always,' he said roughly, remembering the first few fumbling times before he'd met Naya.

He shifted slightly so he wasn't lying on top of her, realising as he did so that he was getting hard again, and that he didn't want to push himself away from her completely. What he wanted was to strip her clothes off her, feast on her naked body until he had her screaming, and then he wanted to be inside her again, feeling the tight clasp of her sex around his, moving inside her until they both lost their minds.

Except that losing his mind had never been part of his promise to Naya. Children, he'd promised her, nothing more. Then again, it was just physical pleasure, that's all, and certainly nothing lasting.

Enjoying sex with Rose didn't mean anything.

'What is it?' she asked, a crease between her brows, obviously noticing his abstraction. 'I'm sorry. I shouldn't have kissed you—'

He laid a finger across her mouth to silence her, because it hadn't been her that had been the problem. 'Kissing me is exactly what you should have done.' He removed the finger. 'I'm only sorry that it was so quick. I had intended our first time to be...different.'

The crease between her brows deepened. 'You said you haven't...been with anyone since your wife died...?'

Instantly he tensed. He didn't want to talk about this,

not now, but he owed her an explanation for why he'd been so rough. Especially when she hadn't deserved it.

'No,' he said.

Rose hesitated a moment, then asked, 'I know it's none of my business, but…how long? You said years.'

'Yes, it has been years.' He knew he'd sounded sharp, but he hoped she'd got the message that he wasn't up for a conversation about this now. Perhaps one day he'd tell her about Naya, but not now. Not today.

'Oh,' she said softly, her big golden eyes searching his face, looking for what he didn't know, but he could see she had more questions. 'Ares,' she went on. 'How were you burned?'

He didn't want to answer that one either, not given how linked that subject was with Naya.

'I only ask,' she continued quickly, 'because I wasn't sure if it was okay to touch them or whether they hurt you or…'

It's a valid question. She should know if you want her to stay married to you.

No, she shouldn't. And he wasn't even sure he wanted her to stay married to him himself. Regardless, knowing wasn't necessary for the getting of heirs. She didn't need to know about his wife or the circumstances that lead to her death. About his pride and the hard lessons he'd had to learn.

About your failure.

Yes, that too.

Her past was shrouded in mystery, they didn't and couldn't talk about hers, so why should he have to reveal his? That wasn't her fault admittedly, but still.

'You can touch the burns,' he said shortly. 'They don't hurt. Some places have no sensation because the nerve endings have burned away, so I might not feel it if you touch me there.'

She was silent a moment, clearly waiting for him to elaborate, but he didn't.

A flicker of emotion passed over her face. 'I'm sorry, I shouldn't have asked.'

'Rose,' he began.

But then she touched the side of his face again, where the scar tissue was thick and twisted. He couldn't feel her fingertips, but he knew they were there, and something shuddered in his chest. 'Thank you for showing me about…desire,' she said. 'But I wonder…could we possibly explore the subject more?'

He was glad that was the subject she wanted to pursue and not anything else. More sex might be a mistake, but he was getting hungrier by the moment, conscious of how soft and warm her body was, and the scent of sweet feminine arousal heavy in the air around him.

Yes, he had missed sex and he wanted it. What was the point in holding back now?

'We could,' he said, shifting once again, going back onto his knees. His hands dropped to the hem of her jumper. 'But understand, Rose. If you want this, if you want me, you cannot go back.' He stared down into her eyes, so she could see the intention in his. 'You are the only woman I have wanted since my wife died, and if you cross this line with me now, I will want more.'

For a second, she only stared back. 'Why me?' she asked suddenly. 'What's so special about me? I'm just a girl you bought from your father-in-law. A girl who doesn't even know her real name. Why should I be the only woman you've wanted?'

He'd only alluded to the truth the last time she'd asked. But she deserved more than that from him now.

'Because regardless of who you really are, regardless of your past, we have chemistry. And because, little maid, even though you grew up in a terrible place, you are fearless. A warrior through and through.' His fingers tightened in the soft wool. 'Or am I wrong?'

The gold of her eyes glowed bright and he had the sense he'd just given her something she liked. A gift that she'd needed. He liked that, but it also made him want to ask her why being fearless, why being a warrior, was so important to her.

Except then she lifted her arms up in wordless invitation and all the thoughts vanished from his head.

Ares jerked her jumper up and over her head, then tore her bra off. She made no move to stop him or cover herself, her gaze never leaving his face, a fierce expression on hers.

No, he wasn't wrong. She *was* a warrior.

He shifted so he could take the rest of her clothes off, so she was finally lying on the silken rug in front of the fire the way he'd fantasised about: naked. And she didn't move as he leaned over her, bracing himself with one hand beside her head so he could pull out the tie of her ponytail and spread her golden hair out all around her.

Then he just looked at her. Looked at her for a long, *long* time. Because it had been years since he'd had a naked woman stretched out beneath him, ready for him and wanting his touch. A woman all gleaming and gilded, painted in shades of gold by the fire. Warm skin, silken hair, molten eyes. All for him.

She was flushed and her nipples were hard, and she didn't look away. So many people couldn't bear to look at him, a man scarred and ruined and harder than iron. A pitiless man. A man whose heart had died in a fire long ago.

She wasn't afraid of that man. She had never been afraid of that man. And she didn't need gentleness from him, or tenderness. She didn't need him to be careful, because she was strong enough to take anything he could throw at her.

And as if to prove it, she reached up and thrust her fingers into his hair and pulled his mouth down on hers.

This kiss was hotter than the one she'd given him just before and hotter than the one he'd returned. Hotter even than the flames in the grate. Raw and wild, a firestorm.

He kissed her back without restraint, just as hungry, ravaging her mouth, gorging himself on the taste of her, mint and strawberries and something else sweet. Then he took her bottom lip between his teeth and nipped her hard, drawing a gasp from her and making her fingers tighten in his hair. And he didn't stop there.

He moved down her body, kissing the stubborn line of her jaw and the graceful arch of her neck, the pulse that beat at her throat—he concentrated on that for quite a while—before moving down to the lush curves of her breasts. He nipped and sucked on each one, even as his hands moved over her, relishing her softness and the silky feel of her warm skin. She twisted and shifted the lower he went, every touch of his mouth drawing tortured gasps and soft little pleas.

He liked that too much and when she tried to sit up, her hands reaching for him, he pressed a hand to her stomach and held her down, because he wasn't finished. Not by a long stretch. Then finally he settled between her spread thighs and touched the softness between them, all slick and hot, making her writhe with his fingers and then, because he was desperate to taste her, his mouth.

It had been too long since he'd done this too, touched and tasted a woman, taken his time building her pleasure. He'd forgotten how hard it had made him, how like a god he felt when she pleaded for release.

He'd perfected the art of violence, knew a hundred different ways to kill a man. Had built a billion-dollar company in the space of fifteen years, yet he hadn't realised, until right this minute, how all of that had been for someone else. For Naya.

He hadn't had anything for himself. Yet this woman beneath him, Rose, she was his. Tonight, in this moment, she was utterly and completely his.

Perhaps it was wrong to be glad of that so savagely, but he let himself have it.

He let himself glory in the sweetness of her, and she was so very sweet, the taste of her heady as any drug. She cried out as he pushed his tongue inside her, exploring her slowly and with great relish, his hands firmly pressing down on her thighs so she couldn't move. So, he had her exactly where he wanted her. And he took his time, because it had been so long, and her cries were music to his ears, the shudder and shift of her hips a dance he'd never tire of.

And as he brought her finally to the edge and pushed her off it, amid her cries of pleasure, he knew that he wouldn't be able to bear any more distance between them.

This was how it would be from now on and he would brook no argument.

Rose stared at the ceiling and tried to determine how she could put herself back together again since she was pretty sure Ares had shattered her into little pieces. Not that she cared. She could lie here like this for ever, the effects of that orgasm pulsing through her, pleasure glittering like a net of sparks laid over her skin.

She'd had no idea she could feel so intensely, that her body could give her so much ecstasy, and all it had taken was his rough hands and his wicked mouth on her. It might have been years since he'd done that, but it was clear that he'd either been born with a gift or whatever lessons he'd learned about how to please a woman he'd forgotten none of them. And he'd practiced a *lot*.

Yes, of course he did. With his first wife.

A small, edged kind of feeling wound through her at the thought, like the needle-fine and sharp edge of a bit of paper, cutting at her, but she ignored it. Now wasn't the time to be thinking about his first wife, not with him suddenly rearing above her, still mostly clothed and his shirt open.

He knelt and reached for her hips, hauling her up and over his hard thighs, her legs spread on either side of his waist. And he gripped her firmly as he pushed himself inside her. She shuddered, the net of sparks pulling tight, sensitive tissues stretching with the most exquisite burn. She closed her eyes as he moved, long and deep, her entire world narrowing to the heat of him inside her, beneath her, holding her fast.

His hands were red-hot brands on her hips, and it felt as if he was imprinting himself on her, leaving scorch marks. Turning every part of her into flame.

It was so intense, so wonderful, she didn't think she could bear it. But she was a warrior, wasn't she? That's what he'd called her, that's what he'd said. That's why he wanted her, because she was a warrior, a fighter, not

a victim and not a servant. Not a passive woman waiting
for her next instruction, too scared to leave her prison.

As the pleasure climbed between them, Rose opened
her eyes and put her hands over his where they gripped
her and pulled herself up so she was sitting upright in
his lap. His tarnished silver eyes were right in front of
her, the iron-hard plane of his chest pressed against the
softness of her breasts.

He didn't stop, he kept on moving, and she didn't stop
either. She moved with him, watching the signs of pleasure chase over his scarred face, because she knew what
to look for now. The lines around his eyes tightening, the
powerful cords of his neck standing out, his mouth hard.
The fire leaping and blazing in his eyes.

She gripped his shoulders, dug her nails in, and they
moved together, building the pleasure between them so
sharp, so acute, she was trembling. Then he pushed his
hand down between them for that sweet extra friction and
she was shattering once again, his name a scream gathering in her throat. But his mouth covered hers, swallowing the scream as she felt his big body thrust once and
then again, hard and deep. Then his arms were around
her, crushing her against him, holding her as he roared
out his own release.

For long minutes afterwards, he held her like that,
and she didn't want to move. Her head was resting on
his hard, scarred shoulder, while one of his hands had
buried itself in her hair. His arm was like iron around
her waist, and she could hear the beat of his heart, loud
and strong and steady.

She drifted a few moments, her thoughts returning
to what he'd told her earlier, about the burns, and about
what he hadn't said too. He hadn't mentioned how he'd

got them, and she thought it was deliberate. He hadn't forgotten her question, he'd just chosen not to answer it, though she could guess why.

It had something to do with his wife, she was sure. Perhaps those burns had happened at the same time she'd died. Perhaps their home had burned down, and he'd got out and his wife hadn't.

Or he got them trying to save her.

Her heart felt tight, as if someone had pinched it suddenly and hard. On the surface he seemed impassive as stone, but just now he'd betrayed a passion and a possessiveness that ran deep. If he'd loved his wife with the same intensity of feeling, then of course he would have tried to save her.

Yet something had gone wrong, and she'd died.

That must cause him a great deal of pain.

The pinch around her heart became more acute. No wonder he didn't want to talk about it and no wonder he hadn't been with anyone else. If he'd tried to save her and failed, that must have been…devastating.

Before she knew what she was doing, she'd turned her head slightly and pressed a kiss to the scarred skin beneath her cheek, her heart aching. She wouldn't push him about this. She had no experience with grief—she hadn't ever lost a person like that. She hadn't ever had a person to lose, but that was beside the point. She didn't know anything about normal human experiences and could offer him no advice. All she had was the comfort of her body, and if he wanted that, then he could have it.

It would be her pleasure—literally.

His hand tightened in her hair, pulling her head up gently, his gaze moving over her, assessing her. 'Everything okay?'

'Yes.' She smiled, giving in to the heady feeling of being drunk on sex and on him. 'Everything is fantastic.'

His hard mouth softened a moment, amusement flickering in his silver-green eyes. But then both were gone, his expression implacable once again. 'First thing, little maid, is that I didn't use any protection.'

A shock went through her. Protection, of course. She hadn't even thought about it.

You could end up being pregnant. Already.

Her muscles tightened as a strange shiver went through her. And it wasn't dread. What would it be like to have a child? *His* child?

You have no idea how to be a mother. You don't even remember your own.

'Second thing,' he said before she could speak, 'no, I didn't plan on not using a condom the first time. Or the second time either. I wanted us to have more discussion about the subject. However...' His eyes glinted. 'It seems my control where you're concerned isn't as good as I'd thought.'

She swallowed, the warm glow of orgasm fading, something colder taking its place. She didn't remember her own mother, that was true. And she had no idea what being a mother even entailed, just as she had no idea about being a wife. Every time she thought she knew what was going on, something would happen to show her that she didn't, that she was still that ignorant, scared servant girl he'd rescued. The girl who didn't even know her real name.

'I see.' Her own voice sounded small and colourless in the warmth of the room. 'And what if I am pregnant? What will that mean for the year you promised me? Does it mean I don't get to choose? Will we have to stay married?'

His gaze narrowed, became sharp, a storm-tossed silvery sea. 'If you're pregnant we will be keeping the child, understand?'

There was a fierce undertone in his voice, a note that vibrated just on the edge of fury, though she didn't think it was directed at her. Whatever it was, though, it shocked her. Because when he'd mentioned children before, he'd done so very casually and in conjunction with bloodlines, rather than out of any desperate desire.

'Yes,' she said sharply. 'But that's not what I asked.'

His gaze flickered and the ferocity seemed to die out of his eyes. 'Apologies, little maid.' His voice was softer this time, yet no less rasping. 'I didn't mean to be quite so…vehement.'

And now she wanted to know why he was so 'vehement,' especially when he hadn't been so before, but then he went on. 'There is no need to discuss it now, not when we do not know if you even are pregnant. We can cross that bridge when we come to it.'

Briefly she debated pushing him for more of a plan, but then decided to let it go. She was relaxed and warm and sated, and so was he, and she didn't want to ruin the moment with an argument. Besides, she liked being held against him like this. She'd never been held before, and it made her feel safe. As if here in his arms, nothing could touch her, nothing could take her.

'It's okay,' she murmured, running her fingers over his chest. 'I shouldn't have been so sharp. It's only… I've only had six months of freedom and… Well. Call it cold feet.'

Again, there was a slight softening around his eyes

and his mouth. The hand in her hair shifted, so he was cradling the back of her head, his fingers pressing lightly yet firmly against her skull in a way she found pleasurable. 'I can understand that. But should we end up having a child, it would not necessarily mean you'd be tied down.' His mouth curved. 'I am, after áll, very rich and can afford any number of staff to help with its care.'

Its care…

Her stomach lurched again, the cold sensation returning. She had never felt her lack of past so acutely. She had no medical records, no family history… What if she passed on some terrible illness to her child that she hadn't even known she had?

She turned her head away, trying to hide her reaction, because she didn't want to talk about that. She didn't even want to think about it, but the long fingers cradling the back of her head firmed, keeping her in place. His gaze speared through her, pinning her. 'What is it?'

He wouldn't let her not answer, that was clear, and she supposed she might as well talk about it. After all, in a month's time she could already be pregnant. This was what being married was all about, wasn't it? Discussions about children.

Rose swallowed. 'I don't know who I am, Ares. I don't have a mother. I don't have anyone. No family history. What if I'm a carrier for some awful disease? And what kind of mother am I going to be when I can't even remember my own?'

He lifted one shoulder as if it didn't matter. 'You will be a perfect mother. You're a warrior, I told you that, which is exactly the kind of mother I want for our child. And as to your past, well, we will find out.'

He said it like it was already a foregone conclusion.

As if *all* of this was a foregone conclusion. As if they already had children and they'd found out who she was, and it was easy and not a problem in the slightest.

None of this was what you thought it would be. None of it.

She had chosen to marry him, it was true. She was the one who'd demanded it. Yet had it been something she'd have insisted on if she'd known what it truly meant? That she would end up here, lying in his arms, aching with feelings she didn't quite understand?

The unprotected sex had been stupid of her. Because sure, while he might have taken responsibility for that, it went both ways. She was a virgin, but she'd done her research over the past three months. She knew what condoms were. She could have stopped him and demanded he put one on, but she hadn't. She'd been as lost to what was happening between them as he'd been.

Yet another thing you didn't know that you didn't understand.

But that thought wasn't a useful one. Right now, she was in his arms, and he was hot, and he felt good against her. And she wanted more of his heat, more of his passion. She wanted to explore him as thoroughly as he'd explored her, see if she could make him tremble, make him call her name. Exert her feminine power over him, bring him to his knees.

Yes, that's what she wanted.

She stared into his eyes, relaxing against him, her fingertips stroking his hard muscled chest, glorying in the feeling of being surrounded by his heat and his power. 'So, what about now? What do you want to do now?'

His mouth curved deeper, his attention dropping down to her throat and her breasts pressed hard to his chest. 'I think you can guess what I want.' He lifted his gaze back to hers. 'But it has to be what you want too. If not, then no matter what I told you earlier, you can walk away.'

Something fluttered hard behind her ribs, an unexpected emotion tightening in her throat.

It was as if he'd somehow known all the doubts about understanding and choices that had been going through her head. It was as if he knew her, and not just as the stranger he'd married or the trafficked woman he'd married, but her. Rose. Knew what she'd be thinking about now and what would distress her. She didn't know how he knew since they hadn't had much to do with each other these past six months, nevertheless he knew.

And perhaps it wasn't a good thing. Perhaps it was dangerous to be known in that way, yet it didn't feel dangerous. It felt reassuring. Comforting. She had always been a mystery to everyone including herself, a mystery that no one had ever wanted to get to the bottom of. But he had.

A warrior, he'd called her, as if he could see her soul already. And she liked it.

A warrior was exactly what she wanted to be.

So, she stared back at him and let him see her fierce spirit in her eyes. 'What happens is that you will take me up to your bed and you'll let me do whatever I want with you. And then in the morning, since it's only fair, you can do the same to me. And then after that, we'll start all over again.'

His smile widened and those silver-green eyes of his warmed, the green deepening, becoming less an arctic sea than a tropical one, making her catch her breath at his beauty. At the warmth of his smile and the scars that pulled at his skin, all melted and twisted and yet a part of him. She still didn't know why he had them, though she suspected, but they were beautiful too in their way, because they were part of him.

Again, this is dangerous. You shouldn't be thinking of him like that.

But she didn't know why it was dangerous to admire him, and she didn't want to think about it now. What she wanted was him and his smile, his beauty and his passion. She wanted the warrior in her to do battle with the warrior in him. A sensual battle full of pleasures she could only dream of.

'In that case, little maid,' he said softly. 'I think I can definitely accommodate you.'

Then she was caught up in his arms as he got to his feet and took her up to his bedroom. And as the afternoon descended into night, a fiery, hot, feverish night, one thing stayed stuck in her head. That this time she'd understood fully what she'd chosen downstairs in his arms, to have this moment, this night, with him.

And she had no regrets.

CHAPTER SEVEN

'No,' ARES SAID. 'Your hand needs to be like this.' He took Rose's small fist in his, extracted her thumb and tucked it over her clenched fingers, then he turned it so her knuckles were facing up. 'Then when you strike, you twist your arm like so.' He demonstrated, extending her arm, then turning it.

She watched him with unwavering focus, as if this was the most important thing she'd ever done, which was the way she approached most things, as he'd discovered.

They were in his gym at the manor, and he'd been teaching her some self-defence. He had a protection detail watching her in Paris, of course, but he'd thought it prudent to teach her how to defend herself. She'd been very keen to learn. In fact, she was very keen to learn about everything.

She was a quick learner too, never had to be told anything twice, and was stubborn when she didn't get it right the first time, trying and trying until she had it. The lessons he'd particularly enjoyed had been the ones he'd given her in bed, though after that first night, where he'd taught her all the ways in which to pleasure him, they'd discovered a few more things together and those had been particularly sweet.

He had to admit that he couldn't get enough of those lessons, as if all the long passionless years had created a need in him that couldn't be quenched by a couple of nights. Or even a couple of weeks. He was already wondering what he was going to do when her two weeks was up, and she went back to Paris. It would mean three months of celibacy for him and everything in him roared with denial at the thought of it.

Even right now, as she created the fist he'd taught her, that look of fierce concentration on her face, he could feel the burn of desire.

It's not just about desire, though, is it? You want to spend time with her.

He liked her, it was true, and he liked spending time with her. But this desire had nothing to do with that. It was completely and utterly physical.

Today Rose wore tight-fitting black yoga pants and a black athletic bra, her lush curves and golden skin on full display, and already he was imagining laying her down on the mat they stood on and pinning her there with his body, getting her to fight him until she finally surrendered in the most sensual of ways.

Maybe he would once he'd finished with their lesson. He didn't see why he couldn't indulge himself, not when she wanted it as badly as he did.

'Now,' he said. 'Punch me.' Her gaze flickered, a smile curving her mouth, and he grinned. 'Bloodthirsty, little maid. You don't need to look quite so pleased at the prospect.'

Her smile deepened and then her fist came out at speed. But he was still ex-Legion and he blocked it easily enough.

She sniffed, obviously dissatisfied with her performance. 'I want to try again.'

Ares released her fist. 'I've had years of experience at this, Rose. You've had all of an hour. You won't hit me if I don't want you to.'

She readied herself, elbows bent, her fists tight and drawn back at her sides. 'What experience? You were a soldier you said.'

'I was in the French Foreign Legion, spent years fighting in Africa.'

'Yes, I read about that. It's—'

'Not as romantic as it sounds,' he interrupted, because it hadn't been. War wasn't romantic. It was blood and desperation and fear and death, and there was nothing romantic about any of that. Not that it had been romance he'd wanted. He'd wanted escape from grief, pure and simple.

'Why?' She'd straightened a little, her curiosity caught. 'What made you join up?'

This was edging into territory he didn't want to get into, but it was inevitable the topic would rear its ugly head. And given that the purpose of these two weeks with each other was to get to know one another, it seemed churlish not to tell her. Besides, those years in the Legion where his life had boiled down to eating, sleeping, patrolling and obeying orders without question had been good years. Simple years. He hadn't had to think. His pain and suffering had only been physical, and he'd embraced it, pushing himself to his physical limits and beyond. He'd wanted to stay there for ever, but a bullet wound and difficulties with his burn injuries had prevented him.

'I joined because I wanted to test myself.' He reached for her fist again and adjusted it. 'My burns had healed but I wanted to get stronger, both physically and mentally, and the Legion seemed like a good fit.' Not exactly the truth, but not a lie either.

'What about the regular army?' Her gaze was on him as he adjusted her thumb. 'You were born in Greece, weren't you? So why didn't you go into the Greek army?'

'Because I didn't want to be in Greece. And the Legion takes men from every country.'

There was a crease between her brows. 'So why did you leave?'

'I was wounded in action in French Guiana and had some issues with the burn injuries, so that was my military career over.' The hospital there had been badly equipped and poorly staffed, and he'd suffered a post-surgical infection. They'd given him the last morphine they'd had, but that had been worse than the pain, causing him nightmares of burning buildings and hearing Naya calling for help, and him trying to batter down a door that wouldn't budge…

Your fault. Your failure.

He shoved the thought away and stepped back. 'Again.'

Rose's fist came out, faster this time, but still he blocked it easily.

She made an annoyed sound. 'So, is that when you started building your company?'

Another difficult subject. Still, he could give her some half-truths. 'I liked the Legion. Life was simple in it. And after I got out of hospital and realised my military career was over, I decided to recreate my own private military, so to speak.'

Rose was readying herself again, though her gaze was still fixed on him, curiosity burning bright in her beautiful eyes. 'Is that what Hercules Security is? I couldn't find much about it online.'

He grinned. 'You researched me?'

Colour stained her cheeks, which he found he liked very much. 'You're my husband and I didn't know anything about you. So yes, I looked.'

'You wouldn't have found much.'

'Hardly anything,' she agreed. 'Apart from Ares, God of War.'

He snorted. 'A stupid name. But no, there isn't much because my clients do not like publicity when it comes to military matters.'

'So…what do you do exactly?'

'We provide services to governments who cannot use their own military for various reasons, as well as helping out in times of civil unrest or natural disasters. There was an earthquake in China a month ago, for example, and I provided a team to help with digging survivors out of collapsed buildings.'

She frowned. 'But what does "services to governments" mean? Do you kill people they don't like or something?'

Anger shifted inside him at the note of censure in her voice and the hint of disapproval in her golden eyes.

He shouldn't let it get to him, but his company was Naya's memorial, her legacy, and she'd be proud of what he'd accomplished, all the people he'd helped. It was not for Rose to judge.

'No,' he said, more terse than he'd intended. 'There are times when governments cannot be seen to intervene in a country's problems but need to in order to protect people. We help rescue citizens, protect civilians and try to contain dictators. Protecting the innocent is our aim, so do not be so quick to judge.'

Rose scowled. 'Well, how was I to know any of that? All I have to go on are a few articles on the internet that don't say anything, because you don't talk about yourself.'

She has given an awful lot of herself to you, while you have given her nothing.

All his muscles had gone tight, and he was very conscious of a defensive anger that he didn't want coiling inside him, along with a deeper guilt that he also didn't want.

Mainly because it was true.

'I did not think you would be interested,' he lied, trying to ignore both the anger and the guilt, and failing. 'Why I built my company doesn't matter anyway.'

But she didn't back down, because of course she wouldn't. 'Of course I'm interested. You're my husband and I want to know about you. Wasn't that the whole point of spending two weeks with you every season?'

Ares scowled, the anger inside him gathering tighter and for no discernible reason. He didn't understand why his usually perfect control was frayed as old rope. So she'd got a little closer to the subject of Naya than he was comfortable with, and now she was pushing him harder for answers. So what? He could ignore it, couldn't he?

'My past is irrelevant,' he said curtly. 'For your purposes, all that matters is that my company makes me a lot of money. Money that you are enjoying right now.'

Sparks glittered in her eyes. 'I don't want your money, Ares. I never asked for it. I never asked for any of it, if you recall.'

But no, he wasn't having that. 'You did, though, little maid. Don't you remember? You asked for my help. You insisted that I marry you, and then agreed to my terms. I never forced anything on you.'

Some part of him was aware that the conversation had got out of hand somehow, and he didn't know how or why, but they were both angry and neither wanted to back down. And he suspected that it went deeper than what they were actually talking about, and that there was something they were both skirting around.

She is making you feel things again. She is making you remember what it was like to have a heart, and you do not like it.

But he didn't have a chance to think more about that because the bright little sparks in her eyes became embers, burning bright, and that was the only warning he got. Her fist came out like a shot, and she punched him squarely in the stomach.

He grunted and went back a step, muttering a curse in Greek because despite her size she was surprisingly strong and hadn't held back. He could have avoided the blow and he may well have blocked it, but he let her have the hit since part of him knew he deserved it.

'Look, I don't even know my mother, but even if I did, that's not a very nice thing to say about her,' she said accusingly, the colour in her cheeks blazing. 'You let me have that.'

He frowned, his attention caught. Had she understood the curse he'd muttered? 'Rose, do you speak Greek?'

'No,' she said. 'Why do you ask?'

'Because you understood what I said after you punched me.' And then he said it again for good measure.

A look of shock crossed her face. 'But I... I...we only spoke Russian in the compound. Where would I know Greek? How?' Her fists dropped. 'In Thailand you had a library and some of the books were in a language that looked familiar to me. I couldn't read them, though.'

Ares shoved aside his anger and the subject of Hercules and what he had and hadn't told her. 'Do you have any memories of your life before the compound?' he asked sharply. 'Any at all?'

Rose's anger had gone now too. She lifted a hand and rubbed at her temple. 'The only memory I have is of looking at some kittens in a shop.' She swallowed and then added, almost wonderingly, *'Gataki.'*

It was Greek for kitten.

A surge of an emotion Ares didn't recognise swept through him then, and he wasn't sure why it should matter to him that she must come from his own homeland, or had connections there at least, but it did.

'Perhaps you are Greek, *matia mou,*' he said softly.

Her gaze shifted to his, her big golden eyes wide with hope. 'Do you think?'

It wasn't until then that he understood how much the not knowing had affected her. She'd mentioned it a week ago, that first night beside the fire as they'd discussed a potential pregnancy, and she'd been worried about her family history. Yet that had only been the tip of the iceberg, he could see now. That hope in her eyes was desperate and he hadn't known, hadn't fully realised, just how desperate she was for her past.

That surge of emotion, inexplicable and powerful, tightened its grip, and before he even knew he was going to say it, he said like a vow, 'We will find out. I promise you, we will.'

Ares meant every word, she could see it in his gaze, hear it in his rasping stony voice. And he'd said 'we.' Not 'you' or even 'I.' It was a 'we,' as if she wasn't alone in this. As if they were going to find out together.

Her throat closed up, her anger at him and the relentless way he'd reminded her that she was the one who'd insisted on this marriage, that she hadn't had to do any of this, that the whole reason she was here and feeling all these big, complicated emotions about him was because of the choices she'd made, had drained away.

She'd shoved that unpleasant truth aside the instant he'd asked her whether she understood Greek. Because she'd understood his curse instinctively and had responded before she'd had a chance to think it through. Then the Greek word for kitten had just been sitting there in her brain, a thread of memory with it. Of kittens in a shop window and pleading with someone to let her stay there to watch them. And then a voice, a boy's, saying, 'Okay, but you have to stay right here. I won't be long.'

Greek. She might be Greek. And Ares was going to help her find out.

She tore her gaze away, her throat tight, a wave of intense emotion flooding through her so tangled she couldn't puzzle it out. Fear and hope and worry all twisted together, and the hard pinch of grief, and more she couldn't even begin to name.

Ares stepped forward and took her hands in his large, warm rough ones. 'Rose?' he said softly. 'It will be all right. We'll find out.'

She looked up at him, the hard knot of emotion pulling tight. 'What if it's terrible? What if I…have no one? What if my family is awful and I'm—'

'It will be all right,' he repeated, and it sounded like an order, as if whatever he willed, so it would be. 'We will deal with it when we get to that point, okay?'

Again, 'we' will deal with it.

Do you really want him involved with this?

She'd never expected him to help find out who she was. She'd thought she'd have to do it on her own. Except, as it turned out, now she had him. And not only his help, she understood, but his support too. Whatever she found about her family or where she came from, or anything else, it would be okay, because he would be there.

It shouldn't have made a difference and perhaps she shouldn't trust him with any of this, but...she did. She just did.

'You don't have to be part of this,' she said, giving him an out if he needed it. 'I'm sure you have other things to do.'

'I do,' he said, his hands so warm and reassuring around hers. 'But I always have other things to do. And you're my wife and this is important. So, yes, I do have to be part of this.' Amusement glinted unexpectedly in his eyes. 'Besides, I'm interested now. I want to know what kind of woman I married.'

She took a shaky breath. It was dangerous to allow him to see how afraid and yet hopeful she was about this, and maybe it would be better if she kept this part of herself hidden. Show no weakness. Don't be a victim.

He'll know. You can't hide from him.

No. He was too sharp, too perceptive, and even back in the compound, he'd seen right through her. He'd always had the ability to get under her skin. Perhaps that was why she'd asked him to help her in the first place.

Yet that was all beside the point. The real truth was that she didn't want to hide this from him. She *wanted* him to know how she felt. Because for the first time she *didn't* have to do this alone, she had someone to help her, someone to lean on…

Ares's gaze narrowed. 'What is it? There's something else you're worried about. I can see it in your eyes.'

She swallowed and looked at him squarely. 'What if the problem isn't them? What if the problem is me? What if I find out who my family is and they…?' The words stuck in her throat, that most secret fear hard to get out. But she forced herself to continue. 'What if we contact them and they…they don't want me? What if they don't want to know?'

His expression didn't change as per usual, but something in his silver-green eyes flared. 'Why would you think that?'

She couldn't look at him all of a sudden. She didn't want him to see the fear that gripped her. The terrible fear that had haunted her at nights sometimes when she couldn't sleep. When loneliness had set in and her future stretched out before her, a future that contained nothing but basic survival, years of being told what to do and cleaning rooms and being treated like dirt. Years of being trapped in the same place and never being able to leave, never being able to see the outside world. No hope. No dreams. Just endless loneliness.

The fear that no one would come for her, because no one had wanted her. She'd been abducted and trafficked, and her family had simply let her go. Intellectually she knew that might not be the case, that maybe her family had been searching for her all this time, but…how would she know? And, more importantly, when the time came to find out the truth, did she want to know it?

She stared down at his large, scarred hands and her own engulfed in them. His touch was warm, the strength in those hands reassuring. Strength enough to keep her safe and hold her together, warmth enough to chase away the cold loneliness that curled inside her even now.

'No one came for me, Ares,' she said, her voice gone nearly as raspy as his. 'And I know, perhaps they just couldn't find me. The traffickers hid their tracks well. But still, no one came. Some nights I used to wonder why that was, why I was just left there in the compound to rot.' She swallowed hard against the sudden lump in her throat. 'And I wonder sometimes if I'd done something wrong and this was a punishment. That I didn't deserve to be rescued.'

There was a moment of silence and in it she heard her own stupid, ridiculous voice, all hoarse with fear and pain. A victim's voice.

He must think her so pathetic. He was a warrior and he valued strength, and she wasn't being strong. She was being broken.

Rose jerked her hands from his abruptly and turned to go, unable to even be in the same room as him while she felt so small and weak. Yet she only took two steps before iron fingers wrapped around her upper arm and she found herself pulled up against his big, hard body.

Her back was to his chest, his heat burning through her sports bra and yoga pants as if they weren't even there. She strained at little against his grip, but then his other hand gripped her other arm, and she was held fast.

Her heartbeat thundered and there were tears in her eyes. She didn't want him to let her go, but she couldn't bear him to see her vulnerability. She thought she was fine with it, but she wasn't. It felt too raw and too painful.

But his grip only tightened, keeping her right where she was.

Then his mouth was near her ear, his warm breath on her skin, making her whole body burn with that desire, a heat that was always smouldering, ready to burst into flames at any moment.

'Listen to me,' he murmured. 'You were a child. You did not deserve to be abducted from the street and sold to the highest bidder. No child deserves that. No *person* deserves that. *None* of what happened to you was your fault.'

Rose closed her eyes, feeling tears start in them, which was silly. She didn't know why she was crying. She didn't know why what he said hurt, because it did hurt. 'Then why did it happen?' She sounded like a wounded bird, desperate and afraid, and she hated it, yet she couldn't seem to keep herself from speaking. 'Why did it happen to me?'

'Because it did.' His voice was harsh, a note of ferocity in it. 'Because sometimes bad things happen to people who do not deserve them. That's life. But that's not the end of the story, Rose, and that's *not* the end of yours. It's what you do after that matters. That's the only thing that matters. You endured and you survived, and you got out, and you did that all on your own.'

'No, I had you—'

'But you had to ask me first. You had to find the courage to ask a man you'd never met, a man with the most terrible scars, for help in a place where no one was your friend. Where even saying the words could get you a terrible punishment. And you found that courage, little maid. You took it in both hands, and you looked me in the eye, and you asked me.' His fingers tightened on her upper arms, just on the edge of pain. 'That's why I called you a warrior. Because it was a warrior I saw

that day. Not a victim. Not a servant. Not a girl someone left behind, a person that no one wanted. A woman
who knew her own worth and refused to play the hand
life had dealt her. A woman who was going to play her
own game, with her own rules.'

There was no hesitation in his voice. Only certainty.
As if he was stating facts and nothing more, and it made
her throat ache, made tears slide gently down her face.

'I don't want you to think that I'm weak,' she said
hoarsely. 'I don't want you to think I'm a victim. You're
so strong and I—'

'And you are too. I told you that.' Then, shockingly,
his teeth closed around one of the cords of her neck, the
gentle bite sending a shock wave of sensation through
her. 'So why don't you show me? Show me how strong
you are, little maid. Right here, right now.'

And he bit her again.

Rose shuddered, the heat already beginning to build
inside her, and that was better than this other feeling, this
intense, powerful, dizzying feeling that was coiling in
her heart. That had felt every single word he'd said and
had carved them into her soul. So she wouldn't forget.
Because if he saw that in her, then it must be true.

She *was* that warrior. And maybe it was time for her
to own it.

Except Ares let her go, the heat of his body at her back
vanishing, and she spun round in surprise.

He'd taken a couple of steps back and was staring at
her challengingly. Then he arched a brow. So, she came
at him, one fist flying out. His fingers closed around her
wrist yet again, but this time he pulled her into him, his
other hand grabbing her ponytail and holding onto it as
he took her mouth like the conqueror he was.

He was not holding back, she knew that immediately. Also, that he was expecting her to give as good as she got, so she did, kissing him back as if she owned him, as if he was hers and always had been.

Her teeth sunk into his bottom lip, and she bit him hard. He made a growling sound deep in his chest and then they were down on the mat, her on her back with him on top of her, a heavy weight pressing her down.

She loved the feeling, loved how he surrounded her and anchored her, making her feel safe and protected. Yet today she didn't need anchoring or protecting, today she wanted to be his match in every way, so she growled at him and shoved, and then they were turning over, with her on top and held astride him.

He sat up, pulling off her black sports bra with ease, while she clawed at the black T-shirt he wore. Then she pushed him onto his back again, her hands going to the athletic shorts he wore, trying to pull them down. He murmured a curse, and they were rolling over once more, him on top, his hands firm and strong as he tugged down her yoga pants and underwear.

She panted, writhing naked beneath him, his hands stroking and pinching and caressing, while she bit his shoulder and pulled at the waistband of his shorts. There was another curse and they rolled yet again, him on his back, her above, and the rest of his clothing gone. He was naked as she was, and her hands found the long, thick length of him. He was smooth and velvety and iron hard, and when she stroked him, he cursed yet again. She wanted to drive him as insane as he drove her, except she had no patience for that, not today. Instead, she gripped him and shifted her hips, letting him push inside her, the long, sweet slide of him making her shudder and shake.

Then his hands settled like brands on her skin, gripping her tight, showing her how to move with him, how to ride him to bring them both the greatest pleasure.

It was intoxicating, heady, to be astride this powerful man, to brace herself on his broad scarred chest, watch the flex and release of all those hard, carved muscles. Erotic too, to know that those muscles honed by violence could yet bring her the most intense pleasure.

His eyes were bright silver as they stared up at her, his face tense with hunger. The push and pull of him inside her was too much, too intense, and yet not enough.

'Ares,' she groaned, shaking. 'More.'

Again, they rolled, and then she was being pressed down hard into the mat as he lifted her legs up and around his waist, driving himself inside her, over and over again until the whole world was fire.

And she was exploding, melting, coming apart.

Until she was nothing but sparks drifting slowly in the air.

For a moment they lay like that together as they both caught their breath, and then Ares rolled them one last time, onto their sides, with her caught fast in his arms and held against his powerful body. Then he pressed a kiss into her hair. 'We can start searching for where you came from today,' he said. 'We don't have to wait.'

But Rose's chest clenched tight. It was good lying in his arms. Good just being with him and she wanted to enjoy it. They only had another week, and she didn't want to think about anything else.

'Can we do it later?' she asked him. 'I want to have this last week with only you.'

He said nothing, and when she glanced up at him, she met his gaze looking back. Something she couldn't name glinted in his eyes. 'You don't have to be afraid, Rose. I told you it would be all right and it will be.'

'I know. I just…don't want to think about that right now. We only have a week left and I'd rather spend it doing this.' And she lifted her hips for emphasis.

His mouth curved in one of his rare, precious warm smiles that made her heart flutter behind her ribs. 'In that case, it can wait. I am all yours.'

And for the whole of the next week, that's exactly what he was.

CHAPTER EIGHT

Winter

ARES STOOD ON the frozen lake that served as a helipad for the lakefront lodge in Iceland that he liked to retreat to during winter and watched as the helicopter bringing Rose from the airport touched down.

It was a still, clear night, the stars glittering in the black sky above like hard chips of diamond, the temperature well below freezing. Behind him was the lodge, all lit up and warmly welcoming so she wouldn't have to bear the freezing temperatures for too long. He'd hurry her inside, let her get settled and then he'd tell her what he'd found.

Her identity.

His staff had only brought him actual confirmation right before his jet had left the States where he'd been completing some business, so he hadn't had long to contemplate it. But it was good news and he wanted to be the one to bring it to her.

Since leaving the Cotswolds he'd put an entire department of his best people onto finding out Rose's identity. They didn't have much to go on—her general age and the possibility that she was Greek—but it was enough to start a search and he did have a lot of resources at his disposal.

His team had trawled police reports and found evidence of many missing girls in Greece around the time that Rose could potentially have been abducted, and one by one they'd dismissed them, apart from a couple.

Yet Ares knew there was only one possibility from that list: Ismena Xenakis, abducted as a child from the streets of Athens twenty years earlier.

The report had been filed by her older brother, Castor Xenakis, but nothing had ever been investigated.

Ares knew of a Castor Xenakis. He'd once been a notorious playboy known for his various shady criminal underworld connections who'd suddenly cleaned up his act, married a woman who'd once been a supermarket checkout girl—if the press could be believed—and was now a respectable family man.

It had to be the same Castor Xenakis who'd lost his sister. The name was too unusual. Further investigations had also revealed that Castor Xenakis had led a secret life infiltrating trafficking rings and passing the information on to relevant authorities, which virtually guaranteed him to be the same man.

Ares had debated contacting him, but then dismissed the idea. It wasn't his place. He had to bring the information to Rose first before anything else, because the conversation they'd had in the gym at the manor house had stuck in his head, as had the fear in her beautiful golden eyes. The fear that no one had looked for her because no one had wanted her. Even now the memory of the pain in her voice made his own chest tighten, though he didn't want to think about why that was.

What he was clear about was that she had to know she

wasn't alone. That she had an older brother, and that if he was the kind of man he was reputed to be, he hadn't stopped looking for her. That he'd been looking for her for the past twenty years.

The rotors slowed and Ares ducked beneath them, walking over to pull open the helicopter door. And felt something akin to an electric shock as he met Rose's bright gaze. She smiled, her lovely face lighting up at the sight of him, and that strange feeling in his chest, the one that had tightened in response to her pain, now tightened again in response to that smile.

You are getting emotionally involved with her.

No, he wasn't. He was pleased to see her because he liked her and felt empathetic towards her, but that was all. Certainly nothing more.

She was all wrapped up in the thick pale blue parka he'd had sent to her, a scarf and hat to match, plus gloves. She looked so beautiful he could barely hold himself back from reaching for her.

But then she flung off her headset and launched herself into his arms and her mouth was on his, making it very clear that she'd missed him.

You missed her too.

He tightened his arms around her and kissed her back hard. Yes, he had missed her. In his bed. Fifteen years of celibacy had never bothered him, yet the past three months without her had been agony. He'd been counting down the days until winter, until it was time for their two weeks, and once he'd told her about her brother, he was going to take her to bed and keep her there for days. Maybe even a whole week. After all, it was winter in Iceland and there wasn't much else to do.

The lodge staff were already hauling out her luggage,

so Ares lifted her from the helicopter himself, carrying her in his arms across the frozen lake, the chilly air bringing a flush to her cheeks.

'You don't need to carry me,' she protested, not making any attempt to dislodge herself from his grip. 'I can walk.'

'Very well.' He stopped, making a show of letting her down.

She laughed and wrapped her arms around his neck, snuggling into him. 'On second thoughts, it's too cold to walk.'

He grinned and resumed striding towards the lodge, feeling as if a weight had been pressing down on him and now that she was here it was gone. It made him feel ridiculously light.

She nestled against him, turning her face against the thick down jacket he'd pulled on to meet her, and they were both silent as he stepped from the ice to the small wooden jetty that projected into the lake, then went up some stone steps that led up to the lodge itself.

A large wooden deck fronted the lake, with big, sliding glass doors that led into the lodge's main living area. One of his staff pulled open the door for them and he stepped through into the warmth of the living area, the door pushed shut behind him.

He didn't want to let her go. He wanted to head straight up the stairs to the comfortable bedroom and big wooden bed and do all the things he'd been fantasising about for the past three months. But this news couldn't wait.

He let her down and then stepped back as the staff member who'd handled the door discreetly withdrew.

She pulled off her hat as the warmth of the room penetrated, her cheeks flushed and her golden eyes glittering. 'Were you disappointed?' she asked suddenly.

He didn't pretend he didn't know what she meant. 'That you weren't pregnant? No.'

She'd sent him an email a month after their time in the Cotswolds, letting him know that she hadn't ended up being pregnant. He'd told himself it was fine, that if she chose to stay with him, they'd have plenty of time to try for children, then had shoved all thoughts of pregnancy and the fact that this was the last two weeks he'd have with her before she made her choice out of his head.

They had more important things to discuss now.

'Are you sure?' she asked. 'I know you wanted—'

'The pregnancy conversation can wait, Rose,' he interrupted, impatient. 'I have something to tell you.'

She looked like she might say something more, but then clearly thinking better of it, merely raised an eyebrow. 'Oh?'

'I've found out who you are.'

Her face went white. 'What?'

He'd known it would be a shock, so he took a step forward, putting his hands on her hips to steady her. 'I know your real name, Rose.'

She stared up at him, golden eyes wide, as if she'd never seen him before her life.

'Your name is—'

She laid her fingers across his lips, silencing him. Her face was still pale, all the light and happiness she'd shown him in the helicopter gone as if it had never been, her fingertips a gentle pressure.

You fool. Did you really have to spring it on her like that? Especially given her reluctance to talk about it over the past three months.

He'd broached the topic several times in various emails about the search for her identity, letting her know that he had considerable resources and he could help if she wanted him to. She'd replied that yes, if he could help, that would be appreciated, but it was clear she hadn't expected him to discover the truth.

She took her hand from his mouth, then stepped away, moving over to the big open fire that stood at one end of the room. The flames burned brightly, firelight dancing over her pale face, reminding him of that night in the Cotswolds where he'd taken her in front of the fire there.

His body hardened, aware that it had been three months without her, and it was hungry for her.

He ignored it. Now was not the time.

'It's good news, Rose,' he said quietly. 'I think you'd like to hear it.'

There was another silence.

'So, you get to know everything about me, but I know nothing about you.' She unzipped her parka, staring down at the flames.

Ares frowned. 'You know about me. I told you—'

'You told me about you being in the Legion and that you'd lost your wife. That's it.' She pulled off her gloves, throwing them with a sudden, forceful movement onto the nearby couch. 'You know my real name, but I don't even know how you got burned.'

A whisper of the guilt and defensive anger he'd felt during their discussion in the gym, about his company, threaded through him once again. Guilt that he hadn't told her anything about himself and anger because he didn't want to.

Everything was so tangled up with Naya and he didn't discuss her with anyone.

Anyway, he was here with the truth of who she was, and he didn't understand why she didn't want to hear it, or why she was making this about him.

'This isn't about me,' he said. 'This is about you. Don't you want to know?'

She didn't turn, pulling off her hat and throwing it on the couch along with the gloves, a wealth of golden hair tumbling out. It was much longer now, to her waist.

'I don't like that you know more about me than I do about you,' she said, ignoring his question. 'You always did. Why is your past off limits and yet you feel free to pry into every aspect of mine?'

Ares gritted his teeth, his anger gaining a dull edge of disappointment. He'd thought she'd be happy about this. 'You told me you were fine with me helping you discover your origins. I asked you and you said yes.'

'I was fine with it.' She turned her head and glanced at him, her gaze brilliant with temper. 'But I didn't think you'd be the one to discover it first. And I didn't think that you'd have everything of me, while I had nothing of you.'

She's right. You have *given her nothing.*

Yes, but giving her something of himself assumed a relationship that they didn't have. A relationship that they would never have either.

You want it, though.

He ignored that.

'I told you back in England that my past is irrelevant,' he said curtly.

'Oh, and mine isn't?' Sparks glittered like embers from a wildfire in her eyes. 'Why do you get to hold onto your secrets? And anyway, it *is* relevant. The fact that you were married is relevant. The fact that half your body is scar tissue is relevant. What kind of marriage are we going to have if you can't even talk to me about it?'

She'd said it as if staying married to him was a fore-gone conclusion and not a choice she had yet to make, and it made something inside him lurch like he'd missed a step going up a staircase.

He'd thought he wouldn't care if she chose to stay married to him or not. But he did care. He cared very much, and he shouldn't.

'But that is not a foregone conclusion, is it, Rose?' he bit out. 'The year is not yet up. You might not choose to stay married to me.'

Her cheeks were already pink, but he didn't miss how they went a little pinker, as if she'd made a slip she hadn't meant to. 'It's true, I might not,' she agreed. 'But you could give me a reason to stay.'

'I didn't realise that mattered to you,' he said roughly.

'What? Getting to know each other?' One blond brow rose imperiously. 'Not initially, no. But then you went on and on about how important it was that we got com-fortable with each other, how I had to learn what being a wife meant, and blah, blah, blah. So I changed my mind. And yes, it does matter to me. You made it matter with your big song and dance.'

She was angry. He stared at her, trying to see what the real issue was. 'Rose—'

'Tell me, Ares,' she said flatly. 'Tell me what hap-pened to you.'

That is *the real issue. You know everything about her, and she knows nothing about you, and that isn't fair. And besides, since when did it become a big secret?*

It wasn't a big secret. It had never been before, even though he didn't talk about it with anyone, so why was he so reluctant? Yes, she'd probably blame him the way he blamed himself, but what of it? He wasn't supposed to care about anyone's opinion anyway, let alone hers.

It was a small thing to give her, and after all, it was an old grief. He could just tell her and be done, and then the subject would be behind them. She wouldn't ask again.

'Fine,' he said harshly. 'What happened to me? The village I grew up in was full of factions and old feuds. People fighting each other. One of the more powerful groups started demanding protection money from people, but I refused to pay. Naya and I hadn't been married long and I was…very proud. The Aristiades name meant strength and I didn't want to look weak or cowardly in front of her. I thought I could protect her, but… They came in the night, with petrol bombs. Our house went up in flames.' He couldn't remember much about the actual fire, the only mercy he'd been given. 'I had been out with my father, helping him with some livestock, and when I got home the whole place was alight. I went in to rescue Naya, but the flames were too fierce. A beam fell on me, and my father had to drag me out. I spent a couple of years recovering from the burns.'

You failed her. It was your fault.

Oh, he knew that. He knew that all too well. The pain from his burns had faded, but the guilt in his heart never had. It was his punishment to always feel it.

Rose was staring at him, her eyes wide, a terrible sympathy glittering in them.

He had to force the words out, but he managed it. 'Naya died because of me.'

The fire was warm at Rose's back, the heat of the lodge's living room warming her through. Yet it felt as if she'd plunged through the ice of the frozen lake outside and into the water beneath it.

Cold shock swept through her, the fire making no difference to the chill that found its way deep into her bones.

He'd lost his wife in a terrible way and somehow blamed himself for it.

He stood not far from her, dressed for the cold in a thick black parka, and the expression on his face was so hard he may as well have been carved from the granite of the mountains surrounding the lodge. There was no deep green in his gaze now, or sparks of glittering silver. They looked dark as the night outside.

And she was conscious of a tearing grief inside her, for him and what he'd lost, and it was all she could do to shove it aside, but she managed it. This wasn't about her pain, this was about his.

You should never have forced this from him.

She swallowed past the lump in her throat. She'd known pushing him to tell her his secrets wasn't fair, that it wouldn't be a pleasant story, but she'd never dreamed it would be so awful.

Tears prickled behind her eyes, and she had to look away, blinking fiercely. She didn't know what to say, everything seemed so inadequate, even an apology.

Still, she gave it to him anyway. 'I'm sorry,' she said huskily, all the anger and fear that had filled her when he'd told her he knew who she was draining away. 'I didn't know.'

'Of course you didn't know.' His voice was even more raspy than it normally was. 'I didn't tell you.'

'I'm sorry,' she said again, uselessly. 'I only wanted—'

'She went to sleep and never woke up,' Ares interrupted as if she hadn't spoken. 'That's what they told me. Smoke inhalation.' He sounded as icy as the lake outside, as if the terrible facts didn't touch him. 'It was years ago. I have moved past it now.'

Her breath shuddered in and out, the pain sitting just behind her ribs an ache she didn't know what to do with. She blinked her tears back fiercely and forced her gaze back to his, because it was cowardly to look away, to not even be brave enough to witness his pain.

And no matter what he'd said about moving past it, she could still hear that pain. His voice might be cold and his expression hard and set, but she could hear agony in the roughened, frayed timbre of his voice. She could see it in the darkness of his eyes. His physical wounds had healed, leaving him with terrible scars, but this hurt went soul-deep. And it had scarred him inside just as deeply as he'd been scarred on the outside.

She wanted to put her arms around him, comfort him, but he was radiating tension and she knew instinctively he wouldn't welcome it. So, she pushed her hands into the pockets of her parka, and said, 'You…shouldn't blame yourself, Ares.'

'Should I not?' Each word sounded as if it had been carved from ice. 'What I should have done was pay them. But I was too proud. I did not want to look like a coward.'

'But you weren't the one with the petrol bombs—'

'No,' he said flatly, a muscle flicking in his hard jaw, the light making jagged shadows with his scars. 'No, we will not talk about this. I want to tell you what I found out about you.'

Her heart ached, fear seeping through her again.

This wasn't how she'd wanted her final two weeks with him to go. She'd wanted it to be like it had been in England, in his bed, in his arms. Spending time with him, learning how to defend herself, or watching all the movies she'd missed out on. Rambling in the woods. Lying in the huge claw-foot bath that was big enough to accommodate both of them, while his hands roamed lazily over her, relating new things she'd found out or discussing the latest scientific advances, which she'd discovered quite an interest in. She'd loved those days. She'd loved talking to him. He was fiercely intelligent and quick, and sometimes she argued with him purely because she loved doing that too.

She'd been looking forward to seeing him so much that the past three months had felt like they'd dragged. She hadn't been able to stop thinking about him. She'd even been surprisingly disappointed when her period had arrived, though she wasn't sure why when she hadn't wanted to be pregnant.

She'd wanted to discuss that now too, and not think about the wild leap of her heart the moment the helicopter door had opened, and his silver-green eyes had met hers. Or the pure joy that had filled her as he'd pulled her out of the helicopter and carried her over the ice, the frigid wind biting at her nose.

Those things she could examine later, but in this moment, it was the thrill of his presence that she'd wanted. And then he'd told her he'd discovered who she was and all of that had disappeared in a flood of cold shock, followed by an irrational anger.

That she knew her anger was defensive didn't help, because she also knew what lay underneath it: fear. Now the moment of truth was here, and she'd been a coward. And she'd turned that fear back on him. It wasn't fair of her. It wasn't right.

She'd spoiled things.

Her hands clenched tight in the pockets of her parka, and she wanted to apologise for that as well, but that was all about her own insecurities and the time wasn't right for them now, so she ignored the apologies sitting on her tongue. Ignored the flicker of selfish hurt that he didn't want to share his grief with her, even though she knew she had no right to it.

Instead, she braced herself and said, 'Okay. Tell me then.'

'Your name is Ismena Xenakis and you were born in Athens. Your mother appears to be dead, your father unknown. But you have an older brother. His name is Castor Xenakis. He's CEO of CX Enterprises, a multi-billion-dollar company dealing in all kinds of different industries. He is married and has one child.'

'Okay, Izzy. You can look at the kittens,' he'd said, already turning away to the shop next door. 'But you have to stay right here while I get the ice creams. Don't move. I won't be long...'

The kittens had been so cute, and she'd done as she was told, staying right where Cas had said. But then she'd seen another kitten across the street, so small and lost-looking. Cas had been gone a long time, and she'd got tired of waiting. The kitten had needed someone to look after it, and so she'd crossed the street and...

Her heartbeat thudded hard in her head, her skull aching. There was bile at the back of her throat.

She'd bent to pick up the kitten and someone had grabbed her from behind. She'd been so shocked she hadn't made a sound. A bag had been put over her head and she'd been bundled under someone's arm only to be tossed onto something hard. Then a door had slammed

*shut and she'd felt movement. It had been only then that
she'd screamed.*

*By then it had been too late... It had been far, far
too late.*

Rose took a breath and then another, and then Ares's
hand was at her hip, guiding her to sit on the long, low,
black leather sofa.

Her brother. Castor. She couldn't remember his face,
couldn't remember anything about him except a feeling of safety and warmth whenever he was near. And
his voice, newly deepening into a man's, telling her to
stay put.

But you didn't, did you?

She shut her eyes against painful tears, swallowing
the sob in her throat.

'He has spent the past twenty years looking for you,'
Ares went on relentlessly. 'I had several contacts confirm
that he was involved in infiltrating trafficking rings and
passing information on to the authorities, and I can only
assume he was doing that in order to find you. I also have
it on good authority that now he uses his many private
residences as safe houses for women with nowhere to go
and no one to turn to.'

She swallowed again, but that sob wouldn't go away.

Ares didn't touch her, but she wanted him to. She
wanted his strong arms around her, to turn her face into
his chest, press herself against all his reassuring heat.
Because she felt weak and needed his strength.

But he wasn't touching her, and she knew it was because of what she'd said to him. Because of the confession she'd forced from him when he hadn't been ready
for it, uncovering a grief that went too deep.

So, who was she to cry over the discovery of her true

name and a brother she'd forgotten? A brother who'd never stopped looking for even after all these years. Who was she to be upset about finding a family, when he'd lost his wife so terribly? A loss he blamed himself for.

Forcing down the sobs and fiercely blinking back her tears, she lifted her head. Ares was standing next to the couch, his hands in the pockets of his jeans. His face wore its customary granite expression, but anger glittered in his eyes. And, well, he had a right to it, didn't he?

He wasn't there to reassure her, not that she deserved it anyway. Not after what she'd made him confess.

'Th-thank you,' she forced out. 'For finding all that out for me. I appreciate it.'

The hard expression on his face didn't change. 'Do you? Didn't seem like you were all that grateful just before.'

'I… I know. I was just…afraid.' Her jaw ached with the effort of holding back the sobs. 'But I'm fine now and, really, I am grateful, Ares. It's just…a lot.' She pushed herself to her feet, needing suddenly to be alone so she could weep in private. She didn't want to put her grief and fear and apprehension about what he'd just told her onto him. 'I need…to go and freshen up. Is my room up the stairs? You don't have to show me, I can find it myself.'

That muscle in his jaw leapt again. 'There is only one bedroom in the main house. We are sharing it.'

Her stomach tightened. So he'd expected that she would be sleeping with him. Ten minutes earlier she'd have been ecstatic. Now all she wanted was some space.

'Okay,' she said thickly. 'That's fine. Is it upstairs?'

He nodded and gestured towards the stairs. He didn't

offer to show her where it was. Apparently, they both needed space.

A set of wooden stairs led up to the upper level of the lodge, where there was a huge bedroom and an equally huge bathroom. Her luggage had been put at the foot of the giant four-poster bed in the bedroom. The bed faced windows that looked out over the lake. It had a smooth, rustic wooden floor covered with rugs and plain white walls, the bed with its giant posts and white linen hangings the centrepiece of the room.

She sat on the edge of it and allowed herself a few moments to weep, her emotions so tangled and twisted she didn't even know why she was crying.

Her name was Ismena Xenakis and she had a brother. A brother who'd been looking for her all this time.

She hadn't been forgotten. And she wasn't alone.

Ares found this for you. He discovered it.

Tears slid slowly down her cheeks, and she didn't bother to wipe them away. Her chest ached with grief and fear and hope and guilt. Grief for the years lost and fear that her brother wouldn't want to see her. Hope that he would, and she would find him again. Guilt for not doing what he'd said on that street so long ago. Guilt for not staying and watching those kittens, because perhaps if she'd done what she'd been told, she wouldn't have been taken.

And beneath all of that lay a deeper ache. For Ares and what he'd told her and where that left them.

Why does he matter so much? You're married to him, but you're not really his wife, are you? You forced him to marry you. He would never have chosen you.

All of that was true, and she didn't know why he'd come to matter to her so much. It was only that he'd been kind to her. No, not just kind; he'd made her feel like she was more than an abducted girl sold to be a servant in a rich man's house. A powerless victim of human trafficking. He'd given her freedom and helped her make a life for herself, and over the past few months as she'd worked at the cafe, little daydreams of having a family of her own, a family with him, had danced in her head.

She hadn't realised she'd even wanted that until she'd discovered she wasn't pregnant, after all. And had been so oddly disappointed.

Nine months ago, in Thailand, she'd thought she'd never want to stay being his wife. Now…it was different.

It's different because of him. Because you're falling for him.

No, of course she wasn't falling for him. That would be stupid in the extreme, and anyway, she'd never fallen for anyone before so how would she even know if she had?

And apart from all of that, he'd be the worst person to fall for since it was clear he was still grieving his first wife. He might say he'd moved on, but a man of such intense passions didn't move on so easily.

Rose scrubbed her tears away. There was no point in thinking about her feelings for Ares, no matter what they were. She wasn't even sure she was going to choose to stay married to him, and even if she did, she didn't know if he'd want that too. Because it was his choice as well, not just hers.

Regardless, she needed to stop thinking about her feelings and concentrate on the most immediate issue, which was the fact that she now had an identity. She could contact her brother to let him know she was alive.

Except, before that, if she wanted to have the two

weeks she'd initially planned, she was going to have to make things right with Ares. She'd apologised for how she'd pushed him, and then she'd thanked him for finding Castor. She couldn't keep on doing both so perhaps the best way forward was to put the tension of what had happened just before aside and carry on as if it hadn't happened.

She wouldn't mention his wife again. She'd leave it up to him if he wanted to talk about it. Then with any luck they could go back to what they'd had in the Cotswolds, that warm intimacy, along with all the physical affection too.

In fact, maybe she should have a shower, then put on the pretty dress she'd spent some of her savings on, the one the sales assistant had assured her would drive her husband mad with desire. Then she'd show him exactly how much she'd missed him.

Pushing herself off the bed, Rose scrubbed away the last of her tears, then strode decisively into the bathroom and turned on the shower.

CHAPTER NINE

ARES STOOD IN front of the fire and knocked back the rest of the very good vodka he'd poured himself, hoping the icy burn of the alcohol would cool the anger that coiled like a dragon inside him.

He'd been petty with Rose, and he knew it. He'd let his anger get the better of him, and that was not permitted. Another example of him not learning the lessons the past had taught him.

He didn't know how she'd got beneath his defences, but she had, and it was clear to him that he had to stop her from getting any further beneath them. Somehow.

So what if the sympathy in her face and the glitter of grief in her eyes had tugged at something painful inside him even though he hadn't wanted it to? So what if she'd told him that he didn't need to blame himself? She was wrong. She was just wrong.

And he wasn't supposed to care. Yet he'd been angry at having to tell her about Naya, and that anger, both at her and with himself, had made him petty, refusing to comfort her distress as he'd told her about her brother. He hadn't even put his arms around her.

You didn't have to tell her about Naya. That was your choice. It's not fair to take it out on her.

Ares put his empty tumbler on the mantelpiece and stared down into the flames.

It was true, he couldn't say she'd forced him. He'd made the decision to tell her, and it was his own misjudgement that he'd kept it a secret in the first place. Turning it all into a big deal. That was hardly Rose's fault.

He let out a breath, rubbing at his brow. He should apologise, especially if he wanted these next two weeks to be as blissful as the last couple in the Cotswolds had been. She'd been distressed and him not doing anything to ease her or comfort her had been cruel, and yes, very petty.

Ares turned from the fire, intending on going upstairs to find her, then froze.

Rose was standing in the doorway. She wore a crimson silk dress with a deep vee neckline and little straps, cut on the bias to hug every one of her generous curves. The colour made her golden skin glow and brought out the sparks in her eyes, her hair a golden halo around her head.

She looked stunningly beautiful.

His body hardened instantly, the weight of the past three months of celibacy descending on him like an anvil. All he wanted was to stride over to her, shove her against a wall and rip her dress away, pour all this sullen anger into her until ecstasy carried it all away.

But he stayed where he was, tense with the effort of mastering himself, because he had an apology to make.

She gave him an uncertain smile. 'Do you like my dress? I wasn't sure about it, but the saleswoman said my husband would love it.'

Her husband. Him.

It hit him hard right then. He'd had no issues with thinking about her as his wife, but for some reason, thinking of himself as her husband hadn't occurred to him. But he was.

And will you fail her like you failed Naya?

A shiver of an emotion he couldn't identify went through him, chilling him.

He ignored it. 'Your dress is beautiful,' he murmured, letting her see the appreciation in his eyes. 'And so are you.'

She flushed, looking pleased. 'Thank you.'

'I hope you let me pay for that.'

'No.' A little spark glittered in her eyes, a hint of challenge that went straight to his groin. 'I used my own money.'

Part of him wanted to argue with her about it, challenge her the way she challenged him, and then finish their argument in the way they both loved so much: in bed.

But that could wait.

He held her gaze. 'I owe you an apology, Rose.'

Her eyes widened. 'Oh?'

For a second, he wondered if she'd even picked up on his anger earlier. She hadn't reached for him when he'd told her the name of her brother, after all. She hadn't even looked at him, keeping her attention squarely on her hands.

But even if she hadn't realised, he still wanted her to know he was sorry for it.

'You were upset,' he said. 'And I didn't help.'

Her long, thick golden lashes lowered, veiling her gaze. 'It's fine.'

'It isn't fine. I should have been there for you, and I

wasn't, because I was angry. It was petty and unfair of me.' The words were surprisingly easy to say.

'It wasn't unfair.' She smoothed her dress. 'I shouldn't have pushed you about…' She stopped, her hands still moving nervously on the fabric.

She was upset, he could hear it in her voice, and before he knew what he was doing, he'd closed the distance between them, going to where she stood in the doorway and reaching for her. His hands found her hips, the fabric of her dress warm against his skin, and he tugged her close. She didn't resist, her nervous fingers resting at last on his chest, and she looked up at him, something that looked like guilt in her eyes.

'I'm sorry,' she said before he could speak. 'I shouldn't have made you talk about your wife. I didn't mean to hurt you. I just wanted to know you better and I shouldn't have pushed.'

'Again, you didn't know.' He tightened his hands on her hips, the warmth of her seeping into him, familiar and yet new, making him want to do so many different things to her. Things he'd been dreaming about since those two weeks in the Cotswolds. 'And you were right to push. It's not a secret and it's not fair of me to keep it like one. Besides, you didn't force me. I chose to tell you in the end.'

Her big golden eyes were full of sympathy and a compassion that made his heart ache for reasons he couldn't have articulated. Especially when neither sympathy nor compassion was what he wanted.

Not when you don't deserve it.

Ah, but he knew that. He'd always known that.

'You don't have to tell me anything more,' she said with quiet finality. 'I'll never mention it again.'

It was what he wanted. His wife existing only in his memory, in his conscience, in the company he'd built to honour her, the only evidence of his failure the scars on his face. After all, he wasn't going to make those same mistakes again.

He'd allowed his pride and his anger to talk him into thinking he was strong enough to protect the woman he loved, and he hadn't thought through the consequences.

His emotions had blinded him; he couldn't trust them to guide him properly, only the memory of his wife could do that.

Sex, though, that was only physical, and he could allow himself that.

He bent his head and kissed her upturned mouth, let the sweet taste of her fill his senses as he explored her. She gave the most delicious shiver and melted against him, her pliant body pressed the length of his. He adjusted her hips, settling the heat between her thighs against the growing hardness of his groin, and he heard her give a little moan.

He dropped one hand from her hip, finding the hem of her dress and sliding his palm beneath it to the silky skin of her thigh. She felt so warm and her mouth beneath his was so hot.

But what about her? What about what she deserves?

The strange chill that had crept through him before did so again, deepening this time, so that even through the heat of their kiss and the warmth of her skin, he felt it.

She deserved all the things she'd never had, all the things that had been denied her as a prisoner. And if she chose to stay, he would give them to her. Freedom to go anywhere, do anything. Money to buy whatever she wanted or donate to charity if she preferred. Passion to keep her hunger satisfied and support to help her branch out into whichever career she wanted to satisfy her intellect.

That's not all she deserves.

His heartbeat was far too loud and the chill creeping through him was getting wider and deeper. He kissed her harder, pushing her up against the wall and pressing himself against her, wanting her heat to chase it away.

She was rocking against him, trying to ease her own need, her fingers curled in his shirt. Kissing him back so hungrily and so desperately.

Yet all the hunger and the desperation in the world wasn't a match for the ice that wrapped itself around his heart, and before he knew what he was doing, he'd pushed himself away from her.

Her eyes were wide, her cheeks flushed with the effects of their kiss. She blinked. 'Ares? What's wrong?'

He took a breath, fighting his growing sense of disquiet.

That all the things he wanted to give her wouldn't ever be enough. That she should have more than that, that she *deserved* more than that.

She deserves to be treated as a true wife should. With love.

He turned away from her suddenly, striding back to fire and grabbing the tumbler off the mantelpiece. He went over to the drinks cabinet where the vodka bottle sat and opened it, splashing some more into the glass.

'Ares?' Rose's voice was full of uncertainty.

He took a swallow of the vodka and glanced over to where she stood. She looked half ravaged; her pretty mouth was full and red from his kiss, a flush creeping down her golden skin and under the creased silk of her dress.

Theos, how he wanted her. Had he wanted Naya this badly? He couldn't remember.

You know it's true. You know that's what you should give her.

He didn't want to acknowledge it, not any part of it, but it crept through his brain all the same. Somehow, at some point in this past year, the heart he'd thought had died with Naya had started beating again, and Rose was the one who'd restarted it.

And now she mattered to him, which was not what he'd wanted or planned for.

His heart was supposed to stay dead along with his wife.

But he could feel the pull inside him towards her, the need to cross the distance between them once again, to have the pleasure of her silken skin beneath his hands, and the hot clasp of her sex around his. Her breath in his ear and her touch on his body. And it wasn't just physical, because if it had been, any woman would have satisfied him right then.

But he didn't want just any woman.

He wanted her and her alone. And he had from the first moment he'd met her.

But why should you be allowed to have her? You had a woman once before, remember? And you killed her. You do not deserve a second chance.

'Ares?' Rose was closer now, the firelight gilding her gorgeous figure. 'What's the matter? Did I do something I shouldn't?'

'No,' he said roughly. 'Tell me, what are you going to do about your brother?'

The change of subject was so sudden Rose just stared at him. She was still trembling from the effects of that kiss, her mouth hot and sensitive, the place on her thigh where he'd touched her burning. She wanted more of that, more of his hunger meshing perfectly with hers, not this anger. Because that's what it looked like to her. He was angry and she didn't know why.

When she'd appeared in the doorway and he'd turned from the fire, the look in his eyes flaring silver, she'd thought their earlier tension had been put behind them. Then he'd shocked her with an apology before kissing her and every thought had vanished from her head. She'd thought they were okay, that they'd gone back to what they'd had back in the Cotswolds…

Until he'd pushed himself suddenly away from her.

It didn't make any sense. Had it been her? Had she done something wrong? Had he had second thoughts? What?

'My brother,' she echoed, the words not making any sense to her immediately.

'Yes, Castor Xenakis.' Ares sounded impatient now. 'You need to contact him.'

Rose struggled to process what he was talking about, her head still wrapped around his kiss. Then it penetrated.

Her brother. Whom Ares had found. Castor Xenakis.

She took a breath. 'Oh, I… Yes, I will contact him.'

'Tonight,' Ares said flatly. 'You need to tell him to-night.'

She swallowed, studying his face, trying to see what his issue was and why he was suddenly being so ada-mant. 'Actually, I thought I'd wait a little bit,' she said carefully. 'I still haven't got my head around—'

'He's been waiting to find you for twenty years. Don't you think he'd want to know that you're alive?'

'Yes, but if he's waited twenty years, he can wait an-other few hours.' She stared at him. 'Why are you so angry? What is this about, Ares?'

He turned away, lifting his tumbler and draining it. Then he went over to the drinks cabinet and poured himself another measure. He did not look at her.

'You're wrong,' he said after a moment, his attention on his glass. 'I do blame myself.'

'Blame yourself?' she echoed, trying to follow the sudden change in topic. 'Blame yourself for what?'

'Naya's death.' He picked up the glass and stared down into it, as if the liquid contained all the secrets of the universe. 'My father was so proud of the Aristiades line. He always said that we were descended from the great hero Hercules and that's why we were so strong. I shared his pride, thought that the Aristiades name made us better than everyone else. So, when this beautiful daughter of a Russian oligarch agreed to be my wife, even though I had no money and only a mountain hut for her to live in, I was even prouder. Being a penniless shepherd in the mountains is a hard life, and she was everything I'd never had—softness and beauty and compassion. I loved her to distraction. I was always afraid she might discover one day that she'd made a terrible mistake in marrying this poor Greek shepherd boy... Anyway, when Stavros demanded protection money, I refused.' He gave a low, bitter laugh. 'I didn't want her to think that I was a coward, that I was weak. I was an Aristiades and we were the blood of Hercules.'

Rose went cold. He was talking about his wife.

'The night of the fire, I wasn't there,' Ares went on. 'I was helping my father with a ewe having a difficult birth and so they didn't find me until the house was well alight. It was a mountain village—we didn't have a fire engine, only hoses and buckets, so by the time I got there, it was too late. I went in anyway, because I was supposed to be strong enough to protect her, save her, but...' He stopped, then raised his tumbler and downed what was left in there. 'I didn't think the consequences would have been so terrible. She should never have married me. She should have stayed well away.'

The chill had reached her bones now, and was working its way into her heart, that grief she'd felt earlier shredding her emotions once again.

She could see him as a young man, full of youthful pride and arrogance. Yet that wasn't a sin. That was just youth, the feeling of being bulletproof, that nothing bad could ever happen to you because nothing ever had.

It wasn't a feeling she'd ever had. That had been taken from her, just as his had been taken from him. And it had been taken. It wasn't his fault that some awful people had chosen to firebomb his house and he shouldn't think that it was. Yet before she could say anything, he went on.

'I was two years recovering from the burns. People kept telling me how lucky I was to be alive, but I didn't feel lucky. I should have died with her. That would have been a just punishment, I think.' He reached for the bottle again and then stopped, his hand dropping as if he'd had second thoughts. He still didn't look at her. 'Afterwards, when I'd healed, I went straight into the Legion, because that's when I decided that if I had to live, I'd do things differently. I'd let my pride and my arrogance, and my anger, blind me, and so I had to get rid of them. They'd led me astray, they'd caused Naya's death, and so they couldn't be trusted.'

Rose's heart ached at the emptiness in his voice, the sheer lack of expression in it. He sounded so bleak it brought tears to her eyes.

'Ares...' she began hoarsely, wanting to say something, to give him some comfort any way she could.

But he gave a sharp shake of his head. 'Let me finish.'

He reached for the bottle again and poured himself yet another glass, smaller this time. Then he raised and took a small, careful sip, as if he was rationing it. 'After the Legion, I was adrift for a time. The only thing I had left was Naya's memory. That's what made me build my company. I wanted to do something in her name, create a legacy for her. A company that she would have been proud to be associated with. She became my conscience, my guide. Everything I do, I do for her.' He glanced at her then, his gaze darker than she'd ever seen it. 'My father died a few years back and he made me promise that the Aristiades line would not die with me. I promised him it would not. I also promised Naya when we married that we would have a houseful of children, because she was desperate for them.

'That's why I agreed to marry you, Rose. That's why our marriage was to include children. To fulfil my promise to my father and to Naya. But that's all. If you choose to stay with me, that's all our marriage will ever be, do you understand?'

Her throat felt thick and tight, her vision swimming with tears of pain for him. And from somewhere she dredged up her voice. 'You can't blame yourself for any of that, Ares. It's not your fault—'

'Do you understand?' he repeated over the top of her, his eyes darkening into black in the firelight. 'If you want to stay with me, our marriage will only be for heirs, Rose. For the promises I made. That is all. You cannot mean anything to me. You cannot be important to me. I will give you nothing. All I have left is this—' he glanced down at himself and shook his head '—empty shell, scarred with the reminders of my failure. That is what you will be married to. That is all I can offer.'

Rose felt as if the winter from outside had come in

through the windows and was now creeping around her heart, freezing it solid. There was no doubt in those darkened eyes of his, no doubt in his voice either.

'You didn't kill her,' she said hoarsely, because she had to at least attempt to convince him. 'A petrol bomb did. Smoke inhalation did. Not you.'

His gaze didn't waver. 'If I hadn't loved her, I wouldn't have wanted to prove myself to her. If I hadn't been so obsessed with keeping her, I would have paid the money. If I hadn't loved her, she wouldn't have married me in the first place and then she wouldn't have died.'

'Something else might have killed her, you don't know. You can't keep playing "what-ifs" for ever, Ares.' She swallowed past the giant lump that had risen in her throat. 'If I'd stayed put and watched the kittens, if I hadn't seen another kitten in the street and gone to pick it up, perhaps then I wouldn't have been abducted. But I was. Second-guessing won't change that.'

'You're right.' His face was impassive. 'Yet my wife is still dead, and it is still my fault.'

'And it's still my fault I didn't do what I was told. It was my fault I got abducted.'

Finally, the darkness in his eyes shifted, a flickering silver flame glittering there instead. 'That is not what I said.'

'But it's the same thing, isn't it?' She didn't back down. He had to see what he was saying, he had to. 'You should have paid that money and you didn't, so it's your fault. I should have stayed where I was and I didn't, so that's my fault too.'

A muscle flicked in his jaw. 'You were a child. You were—'

'You were young,' she interrupted. 'You thought nothing could touch you. That's not a crime. Loving some-one and wanting to prove yourself to them isn't a crime either. Besides, she loved you too. Or does her choice not matter?'

He only shook his head and said harshly, 'She chose wrong.'

She opened her mouth to argue yet again and then stopped. And looked into his eyes, seeing the silver flames flickering there. Anger, yes, but she could see the grief too. A grief that was still there no matter what he said about getting rid of his emotions.

A grief that unlike his scars had never healed.

You cannot argue with him. You cannot push him. Not about this, not if you care about him.

No, she couldn't, and more, she didn't want to. Be-cause it was true, she did care about him. And it felt as if it was something that had been sitting inside her all along, right from the first moment he'd walked into the room as she was cleaning it. And instead of ignoring her or touching her or even talking to her, he'd sat quietly down in the chair by the fire. He hadn't said a word and she hadn't looked at him, her heart beating so fast with fear, the way it did whenever a guest was around. He hadn't moved or spoken. He'd sat there like a rock, un-moving. And gradually over the course of that first day, she'd begun to realise that he wasn't going to talk to her or reach for her or do any of the things the other guests did. All he was going to do was sit there, watching her. As if he was fascinated and couldn't take his eyes off her.

She'd asked to him to rescue her because he'd felt like someone who would, and she hadn't been disappointed. And over these past few months, as she'd got to know him, she'd come to see that he was a protective man. A man who had kindness in him and generosity, and humour too. A man she could rely on, who would support her and who sparked her passion like no one else. A man who made her feel strong and brave, as if she was the woman she'd always wanted to be.

It wasn't that he didn't feel, that wasn't his problem; she could see that now.

It was that he felt too much; he was still mired in his grief. Living not for himself, but for the woman he'd loved and lost, and who surely wouldn't want to see the agony he was putting himself through.

He stood now beside the fire, the golden light gilding the harsh, scarred lines of his face, somehow making beauty out of the twisted, gouged and roughened flesh. Scars he'd earned trying to save someone he'd loved, because that's the kind of man he was. They weren't signs of the depth of his failure. They were signs of the depth of his love.

And it was in that moment that it hit her, looking at those signs, those terrible, beautiful scars, that she realised she wanted that love too. She wanted his love.

Because it was true the thought that had whispered to her upstairs. She *was* falling for him—or rather, she'd already fallen. And there was no saving her.

She loved him. She loved him completely and utterly without reservation, and while it was probably selfish of her, she wanted him to love her back.

But why should he? You're a silly little girl that didn't do what her big brother told her and got herself abducted? Why should he put aside his grief for the wife he lost for someone like you?

He wouldn't and she would never ask him to. Why make this any harder for him than it needed to be?

He'd lost his wife and he didn't need her wanting things from him. He didn't need her grief for him or her love for him either. What he needed was her body and so that's what she'd give him.

She swallowed, shoved away her own grief and pain, ignored the cold that was threading through her veins. Because she'd made him a promise. She'd told him that at the end of the year she would choose: to stay married to him, to be his wife in all ways, give him the family that he'd wanted or… She would choose to leave.

'If you want children, then you're not going to get them by pushing me away.' She held her arms out to him. 'I've made my choice, Ares. I choose to stay with you and be your wife. So, come and finish what you started.'

He didn't move, his face a mask, his eyes reverting to that dark, stormy ocean with no moonlight on it at all. 'No. My promise to Naya will have to go unfulfilled.'

Her arms dropped, her gut lurching, the cold biting deeper. 'But—'

'You have your brother now, Rose,' he interrupted roughly. 'You should go to him. You don't need me.'

'I don't know my brother.' The words sounded too desperate, but she couldn't stop herself. 'And I want to be with you.'

A flicker of something raw crossed his face, and then it was gone. 'I'm afraid I cannot allow that. Not now.'

It felt like he'd stabbed her, the pain catching her unexpectedly hard deep inside. She stared at him. 'Why not?'

He only stared back, his gaze uncompromising, no give in him at all. A man made of iron, of hard, rigid metal. 'You are free to make a choice, and so am I. And my choice is to annul our marriage. I should never have agreed to it in the first place.'

The knife twisted, making the pain start to radiate like cracks in a broken windowpane, but she ignored it. 'Why? But your promise—'

'Naya is dead.' His eyes glittered blackly. 'And my father is too. They won't know anyway.'

'Ares, don't—'

'Enough.' The word was hard and flat, a sword of iron cutting her off. 'I won't hold you to a marriage that will only cause you distress in the end, and it will, Rose. You deserve more than being the bought wife of a man who only wanted you for your ability to have children. You deserve *better*. You deserve to be loved. That's what marriage means. And that I can never give you.'

There were tears in her eyes, but she forced them back. 'What would you know about what I deserve and what I don't? Perhaps *you* are what I deserve, love or not.'

'Is that what you really want? To be chained for ever to a man who will never love you? Who will never give you the one thing you've wanted all your life—and you have wanted it, little maid, don't deny it. How is that any different to being Vasiliev's prisoner?'

The knife inside her twisted a little more, a little deeper. She'd had years of loneliness, years of unhappiness. Years of having nothing and no one but Athena, and yes, he was right. She wanted more than that.

She *did* want love. But the love she wanted was his.

She felt as if she was falling into pieces inside, but she decided she wasn't going to beg. She wouldn't plead or weep either. She would stand tall and strong and tell him that she loved him, because regardless of what he could give her, she wanted to give this to him.

She was a warrior and there was a strength inside her,

a steel, and now she knew where that steel came from. It came from love. Her love for him.

'I love you,' she said, swallowing her tears and reaching for the fierce part of her. 'Doesn't that make any difference at all?'

He went very still, his gaze focusing on her, something bright glittering there. Then abruptly he looked down at the vodka bottle on the bar instead. 'No. It only makes me more certain that dissolving this marriage is the right thing to do. I will not be your jailer, Rose. I want you to be free.'

She blinked hard against the prickling tears. 'But how can I be free when you aren't? And you're not, Ares. You're letting your grief trap you, can't you see that?'

'I chose my cage. You did not choose yours.'

'But what if I want to? Don't I have a right to choose my own?'

The line of his powerful shoulders radiated tension, his ruined profile harder than stone. He didn't look at her. 'You can. But I'm not going to be the one to close the cage door.' The muscle in his jaw twitched again, his expression hardening. 'I'm going send for the helicopter. There is no need for me to stay here any longer. You, however, may stay as long as you wish.'

Then abruptly he turned away and strode from the room before she could speak.

CHAPTER TEN

Spring

ARES NORMALLY LOVED spring in the mountains of his Greek homeland. He would often allow himself a week in his house there, close to the village where he'd grown up. Where the air was clean and fresh, the sky was deep blue and the cold of winter was fading, yet the baking heat of summer hadn't yet had a chance to settle in.

His house was more of a castle, perched on the side of one of the mountains near his old village. It had been built in medieval times, and he'd had it refurbished at huge expense, the only exceptions he made for modernity being a fast satellite internet connection, power and running water.

Mainly, though, he liked it because it was isolated and there was no one to bother him. Plus, being in the mountains, near the place where he'd been born, was a good reminder of his own failures.

Four weeks after he'd left Rose in Iceland, he'd sent her through divorce papers. She might have chosen to stay married to him, but he couldn't hold her to it. Because regardless of what she'd said about choosing her own cage, about being in love with him, well… What did she know about love? She might know what a cage was, he'd let her have that, but love? No, she had no idea.

He did, though. Love blinded you. It betrayed you. It gouged out your heart and burned it to ashes and left you with nothing. He couldn't trust it, never again. Rose hadn't learned those lessons yet, and with any luck, she never would.

What she deserved was all the love, all the happiness. She deserved everything she wanted, but that wasn't him.

Telling her that in the living room of the lodge in Iceland had hurt her, he knew. And the look on her face, the pain he'd seen in her big golden eyes, had hurt something inside him too. But he was used to pain so he ignored it. Besides, he couldn't see another way.

She loved him and he didn't love her, and he never would. He couldn't allow himself to. The only love he'd ever trusted was Naya's. He couldn't trust his own.

Rose would heal in time—she was nothing if not resilient—and then she'd be free to find someone else who would love her the way he couldn't.

That thought made him want to roar in denial, but he ignored that too, shoving it to one side as he walked in the castle olive grove the morning after he'd arrived. His gardener had some queries about some of the trees and talking about that was an excellent distraction from the subject of Rose.

He had to stop thinking about her. He had to.

Ares had paused beneath a particular tree, his gardener pointing at something on the branches, when one of Ares's assistants came hurrying over the green lawn with news.

Apparently, so his assistant said, his wife was not only *not* going to sign the divorce papers, but she was also never going to sign them, and if Ares didn't like that, he could stick them in an anatomically incorrect and very painful place.

Ares stood beneath the olive tree as his assistant relayed Rose's response, aware of an intense fury gathering inside him. A fury in defiance of his own self-control and out of all proportion to her refusal. Fury that she was making this harder than it needed to be, and how she appeared not to have listened to a word he'd said. He'd told her he would never give her what she needed. Didn't she want to be free?

Obviously, she hadn't been listening, which meant they were going to need to have another little chat. A phone call wasn't enough, and he definitely wasn't going to email her. No, he needed to see her in person.

He didn't ask himself why it was so important she understand, not when he'd been telling himself all this time that he wasn't supposed to care. And he didn't question the need to leave Greece immediately when he'd only just arrived.

He left the grove, took the helicopter back to Athens where he kept the jet, had it fuelled and ready to leave for Paris within the hour. And as the jet powered its way across Europe, he went over in his head again and again what he was going to say to her.

She had to sign those divorce papers. He couldn't keep her. He wouldn't.

Paris in spring was beautiful, but Ares took no notice, heading straight to the cafe by the Seine, where Rose worked. It was just on closing time and most of the customers had left already, but Ares wasn't in any mood to wait.

He had with him a couple of security staff who discreetly got rid of the last two customers, then stationed themselves outside the cafe door. Rose was inside; he could see her through the windows, standing beside the counter and looking down at something.

And he had to take a slow, silent breath as everything

drew tight inside him, the fury that had sustained him all the way from Greece turning into something hotter and more demanding.

He tried to shove it away as he pushed open the door and stepped inside, tried to ignore it as the door closed behind him, but as Rose turned her attention to the door, and those big golden eyes of hers met his, it erupted inside him like a volcano.

He froze, his control hanging by a thread, knowing that even moving one muscle would annihilate that thread and he would be closing the distance between them and dragging her into his arms.

You will never let her go.

He couldn't do that. He wouldn't.

Rose's eyes widened, an expression of shock crossing her lovely features, to be followed by one of pure joy, as if seeing him had been the best thing to have ever happened to her in her entire life. Then just as quickly as it had appeared, the joy faded into something harder, more determined, and her chin lifted, her spine straightening.

The warrior ready for battle.

Instantly he wanted to cross the space between them and bring that battle right to her. Match her and master her and make her his.

But he closed his hands into fists and stayed where he was instead.

'Why did you not sign those documents?' he demanded, getting straight to the point. 'You need to be free, Rose. You do not need to be married to me any more.'

'And I told you that I don't want to be free, remember?' she snapped straight back. 'Not of you.'

'It's been a month. You really still—'

'Nothing has changed.' She looked so fierce as she

took a step towards him. '*Nothing*. I told you I wanted to choose my own cage and I have.'

Frustration curled inside him, made more acute by the feeling rushing through him, the powerful need to get close to her, have nothing between them. 'I can't give you what you want. I told you that. Not to you and not to any children we have—'

'What do you want, Ares?'

'What?' The question was so out of left field he couldn't process it. 'What do you mean what do I want?'

'I mean, what do *you* want?'

'The promise I made to Naya—'

'No. What do *you* want for *yourself*?'

He stared at her, the words not making any sense for a moment. Then they did and his brain instantly provided the answer.

Her. You want her.

It felt like someone had put their fingers around his throat and was squeezing hard, choking the breath from his body.

She only looked at him, all the ferocity gathering into a bright, hot, burning look that rooted him to the spot.

You know why you're here. Why you flew across a continent to get to her. And it's not to sign divorce papers.

It was that feeling inside him, the one he didn't want to examine. The one he didn't want to feel, not again. Because he'd felt it before. He'd felt it with Naya. The same and yet different this time, because it was Rose standing in front of him.

Rose, who wasn't afraid of him. Who matched him will for will. Who laughed with him and fought with him, and in the end trusted him. Rose, who hadn't let any of the experiences she'd gone through grind her into dust, but who'd emerged victorious. Rose, whose courage shocked him and who'd grasped what life had given her and had bent it to her will.

Rose, who touched his scars as if they were more than reminders of his failure.

Rose, whom he knew now he'd fallen in love with despite every part of him trying to resist.

Rose, who'd restarted his dead heart and now it was beating and beating for her alone.

'You,' Ares said, the words coming out of him harsh and raw. 'I want you. I want to keep you. I want you to be my wife for ever. But I can't. Love lies. It cannot be trusted. And my love will kill you just as surely as it killed Naya.'

It had taken all of Rose's considerable will not to cross the distance between them and fling herself into his arms the moment Ares had stepped through the door and into the cafe.

She'd never expected him to come to Paris for her, not even once.

The past month had been a busy one, though he'd never been far from her thoughts. She'd finally gathered her courage to make contact with the brother she'd thought she'd lost, and their reunion had both torn her apart and then put her back together again.

Castor had welcomed her with open arms, and she'd got to meet his lovely wife, Glory, and their son, her nephew. It had been so bittersweet, giving her back parts of herself she'd thought she'd lost for ever. Yet one part was still missing. The part of herself she'd given away.

Her heart.

She'd stayed for a couple of weeks in that lodge in Iceland after Ares had left, not knowing what to do.

Whether to go to him and beg to be taken back or go to Paris and try to forget he ever existed.

Except she couldn't do either of those things. Firstly, even if she'd wanted to beg him to, she suspected he wouldn't take her back, and secondly, she was never going to forget him. She was never going to want another man. It was only and always ever going to be him.

Yet she couldn't let him be alone either. She had a new-found family in Castor and Glory now, but who did he have? No one. He was alone with only that lonely legacy of a company, and she hated that thought more than anything in the world.

So, when the divorce papers had come through, she'd simply refused to sign them, because she'd wanted him to know that she wasn't going to let him go so easily.

She'd just never thought he'd come all the way over here to confront her.

But that meant something, didn't it?

She could see it now as he stood by the door, so tall and powerful and so beautifully scarred. The depths of his love worn proud for the world to see.

'Your love didn't kill Naya,' she said quietly. 'It didn't, Ares. Your love made you go into a burning building for her, made you risk your life for her. Your love built a company in her memory, a company that helps people the world over. You didn't fail her. She was taken from you, that's the tragedy.' She took a soft, shaky breath. 'But you can't go on letting a memory be your own reason for living. And you can't go on living in your grief.'

His eyes were completely dark, his big, muscled body tense as a coiled spring. 'That is not—'

'You were badly hurt. And you're afraid. But you're lonely too, Ares. You need someone.' She stared at him, willing him to see the love that was burning in her eyes, the love she had for him. 'Naya loved you and she would want happiness for you, not this…half-life you're living now. She would look at the scars on your face and see how deeply you loved her, not how badly you failed her.'

His expression twisted, a muscle in his jaw flicking. 'How could you possibly know that? You didn't know her.'

'No, but we both love you.' She was very calm all of a sudden, trusting the feeling inside her. 'And that's what I want for you. And I think that's what she'd want for you too.'

Agony glittered in his eyes, and grief, and anger. So many different emotions, all the ones he'd been locking inside himself that he was finally now showing to her.

And she couldn't stay where she was any longer.

She stepped away from the counter and crossed the distance between them, and he didn't move, watching her as she came. And when she was right in front of him, she lifted her hands and placed them lightly on his chest, looking up into his beautiful, ruined face.

'These are love, Ares.' She reached up and touched him, tracing the lines of his scars. 'These are all love. Can you feel it?'

'Little maid,' he said hoarsely, his rasping voice vibrating with something powerful. 'Little maid…' He turned his head into her hand, watching her as if he couldn't drag his gaze away. 'When Naya died…part of me died too. And I don't know… I don't know if I can do this again with you.'

'I understand. After what you lost…' She touched his hard mouth, looked up into his eyes. 'It must be frightening to risk your heart again. And I know I haven't lost what you have, but… I'm scared too. Yet all I can think is why shouldn't we both get what we want? Don't we deserve it? Don't we deserve to be happy?'

He made a harsh sound. 'Do you really want this? Do you really want to be tied to someone like me? I don't know if what I have to give you will ever be enough. I'm scarred and broken, and…'

'Still grieving,' she finished and smiled. 'You may be scarred, but you're not broken, Ares. You're kind and protective, and whether you like it or not, you're caring. And there is no time limit on grief.' Her fingertips drifted to trace the line of his bottom lip. 'We can work it out between us.'

'Rose…' The look in his eyes had lightened, the moon coming out from behind the clouds and shining on a green sea. Then he took her hand and pressed a kiss to her palm. 'How can I divorce you when I think I'm in love with you?'

'Are you?' Her chest was tight with the pressure of everything she felt for him, the huge, complicated feeling that had tied itself into a knot behind her ribs. But it was a good pressure and it felt right. As if now she was finally whole. 'You can't divorce me. I won't let you.'

Abruptly the look on his face changed, and she was being pulled against his hard, powerful body and he was bending his head, his mouth covering hers in a kiss that consumed the entire world.

'No, little maid,' Ares murmured against her mouth. '*This* is love.'

And he spent the rest of his life proving it to her.

EPILOGUE

ARES LOUNGED ON a blanket in the olive grove just below his castle in Greece, keeping a watchful eye on his son, Niko. The boy had just learned to crawl, and Ares could already tell he was going to be the kind of child who got into everything and caused havoc for his parents.

He couldn't wait.

Not far away, his little maid was playing with her nephew and twin nieces while her brother, Castor, looked on. He and Glory were visiting, and Ares found he quite enjoyed their company, even though he had a healthy disdain for men from the islands, which Castor was. Glory, however, was a delight, and it was true that Castor loved his sister very much, which was a point in his favour. As Rose loved him.

But Castor didn't love her as much as Ares did.

He'd sold his company, and after much discussion with Rose, they'd both decided to invest the money in the mountain villages of his homeland, giving back to many of the poorer communities. Naya would have liked that, he was certain.

Rose had also taken some of his money and, along with Castor, had founded an organisation dedicated to helping the victims of human trafficking. She was very, very good at it, and a fierce advocate.

But what was most important was that she was happy, and he knew because she told him so every day. Just as he told her the same thing. And he was. He'd never thought he would be again, never thought he would have deserved it, but Rose had shown him that he did. She had given him the courage to realise that despite all his talk of legacies and memorials, he'd been doing exactly what she'd accused him of: living in his grief. Using it to keep himself protected, because he knew grief. It was familiar. It was safe. But loving again wasn't, especially loving someone different. Loving Rose was like exploring an undiscovered country: it definitely wasn't safe. There were threats everywhere, and yet also such beauty. Such joy. Such happiness.

He didn't regret a moment of it.

Niko had reached his knee and gripped it with chubby fists, pulling himself up onto his feet for the first time, and grinning madly at his father.

And Ares felt his heart grow bigger, beating strong and hard behind his ribs.

He smiled at his son, and when he looked over at Rose to draw her attention to Niko's brilliance, he found her already looking back, her golden eyes full of light.

She smiled, glowing in the late summer afternoon, the slight breeze blowing the red dress she wore against her figure, the little bump that was their second child already visible.

His heart beat stronger, harder.

She'd restarted that heart again, his little maid.

She'd made it beat.

And every beat was love.

* * * * *

COMING SOON!

We really hope you enjoyed reading this book. If you're looking for more romance, be sure to head to the shops when new books are available on

Thursday 8th December

To see which titles are coming soon, please visit

millsandboon.co.uk/nextmonth

MILLS & BOON®

Coming next month

THE COST OF CINDERELLA'S CONFESSION
Julia James

From the back of the church, footsteps – like nails striking the flagstones of the aisle.

A voice – harsh and strident, breaking the hallowed silence. Heads turning, breaths intaking across the congregation.

A voice calling out –

Announcing. Denouncing…

Luca felt his head turn. Felt his gaze fall on the figure of the woman walking down the aisle. A red suit, exposing every curve of her voluptuous body. A matching pill box hat with a black veil concealing her upper face.

A veil she threw back as she approached.

To his side he heard Tomaso give a snarl of rage, start forward.

But he himself did not move. Could not.

Could only level his eyes on her, with a fury he had not known he could possess, that should strike her to silence if there were any justice in the world – any decency.

But there was no justice, no decency. There was only her voice, ringing out like sacrilege. Freezing him to the very marrow of his bones.

"He cannot marry her!" she cried out. "I am pregnant with his child!"

Continue reading
THE COST OF CINDERELLA'S CONFESSION
Julia James

Available next month
www.millsandboon.co.uk

MILLS & BOON

THE HEART OF ROMANCE

A ROMANCE FOR EVERY READER

ODERN

Prepare to be swept off your feet by sophisticated, sexy and seductive heroes, in some of the world's most glamourous and romantic locations, where power and passion collide.

STORICAL

Escape with historical heroes from time gone by. Whether your passion is for wicked Regency Rakes, muscled Vikings or rugged Highlanders, awaken the romance of the past.

EDICAL

Set your pulse racing with dedicated, delectable doctors in the high-pressure world of medicine, where emotions run high and passion, comfort and love are the best medicine.

Celebrate true love with tender stories of heartfelt romance, from the rush of falling in love to the joy a new baby can bring, and a focus on the emotional heart of a relationship.

Desire

Indulge in secrets and scandal, intense drama and plenty of sizzling hot action with powerful and passionate heroes who have it all: wealth, status, good looks...everything but the right woman.

EROES

Experience all the excitement of a gripping thriller, with an intense romance at its heart. Resourceful, true-to-life women and strong, fearless men face danger and desire - a killer combination!

To see which titles are coming soon, please visit

millsandboon.co.uk/nextmonth

LET'S TALK
Romance

For exclusive extracts, competitions
and special offers, find us online:

f facebook.com/millsandboon

🐦 @MillsandBoon

📷 @MillsandBoonUK

Get in touch on 01413 063232

For all the latest titles coming soon, visit
millsandboon.co.uk/nextmonth